Loretta H. Marion

# THE FOOL'S TRUTH

*The Fool's Truth*

First Edition: September 2016
Registration Number: TXu 1-983-580

Print: ISBN 978-0-9977886-0-0
Ebook: ISBN 978-0-9977886-1-7

Cover and Formatting: Streetlight Graphics



Published by:

Time At Last Books
www.TimeAtLastBooks.com

www.LorettaMarion.com

For my sweet mother,
who always believed in me and whose kindness inspired me.

"Being deeply loved by someone gives you strength,
while loving someone deeply gives you courage."

Lao Tzu

“Long is the night to one who is awake.
Long is ten miles to one who is tired.
Long is the cycle of birth and death
to the fool who does not know the true path.”

The Fool, Lord Buddha

"DESPERATION IS THE RAW MATERIAL OF DRASTIC CHANGE.
ONLY THOSE WHO CAN LEAVE BEHIND EVERYTHING THEY HAVE EVER BELIEVED IN CAN HOPE TO ESCAPE."

WILLIAM S. BURROUGHS

"BABY MINE, DON'T YOU CRY, baby mine, dry your eyes. Rest your head close to my heart, never to part, baby of mine." The woman's placid song voice, meant to calm her child's cries, was proving ineffective. She bent down to offer her tiny daughter a favorite stuffed elephant and caressed away the tears from those terribly sad and sodden cherry cheeks. "Dumbo will keep you company. We'll go soon. Just a few more minutes, honey pie."

She tuned out the child's whimpering and returned to her task, pausing on the path from dresser to suitcase, tapping index finger to chin she closed her eyes. *Now what was it she must not forget?* A ghost of a smile brushed across her lips and she lithely stepped around the unmoving form with the seeping pool that was turning her beautiful blue, hand-hooked rug a deep shade of aubergine. She opened the music box and began humming along with the tune, *Dream a Little Dream of Me.* It was her talisman for escape. She'd perfected her talent for suppressing when as a young girl she'd sneak away to the dark and dusty attic with the ancient turntable and scratched 45 hidden within the cobwebs. Over and over again the record would play and she would lose herself in a safe and imaginary world; a place where the evil tentacles of life could not reach her. It became a well honed survival mechanism that had served her well through troubled years.

But this day was different; the scene more terribly tragic than any before. She had deeply immersed herself in a story that was not her life but one of fiction, created to flee a nightmare reality. But was the chasm she had crossed over to fantasy so wide that she might remain forever trapped in her newly imagined world?

Still humming, she reached down to lift her young daughter from the playpen and hugged her tightly. "Don't you worry, honey pie. I will always keep you safe. I promise."

# PART ONE

## FIRST FLIGHT OF THE FOOL

# CORDELIA

"THE MIND IS EVERYTHING. WHAT YOU THINK YOU BECOME."

BUDDHA

THERE WAS ONLY ONE PERSON who still called me Cord, but how was it that Ramon Alvarez came to be speaking from the other end of the phone line?

"Tell me why you have called, Cord," he persuaded gently.

So I called him. Strange that my subconscious mind would seek out someone I hadn't seen in over a decade. And yet, it wasn't strange at all.

"I am listening, but you must talk to me."

My own tongue had turned to stone, but how reassuring to hear Ramon's beautiful voice, dancing with the soft inflections of his Spanish heritage, almost like a tango with its glides and sudden pauses.

"Cord, you are frightening me."

"Yes, Ramon," I whispered. "It's me."

No sound came from the payphone ear piece. Had I broken the spell of an imagined notion when I spoke his name?

Then finally, "What is it, mi querida? Tell me, please, what is wrong."

Where to begin? I took in a deep breath before the words that would cement my intentions came tumbling from my lips. "I'm leaving Aiden and I've taken Gabriella."

"Whoa. What has happened? Just a few months ago

everything seemed…" he left the thought dangling as if he was trying to bring to mind that last conversation.

He was referring to our most recent Annual 411 call, a sacred ritual that had been born of a childhood pledge. Each year at precisely noon on New Year's Day, no matter what we were doing or where we were, we would find a way to connect. Surprisingly, for twenty years and with many miles separating us, we had without fail followed through on that promise to stay in touch. Even after that disastrous chance encounter nearly ten years ago.

I shook away the unpleasant memory.

"The last time we spoke you were about to board a plane." I was ashamed to admit I hadn't even thought to ask where Ramon was going, so lost in relief was I to have an excuse for not talking about my crumbling marriage.

"Right." He was remembering now. "It had been a quick call. Still, you sounded okay."

"It's safe to say I was more okay then than I am now. I have to leave here. Today." My words started quaking. "Aiden..."

"What has Aiden done? Has he harmed you? Or your daughter?" Tones of panic had replaced mild concern.

"It's less about what he's done" - although there was no denying my husband had become a total sleaze - "and everything about what he's planning to do."

"And that is?"

"I can't think what I did to make him hate me so much that he would take from me what I most love. I can't lose her, Ramon. I just can't." I tried to choke back a sob, but was unsuccessful.

"He was going to take Gabriella away? That is ridiculous. How could he imagine any judge in his right mind would agree to that?"

Again I found myself unable to speak, yet even if I could, how would I describe how Aiden had changed through the years? Or had I simply been blind to his well camouflaged lack of principles? My husband had become an influential man with countless alliances. There'd most certainly be a judge, any number of judges and *one in particular*, who would have a motivation for siding with him.

"You must tell me what is going on," Ramon insisted.

"I can't right now." I nearly dropped the receiver as I dug in my purse for a tissue. "It's too complicated to explain over the phone."

He heaved a sigh of resignation. "Fair enough. Then tell me what I can do to help. Do you need money?"

What I truly needed was something nobody could give me. More time. But what I said was, "I need to come back to the city."

"You never should have been forced to leave in the first place."

I looked across to First Bank where the security officer was unlocking the doors and welcoming the day's first depositors and withdrawers. I would be among the latter.

My delay in responding had been misinterpreted for Ramon quickly added, "I am sorry. That was presumptuous."

"What? No. You're right." In the middle of ninth grade, just two years after adopting me, my parents made the fateful decision to relocate from Manhattan to the Washington, D.C. area. Why I never returned for a visit I couldn't say, but now I had a deep longing to breathe in that heady scent that was uniquely New York City.

"And yet, had you remained here? Well, you would not have your little one."

There was no question it was Gabriella who was keeping my tempest-tossed boat anchored and I understood Ramon was only trying to comfort me. But I had to reign in my emotions quickly because entering a bank with red, puffy eyes and a tear stained face would draw unwanted attention.

"If you want to help, find us a place to hide out for a day or two. Somewhere private where I can work through my thoughts, make some definite plans."

"You can stay with me. My loft is not chic, but it is spacious."

The offer stirred up all the tangled emotions that blurred the boundaries of our friendship. It would be comforting to see him. More than that if I was being honest. But would it be the wise decision? "I don't want to drag you into my problems."

"I will listen to no arguments. It is settled. You will come here."

The hard truth was I had no other options at the moment. How disheartening to be thirty-five years old with only one person to turn to in a time of crisis.

"Okay. But I promise it will be a short stay." *It had to be.*

"When will you leave?"

"I'm already gone." I glanced at my watch, ironically the last gift Aiden had given me. "Right now I have a loose end to tie up, but I'll call you at my next stop and we can sort out the details."

"Cord?"

"Yes, Ramon."

He hesitated for more than a beat before saying, "Stay safe on the roads."

I replaced the phone to its hook and out of a childhood habit fingered the slot where the unused coins drop down. I wondered what Ramon had intended to say, for clearly he had stopped himself. I leaned down to caress my slumbering daughter's cheek before hefting the carrier seat.

"I will indeed stay safe on the roads sweetie, for you are my most precious cargo."

"Can I do anything else for you today," the teller glanced

again at the withdrawal slip, "Ms. Carlyle?" Fortunately, the bank clerk had been keeping her eye on the handsome gentleman behind me in line and paid me little notice. First Bank was a large, bustling bank in the heart of downtown Richmond. It was a two hour drive from my home and in the opposite direction of my destination, but it offered the anonymity I sought. And I'd been careful not to visit with a frequency that would make mine an easily recognized face.

"I need to access my safety deposit box."

"Certainly. Someone will be right with you at the second door on your left." That's where another preoccupied bank employee met me and signed me in, instructing me to buzz him when I was finished.

As I was emptying what I needed from the box, my mother's words of warning resonated loudly in my head. "Look out for yourself, Delia. Keep your money in a separate account. Aiden never need know it exists. If we can't stop you from going forward with this ill-conceived wedding, at least take my advice about protecting your financial future."

It had been one of our last conversations. How long now? Five years ago. Lorraine had been right about the money and she'd been right about the marriage. If ever we mend our fences, I will admit to being glad for listening to one of my mother's warnings. However, I might repent a lifetime for not heeding the other.

# RAMON

"AND TAKE UPON US THE MYSTERY OF THINGS AS IF WE WERE GOD'S SPIES."

WILLIAM SHAKESPEARE, ***KING LEAR***

When Cord called a second time for directions from a payphone outside of Baltimore, Ramon had gently probed to uncover a few more details regarding the disintegration of her marriage. He'd not been surprised when she told him of the affair. It was rare to learn of a relationship that remained untouched by betrayal. Even rarer was the couple who survived the unmanageable weight of guilt from infidelity. Wasn't the collapse of his own marriage a perfect example?

She'd remained composed in the telling, but he couldn't be certain she grasped that the consequences she was facing from her current scheme were far worse than the emotional fallout from an errant husband's transgressions. Cord had always possessed an enigmatic aura, walking through life somewhat detached from her surroundings, an internal defense mechanism to protect her fragile core. When they were younger he'd been charmed by her dreamy aloofness, but right now it had him deeply concerned.

Their friendship had its unlikely beginnings in one of the myriad of small melting pot neighborhoods hidden in the vastness of New York City. The shy Hispanic boy had become fascinated by the daydreaming young girl perched upon the stoop of the apartment building directly across from where the Alvarez clan lived. She'd been ten at the time and had been

Cordelia Richmond when she came to live with her third foster family in as many years. Kim and Chung Wu were a reserved and hard-working Chinese couple who'd provided well for her and exposed her to their Asian Buddhist philosophy.

But two years later, her new adoptive parents had decided that life with them in midtown called for fresh beginnings, so they began to call her Delia. Delia Carlyle. Ronald and Lorraine Carlyle had desires and aspirations for their new daughter: new name, new school, and most importantly, new circle of friends. Although they'd stopped short of forbidding an association with Ramon, her parents threw constant interference in hopes of gradually severing the bond. The approach backfired, for the two determined friends steeled themselves against all attempts to break them apart. Until they'd met with an insurmountable obstacle when the Carlyles uprooted their daughter to Washington, DC.

When Ramon heard Cord's voice earlier that morning, he'd been unprepared for the reawakened surge of long tamped down feelings. It had been almost ten years since he was stranded at Dulles. Who could have guessed one innocent but badly timed phone call would be the first domino to fall in changing their relationship? He'd been thrilled by the prospect of seeing his friend again, but his reaction to Cord had been completely unexpected. A professional chef, she'd whipped up an impressive repast. But it wasn't the Curried Shrimp he'd found irresistible. It was Cord. And his appetite had been voracious. It had taken less than an hour for them to tumble into her lavender scented bed and three days for the freak blizzard to wind down. But their coupling had been ill-fated and the parting messy, for Ramon was trapped by circumstances at home. He hadn't even had a chance to fully explain because the airport closing had been lifted and he had to rush to make his flight. Remarkably, whether from embarrassment on her part or cowardice on his, neither of them had ever broached the subject again.

He certainly hadn't handled it well, but at present he couldn't afford to be pulled down into an unsettling abyss of unanswered *what ifs*. There was a looming assignment to prepare for, but he found himself useless for anything work related. Instead, he kept his senses attentive to the news and began calling in favors from his sources and contacts, people who would be valuable in getting Cord and her daughter safely out of the country.

# CORDELIA

"KNOW WELL WHAT LEADS YOU FORWARD AND WHAT HOLDS YOU BACK, AND CHOOSE THE PATH THAT LEADS TO WISDOM."

BUDDHA

"COULD YOU TELL ME WHERE I went wrong?" I tried to flatten the wrinkled road map across the crowded checkout counter of a *Sunrise Mart.*

The clerk pulled at one of many piercings as he squinted down to where I was pointing. "Yeah. Looks like you made a wrong turn."

A line of impatient shoppers was forming and Gabriella was beginning to fuss again. The man behind us reached around to pay for his soda, tipping it over and spilling it onto the map. As I grabbed some napkins from the dispenser and began to blot the mess with my free hand, I felt a tug on my necklace. It was too late when I realized it wasn't Gabriella's small fingers grasping hold of the heirloom treasure. I heard a snap but before I could react and in less time than it took to turn toward the door, the only hint of the offender was a single gray sneaker thrusting off into a sprint.

"Stop him," I shouted, pushing through the door. But stop who? The thief, if he was still within sight, had blended into the human amalgamation that invaded the city sidewalks at five o'clock.

A moment later a young woman followed me out of the

convenience store carrying the map and the backpack I'd left by the counter. "I think these are yours."

I quickly wiped away the tears. "Thanks."

The stranger set the backpack on a bench and reached a heavily tattooed arm toward Gabriella. "Hello there, cutie."

Instinctively I pulled my daughter closer.

"You can't judge all New Yorkers by that creep." The woman breathed out a weary sigh. "Most of us are just trying to get through the day."

"I didn't mean to be ungracious." My eyes welled up again, this time from shame. Out of habit my fingers searched for the amulet now missing from my neck.

"You could contact the police. But all that will guarantee is several hours spent waiting in a crowded precinct substation." She offered a regretful smile. "You'll give them a description of the item, they'll give you little encouragement of it ever being found. Trust me. I've been through the routine. You'd have better luck checking the local pawn shops over the next few days."

Little did this stranger know, the police were the last people I'd contact for help. Even more an issue, the commodity of time had become more precious than the necklace that had been snatched.

"Shall we try to get you headed back in the right direction?" she asked.

"I thought my route was pretty well planned out, but my GPS let me down."

"Skyscrapers sometimes block satellite signals." The woman unfolded the damp map then asked, "You've traveled from down south?"

My skin prickled. "I was actually born here in the city, but I've been away for years. How could you tell?"

"The accent. What is it? Georgia? The Carolinas?"

Evidently I'd been living among Virginians too long and hadn't been mindful of acquiring their mild southern inflections.

"Kentucky." The lie tumbled much too easily across my lips.

An hour later, my body a gnawing jumble of nerves, I pulled into the parking garage where Ramon had directed me to leave the car.

"What am I doing here?" I covered my face with my hands, suddenly paralyzed by how little I knew about Ramon Alvarez the man. I replayed all the arguments for putting my trust in someone I'd seen only once in the past decade. My instincts were based purely on memories from my youth and one incredible connection as young adults. The memory of that bygone weekend provoked ambiguous feelings. Today I pushed aside hot humiliation. It had taken a long time for the frozen compartment in my heart to thaw, but I'd convinced myself the friendship was too meaningful to let my injured pride win out.

Besides, it had been Ramon who made the first move after that doomed reunion. And if I thought back, wasn't he usually the one to make the 411 call each year? His steadfast effort to keep in touch had to count in the plus side.

I took in several deep breaths to shore up my resolve. It was too late for second thoughts. More to the point, I had nowhere else to go.

The door swung open before I'd even had a chance to ring the bell.

"God, Cord." Ramon's tone pure exasperation as he pulled me and my howling daughter in from the hallway. "Why not just wear a sandwich board with your name painted across it?"

I was flustered, embarrassed and convinced my reluctance just moments before had been valid. To hide my teary eyes I leaned down to free a bottle from the backpack, which Gabriella grasped hungrily and that at least put an end to the shrieking.

"Sorry. It's been a long day for a two and a half year old and it's well past her dinner time." I rubbed my arms, quickly taking in the expansive loft with its unique furnishings. But the heart of the space was the collection of enormous, prominently displayed canvases, bursting with vibrancy like nothing I'd ever seen. Ramon's ex-wife was an artist and I imagined these were her works, which left me speculating why he'd retained custody of her paintings.

Ramon opened the door again, apparently checking to see if any of his neighbors were sufficiently curious to rouse themselves from their television viewing to take a peek at the drama unfolding in their own building.

"What is this?" He hefted the animal carrier into the apartment and quickly closed the door.

"Our cat."

Ramon grimaced.

*Was it too late to turn around and leave?*

"I couldn't bear to leave her."

Gabriella toddled over, still attacking the bottle, and began petting the crate.

"Ting," she gurgled in her tiny voice.

I unlatched the door and lifted the fur ball out of its prison. "See sweetie. Ting is fine."

The echo of a soft canine growl from the far end of the loft grew nearer, accompanied by the clicking of clawed feet against the hard wood floors. It was approaching rapidly and before I could secure Ting, she let out a screech and leaped atop a rustic armoire and disappeared behind some exposed ductwork.

"Oh, no." I turned to fend off the tantrum certain to be brewing, but to my surprise Gabriella had become enthralled with the little pooch and wasn't in the least fazed by the cat's escape. I kept my eyes trained on my daughter and the strange looking dog, purposely avoiding a glance in Ramon's direction, not wanting to witness his disdain.

"Quite the ice breaker, was it not?" He chuckled.

It was the voice of the Ramon I remembered; charmingly formal with the soft nuance of a Spanish accent. And when I brought my gaze up to look directly at my old friend, although his handsome face was a tad sun weathered and there were crinkles at the corners of his eyes, the familiar smile was warm and sensuous, prompting a thrilling flutter deep within.

"Look, I am sorry I reacted so..." He made a face and waved his hand as if that was enough.

"Panicked?" I finished the thought left hanging.

"No doubt." Ramon shook his head and then lowered his voice. "There is an *Amber Alert*."

Instinctively, I kneeled down and folded Gabriella into my arms. An *Amber Alert* made everything all too real. I deeply inhaled the intoxicating scent of my child until she squirmed free to resume her playful attentions to the dog.

"It was alarming to see your pictures pop up on the screen so soon," he continued to explain. "And then moments later, there you were at the door."

In just a few short minutes my troubles had grown exponentially. There would be people looking for us - law enforcement officials, airport security, border patrols. I stood slowly, hoping Ramon wouldn't notice how shaken I was by the news.

"Did you not say Aiden was out of town for a few days?" he asked.

"Yes, he's in California."

"How do you imagine he found out you had taken Gabriella?"

I rubbed my temples as I tried to come up with a plausible explanation.

“I have no clue, unless he came back early. But I don’t see how that’s possible. He flew to LA this morning. There’s no way he could have returned by now.”

“Could he have lied to you about the trip?”

I brought fingers to my lips as an involuntary moan escaped.

# RAMON

"IGNORANCE IS THE CURSE OF GOD; KNOWLEDGE IS THE WING WHEREWITH WE FLY TO HEAVEN."

WILLIAM SHAKESPEARE, ***HENRY VI***

"LOOK, THERE WILL BE TIME later to speak of your... situation. Maybe you are hungry? I have something special for you."

Ramon walked in the direction of the open kitchen and motioned for Cord to follow. She plodded numbly behind him and leaned dejectedly against the large kitchen island for support.

"I am sorry about your cat," he said, removing a pan from the oven.

She looked up to where Ting had disappeared. "I hope we can lure her back down."

"She will come out when she gets hungry."

"You never mentioned having a dog."

"A new acquisition, if you can call him that. I found him rooting around in an open garbage bin in the rear alley. You think he looks skinny now?" He moved with ease from oven to stove.

"With all the traveling you do, I didn't think a pet would be practical."

The dog seemed to know he was the topic of conversation and wiggled loose from Gabriella's grasp to pay homage to his benefactor.

"I have...a friend, who takes care of him when I am away."

"What's this mutt's name?" Cord was looking at the creature with mild distaste.

"Oh, but you are wrong. This little man has a pedigree." He offered the pup a biscuit. "Guapo is a purebred Portuguese Podango."

"Guapo?" She smiled for the first time. "I remember your mother pinching your cheeks and calling you *mi'jo guapo.*" Her handsome son.

"What do you think?"

"He's handsome, all right." She rolled her eyes at the contradiction and the dog scampered back to the adoring arms of her daughter.

Ramon turned his focus back to the chore of assembling the meal.

"How is your mother?" she asked warily.

"Sassier than ever." He swiveled around to display a filled platter, eyebrows raised in a taunt. "Still makes the best empanadas in the city."

"Nothing like empanadas to heal an ailing soul." Cord was quoting Mrs. Alvarez. Ramon and his brothers had always boasted their mama's Spanish dishes as the real definition of soul food. "So, she finally taught you to make them?"

"Me?" He made a face. "I am useless in a kitchen. These are the real deal."

She grabbed the side of the polished concrete countertop. "Your mother knows I'm here?"

"I wish I could have told her, but, you know." Ramon concentrated on the task of dishing up the food to avoid looking at her. How could he put his mother in a position of having to lie?

"Of course." In a cautious tone she asked, "Do you think she's heard the news?"

"For sure she has not or I would already have a hundred voice messages from her."

Cord hesitated a moment before declaring, "When this mess blows over I'll come back to the city to see her."

Ramon reflexively jerked his head.

"What's wrong?"

"Nothing." He recovered and made the charade of shaking his hand. "I burned myself on this hot pan. Shall we eat?"

After they'd finished the meal and Gabriella had been put to bed, Ramon studied Cord closely as he swirled a glass of Rioja.

"The haircuts were a good idea," he said, thinking how young she looked and being momentarily assaulted by a surge of nostalgia from their teenage years together. "It suits you."

"I'd always wanted to try going blonde." She ran her fingers through shorn flaxen pixie locks. "It still feels strange. But it's just hair, right?"

"Right." And surely the least significant consequence of this whole mess. It was time to get serious. "So now tell me the whole story."

"I don't know where to begin, but I can show you these." She produced a folder of documents she'd removed from Aiden's safe: a letter from his attorney outlining a legal strategy to obtain full custody, a damning child welfare report and the accompanying depositions from the babysitter who'd falsely accused Cord of abusing Gabriella.

"Why not take this to the police?" he asked after a quick glance at the attorney's letter.

"My husband is a clever and well connected man. Besides which, the woman he'd had the affair with is a high ranking judge. Who could I trust? And up until two days ago I was under the false impression the abuse claim had been dismissed and expunged from all records." She pointed to the pile of documents. "Obviously, that didn't happen."

"Did you not have your own attorney?" A perfectly reasonable question.

Her face grew red. "I've been naïve and foolish and allowed myself to be manipulated. We'd been on the threshold of reconciliation when our babysitter made the ridiculous claim of witnessing me brutally shaking Gabriella. Aiden seized control and with the help of some of his cronies managed to have it all *swept under the rug*."

She paused to drink deeply from the wine glass then wiped her lips with the back of her hand. "He'd had help all right, but it wasn't to get the charges against me dismissed. Instead he arranged to have the hearing pushed back to a date that suited his own underhanded purposes. It was a well staged ruse, a superb performance to regain my trust. And I fell for it."

"It will not be beneficial to beat yourself up," Ramon gently admonished as he began creating a flow chart showing the dates of all the documents. He held up the first deposition dated over four months ago. "Gabriella was not seen by a doctor after this?"

Cord bristled. "Do you really think I'd ever do anything to harm my baby?"

"Not at all. I am trying to think like Aiden might and it seems strange that he would not have taken her to a medical professional to verify these claims. I would also assume that an evaluation would be required in any child abuse allegation."

"I don't even know how or when DCYF became involved. I was never interviewed by a case worker, but magically there's documentation of such a meeting right here." She flipped through the report. "To my knowledge she was not seen by a doctor, but I'm a working mother so there would have been opportunities for Aiden to take her. But because *nothing happened* there would be no physical evidence of abuse."

"We cannot assume, just because there is no doctor's report in this folder, that it does not exist or that it will not be created at some point. Anyone can be bought."

She reached back to rub her neck and then handed him a second fabricated deposition. "It's clear Aiden was setting the stage to act the part of the stunned and betrayed husband when he presented this to a family court judge."

He began to add the date to his chart but stopped to scrutinize the statement more closely. "How can this be? It has been notarized with tomorrow's date."

"Yes, I know." She collapsed into a sigh of defeat. "It's easy to predict how my husband intended this maze of deceit to play out. First, there'd be proof he was out of town on the date of the purported second abuse episode. He'd pretend to be devastated for putting his little girl in jeopardy after giving me a second chance. Aiden would have no choice but to take the evidence to the authorities, incompetency charges would be filed against me and he'd sue for full custody. Nobody would find fault with his actions and he'd win on all fronts."

Ramon closely compared the two depositions and indicated the signatures.

"So this babysitter, she remained under your employ?" he asked with more than a hint of skepticism.

"We dismissed her immediately." A cynical little laugh escaped her lips. "But evidently she's still on Aiden's payroll, and probably being paid handsomely for her role in all this."

"How then would this second deposition have any validity? Surely friends and family would know that she had been fired."

Cord shook her head. "Aiden and I socialized almost entirely within his world: his family, his work associates, his friends. I didn't feel I could confide in any of them."

"Your parents?"

"They don't know." She waved her hands to signal she didn't want to go there.

The Carlyles had always been a thorny subject so he let it go. "Had you found someone else to look after Gabriella?"

"I could never trust another stranger, no matter how glowing the references. My first instinct had been to quit my job. But Aiden persuaded me not to make a rash decision and arranged for his sister to watch her while we sorted through what to do."

"And this sister?"

She shrugged. "We'd always been cordial and I had no reason to mistrust her. Still, her loyalties would lie with Aiden. Look, I know this is going to sound paranoid, but who knows what he's lead everyone else to believe about me. He's lied to me, what would stop him from lying to the rest of his family?"

Ramon nodded solemnly then perused the documents for endless moments before assembling the papers and tapping them into a neat stack. He blew out a deep breath and nodded.

"We have much to do."

Her eyes welled up and she reached across the table, gently entwining her fingers with his. He held on for a moment before reluctantly releasing his grasp.

"You have been fortunate to make it this far before the *Amber Alert* was issued," he told her. "Now, we must capitalize on that head start and figure out how to get you to a safe haven. Luego luego." *Without delay.*

He wanted to believe everything Cord had told him, but he could not shake free of a suspicion she was holding something back. Why hadn't she hired an attorney and why had she not sought out her parents' help? He'd try again tomorrow to pry loose some additional details. Regardless, he'd need to set aside any misgivings if he was going to help facilitate her departure.

# CORDELIA

"WHY DO WHAT YOU WILL REGRET? WHY BRING TEARS UPON YOURSELF?"

BUDDHA

WE STAYED UP LATE INTO the night, making plans and decisions, occasionally digressing to take up a thread from that long ago time when the friendship of our youth came to bud.

When Ramon asked about Loraine and Ronald, my hand was automatically drawn to my neck. Instead of telling him I'd not seen or spoken with my parents for several years, that they hadn't even met their granddaughter, I segued into a recounting of the earlier events of the day.

"I am sorry about the necklace. It was meaningful to you?"

"A family heirloom given to me as a peace offering of sorts."

"From your mother?" Ramon raised his eyebrows. He didn't need reminding of how often my parents had been disappointed by my choices.

I nodded. "My mother only wore the necklace on special occasions, but I never took it off."

"It was beautiful?"

"Yes. But more than that, it was an everyday reminder of how lucky I'd been that Ronald and Lorraine Carlyle happened to be watching the news when my three minute *Tuesday's Child* segment aired. I mean, who chooses an unfocused teenager who'd been stranded in foster care for five years? If not for them," - I held up my arms - "I would have been permanently deserted in the system. They took a big chance on me and for that I have always remained grateful."

"Even if you didn't always see eye to eye. ***Delia***?" He was teasing now.

"Ugh." I shuddered at the ill fitting mold I'd been forced into. "They never understood how much I disliked being called Delia. Even when I began using Cordelia professionally, they refused to honor my wishes. Lorraine had this irrational fear that changing my name back signaled a wish to reconnect with my birth mother. I could never convince her otherwise."

I wished to depart from the subject of my parents before Ramon delved too deeply with his questions, so I quoted Buddha. "The things we touch have no permanence. Only by letting go can we truly possess what is real."

"Are you channeling Chung Wu?" he asked.

The mention beckoned bittersweet emotions. Only recently had I learned of my beloved Chinese foster father's death. I blinked hard and Ramon reached across and enfolded my hand in his. I'd been unprepared for the flutter deep within.

"Thanks," I whispered, more to hide the quiver in my voice.

He gently pressed my hand in a gesture of sympathy but then pulled back and cleared his throat before asking, "So, you continued your study of Asian principles. Buddhism, right?"

"Yes. And Taoism. A little Tai Chi. Those ancient philosophies satisfy my spiritual needs in a way Christianity never could."

I could never get past the irony. The woman who abandoned me never missed Sunday mass and forced me to attend weekly catechism classes in preparation for the momentous First Communion. It was less than two weeks after the sacred event that my mother deserted me, and that's when I dispensed with all things God. I'd been seven years old, *the age of reason* according to the Catholic Church. And my seven year old mind had been able to reason one truth: If God was the omnipotence everyone claimed, then I wouldn't have ended up forsaken to foster care.

"I never told you how I'd invented my name."

"Cordelia is not your real name?" Ramon frowned.

"Cordelia is the rightful part of my name." I was fond of the name my birth mother chose, especially after reading *King Lear*. Cordelia had remained truthful and I always tried to emulate my Shakespearian namesake. That is until recent events began leading me down a back alley of deception.

"So tell me, where did Richmond come from?"

"On the night my mother abandoned me, the police officer who'd been called to the movie theater had been tired and grumpy or perhaps he would have noticed the marquee and made the connection. She'd left me at the old Richmond Theater on Tenth Avenue. When I first saw the policeman, I was certain he'd been sent by my mother. But when I learned instead it had been the theater manager who called to report an unaccompanied child, I'd been mortified and wished never to see my mother again. So I lied about my last name."

Ramon's handsome face was contorted by perplexed sadness. "No, you did not tell me this story."

"I was probably too embarrassed."

"You should not be ashamed for lashing out in anger. What kind of parent leaves a young child alone in a movie theater and then never returns? You were only seven years old and you were frightened."

Of course, Ramon was right. But the unspeakable wish had been granted. I never saw my mother again, and the consequences had been severe. A few days later when I'd awakened to the nightmare of foster care, I convinced my case worker to help me. I recited the telephone number of our apartment which my mother had insisted I memorize. But by then the phone had already been disconnected and the apartment had been rented to a new family. Poof! She was gone.

"Hey," he gently interrupted my reflections into the haunting past. "You wear the name well. I cannot imagine you as anyone other than Cord Richmond."

But I could feel Delia Carlyle's pull, drawing me back into the morass of my present reality. Whether it was simply a desire to escape my troubles, or the resurrection of a decade-long, pent-up ache for Ramon, my mind flooded with wildly intimate notions to which my body was eagerly responding.

Ramon pushed his chair back and stood. "You are tired from your drive and tomorrow will be a busy day."

True, I was exhausted, but not even extreme fatigue could calm the quaking need that had surfaced. It was so tempting, the thought of an indulgent night of passion.

"Not sleepy yet." I impulsively reached up to stroke his face.

He stiffened and stepped away.

"And yet, sleep is what we both need."

I hadn't presumed he'd be willing, but I also hadn't thought to repel him either. After an awkward dance of parting for the night, I'd been left burning from the indignity of another rejection.

Sleep was elusive and the echo of Ting's unhappy mewing somewhere above the ceiling was not helping. Add to that, the more than usual wine I'd consumed had clouded my ability to meditate, which was my customary method for pushing aside anxieties. *What must Ramon think of me?* Isolating myself within Aiden's wicked world, no close friends of my own, and certainly not good judgment when it came to looking out for myself and my daughter. *And then in the midst of all these troubles I come on to him?* No wonder he'd retreated.

I didn't want to think about Ramon anymore, so I returned

my thoughts to the incident with the necklace. I tried to concentrate on the words of Buddha: *You only lose what you cling to.* But the image of my mother's worried face projected against my closed eyelids. Lorraine Carlyle, crusader in the *Just Say No* campaign against drugs, would be heartbroken to know her great-grandmother's delicate diamond pendant would be exchanged to satisfy some junkie's fix.

Add one more failing to the list.

Yes, I'd been a disappointment. I'd forsaken my parents' desires for me. But they had always, *always* stood by me. Until my obstinate disregard for their wishes propelled me down the aisle toward a man they deeply mistrusted. For not the first time, I was filled with regret for not heeding their warnings and for causing my parents such pain. How devastated they must be now that they've surely heard the news.

# RAMON

"WHO EVER LOVED THAT LOVED NOT AT FIRST SIGHT?"

WILLIAM SHAKESPEARE, ***AS YOU LIKE IT***

RAMON'S AGITATION WAS PREVENTING HIM from finding serenity in his usually comfortable king sized oasis. How could he expect to get any sleep with Cord laying an arm's length away? He placed his hand on the wall separating them, but the coolness of the bricks did nothing to calm the fever of desire. He'd been unbalanced by the unexpected early morning call and the vulnerability of her trembling voice had invoked a brotherly reaction to protect her. But then seeing and being so near to her had aroused a long suppressed need to possess her.

He flailed his body away from the wall and trained his thoughts on Cord's dilemma.

Now, having reviewed the evidence procured from Aiden Martelli's safe, he was glad he'd taken the initiative and gotten a head start. Still unclear were the motives behind such nefarious intentions, but the man's accusations had to be invented. Regardless of the questions surrounding Cord's story, he was convinced she would never hurt her daughter.

In the morning he'd put in another call to Badger, a tenacious investigator who'd earned the fitting nickname early in his career. His colleague and friend would undoubtedly close the gaps in Cord's story. There were enough leads to follow, including connections between the judge, the babysitter, the

DCF caseworker and Gabriella's pediatrician. And then there was the issue of the pre-dated, notarized deposition. It was an important clue. He'd have Badger check out the notary as well. Tomorrow he would collect the new driver's license, passports and travel documents he'd initiated earlier today. There was also a need for a new cell phone, and of course, a change in vehicles.

Putting his mental To-Do list aside, Ramon's thoughts made the inevitable return to Cord. When he'd opened the door a few hours earlier, his subconscious mind had been expecting the same skinny girl with hair the color of pecans who'd fascinated him since the day he first noticed her in front of the Wus' apartment building. Even though he'd also seen her once as a grown woman, it was the image of a withdrawn teenaged Cord that remained embedded in his memories. No doubt a defense mechanism. He'd go mad if he envisioned her as she'd been that one crazy weekend when they'd come together so unexpectedly. He'd often wondered how something so exciting and wonderful could also bring such misery to his life. But thoughts like these were unproductive. He must shove aside the haunting ambivalence and concentrate on getting her out of this mess.

# CORDELIA

"YOU CANNOT TRAVEL THE PATH UNTIL YOU BECOME THE PATH ITSELF."

BUDDHA

"Come on Ting." The sorrowful meows were heard high in the rafters. Yesterday she'd finally appeared from her retreat for some food but that ugly little dog began to bark furiously and chased her away again.

"It is time to go." Ramon tapped his wristwatch when he returned from carting our belongings to the garage. It was only four o'clock, but the plan was to get on the road well before gridlock set in on the busy streets of Manhattan so I could cross the border into Canada before dark. And Ramon needed to catch an early international flight out of JFK.

Thank goodness we'd managed to ease the awkwardness from the night I'd arrived. Yesterday had been a working day, with Ramon gathering all the counterfeit documents Gabriella and I would need and combing used car lots for a suitably nondescript vehicle.

I'd been astonished when he'd returned with not only a new passport, a Green Card and a New York state driver's license with his loft address and my former name, but also a birth certificate for Gabriella. I examined the official paper; confirmation of the birth of Ella Richmond. He'd suggested shortening my baby's name to Ella since Gabriella would be printed on issued flyers and alerts.

"Who do you work for?" I'd asked then quickly followed with a disclaimer. "On second thought, I don't want to know." Ramon was a photojournalist and his job involved extensive travel, occasionally landing him in some dangerous destinations.

"You are right." He'd responded with a mock menacing smile. "Once you learn my secrets? I will have to silence you forever."

My stomach lurched. Even though he was making light of the occupational hazards of his job, I didn't need to be reminded that unearthing people's secrets was a dangerous game.

"*Cordelia Richmond* returns," I said, flipping through the documents, proof of my new - or old depending on how you looked at it - identity. Truthfully, it felt more like coming home than pretending.

"Did she ever really go away?" He averted his eyes and spoke reminiscently making me wonder if I'd completely misread his earlier indifference. "Do you have your route mapped out?"

My assignment had been to submit a MapQuest for a strategic and circuitous route to my destination. When finished, I'd innocently clicked on the *My Pictures* icon of Ramon's computer expecting a peek at his brothers and their families, and maybe even a recent shot of Mrs. Alvarez. But there were just three photos in the file, all candids of the same woman, luxurious brunette curls cascading around a simply stunning face. Who else but Ramon could have captured these snapshots? And the expression looking back was filled with an irresistible quality. Pure devotion. I was fighting back an irrational dislike for the adoring woman as I considered who she could be. His ex-wife? Someone new to his life?

But those questions were left unspoken in the interest of preserving the tenuous peace Ramon and I had established. Besides which, my current dilemma was more pressing. Ting was simply not cooperating and I needed to get on the road.

"Even with the dog locked up, your cat is not feeling secure enough to come out of hiding."

"I can't leave her here." I was not ready to admit defeat, but could feel hot tears brimming as I continued to shake the favorite catnip toy with the small, tinkling bell. "Ting has been with me through all the bumps in the road."

"It will only be a couple weeks. Besides, the *Amber Alert* reports you are traveling with a Bengal cat, a fairly exotic breed if I am not wrong, and that has me worried."

"Who would take care of her while you're away?" I asked in a voice so meek I hardly recognized it as my own.

"I need only make a call to my friend who was going to take care of Guapo and explain the situation. So please do not worry. When you get settled in Canada, I will make the trip up and hand deliver your beloved Ting." Ramon gently removed the cat toy from my grasp. "Look, I was serious when I suggested this before. Why not take Guapo instead?"

My shoulders slumped in a dramatic gesture, but this did not deter Ramon from pleading his case.

"Hear me out. It might enhance your cover. In addition to changing your appearances, your car and your identification, by throwing a dog into the mix it is entirely unlikely you will be connected with the missing person description."

I shook my head in refute of his argument. "I'm not really a dog person."

"You are a Buddhist. Are you not supposed to love all creatures equally?" He began collecting the dog's food, bowls and treats. "Think about how your little one is going to react when you leave here not only without Ting, but also without her new best friend. Besides, your kitty may never come down until Guapo is gone."

"Why do I think you're just trying to get rid of him?"

"You are wrong about that," he said as he opened the bathroom door where the pooch had been incarcerated. The dog summarily leaped up into his arms and began licking his face. "Mi'jo guapo. I will miss my boy."

Then he released the dog who ran immediately to Gabriella and she squealed with delight.

*Poor forsaken Ting.* I sighed in resignation. "All right. I guess you can come with us *Handsome*."

"Hansome!" My daughter clapped her hands giving her approval to the new name.

"I will walk you down to the garage." He clipped on the leash and tried to hide a triumphant smile. After I secured Gabriella in her car seat the dog hopped right in beside her as if it was his rightful place.

"Adios, mi pequeňa, Ella." Ramon reached in and gently patted her head and tossed a treat to the dog. "You take care of these ladies, you hear?"

Then he ruffled my short blonde hair and smiled. "You will be fine."

"Promise?"

"I promise, mi querida." He brushed my cheek with the back of his hand.

"Shall I call you when I arrive?" I asked to cover the involuntary sharp intake of breath.

"I will call you."

"That's right. You'll be on a dangerous mission." I brought my fingers to the corners of my stinging eyes.

"Come here." He pulled me into his arms, and said more earnestly, "Promise me you will be most cautious of your surroundings. Be wary of who you trust."

I nodded into his shoulder but could not speak. After a few moments, although I was reluctant to let go, Ramon gently disengaged from the embrace. He lifted my chin and tenderly touched his lips to mine.

"Tanto tiempo," he whispered.

No longer able to defend against an upsurge of emotions, ranging from panic to passion, I quickly climbed into the car and buried my head in my hands. How I rued this mess I'd gotten myself into. Maybe it was wrong not to tell Ramon everything. With my hand on the car door I glanced in the rear view mirror. But he was already gone. I took it as a sign. My only option now was to push on.

Pausing to reconsider my path for escape, I wondered if I'd ever see Ramon again? Or if I even should? I shivered from a dark sense of despair as I turned onto the strangely quiet street, setting out on a different route from the one Ramon had so carefully laid out for me.

# PART TWO

## THE FOOL LANDS ON THE MIDDLE PATH

# HOMER

"IT IS MY BUSINESS TO KNOW WHAT OTHER PEOPLE DON'T KNOW."

SHERLOCK HOLMES IN ***THE ADVENTURE OF THE BLUE CARBUNKLE***

"ANOTHAH CUP, SHERIFF?" THE PROPRIETOR of *Becky's Diner* hovered with a fresh pot of coffee.

"When have I ever said no to a free refill?" Homer Pruitt looked up from his newspaper and lifted his mug for the brew that poured like molasses.

Elwood Beckwith, *Becky* since grammar school days, set the pot on the burner and took the pencil from behind his ear and began scratching it against his order pad.

"I'm making out on this deal, seeing as I'm getting round the clock police protection."

"And when exactly was the last time this place was robbed, Becky?" Homer already presumed to know the answer.

The man rubbed his stubble and gave the question a good long thought before replying. "Well, let's see. The year before you came to Murphy, Curtis Melton picked up a tennah from table seven and made it all the way to the bus station in Four Corners. So I'd say this arrangement of ours is working out on my behalf. Anothah?" Becky winked, reaching for the pot again.

"I'm okay," Homer held his hand atop the already filled to the brim cup and glanced out the window just in time to catch a glimpse of Rebekah Winchell, her long witch-like hair flowing behind as she scurried into the Hannaford Market on one of her rare forays into town.

Becky followed the gaze and as if reading his mind remarked, “She is a strange one.”

The tinkling of the bell announced another customer, saving Homer from further commentary about the eccentric hermit. His detective mind had been intrigued by the Winchell woman ever since she arrived, not long after he had relocated his own family to the quiet burg of Murphy, Maine. But his current reflections were interrupted by an annoying arrival.

“Might I join you, Guv?” The cockney accent didn’t fit the refined and impeccable appearance of the man who slid into the antiquated booth across from him. Russell Payne, a middle aged Cary Grant caricature, had been forced to abandon a lavish life in London when his exceptionally popular gossip weekly was bankrupted by one too many libel lawsuits.

Homer pushed the *New York Times* to the side and tapped his pen impatiently against the worn Formica table top.

“Feeding your crossword addiction I see. And not even using a pencil and eraser.”

“A sharp mind,” Homer said, pointing the pen to his head. But the challenging puzzle was the least of reasons he subscribed to the paper. His roots were pure New York and he liked to keep abreast of what was going on in his hometown. He picked up his copy of *The Times* and said, “This, unlike your slimy rag, is a credible newspaper.”

Homer liked to bring up *The Weekly Informer* whenever he could to keep Russell’s oversized ego in check. The British tabloid had represented both the pinnacle of the journalist’s success and his undoing.

Russell cleared his throat. “Water long under the bridge.”

“Once you swim with the sharks you never lose your taste for blood. If I'm not wrong, you're trolling as we speak. Unless you just popped in to check the daily special board."

"Pot roast." Russell grinned. "So what have you got for me this week?"

"Aren't you tired of digging up dirt around here? Such small potatoes compared to the latest Royal scandal. When are you going to resign from your gig at the *Murphy Post* and return to the excitement of jolly old London?"

"Country life suits me." Russell had returned to the same cabin in the wilds of Maine where he'd secluded himself to write his first novel after graduating from Columbia. Failing in his dream to become a world famous author, he'd returned to England to try his hand at newspaper reporting. He'd become seduced by tabloid journalism and ended up as managing editor of *The Weekly Informer* where he earned his nom de plume, *The Pagan Fox* for his wily ways. "I'm becoming a Yank through and through."

"You know as well as I, we could both live here another fifty years and still neither of us would ever be considered anything except *from away*."

Homer's gaze automatically tracked Rebekah as she exited the market and the sly reporter didn't miss it.

"Did you ever figure out her story?" asked Russell.

He knew better than to feign ignorance for it would only heighten the bloodhound's curiosity. "No story far as I know."

"Oh, there's a story all right, mate. Everybody has a story. Some worth telling and others" – he shook his hand – "I wouldn't offer a ha'penny bung for."

"I just thought of some news that might be worth mentioning." Homer wanted Russell off the scent of Rebekah Winchell. She was an odd bird, but he didn't see a reason for her private world to be upset by a newshound's snooping. "Remember Samuel Rawlins?"

"The fellow serving time for that vicious assault case?"

"That would be the one. He's getting out on parole next week."

Russell raised his eyebrows. "Awfully quick for felony battery, isn't it? As I recall it was a longer sentence. Ten, twelve years? He's served less than half. Why so light?"

"Apparently he was a model prisoner and one the parole board felt confident about releasing back into society." Homer's tone dripped with sarcasm.

"I don't envy you. A pretty dangerous chap, that one. I guess you're going to have to start earning that large paycheck the town sends your way every two weeks. Hmm? I wonder, when will you find time to consume copious quantities of Becky's dregs and complete your little puzzles?"

"Rest assured, Rusty, I'll be keeping a close watch on Samuel Rawlins for you. No need to go out and buy a night light." Homer could return a good lob.

Russell had the good sense to let the comment drop and took from his pocket the little red notebook he was never without to jot details about the soon to be released criminal. With Russell's hunger for a story satisfied and Homer's mind back on Samuel Rawlins' return to town, Rebekah Winchell was forgotten for the moment.

After Russell departed, Becky returned to offer one last refill.

"No, thanks. I've got to drive over to the courthouse for a hearing." Homer was gathering up his papers.

"You be careful out there, Sheriff. That's some fog creeping in. A real pea soup-ah."

Homer approached his cruiser just as an unfamiliar car passed down Main Street. He took note of the New York plates and was tempted to wave them over for a quick hello, see if they were from the city. One check of his watch and he knew he'd have to deep-six that thought, especially with this fog thickening up.

# CORDELIA

"THERE ARE TWO MISTAKES ONE CAN MAKE ALONG THE ROAD TO TRUTH... NOT GOING ALL THE WAY AND NOT STARTING."

BUDDHA

I HAD TO HOPE MY LUCK wasn't running out, having glided through most of New England without a snag before managing a wrong turn when a sea fog drifted in along the coast of Maine. I'd been about to stop and ask for directions when that sheriff appeared and gave me a double take. It was best to press on. There had to be another town nearby.

I crept along in the murkiness far too long without passing another car or seeing any houses. Without warning a force hit the car sending it spinning. When the Corolla came to a stop, Gabriella let out a panicked shriek while the ugly mutt hopped between the front and back seats to check on the two humans under his watch. The impact had not been severe enough to employ the air bags, but an adrenaline rush had my heart racing. With trembling hands I found the door handle and stumbled out on shaky legs.

"Hush, honey girl. You're okay." I checked to make certain that was an accurate statement and was relieved to find my daughter securely strapped into her car seat and in perfectly fine shape.

Handsome, if there ever was a misnomer, jumped from the car and began sniffing the front bumper. I joined him to inspect the damage, but could see no sign of what caused the accident. It happened so quickly and the visibility was poor, but my guess was a deer had grazed the car.

"Just a fender bender," I said to the dog, now happily relieving himself on a nearby bush. Yet when I tried to restart the engine, an unwelcomed grinding sound quashed my hope. It stubbornly refused to engage and after several further attempts the starter sputtered its death rattle.

I leaned my head against the steering wheel. Hemmed in by limited options, I craved the luxury of time for some meditative clarity. But there would be no path to enlightenment today. I hadn't a clue where I'd crash landed, so calling information for a local repair shop would be fruitless. Dialing 911 would connect me with the police and was therefore a last resort. I could wait for a Good Samaritan to drive by or I could start walking. I reluctantly leashed Handsome, grabbed my backpack and hefted Gabriella onto my hip before continuing on foot in the direction I'd been driving in hopes of coming across a house, a phone or maybe even somebody handy with cars.

The fog was in pockets now, offering small stretches of clearing, but there wasn't a hint of life on that unpaved road in the backwoods of Maine. Soon it would be dark. Who knew what fearsome nocturnal creatures would be rising from their dens? Coyotes? Bear? Maybe it would be prudent to make that 911 call after all. I set Gabriella down to ease my cramping arm for a minute when the dog's leash slipped from my grasp.

"Shoot. Come back here," I hissed as he scampered off into the fog, snarling a warning to whatever he was pursuing. Taking Gabriella's hand I followed quickly and wandered out from a blanket of mist into a meadow. A mere ten yards away, a woman with waist length, gray streaked hair stood near a small campfire, holding a sling shot aimed straight at Handsome.

"NO! Please!"

# REBEKAH

"HE THAT PASSETH BY AND MEDDLETH WITH STRIFE NOT BELONGING TO HIM, IS LIKE ONE THAT TAKES THE DOG BY THE EARS."

PROVERBS 26:7

"Sing to the Lord of harvest." Rebekah Winchell dipped her hand into a burlap grain bag and began to scatter seeds as she sang and danced around the fire over which a handmade spit held the small body of a charring animal. "Bring to His sacred altar the gifts His goodness gave."

She stopped abruptly, her senses quickened at a peculiar sound from within the fog hovering around the open meadow. She knew her land as well as she knew her own face, but the inability to see into the surrounding woodland was disorienting. She closed her eyes to sharpen her hearing. Nothing.

After several uneasy minutes she returned to her worship ritual, but kept a wary eye to the woods and her singing voice lowered. "To God the gracious Father, who made us very good, to Christ, who when we wandered, restored us with His blood, and to the Holy Spirit, who doth upon us pour His blessed dews and sunshine, be praise forevermore."

When she'd finished her ritual, Rebekah sat cross legged by the fire and picked up the skin of the animal that was burning over the fire and began to scrape it. A tear moved slowly down the side of her face which she briskly wiped away then muttered, "De-ah old Griselda."

Griselda had been her best little goat, even though she had quit kidding and giving milk a long time ago, she was the matron of the flock and kept the others in line.

"I put it off as long as I could, but today there was no choice. I need my studs and kids and the other girls are pregnant." She sniffed and rubbed her nose. "Let's face it. You weren't long for this world anyhow. But I sure am gonna miss you old lady."

When she completed her work with the pelt, she laid it aside and bowed her head over clasped hands, her lips forming words but producing no sound.

It was the low growl of an animal that awakened her from the prayerful state. Probably an old coyote smelling the burning flesh. Such a nuisance. She stealthily grabbed her slingshot and began to pivot in the direction of the sound.

Rebekah held her weapon taut as the critter circled the field then returned to a figure that was emerging from the fog. She narrowed her aging eyes to focus on what she thought to be a young boy.

"No! Please!" Came the surprising pleas of a female voice.

"You just stop right the-ah," Rebekah yelled out, inching closer to the trespasser.

"Come Handsome." It was an urgent command, but the dog was doing nothing to help its case as he continued the charge and retreat tactics.

That's when she first caught a glimpse of the small child clinging to the stranger's legs and promptly tossed aside the stone, wound the loop of leather around the y-shaped prongs and stuffed the sling into her pocket.

"I'm sorry about the dog. He's very protective of my little girl." The young woman took a step forward and tentatively offered her hand. "My name's Cord. Cord Richmond."

She nodded briskly but ignored the outreached arm.

The toddler stayed hidden, one arm wrapped around her

mother's leg and the other hand grabbing on firmly to the mangy little dog's collar. "Well, anyway, this is my daughter, Gab...I mean, Ella."

"This land is private. How'd you get he-ah?"

"I'm so sorry." The young mother gently petted the little girl's blond hair. "I was heading north along the coast when this sea fog came in and I got lost."

"You-ah a good ways from the coast now. Where's your car?"

"Back that way." The woman pointed in the direction from which she came. "I hit something, a deer I think. Anyhow, my car won't start. How far would it be to the nearest mechanic?"

Rebekah had known in her bones the dog was a shadow of trouble. You could set your watch by Fred Taylor's five o'clock closing time and it would take more than a Nor'easter to move him from his barstool at *Moody's Grill Room* back to his auto repair garage. What was she supposed to do now? Leave them to fend for themselves with dusk descending and the fog thickening up again? If it weren't for the little girl she might have been tempted, even if it wasn't a Christian attitude.

"Nothin' can be done tonight. I'll drive my truck over in the mornin' and take a look. Hopefully the fog will lift by then." She turned and started walking back to collect poor old Griselda's remains and called over her shoulder, "I can offer you some food and a bed for the night."

# RAMON

"SPEAK LOW IF YOU SPEAK OF LOVE."

WILLIAM SHAKESPEARE, ***MUCH ADO ABOUT NOTHING***

"We'll be landing soon, Mr. Alvarez." The flight attendant reached for his half empty drink.

Ramon downed the rest of his Bloody Mary before surrendering the glass. He'd had several hours to catch up on lost sleep from the past two nights, but his mind had been in overdrive. He was not usually one for having regrets or looking back. He made his decisions and he lived with them, accepting the consequences. Why then was he having such a hard time shaking off the frustration of Cord's sudden return to his life? Although if he was being truthful, hadn't she always been a presence, at least on the periphery? But she had also been safe, at a distance both geographically and emotionally. Untouchable because she was married. Now, without warning she was back, and yet again their timing out of sync because of this mess she'd gotten herself into. He couldn't help wondering, was that what made her all the more tempting?

When the plane began a descending bank he checked his watch. Cord should be within striking distance of the Quebec border by now. His confidence that she'd make it safely out of the country had been buoyed when he spoke with Badger before boarding. His friend had created a couple of diversionary tactics that would send officials in the opposite direction. First, tickets on a flight out of Miami to Hawaii had been purchased in the names of Delia Carlyle and Gabriella Martelli for the following morning. And then a report sighting the mother and daughter at a hotel near the airport had been leaked.

He reached under the seat for his messenger bag from which he pulled a battered envelope. It was the letter he'd written to Cord after his abrupt departure that decade ago weekend in Washington. A letter he never found the courage to send, nor bring himself to destroy.

Looking back through more mature eyes, Ramon now understood it was a self-destructive mix of pride and shame that had prevented him from posting the letter. He'd waited for Cord to make the move, but what a careless gesture that had been. After all, he hadn't even told her about his engagement until moments before he left. What had he expected her to do? Thank him for taking her to bed when he was committed to another? Beg him to call off his wedding?

He perused his words for the third time in as many days, the same maddening question cropping up. How would life be different if he had sent the letter?

He returned the envelope to his bag and took out the small box from *Simmons Jewelers and Pawn Shop*. He lifted the lid and fingered the pendent. Yesterday he'd returned to the area where Cord's necklace had been stolen. She had described the engraving so it was easy to identify and it hadn't taken long to track it down. He'd intended to give it to her this morning but completely forgot because the whole Ting debacle had consumed precious time. He reflected on Cord's screwed up childhood and the story she'd told about her invented name. No wonder she always had her head up in the clouds as a teenager. Who wouldn't want to escape to a fantasy world if they'd been abandoned by a parent to the horror of foster care? His affection for her intensified with each painful truth she shared.

In his mind he had reconciled his intentions. When he returned from this assignment he would give Cord the letter. This time he would place destiny in her hands.

Of course, there was still one added complication. Gina.

# CORDELIA

"IT IS BETTER TO TRAVEL WELL THAN TO ARRIVE."

BUDDHA

I WAS NOT THE LEAST BIT comfortable staying in a remote farmhouse somewhere in the boondocks of Maine with this peculiar woman.

"We couldn't possibly impose. Is there a motel somewhere nearby?"

"It would be two hou-ahs round trip to the Inn at Four Corners," the woman grumbled as she removed the body of a small animal from a makeshift spit and wrapped it in an animal pelt.

*Could that charred carcass possibly be the mainstay of the meal that had been offered?*

"I can pay you for your time and trouble."

The woman grimaced then wrapped herself in a thick but tattered shawl and twisted her long mane into a knot at the base of her neck. "I won't take any chances with my truck in this fog."

Once again I was constrained by a shortage of alternatives and none that appealed. So I picked up my shivering child, and with Handsome trailing behind, I followed the strange woman.

"What would you like us to call you?"

The clipped response came so belatedly I thought I might have broken some backcountry rule of etiquette.

"Rebekah. Winchell."

"How far of a walk is it to your home, Rebekah?"

"I imagine we'll make it before dark."

And not another word was exchanged on the long hike to our lodgings. It was just as well because my hostess for the evening bore too strong a resemblance to a character straight out of *Murder She Wrote*. For years I'd been pressed to join my mother in front of the TV on Sunday nights and wonder - *duh* - if Angela Lansbury would be able to solve Cabot Cove's murder of the week. But right now I didn't want to be thinking about my mother, in fact I was trying mightily to suppress the mental image of Lorraine Carlyle's anguished face.

"This is cozy." The farmhouse was sturdy and clean, if not a bit cluttered. I sat on the floor with Gabriella on my lap in front of the wood burning stove. The warmth was welcomed after walking a fair distance in the chilly evening breeze. But the quiver of ghost fingers crept up my spine as I studied the room more closely. On the table by the rocker were several prayer books and a large, well used Bible. A praying hands sculpture was displayed prominently in the center of the hearth mantle flanked by a pair of crucifix candlesticks. And scattered throughout the large living space were numerous crosses, pictures of Jesus and other religious statues and symbols. As a practicing Buddhist, I found it somewhat eerie to be sitting in the midst of this shrine to the Christian savior.

Within minutes the aroma of fried onions and garlic set my stomach grumbling. Handsome was whining, and although Gabriella hadn't begun to complain yet, an empty tummy could soon send her into a rage. I pulled some snacks from the backpack which were gulped down immediately.

"So what's your story?" Rebekah asked as she tended the frying pan.

"My story?" I was taken aback by the abruptness of the question. "I don't really have a story."

I settled my daughter on a faded chintz loveseat and removed from the backpack the tennis ball that assuredly would keep her and the dog entertained.

"Can I help you with anything?"

"Where you from?" Rebekah asked, tapping a wooden spoon against the large skillet on the antique cast iron range.

"Originally, I'm from New York, but when I was a teenager my family moved to Kentucky." I began to recite the details of the history Ramon and I had invented. Leaving him had proved more difficult than I could have imagined and such thoughts were reawakening the ache to my heart. But I pressed on with the fabricated details. "After my parents died, that was about five years ago, I returned to the city."

"Where's your husband?" Her tone was sharp.

"I, um, never married."

Rebekah's judging eyes wandered in the direction of my daughter.

"After I became pregnant, her father flew the coop." I wasn't sure why I felt the need to justify the fictional story.

"What do you do in New York?" Rebekah was cracking eggs into a bowl.

"Do?"

"To make a living?"

"Oh. I was a legal secretary for a Wall Street brokerage firm."

"Was?"

"It had become too hard to make ends meet. After paying for day care and rent, there was barely enough left to cover necessities. Like food. Are you sure I can't help with anything? Maybe set the table?"

Rebekah opened a cupboard and took down some dishes.

The china was of a surprisingly high quality and a curiosity briefly fluttered through my mind as I took in the *C* monogram.

"What brings you to Maine?"

"Well, Maine was never my intended destination." *Why hadn't I stuck with my original route through Vermont?*

"Oh?"

"I'm passing through on my way to Canada." And had I not taken that imprudent detour, I'd most likely be safely settled in an apartment arranged by Ramon's contact, and almost certainly one without these creepy crucifixes.

"Same thing according to folks in these parts." Rebekah offered her first, albeit fleeting smile as she took out a cutting board and began to slice a misshapen loaf of homemade bread. "Maine used to be the lower half of Quebec."

"No kidding?"

"Every year Maine and Quebec get together and vote to leave the unions and join forces. Every year the U.S. and Canadian governments overthrow the votes. Native Main-ahs hate being part of the United States. And fair warning" - she pointed her knife at me - "Main-ahs also don't take much to outsiders."

*All the more reason to get on our way*. If not for the fog and a deer on a collision course with the Corolla, we'd be out of Maine by now.

After the dishes were cleaned up, Rebekah offered to keep an eye on Gabriella while I took Handsome outside for his evening constitutional. The mist had lifted and the moon was casting a glow upon the farm yard. Beside a bustling chicken coop stood a large red barn from which the heads of three llamas peeked out curiously. In the surrounding fenced area a small herd of goats was huddling together by the door waiting to be let in for the night.

"So how did you like your meal, Handsome?" Following a

lengthy prayer of thanksgiving, Rebekah served a delicious egg dish made with onions grown in her garden and wild forest mushrooms she'd collected in the surrounding woods. She then offered the dog some of the meat from the carcass she'd toted back from the meadow. "I'll bet you never had goat before."

The dog was sniffing around the fence as an inquisitive kid wandered over for a closer look. The two animals sized each other up for several minutes before bringing their noses together. When the goat's tongue suddenly slipped through to lick Handsome's chin he spun around, wagging excitedly.

"Have you found yourself a girlfriend?" I reached down and petted the little mutt for the first time since Ramon coerced me into taking him. The wiry looking coat was surprisingly soft.

"I have to admit, you were quite the brave one today, ready to take a sling shot to the head for us." As he writhed with pleasure I shuddered to think what could have happened out in that field. Ramon was quite fond of the ugly little pooch, and that was incentive enough to keep him safe.

When Handsome and I returned to the sitting room, my daughter was sleeping peacefully as Rebekah rocked her.

"Shall we get her to bed?" I whispered.

I found the woman's rapt expression disconcerting as she carried Gabriella to a second floor bedroom and gently placed her under the worn but downy soft quilts. But what was most disturbing was the sound of the door being locked from the outside after Rebekah left the room. I flipped open my phone for reassurance, but didn't find it there. The farm was obviously beyond cell tower range. I tried to calm my fears by reminding myself that we were in fact the strangers in this situation.

# REBEKAH

"TRUTH, LORD, YET THE DOGS EAT CRUMBS WHICH HAVE FALLEN FROM THEIR MASTER'S TABLE."

MATTHEW 15:22

REBEKAH WAS BY NATURE A suspicious being and was convinced the young woman was spinning a tale of deceit. First of all, the accent was much too refined for the hills of Kentucky. Her Mummy's family came from that neck of the woods and spoke nothing like the woman called Cord. And her left ring finger bore an unnatural indentation where a wedding band might have been worn. Rebekah unconsciously touched her own naked ring finger as she considered her lodger's story.

"That poor little Ella," she thought. "Wonder what trouble her mama's gotten mixed up in."

She closed her eyes and hugged herself, reliving the moment when she held that sweet little one in her arms. It had felt so natural, so good.

She shook her head to shove aside memories that were hovering dangerously.

"Best to get them on their way quickly," she mumbled as she wrapped up the remainder of old Griselda and placed the meat in the icebox. Might as well go to the mangy mutt. After all, she could never have brought herself to eat the flesh of her dear old friend.

# CORDELIA

"LONG IS THE NIGHT FOR THE SLEEPLESS. LONG IS THE ROAD FOR THE WEARY. LONG IS THE CYCLE OF REBIRTH FOR THE FOOL WHO HAS NOT RECOGNIZED THE TRUTH."

BUDDHA

IT HAD BEEN A FITFUL night's sleep but I must have dozed off at some point because I was awakened by Handsome's soft growl followed by the unlatching click of the door lock. I hadn't undressed in case the need arose to flee via the escape route I'd worked out last night. The roof to the porch was just outside the window and it appeared to be an easy climb down from there.

I slipped my shoes on and peered out the window. There was just enough light in the sky to make out a figure filling grain buckets in the pen.

"There's oatmeal simmering on the stove," Rebekah called out when she saw me with Handsome on the far side of the house. "And some more meat scraps for the mongrel. I'll be finished here shortly. Then we'll take a ride over to your car."

I quickly downed some oatmeal and gave a hearty serving of goat meat to Handsome before collecting my still slumbering daughter and my backpack. I grabbed a banana from the kitchen counter for when Gabriella woke up and climbed up into the truck alongside Handsome to wait the few minutes it took Rebekah to finish her chores.

"In a hurry to leave?" the woman asked gruffly, hoisting her body up into the driver's seat.

*Indeed I was.* But I said, "Just hate being an imposition, that's all."

Daybreak offered a better view of the stretch we had traveled on foot the day before in foggy darkness.

"So all of this land is yours? Isn't it a lot to take care of on your own?"

There came no reply and I was fairly certain it wasn't because the driver couldn't hear over the sound of the muffler. Gabriella and I had landed at a most uncomfortable docking station on the way to starting a new life and I'd be glad to have the car repaired and on our way again.

When we arrived at the Corolla, Rebekah inspected the damage.

"Looks like you grazed some of these boulders." The engine still wouldn't turn over but she somehow managed to shift the car into neutral. "I'll hitch it to the truck."

The woman was amazingly strong for her age, easily hefting a sizeable chain from the back of the truck and hooking it to the front of the Toyota.

"How far to town?" I asked.

"Maybe an hour."

"That far?" It hadn't seemed quite so long a drive yesterday.

"It's a bumpy road. I'll have to take it slow or do worse damage to the bottom of your car. Then you might be stuck here a while."

*Now that was a disconcerting thought.* Even more perplexing was to see that we were returning to the farm.

"Aren't we going straight into town?"

"I'll tow the car from here after you unload your things."

"That seems unnecessary," I argued. "You can just drop us at the repair shop and we'll wait until the car's ready."

Rebekah scoffed. "If you take it in they'll fleece you good for the work. I'm more likely to get a fairer price."

"I don't mind paying more for the repair." *Especially if it gets us out of here faster* was what I did not add.

Rebekah stared hard at me. "I thought you'd been having a tough time making ends meet?"

Having landed squarely on the sticky flypaper of deceit, I tried to backpedal. "It's not that I don't appreciate your trying to save me money, because I do. But we've imposed on you enough."

"Another day won't make much difference." She came around to open the passenger door. "Now let's get what you need out of the car."

Slowly I began to remove the essentials, trying to buy time and come up with a reasonable counter to the plan.

"Could we tag along to town? I need to pick up some food and diapers."

Rebekah sucked in an irritated breath. "Write up a list and I'll gather the things ya need."

I was wary of her insistence on leaving us behind, but then recalled the sheriff I saw when I drove through the last town before getting lost. Maybe it was best to stay off the radar. I searched for some paper and pen in the drawer of a small side table, but only found a deck of playing cards.

"What are you doing?" Rebekah barked, toting in a suitcase, the harshness of her voice making me jump.

"I was just looking for something to write the list."

She pointed her chin toward the kitchen. "You'll find a notepad and a pencil in the middle drawer of the sideboard."

I quickly jotted down some useful items and handed her some money.

"Could I use your phone while you're gone?" I looked around the room to locate it.

"You could if I had one."

"You don't have a phone?" It shouldn't have surprised me. Besides electricity and running water, there were no other modern conveniences in this house. No television, no dishwasher, no microwave and evidently no phone.

"Pshhh. Don't need one." Rebekah walked toward the door, and in a gesture incongruous to her stern nature, she tenderly cupped her hand over the top of my daughter's small head. "I'll be back."

I waited for the engine to start before emerging from the house to watch my vehicle for escape vanish in a cloud of dust. Rebekah's steadfast stance against our joining her in town was worrisome. Had she detected something amiss in the tale I told. And if so, what might she do about it?

As I considered my circumstances, the sharp edge of dread sliced through me. Stranded on an isolated farm in the backwoods of who-knew-where Maine, locked in by a suspicious religious zealot, and with no means of communicating with the outside world. I thought about the business card for B.T. White, securely tucked away in my backpack. It was the emergency contact Ramon had arranged for while he was out of the country. But what use was it to me without a phone?

Gabriella and Handsome were playing their favorite game of toss and fetch so I did a little poking around, starting upstairs. I gently pushed open the creaking door to a second bedroom which was even more austere than the room we'd been given. There was a framed painting of Jesus above the bed and another Bible on the bedside table. I admired a beautifully carved music box atop the bureau before peeking into the open closet which revealed a limited wardrobe of jeans, khakis, long sleeved white and chambray shirts and several pairs of work boots. Hanging from a hook was the long skirt and woven shawl Rebekah had been wearing the day before.

Back downstairs I opened a door at the back of the house where I was greeted with an explosion of color. Nearly every inch of the walls and ceiling was covered with racks and hooks from which a rainbow of large spools of yarn were stacked or hung. Also crowded into the small room were three looms of varying sizes, each with a work in progress. To my inexpert eye the weaving appeared to be of excellent quality.

Nowhere in the house were there any family photographs or keepsakes to offer a personal glimpse of the woman. I wandered back to the kitchen to brew a cup of soothing tea. When I couldn't find the sugar, I tried the door where Rebekah had retrieved the onions last night, but found it locked.

*How odd. Who locks their pantry?*

I remembered the deck of cards in the side table and thought perhaps a game of solitaire would relieve my edginess. But upon opening the box, I discovered it was no ordinary deck. Yet it seemed entirely unsuitable for the obviously devout Rebekah to have Tarot cards secreted away.

The *Hanged Man*, *Empress*, *Magician*, *Ace of Cups*, the *Sun* and the *Moon*. I flipped through the cards trying to summon to mind their meanings. Not long ago, a group of the waiters at *Futasia Grill* had persuaded me to join them for a psychic reading by Miss Crystal who'd become all the rage in Georgetown. As head chef, I'd gone along to foster a spirit of camaraderie among the staff. When I turned the next card to reveal *The Fool*, my hands began to tremble at the memory of Miss Crystal's severe warning.

"*The Fool* is the most powerful of all the cards, my dear. Do not be blindsided. Take great care on your pending adventure. One wrong turn could lead to perilous consequences."

There was a poem printed on the flip side of the card:

> With all his worldly possessions in one small pack,
> The Fool does travel he knows not where.
> So filled with visions and daydreams is he,
> He cannot see the edge of the cliff is there.

But close to his heel, a small dog does nip,
Warning him of a possible mis-step.

Gabriella had toddled over for a look at the colorful picture and giggled, pointing to the ugly dog nipping at the Fool's heels. "Hansome!"

The resemblance was unnerving and upon closer inspection of the image, I noticed other parallel traits. *The Fool* had feminine features and short blonde hair very similar to my newly shorn locks and even wore a red jacket not unlike my own. And *The Fool* was indeed oblivious to the precariousness of the cliff upon which he teetered.

I shoved the cards back into the drawer. Inhaling deeply, I closed my eyes and tried to push aside the superstitious nonsense. *Does not the Buddha reject superstitions and urge us to pursue wisdom?* But these meditations did nothing to restore my confidence.

I needed to get to a phone.

# REBEKAH

"DO NOT FORGET TO ENTERTAIN STRANGERS, FOR BY DOING SOME HAVE UNWITTINGLY ENTERTAINED ANGELS."

HEBREW 13:2

REBEKAH'S PULSE WAS RACING. WHY did it have to be on her property these people got lost and wrecked their little foreign car? And why did the woman have to pester her about coming to town? She didn't like attention being drawn to her and that's exactly what would happen if a young woman and child came along. Everyone sniffing around, asking questions. Though she hated to lie, maybe she'd tell Fred Taylor the car belonged to her niece who was passing through. If she was lucky, she'd get them on their way before anyone even discovered they'd been there.

"Ah, but that sweet child. So much like my Gemma," she whispered as she once again lost herself in the memory of how perfectly wonderful it had been to hold the little girl in her arms. Unconsciously she began humming the special song.

Rebekah felt the beginnings of an old familiar throbbing at her temples as the truck bumped along deserted Old County Road toward Murphy. The battle taking place in her mind would surely provoke the return of the headaches, her curse for so many years. A solitary life had been the only cure.

She brought the truck to a full stop for prayerful reflection.

"Dear Lord, if you are looking down upon my wretched self at this moment, I pray it is without shame. To repent for my sinful thoughts, I will do my best to make a nest for the wounded birds. In thy name I pray. Amen."

# HOMER

"WOMEN ARE NEVER TO BE ENTIRELY TRUSTED, - NOT THE BEST OF THEM."

SHERLOCK HOLMES IN ***THE SIGN OF FOUR***

"HE-AH YOU ARE. GRILLED CHEESE for the kiddies, a chef salad for the lady and one BLT for my best customah." Becky brushed his hands together as if dusting crumbs away. "Can I get you fine people anything else?"

"We're all set," Homer said, sliding aside today's issue of *The Times*.

"Thanks, Becky." Frannie had brought the grandkids to the diner for a rare treat. Homer didn't like to be distracted by family when at his unofficial post. The Sheriff's Office was located on the end of a side street which didn't afford him a good look at what was going on in town. So after his morning calls and paperwork had been tended to, he parked his cruiser in front of the diner and with his cell phone at the ready, he set himself up at the corner booth which gave a good view of Main Street Murphy. Everyone knew where to reach him in case of emergency and fortunately he had an efficient deputy assistant. Truth be told, Olivia Bishop could handle any problem that arose as well as he could.

"So what's on tap this afternoon?" he asked the two grandchildren he and Frannie had legally adopted five years ago when they'd been taken into protective custody by DCYF. Their daughter, Sophia, had chosen a regrettable path with a string of unsavory boyfriends including the controlling low-life rock singer who'd left his physical mark on her innocent children.

Benjamin, the older at age ten, muttered with little enthusiasm, "We're going to the library."

"So you don't wanna do that? Improve your mind?" Homer asked, tapping the young boy on the head.

"I'm too big for story time, Pops. Can I stay here with you?"

"I like story time," Sara chimed in, hugging her tiny seven year old body. "Today Mrs. Nichols is going to read *Cloudy with a Chance of Meatballs* and that's my very favorite."

Benjamin made a face and silently mimicked his little sister.

"That's rude." Frannie chastised. "If you can't be polite then we'll just skip the stop at *Mike's* afterward."

At the mention of *Mike's Toy and Hobby Shop*, Benjamin perked up a bit.

"Sorry," he said in his most humble voice. "But can I stay here for a little while? Just during story hour? Please Pops?"

"I'll be busy working."

Benjamin glanced at the unfinished crossword puzzle, then at his grandmother who gave a subtle cautionary shake of her head to keep his thoughts to himself. Surely he'd heard his classmates repeating their parents' opinions about the sheriff's easy life in Murphy. Homer's addiction to puzzles was a running joke in town, but Frannie understood his public image of the laidback sheriff was entirely misleading. In fact, it was a ruse he preferred to perpetuate.

"Better for a criminal to be lulled into believing they can get away with something," he'd said on more than one occasion. "They have a false sense of security which makes it easier to catch them in the act."

But there weren't many criminals in Murphy, Maine. Frannie was almost glad Samuel Rawlins would be out on parole soon. *Almost.* At the very least it would give her husband's shrewd detective mind something on which to keep itself honed. It had nearly killed him when he left the NYPD twenty years ago after taking the fall for being in the wrong place at the wrong time in the company of a corrupt fellow officer. He'd been offered early retirement and the financial security of his pension if he pled no contest and walked away. Frannie had wanted him to fight it, but Homer clammed up whenever she broached the subject. "What's done is done," he'd told her. "No muss, no fuss."

Russell Payne approached the booth with a rolled up edition of that week's *Murphy Post* which he rapped against his free palm, startling Frannie out of her brooding.

"Just thought I'd stop by and pay my respects."

"Hello, Rusty." Although Homer had observed the newsman taking a seat at the counter earlier, he was hoping he'd keep his distance.

"Sheriff. *Francesca.*" Russell, the only person who didn't use the shortened nickname, bowed slightly and offered his most enchanting smile. "Always a pleasure."

Homer didn't miss the blush that came to Frannie's cheeks whenever Russell Payne was in her presence.

"Good afternoon, Russell. Children, say hello to Mr. Payne."

They both mumbled a polite hello.

"Playing hooky today?" he asked.

"No. It's a teachers' professional day," Benjamin announced with a tinge of defiance in his voice.

Under normal circumstances Homer would have scolded the boy for being fresh, but since it was Russell, he let this one slide.

"Well, I shall shove off. Cheerio."

"Cheerios!" Sara replied with amusement.

As the Pruitt family finished their lunch and Benjamin continued to negotiate plans for the afternoon, Homer saw Rebekah Winchell's truck pull up in front of *Jake's Hardware Store*. Twice in as many days? Now that *was* odd. And mere minutes after entering the store, the woman charged back out, visibly disturbed and not carrying any purchases. When she got back into the truck she rested her head in her hands for a moment and then made a hasty exit.

"So what do you say, Pops?" Benjamin's voice was hopeful.

"Here's the deal. You go with Granny to the library, but instead of story time, you can look for your summer reading selections. And I suggest you pick at least one book by Mark Twain. I think you'll thank me. Then when Sara's story time is over you can go to *Mike's*." He took out his wallet and withdrew some cash. "My treat. Now if you'll excuse me, I've got some business to attend to."

"Thanks, Pops!" Benjamin pocketed the bills with glee.

Homer kissed both kids atop the head and then leaned down to plant one fully on Frannie's lips. He was not one for public displays of affection but he liked to keep people guessing. Especially his wife.

# CORDELIA

"THE WHOLE SECRET OF EXISTENCE IS TO HAVE NO FEAR. NEVER FEAR WHAT WILL BECOME OF YOU, DEPEND ON NO ONE. ONLY THE MOMENT YOU REJECT ALL HELP ARE YOU FREED."

BUDDHA

I NEEDED AIR. THE TAROT CARDS had been unnerving and the walls of this backwoods shrine were closing in on me.

"How about a walk?" Gabriella clapped her hands and Handsome wiggled with delight at the prospect. I guess we all had cabin fever.

With my daughter in the backpack carrier and Handsome taking the lead, we found a short trail through the woods which brought us to a rushing river. The path continued along a contrasting landscape of towering trees and wild ferns on one side and the rocky descent to the cascading stream of water on the other. The beauty of the scenery was marred only by the presence of a severely weathered cabin across the way. However, the presence of phone lines leading to the house was a detail I didn't miss.

"Let's hope Rebekah returns with a repaired Corolla so we can get back on the road pronto," I said aloud. Otherwise I'd have to find a way to get in touch with B.T. White.

I hadn't had much of a chance to think about Ramon since crash landing in Podunk, Maine, but I'd thought of little else on the drive up through New England. The years had done nothing to diminish the attraction. Just the sight of him had awakened old stirrings for which I'd been unprepared. Had it only been two days ago? I closed my eyes to savor the memory of when he held me during our goodbye embrace.

I opened them again in time to watch Handsome dart back into the woods, probably to chase a rabbit or squirrel. A city dog might never have encountered such furry wild creatures. Moments later the dog returned to the path ahead of me with a strut of self importance.

"Buddha would not be pleased if you harmed another animal. I'm pretty sure there's such a thing as doggie karma, too."

The dog tossed a haughty look over his shoulder as if to say, "Worry about your own karma."

*How true.* The discomposing emotions that arose from seeing Ramon and the agonizing thought of him discarding me again had me running scared and making the fateful decision to change course. And look where that had gotten me.

The trail ended at a small meadow with a backdrop of rolling hills ascending to a range of rocky peaks glimmering in the morning sun.

"This is spectacular." I removed Gabriella from the carrier so she could run amid the wildflowers and chase after Handsome. When she started to get sleepy, we sat down in a shady spot overlooking the riverbank where I began to rock her, humming a favorite lullaby. The vantage point offered a good view of the house across the river and I deliberated on how difficult it would be to traverse those rapids if the desperate need arose. I had a pretty well formed Plan B for getting to a phone when I spied a figure approaching.

"Looks like you did a bit of exploring." Rebekah wasn't the least bit winded from the trek.

"It's so beautiful and peaceful here."

"There was a cottage here long ago," she said, in a wistful tone.

"It would be an idyllic spot." Then I asked casually, "Anybody live in that house across the way?"

"The Rawlins boys. Nothing but trouble," Rebekah tutted. "A real life Cain and Abel. One's been serving time in prison and the other'n? He's just not right in the head. Poor Timothy. I don't think he's seen anyone 'cept Pastor Josh for the past six years."

"Pastor Josh?"

Rebekah's expression soured. "Minister of Union Church over to Laurel. Timothy's mother was organist there until she died and the congregation takes a special collection on Sundays so Pastor Josh can bring him groceries every Monday morning."

"How did she die?"

"Either from fatigue or shame. She passed the very day they sent Samuel to prison."

"What was the crime?"

"You don't want to know. And it would have been best for everyone if the monster stayed locked up forever. But he'll soon be free."

"Is the other brother...Timothy, did you say?"

Rebekah nodded and tugged on the cuffs of her shirt. It was a frequent tendency.

"Is he also dangerous?"

"I don't imagine he'd intentionally bring harm to anyone. But like I said, he's just not right."

"Does anyone ever go rafting on this river?" I asked to change the subject from monsters and the mentally unbalanced.

"Too remote. Anyway, it's only rushing now because of spring melting. The rapids will calm any day now. Then it will be crossable."

I felt as if the woman had been reading my thoughts.

However, after hearing the description of Rebekah's neighbors, I hoped there would be no need to execute Plan B.

"Maybe we should get her back." I kissed the top of my daughter's head and she began to stir.

Rebekah's often severe expression softened as she reached out to take Gabriella so I could stand up. "Can I carry her for a piece?"

"If you'd like." I gathered the backpack and we began to retrace our path to the farm. "So, is my car fixed?"

"'Fraid not. Fred Taylor has to special order a part."

Not what I wanted to hear. "How long will that take?"

"Three days, maybe."

"Why so long?" *It was a Toyota for crying out loud.*

"You're on Maine time now."

"There must be an inn or a motel somewhere nearby where we can go to get out of your hair."

"Unfortunately, there's a retreat over at the camp this weekend, and there won't be any rooms available this side of Bangor."

"What kind of camp?"

"Camp Davis. It's a spiritualist camp."

"Like a church camp?"

"Of a fashion." A pained expression crumpled her brow.

"Are there cabins there? Maybe I could rent one while we wait."

"It's a popular retreat. Cabins are booked well in advance."

We walked along in silence for a few moments. As had been the case since I set off on this course, alternatives were not plentiful. I could try to buy another car, but I'd need to involve Rebekah and that would foster suspicions. Not to mention, the initiation of a paper trail using false documents could certainly open Pandora's Box. And with no access to a phone or cell service I couldn't get in touch with Mr. B.T. White for help. Of course, if I did find a way I'd be forced to explain my reasons for abandoning the original plan. And how could I do that if I didn't fully understand myself?

"Are you handy with a paint brush?" Rebekah asked offhandedly.

"What?" My mind had been drifting and I wasn't certain I heard her correctly.

"My house needs painting. You can stay on here until your car's ready and help me get a start on the job to earn your keep."

"It's a kind offer, Rebekah." It would only be for three more days and the isolation of the farm was nearly as good as being in Canada. I mean really, who'd think of looking for us in these remote woods of Maine? "Sure, I'll do it."

# HOMER

"THERE IS NOTHING MORE DECEPTIVE THAN AN OBVIOUS FACT."

SHERLOCK HOLMES IN ***THE BOSCOMBE VALLEY MYSTERY***

"AFTERNOON." HOMER STROLLED INTO THE hardware store with a casual air.

"Sheriff." Jake nodded and nosey customers were drawn to the counter like nails to a magnet.

Homer glanced above the checkout register where the television was tuned to the Bangor station and saw the conceited mug of the either loved or abhorred anchor, Phillip Videlle. Homer knew which side of the fence this crowd sat.

"So what does A-hole have to say today?" A chorus of smirks ensued.

Jake imitated the pretentious way the newscaster combed his fingers through his wavy bleached blond hair. "Let's see. There was a bit of a ruckus out at Camp Davis with that Spiritualist convention going on this week."

"What kind of ruckus?" The camp was not under his jurisdiction, but Homer was curious.

"Protestors from *The New Christian Soldiers* became a bit zealous in their hate chants."

"Hate is job security for law enforcement. And greed."

"True. Anyhow, there's a popular shaman attending this year who says he's made spiritual contact with Jesus."

"No wonder he's popular."

"Anyhow, the *Christian Soldiers* strongly object to what this guy claims Jesus told him. Things got heated. The state police were called in to settle everyone down."

"Good to know the troopers have the situation under control."

"Hey, did you know Samuel Rawlins was being released today? I thought the *Murphy Post* article said it wasn't until next week."

Homer frowned. "News to me."

"The D.A. is livid. And guess who's been assigned as his new parole officer? Jimmy Kramer. And he's none too happy about it."

"Neither am I." Not only would Homer be giving up his weekend but he'd also have to contend with Russell Payne who would surely call him on the inaccurate information he'd provided. "That's it for local news." Jake flattened his palms against the counter.

"Who won the Bo-Sox game?" Homer grinned, knowing that his Yankees had swept the Red Sox in the series ending last night.

"Not funny. So, what do ya' need today, Sheriff?"

"Two cans of mace and a new fire extinguisher. Put it all on the department's bill."

"Coming right up."

On the walk back to his perch at the diner he put a call in to Olivia. "Did you tape the twelve o'clock news today?"

"Always do. There are problems out at Camp Davis. Oh, and Samuel Rawlins…"

"Is being released today. I know. Has Jimmy Kramer called yet?"

"No. But he will."

"I'd like to have a look at that tape."

"What are you looking for?"

"I'm not sure, but I'll be over to the office in 'bout an hour. Don't mention this to anyone."

"I never do."

"I know, Liv. You're a peach."

# RUSSELL

"PERSONAL COLUMNISTS ARE JACKALS
AND NO JACKAL HAS BEEN KNOWN TO LIVE ON GRASS ONCE HE HAD LEARNED ABOUT MEAT
- NO MATTER WHO KILLED THE MEAT FOR HIM."

ERNEST HEMINGWAY

HOMER PRUITT WASN'T THE ONLY person who'd witnessed the strange behavior of the hermit weaver. Russell Payne had been standing by the counter shooting the breeze with Jake when the Winchell woman entered the store. She fidgeted as she waited for the men to finish their conversation but then something on the news caught her attention and not in a good way. Russell was an expert in reading expressions and Rebekah's blended shock and recognition. When he followed her gaze, footage of the scene at Camp Davis was concluding and the mug shot of Samuel Rawlins flashed on the screen as Phillip Videlle segued from the protest rally to the early release of the local criminal. Seconds later the odd woman dashed out the door.

"What got into her?" Jake asked, shaking his head.

"Maybe she just got tired of waiting," Russell suggested, but didn't believe. He strolled to the door to study Rebekah, her anguish obvious as she recklessly reversed the car and sped off.

Before he turned back to the business of buying a new set of screwdrivers he spied Homer ambling from the diner in the direction of the hardware store. While Jake was waiting on another customer Russell ducked down one of the aisles out of sight but within earshot of the checkout counter. He listened intently to Homer's questions, trying to decipher an agenda. The sheriff's displeasure about the change in Samuel Rawlins' release date was apparent, as was the fact he'd not been informed. He'd also expressed a genuine curiosity about what was going on at Camp Davis. Somewhere in the mix there was a scent of a story brewing. But was it worth telling? And was Rebekah Winchell somehow involved?

He'd have to do some digging around and he might as well start here at Jake's with the group of old timers who congregated on the porch after lunch. They'd all have their own views about the loner and where she came from. He felt confident somewhere in those opinions would be a lead to track down. God, that old familiar adrenaline rush felt good. *The Pagan Fox* had lain dormant far too long.

# REBEKAH

"THE WOLF SHALL DWELL WITH THE LAMB, AND THE LEOPARD SHALL LIE DOWN WITH THE YOUNG GOAT, AND THE CALF AND THE LION AND THE FATTENED CALF TOGETHER; AND A LITTLE CHILD SHALL LEAD THEM."

ISAIAH 11:6

REBEKAH COULDN'T CARE LESS IF her house got painted and though her instincts were sending a clear message to avoid getting involved, every time she looked at that little Ella her heart overruled her good sense. She had a strong hunch the young mother was running away from trouble and she felt compelled to protect the child.

Of course, tomorrow she'd have to return to town and buy paint, a task she didn't relish. She tried to avoid being a regular presence in Murphy, but far worse she'd have to face Jake and his good old boys after running from his store like a chicken being chased with a hatchet. She couldn't help it. It had been a shock to see Aunt Lucinda on the television news, being interviewed because of some problems out at the camp. Her heart had been flooded with a mix of love and hurting so much that she couldn't bear it. How many years had passed since she'd seen Lucinda? Too many to count.

"Can I help?" Cord interrupted her thoughts.

"Just finishing up." She'd been chopping vegetables for a stew. "Where's the baby?"

"Napping on her blanket under that old rhododendron out front with Handsome. She fell asleep while I was reading to her."

"Why don't you take that dog of yours out on the river trail for some exercise? Let the little one sleep. I'll keep an eye on her while the stew simmers." Rebekah dragged down the old porch rocker and settled herself next to where Ella was slumbering peacefully and began finishing work on the table cloth she'd just taken off the loom.

Cord whistled to get the dog's attention. "Let's go for a walk."

But Handsome wouldn't budge.

"Off with ya' now." Rebekah shooed away the mutt.

But the dog stubbornly curled up at the child's feet, offering the closest expression to a glower of which any animal is capable.

"Not an obedient creature," she clucked disagreeably.

"He grows on you." Cord stretched and stepped off the porch. "Maybe I'll just take a short stroll around the farm yard."

Rebekah felt a sinking in her gut when the young woman approached the barn and hesitated at the door. She sighed with relief as Cord moved on to where the llamas were eagerly awaiting an afternoon snack. It might be wise to padlock that door for the time being. Another item to add to the list for Jake's tomorrow.

# CORDELIA

"YOUR WORST ENEMY CANNOT HARM YOU AS MUCH AS YOUR UNGUARDED THOUGHTS."

BUDDHA

As I walked between the farm buildings a memory of Aiden flashed into my head forcing me to lean against the barn for support.

"You're too cavalier with the baby," he'd accused me at one of the last family dinners. Of course, it wasn't true. I was always very watchful of Gabriella. My husband had been advancing his nefarious plan by instilling doubts in those close to us. But I hadn't stood up for myself.

I grabbed some apples from a basket and began feeding them to the llamas.

What a mess I'd gotten myself into. I'd suffered a severe case of myopia when I fell for Aiden. How had my parents seen so clearly what I had not? I should have admitted they'd been right. I should have told them I was leaving. And I should have told Ramon everything. But it would have been unfair to involve him further in my problems. Still, someone should have been given a copy of the evidence. Just in case.

I closed my eyes and repeated a favorite Buddhist quote. "*Do not dwell in the past; do not dream of the future; concentrate the mind on the present moment.*"

I returned from my walk to find a vacated blanket and

rocking chair. While Handsome, who'd been left tied to the porch, was whimpering unhappily.

"Sorry bud." I untied the rope from his collar and when freed, he turned and pressed his nose against the door. I reached down to scratch him behind the ears. "I don't have much experience with little doggies, but Ting used to like this."

I moved my fingers to the top of his head and he responded with a slow forgiving wag. Then he plopped down submissively for a tummy rub. "I'm glad you don't bear your grudges long. I promise, no more ropes."

I smiled, remembering how vigorously I'd protested Ramon's suggestion Handsome join us. Now I was kind of glad to have him along.

"Do you miss Ramon?" The dog licked my hand. "Yeah, me too."

But I couldn't forestall the punch-to-the-gut feeling that came upon me whenever I thought of those photos on Ramon's laptop. Whoever the gorgeous woman was, she obviously meant something to him. *But what? And what difference did it make anyhow?*

I pushed aside those tormenting questions and peeked through the window before entering the house. Gabriella was sitting on Rebekah's lap as the woman read to her, but was so captivated by the story she didn't even notice me.

"Jonah sat in the belly of the whale for three whole days. Can you imagine?" Rebekah asked.

My daughter shook her head, eyes wide in awe of the tale.

"Me neither. But he prayed and prayed and God answered."

I rolled my eyes and headed to the kitchen to check on the stew. Right now I felt I had a lot in common with Jonah. Three days to sit in the belly of the whale while waiting for the Corolla part to arrive.

# RAMON

"LOVE IS A SMOKE AND IS MADE WITH THE FUME OF SIGHS."

WILLIAM SHAKESPEARE, ***ROMEO & JULIET***

"IT IS ME. HAVE YOU heard anything at all from my friend?" Ramon spoke softly into the only phone available for miles while he kept a vigil of his surroundings. He'd had an unexpected opportunity to call Cord, but she hadn't answered her cell phone. After several attempts he gave up on her and put in a call to his colleague and confidante.

"No? Hmm. Tell me, Badger, has there been anything else relating to her disappearance in the news?"

He listened as he kept his eyes on alert for trouble.

"I do not think she would have abandoned the plan." He'd called in a favor from a former associate in Montreal to find Cord an apartment to rent in a small town outside the city. But evidently the woman hadn't heard from her either.

"She did not tell me that." He blew out a breath of frustration and said under his breath, "But it does close one of the gaps in her story."

"What?" Ramon rubbed his forehead while listening to more troubling news, then said, "No, that is most definitely not good." He paused to listen again. "Okay, yeah, but if she does get in touch with you, do anything you need to make sure she is safe. If I can, I will try to contact you again. Otherwise, I will see you on Tuesday. Adios."

Cord should have made it to Canada by now. And although he could think of a dozen logical reasons why she might not have answered her phone, Ramon's instincts were settling on more disquieting possibilities. Why hadn't he blown off this assignment and personally seen to it that she and her daughter made it safely out of the country? A well-oiled defense mechanism to protect his heart had obviously interfered with his logical thinking.

He needed to put to rest the growing doubts about Cord's story and her reasons for running away, especially in light of this new information Badger had dug up. He would try to finish his assignment quickly and get back to the states and to the bottom of this mystery, of which the most pressing aspect was finding the woman who had stumbled back into his life and reawakened a long buried yearning.

# HOMER

"TEMPTATION TO FORM PREMATURE THEORIES UPON INSUFFICIENT DATA IS THE BANE OF OUR PROFESSION."

SHERLOCK HOLMES IN ***VALLEY OF FEAR***

"Here you go, boss." Olivia pushed aside the piles of mail and set before Homer a cup of steaming green tea. "I don't know how you can drink Becky's dreadful coffee."

"That I love. This?" Homer grimaced but took a sip in spite of his disinclination.

"Someone's got to make sure you take care of yourself," Olivia scolded. "And it sure as right won't be Becky or…" his assistant stopped abruptly, her cheeks taking on a rosy tinge.

"Or?" He raised his eyebrows. Olivia, who was outgoing and lively by nature, had never really approved of or felt comfortable around his introspective and often times aloof wife. A palpable tension materialized whenever Frannie stopped by the office.

"Pardon me, boss. I misspoke." She pointed to the TV monitor in an attempt to take the attention off her gaffe. "Something of significance on that newscast?"

"Why do you ask?"

"Because you've replayed that video half a dozen times."

Homer clicked the pause button of the remote control and rubbed his eyes. "Do you know anything about Rebekah Winchell? Where she came from? If she has any family around here?"

"Ms. Winchell? What's she got to do with the price of eggs?"

"She's been to town three times this week."

"That's odd." Frown lines wrinkled Olivia's forehead.

"Does she have any connection to the Rawlins boys?"

"Oh, so this has to do with Samuel Rawlins? I don't know of anything. Except..." Olivia raised her index finger and left his office for a minute, returning with a map which she laid flat on the desk.

"Let's see, now." She searched the map. "The Winchell property is on the western side of the Argyle River at the end of Old County Road. And I believe, the Rawlins boys live just across the river." She pointed for Homer to see. "Enough of a connection?"

He thought about it for a minute then asked, "What about the boys' mother? Remind me what she did before her death."

"Pearl? She was organist at The Union Church over to Laurel. A talented musician from what I understand."

"In that case I suppose I'd better pay a little visit to Pastor Josh." Pastor Josh was a bit of a celebrity in the county because he'd formed a popular folk rock band with three other local ministers. But Homer knew him because he was on the chaplaincy board for the Maine state prison system and was involved in programs at the nearby Charleston correctional facility.

"Is that all you're going to give me?" Olivia stood, arms akimbo.

"I'm working on a hunch here. Nothing more. So you don't know where Rebekah's from?"

"I don't believe I ever heard mention. Of course, she's not exactly a frequent topic of conversation either. I can do some poking about; see what I can uncover."

"Be discreet." They said in unison before Olivia sashayed toward the door.

"Wait. These just came in." He handed his assistant several

*Amber Alert* flyers. "Can you post them around town? The usual places."

"Sure thing, boss." She gave the flyers a cursory look. "I've always wanted to see this part of the country, but so far I haven't made it south of Jersey."

The sheriff played the video one last time trying to discern which news segment could have provoked a reaction like he'd witnessed. Of course, he also couldn't rule out the possibility Rebekah had been upset by a remark made by Jake or one of the other customers. Either way, his gut was telling him there was something amiss with the reclusive Ms. Winchell, and only once had his instincts failed him. He shook his head as if the gesture could push away the dark shadow of a distant memory.

He must focus on matters at hand. Still, he'd keep a watchful eye on Rebekah and make a point of touching base with Pastor Josh to see what light might be shed on the mysterious woman. He had the perfect excuse to check in with the good reverend who was a benefactor of sorts for Timothy Rawlins, particularly now with big brother Samuel's looming return to Murphy.

Homer leaned back in his chair and grinned with satisfaction. He was thrilled to have a real life puzzle to solve and was reveling in the high that accompanied an investigation. He'd been idling in neutral far too long.

# CORDELIA

"THREE THINGS CANNOT BE HIDDEN LONG: THE SUN, THE MOON, THE TRUTH."

BUDDHA

While Rebekah was in town buying paint I took advantage of the free time for another hike along the river. But before leaving I was drawn into the weaving room by vivid shades of green and blue yarn being spun into a gorgeous piece resembling the sea. Woven into the center was the letter G in a soft rose color. I couldn't resist touching the downy soft blanket.

*She must be making this for someone special. I wonder who.*

The enigma of Rebekah occupied my thoughts as we climbed to the beautiful meadow we'd visited yesterday. There were stacks of finished goods in the weaving room, but for whom did she make them all? Any questions I'd asked about her family or friends had been met with curt and evasive responses. She had no phone and therefore no contact with anyone. My initial impression was an absence of loved ones and chalked that up as the primary reason for her solitary existence. But maybe there was more to the woman's story.

I should just let it go. In a couple of days, Gabriella and I would be on our way to Canada and the mysterious Rebekah Winchell would be but a speck in the rearview mirror.

"Let's hope the car part comes in sooner rather than later, huh Handsome?"

Gabriella had fallen fast asleep by the time we reached the clearing. I gently laid the slumbering angel atop my red jacket in the shade of a crabapple tree. I caressed my daughter's cheeks and whispered, "We will have a wonderful new adventure."

Handsome curled up beside his charge and sighed with contentment.

"You stay here, buddy." I patted his head then walked to the middle of the small meadow and began to perform some standard Tai Chi movements.

"Yield and overcome: bend and be straight," I spoke softly in harmony with the fluid movements. Oh, how I'd missed what had once been central to my daily routine. And I couldn't even remember the last time I'd meditated. How had I gotten to this place? The philosophies I'd centered my life around were about being natural and honest and of late I had possessed neither of those qualities.

I crumpled to the ground in a heap of misery. After indulging my self-pity for several minutes, I pulled myself together and walked to the edge where there was a good view down across the river to the dilapidated shack. An official looking car drove up and two men emerged. There was a brief verbal exchange before the driver got back into the car and pulled away. The wiry, scruffy man who remained nonchalantly flicked a cigarette butt to the ground before picking up a small bag and entering the house. Another man, tall and sturdily built, came into view from the side of the barn and ambled cautiously toward the house. He climbed the porch steps and slowly turned to gaze in my direction. I hadn't realized I was visible until he offered a quick wave. But seconds later the smaller man came back out and roughly dragged the gentle giant into the house.

It was Handsome's soft murmur and cold nudging nose that awakened me from deep contemplation.

"Did I leave you for a while?" I reached my hand to smooth back the wild fur sprouting from around the dog's face. Out of the corner of my eye saw a figure approaching, jolting me alert. Fortunately it was only Rebekah. Still, Handsome was proving himself to be a very useful companion after all and I was beginning to understand why Ramon was so crazy about the little critter.

"Seemed like you were a million miles away from this place," Rebekah observed.

I smiled up at her, but she wasn't smiling back. In fact, the woman's severe and angry expression was so disconcerting I felt compelled to explain.

"It's a habit that started when I was quite young. I'd flee to fantasy worlds. Daydreaming was a means of coping, escaping troubles. Then as I became older, I began to meditate as a way to tackle my problems. Sometimes I immerse myself so totally in thought that I lose track of time."

"Like today?" Rebekah spit out the question.

I glanced up at the sun. We hadn't been gone so long to warrant such a harsh reaction. "Is it late? I'm sorry if I worried you."

"Not worried. Just curious." She shoved her clenched hands deep into the pockets of her jeans. "What troubles were you trying to escape from today?"

"I wasn't. I don't need to..." I was flustered. "I'd been rocking Ella and thinking about getting to Canada. I want to show my baby a happier life than what I had as a child."

"So you have nothing to hide, Cord?"

I opened my mouth to respond, but she cut me off before I could finish.

"Oh, but got that wrong, didn't I? It's *Delia,* isn't it? *Delia Carlyle.*"

The events of the past few days quickly reversed through my

mind. *What I wouldn't give to step back in time and begin this journey over again.*

# REBEKAH

"BEHOLD, I AM SENDING YOU OUT AS SHEEP IN THE MIDST OF WOLVES, SO BE WISE AS SERPENTS AND INNOCENT AS DOVES."

MATTHEW 10:16

"THOU SHALT NOT BEAR FALSE witness against thy neighbor. Thou ***shalt not*** bear false witness." Rebekah was pacing furiously. How dare this young woman take advantage of her generosity by deceiving her?

"Please calm down. You're upsetting Ella," Cord pleaded, holding her tearful child to her breast.

"Ella? But that's not her name either now, is it?"

"Gabriella," Cord whispered.

"What did you say?"

"Her name is Gabriella. I was calling her Ella, for short."

"Gabriella *Martelli*. And you said you never married her father." Rebekah pointed an accusing finger.

"I lied about that."

"And what else have you lied about besides being a fugitive and a kidnapper?" she hissed. Rebekah had immediately recognized the little girl in the flyer posted outside of *Jake's Hardware Store* when she'd gone to town for the house paint. But not wanting to be obvious she was only able to take in the key points on the bulletin.

"Let me explain," Cord pleaded

"Whatever you have to say better be pretty convincing

because who knows when the law will arrive on their door-to-door manhunt." She thought it unlikely Sheriff Pruitt would be showing up and sticking his nose in her business with Samuel Rawlins out on parole, but Cord didn't need to know that.

The young woman cowered but the little dog was hopping about in a frenzied state.

"I promise to tell you everything. The complete truth. If you'll just give me a chance, I'll make it right. I shouldn't have lied to you. I shouldn't have lied to anyone..." Her voice trailed off.

"You will burn for your sins. Yes, indeed, the Lord will punish you later. But I've got to figure out what to do with you right now."

"I'm so sorry," the woman sobbed.

Rebekah had not been prepared for the tearful outburst and she couldn't prevent her hardened heart from softening when the small child reached up to pat her mother's cheeks. She gave Cord a moment to compose herself and walked to the edge of the clearing and gazed across the river. There stood Samuel Rawlins on his mother's rickety old porch, looking completely satisfied with his new found freedom.

"Lucky cuss," she whispered into the wind before turning back around to face the other lawbreaker in town. "Let's not do this in front of the little one. You can tell your side of the story back at the house."

The young woman stood in silhouette against the window as the sun's rays streamed in from behind giving her a beatific aura which Rebekah found unsettling.

"I'm sorry I wasn't honest with you," Cord admitted. "But you have to understand. I never thought I'd be here longer than a few hours to get my car fixed."

"That's your excuse for breaking one of the Lord's commandments?"

"It was simply too painful and personal to share with a stranger." Cord left the window and slumped down into the chintz sofa across from Rebekah's rocking chair. "My husband. Well, I was frightened of him."

"Why?"

She closed her eyes tightly and gave a slight shake to her head.

Rebekah looked on intently, trying to determine if this outward show of struggling was genuine or a pretense to garner sympathy. The young woman breathed in deeply before opening her eyes and offered a perfectly guileless expression. "Have you ever looked into the eyes of somebody who was purely evil?"

The answer was yes. She pressed her hand to her stomach to settle the bile that was forming. She'd most certainly faced the devil squarely. Many times. But she didn't want to be reminded. Not now. Not ever.

The two women sat uneasily for several moments until Cord breached the silence in an eerily raspy voice. "He was planning to have me killed."

"That's a pretty strong allegation," Rebekah clucked then challenged, "You have proof?"

Cord nodded. "But first, he was plotting to take my baby away from me."

In an automatic reflex, the back of Rebekah's hand flew to her lips to stifle a gasp. She felt as if this stranger had somehow trespassed on her past. Needing a distraction to block the reminder of the most painful moment in her own past, she sprang from her chair and with a quick step walked to the kitchen and busied herself with rinsing out the morning coffee mugs.

"Aiden's a despicable man who gets what he wants whatever the cost."

Rebekah cringed as hate and bitterness transformed the young woman's usually lovely features. "At one time he must have wanted you."

"That's right. And to conquer my heart he wove a story about himself he knew I would find irresistible. He was both charming and clever in his pursuit. But men like Aiden become easily bored. He tired of me and cast me aside for a shinier toy."

Rebekah dried her hands on a faded dish towel and retook her seat.

Just then the dog jumped up and began to sniff at Cord's hand and within seconds the soft crying of the young child could be heard from the room above.

"I'll just go get her." Her voice was resigned. But before climbing the steps she turned and said, "And just for the record, in the time we've been gone, not once has my little girl asked for her father."

The dog didn't follow his master up the stairs, which was unusual. Instead, he set his eyes on Rebekah and let out a soft growl.

"I don't care much for you either, buster." She rose from her chair and walked to the door. "Go on now. Git. I don't need to take your guff."

But the stubborn creature wouldn't move until Cord returned with her sleepy-eyed little girl and he curled up at their feet.

"I'm begging you, please don't turn me in. If you drive us to the nearest bus station we can disappear and you can forget we were ever here."

Now the child had turned her head and was offering the most pitiful expression. Normally Rebekah's instincts were like that of a cat, and learning to anticipate had been key to her survival. Although she was suspicious of this newly spun story, those carefully honed instincts were becoming clouded as her fondness for the child continued to deepen.

After several moments of silent prayer, Rebekah made her decision. "You'd best stay here and lay low until your car's ready."

"Thank you." Cord's relief was palpable.

Rebekah hefted herself up and when she did the child reached out both arms as if in her own way offering thanks. She picked up the little girl and held her close breathing in the beguiling scents of innocence and baby powder and could have done so for hours had that darn dog not begun a low pitched whine.

"Stop being so jealous," Cord gently reprimanded while at the same time rewarding the dog with a scratch behind the ears.

Rebekah reluctantly returned the child and picked up the keys to her truck. She needed to figure out what to do next.

"I have an errand to run. I'll be back in a few hours."

# PART THREE

## DEAD RINGER

# RUSSELL

"IN THE REAL WORLD, NOTHING HAPPENS AT THE RIGHT PLACE AT THE RIGHT TIME. IT IS THE JOB OF JOURNALISTS AND HISTORIANS TO CORRECT THAT."

MARK TWAIN

Russell had driven out to Camp Davis to see what was happening with the protestors. It would make a noteworthy piece for the *Murphy Post*, but it also gave him an opportunity to do a little digging around for the book he was writing. Spiritualists had been convening at Camp Davis for well over a century and embraced a doctrine postulating the existence of a spirit world and the ability of mediums to make contact with those who had crossed over to an afterlife. He'd been fascinated by the kooky disciples of Spiritualism ever since coming to Murphy, so much so that it served as the backdrop for his novel.

Although none would be quick to admit it, his research had uncovered connections between ancestors of some prominent Murphy residents to the Spiritualist movement. But these days, devotees to the principle came from parts as far away as his home country to celebrate the mystic tenets and he hoped for a chance to interview a few of the participants while he was out here. When he pulled up to the gate, the protestors had laid down their signs and were gathered at a picnic table. He'd let them enjoy their break.

Russell parked his Aston Martin beneath the shade of a maple tree and took out his little red book to jot down some notes from his breeze shooting session with three of the regular porch sitters at *Jake's Hardware Store*. Not much to go on. He tapped his pencil on the steering wheel as he replayed the conversation about Rebekah Winchell.

"The woman just showed up one day shortly after the old Wakefield homestead went up for sale," Harry Mullner answered the query first. "When was that George? Nineteen ninety?"

George Kepler stroked his chin then said, "Mary Ruth Wakefield died the same year my first grandson was born. I remember havin' to stop by the funeral home on the way to the hospital. And young George will be twenty-two this fall. As I recall, the farm sold the followin' spring. So that would have been nineteen eighty-nine."

"Close enough," Harry grumbled as he tapped his pipe. "She's an odd bird, but she doesn't both-ah anyone."

"She's a hard worker. I'll give her that. Runs that farm by herself."

"Does she have any family?" Russell asked.

The three men shrugged in unison.

"Friends?"

"That one's a lon-ah. I've never seen her in the company of another soul."

"So you think she's from Maine originally?"

"Talks like a Mainah." Harry raised his eyebrows.

"Acts like one, too," George agreed.

"She might have been born here, but she's been away. I can tell." Luke Windsor, who had been silent up to this point of the conversation, finally offered his commentary.

"How's that?" Russell asked.

"I just can."

And Luke's cohorts had nodded their assent.

Talk about some odd chaps, Russell mused. As the protestors began to stir, a familiar green vehicle approached the camp entrance. He ducked down a bit to avoid being seen but he needn't have worried. Rebekah's eyes were focused straight ahead as she sped through the gates of Camp Davis.

"Indeed, this is becoming quite fascinating." Russell cocked his head, one eyebrow arched to give him a creepy aura. Was this a gift from heaven? Or perhaps the devil was at work.

He saw a bicycle propped against the stone wall so he jogged over and asked if he could borrow it, tossing a twenty dollar bill in the direction of the young owner. His sleek silver sports car was far too conspicuous for this crowd of Volkswagen camper vans and the like.

Russell lost sight of Rebekah's truck but spied a cloud of dust just beyond a dip in the road. He followed his hunch and made it down the long dirt path in time to watch his target being led into an old stone cottage by an aged woman wearing a long flowing cape.

"Pay dirt."

# CORDELIA

"WORK OUT YOUR OWN SALVATION. DO NOT DEPEND ON OTHERS."

BUDDHA

THE SILVERADO DISAPPEARED IN A cloud of dust while I was left to ponder on which side of the coin my luck would land. Where, if not straight to the authorities, was Rebekah headed? And I was in the unenviable position of being helpless to do anything about it.

"Play, Mama!" A little someone was begging to be entertained and I welcomed the opportunity to escape my well founded fears.

I rolled a red rubber ball across the floor. "How about this, sweetie pie?"

Gabriella happily pushed the ball toward Handsome, who was sniffing around the pantry door. At the prospect of play, the dog spun around and in doing so his body bumped against the door and it came ajar.

I was surprised the pantry had been left unlocked, but thought little more of it until moments later when I spied a mouse peering out from the door. Unfortunately, so did the dog and a feverish pursuit of the little fur ball ensued during which boxes were upended, spilling their contents onto the floor.

"Handsome stop!"

It took some doing, but finally I managed to take hold of the dog's collar and tug him to the porch so I could deal with the mess he'd left in his wake. I grabbed the much loved *Baby Stella*

*Peach* doll and the toy tea set I'd thought to remove from the car and set them before Gabriella as a distraction while I gathered up the contents of the overturned boxes. One pile was religious books and Bible study handouts.

"No surprises in here." I flipped open one of the workbooks and took note that this particular session had been conducted in Kentucky by a Chaplain Morely. There were no dates but the pages were yellowed and curled.

Another held an array of books and articles about the afterlife, mysticism and mediums. Just like the Tarot cards, the subject matter was oddly out of character for someone so devout in her Christian beliefs.

I skimmed through the articles, trying to replace them in an organized fashion. There was a book entitled *The History of Spiritualism* written by Arthur Conan Doyle. Who knew? *A Stellar Key to the Summerland* was an intriguing title and my eyes were drawn to a highlighted passage:

> Death is but a door which opens into a new and more perfect existence. It is a triumphal arch through which man's immortal spirit passes at the moment of leaving the outer world to depart for a higher, a more sublime, a more magnificent country. Our entire existence is one of spiritual development that started on planet Earth and will continue in the Summer-Land. Evil converts the present life into a stormy winter, and the darkness of ignorance and the suffering flings sadness over the whole race: but in the next world there is a summery bloom on the cheek of everyone from the least to the greatest, and the song of the thronging millions is filled with the music of perpetual

> summer. It will be natural and truthful to think and speak of the spirit world as the SUMMER- LAND.

"Weird, weird, weird."

There was a folder of articles about a group of theology students who were interviewing descendents of members of a local sect. One article presented an interview with an anonymous present day practitioner of Spiritualism. The most recent was a posting of an annual gathering of practicing spiritualists. I was thinking this must be the retreat Rebekah mentioned.

After putting to order the boxes Handsome had knocked over, I pulled another box from the shelf. *So here are the family photographs.*

There were several framed pictures of an austere middle-aged couple dressed in black, the formidable man holding a large Bible and the woman's posture submissive. Stuck to the back of one was a snapshot in which the same couple was accompanied by a young girl, cupping a small Bible in her hands at waist level and wearing an impish grin that contrasted the dour expressions of her parents. A young Rebekah.

In another photo a twenty-something Rebekah was standing with a woman twice her age, but not the woman in the other pictures. They could have been dressed for a costume party for they were both sporting gypsy-like outfits. Rebekah, with a flowing scarf wrapped around her head and long dangling earrings, an off the shoulder dress of a light, cascading floral fabric cinched tightly at the waste. Atop the older woman's head was a turban held together by a large, fake gemstone and a floor-length velvet cape draped from her shoulders. The two were smiling mischievously at the lens.

I contemplated the two photographs of the young girl and the woman at full bloom. How did such a pretty and vibrant young woman end up a religious fanatic farmer in the wilds of Maine?

There was one last picture at the bottom of the box. It was of a ginger-haired little girl close to Gabriella's age, in a silver frame engraved with *My Little Gem*. I pulled open the backing of the frame to check the date of the photograph. June 1982.

I took care to replace the contents of the box in the same order in which I'd removed them. But when I tried to return the box to the shelf it wouldn't fit back into its original space because a thick envelope had fallen down from where it had been wedged for safe keeping. Inside was a bundle of letters addressed to a woman named Betsy Cooper. I started to read them but was interrupted by Handsome's frantic barking. I rushed to the window and saw the truck rounding the bend of the dirt road.

"Handsome, you are a life saver. All is forgiven." I let the dog back in the house then hurried back to the store room, cramming the envelope into the space from where it had dropped so I could push the box back into place. After a quick check to ensure nothing was out of order, I secured the door and gathered up the toys. However, a little someone didn't appreciate having her playtime disrupted and began to wail in protest.

Just as the thud of the truck door sounded I noticed the pile of letters I'd left on the side table by the window. I made it to the other side of the room just in time to quickly slide the bundle into the back of my pants and untucked my shirt for further camouflage. I picked up Gabriella and was rocking her when Rebekah entered the room.

However, this was not the same angry woman who told me a few hours ago I'd burn in hell for my sins. No, the Rebekah who just walked through the door had a serene, almost entranced bearing. I honestly didn't know whether to feel reassured or frightened.

# HOMER

"BUT LOOK AT THESE LONELY HOUSES, EACH IN ITS OWN FIELDS, FILLED FOR THE MOST PART WITH POOR IGNORANT FOLK WHO KNOW LITTLE OF THE LAW. THINK OF THE DEEDS OF HELLISH CRUELTY, THE HIDDEN WICKEDNESS WHICH MAY GO ON, YEAR IN, YEAR OUT, IN SUCH PLACES AND NONE THE WISER."

SHERLOCK HOLMES IN ***THE ADVENTURES OF SHERLOCK HOLMES***

Sheriff Pruitt had asked Pastor Josh if he wouldn't mind driving out to the Rawlins' place with him to meet with the newly released prisoner and his parole officer, Jimmy Kramer.

"So I hear the congregation has been real generous to Timothy while his brother's been…away."

"His mother was the organist at Union Church for many years. Besides, with Timothy being as he is." The minister let the sentence drop and shrugged.

"How do you mean?" Homer knew that Timothy Rawlins was a strange young man, but he preferred to hear Pastor Josh's perspective.

"Timothy is, well, I wouldn't really know how to describe it. He's an oddity for certain. Many people around here call him slow-witted, but he's not intellectually disabled. In fact, he's rather well-informed on subjects that interest him."

"And what would those be?"

"Nature. Mainly plants. He can tell you the name of any wildflower, shrub, tree or weed. He might have made something for himself in the field of natural science had he not been so peculiar."

"Peculiar in a dangerous way?"

"Dangerous?" Pastor Josh was clearly startled by the question. But he didn't respond as he gazed out the window at the passing farm land. "I guess I'm trying to determine if Timothy is anything at all like his brother."

"If it weren't for a facial resemblance to their mother, it would be hard to imagine those two boys coming from the same gene pool."

He hadn't exactly answered the question, but Homer would let it drop for now and move on to another subject of interest. "So, tell me, do you know anything about Rebekah Winchell?"

Pastor Josh looked sharply askance. "Why do you ask?"

"Well, her property abuts the Rawlins place, doesn't it?"

"Oh, yes, I see. That it does."

"How well do you know the woman?" Homer turned slightly to observe the minister's reaction and was surprised to see his color rising.

"She was a parishioner for a while, back when I first came to Laurel."

"And?"

"Why the interest in her?"

Homer was tiring of having all of his questions answered in kind. "You've been spending too much time around law enforcement and corrections personnel. You're beginning to sound like one."

The minister smiled sheepishly. "Sorry. I just find it strange for you to be inquiring about Ms. Winchell. All I can tell you is she stopped coming to church shortly after I was called."

"Was she friends with Mrs. Rawlins?"

"I'm not sure how close they were, but Rebekah did drive Pearl to church on Sunday mornings until she stopped coming."

"Do you know why she stopped coming?"

"I know my side of the story."

But Homer didn't have the chance to hear it because they'd arrived at the Rawlins' homestead, if you could call it that, and Jimmy Kramer was pacing beside his jeep.

"Sorry to be late, Jimmy," Homer said as he got out of his vehicle and walked forward, his hand outstretched.

"Sheriff." Jimmy nodded hello. "Pastor."

"Have you spoken with Samuel yet?"

"Looks like we might already be closing in on a violation of parole. Mr. Rawlins has failed to show and I've already given him a generous grace period." He grinned and tapped the crystal of his watch. "By my calculation he has three more minutes to show."

Obviously, nothing would gratify Jimmy more than to send Samuel back to the slammer. It was a standard condition of parole for the prisoner to report to his parole officer within 24 hours of being released.

"I thought we were meeting him here because of his lack of transportation."

"That's correct. We made a special concession and scheduled a meeting out here for" - Jimmy checked his watch again - "28 minutes ago. The boy doesn't play nice."

Homer walked around to the river-facing side of the house and there sat Timothy Rawlins swaying steadily back and forth upon the porch swing, the movement as constant as the beat of a metronome, his eyes focused straight ahead.

Homer gave a silent cue to Pastor Josh to speak to the young man.

"Hey there, Timothy."

The swing stopped, but still the young man's eyes remained averted.

"These gentlemen here have driven out from town to visit with Samuel. Is he here?"

Timothy nodded and pointed in the direction of the barn or the wooded area beyond, it was hard to tell.

Jimmy swore under his breath. "Why didn't anyone answer my knock? I called out several times when nobody answered the door."

Timothy simply shrugged, evidently not in the mood to be helpful.

Homer walked to the barn and opened the door. "Samuel Rawlins? This is Sheriff Pruitt." But there was no answer.

"He's got one minute." Jimmy was looking at his time piece as if urging the second hand to move faster. But Samuel Rawlins wasn't going to be sent back to prison just yet. With mere seconds before his deadline elapsed, an old Schwinn squeaking with rust tore through some shrubs at the side of the barn and screeched to a halt right before Jimmy Kramer, kicking up enough dust to set the officer to coughing.

The man wore a nasty expression as he jerked himself off the bicycle and practically threw it against the porch.

"Why didn't you ring the God-damned bell you big fat sissy?" the parolee screamed at his brother.

A thought came to Homer's mind that maybe Timothy understood the ramifications of his brother missing a meeting with the parole officer. If so, he was far cleverer than anyone gave him credit.

Samuel confirmed the sheriff's suspicions as he jumped up on the porch and brought his enraged face within an inch of Timothy's. "You fuckin' rat! You knew I had to be back here by ten. You'll be sorry for this one, bro."

But Timothy remained impassive.

Homer cleared his throat loudly. "Mr. Rawlins, you do

understand refraining from threatening behavior is one of the conditions of your parole?"

Samuel froze for an instant, probably gathering his wits, before turning to face the group, his malicious expression morphing into a calmer, yet insincere façade of respect.

"Just a bit of sibling rivalry. We've tussled all our lives, haven't we Timmy-boy?" He tried to ruffle his brother's hair, but Timothy ducked his head away. An attempt at a smile came off a sneer. "But we always kiss and makeup."

Homer was incredulous and outraged that Samuel Rawlins had somehow been able to mask an unmistakably depraved nature and convince a parole board he had reformed and was ready to return to society. If he had been Timothy, he wouldn't have sounded the warning bell either.

Following a review of all the conditions set forth by the state of Maine for convicts paroled from their prison system, Jimmy declined his right to search the property. Homer suspected this was a tactic to lessen the ex-con's guard, and he for one hoped it worked. To his mind the sooner Samuel Rawlins was back behind bars the better for everyone.

"It's Timothy I worry about," Pastor Josh said on the return drive. "His quiet existence is going to become a hellish nightmare."

"Can we get him out of there?" Homer asked.

"To where? He has no family, at least none anywhere near to Maine. And it wouldn't be easy for him to assimilate into another situation. This has been his home since he was a young boy. Why should he have to leave it?"

"Where'd the family come from?"

"I'm not certain. Pearl had an ever so slight accent, but it wasn't discernible. Mid-west, maybe."

"What about the father?"

"Pearl Rawlins came to Maine to get lost, if you know what I mean?"

Homer understood intimately how Murphy was as good a hiding place as any. "So she'd run away from an abusive situation?"

"That's my impression, though Pearl was guardedly private. I could never persuade the entire story out of the woman."

"Speaking of stories, you were saying something earlier about Rebekah Winchell. Care to elaborate on why she left the church?"

Pastor Josh's cheeks again took on a flush. "Apparently, she didn't appreciate my interpretation of the scriptures. In fact, she took me to task every Sunday following service. I was supposed to be enjoying what we in the clergy call the honeymoon phase where a newly called minister can do no wrong. Well, I have to tell you, it was very uncomfortable to be dressed down each week in full view of the other worshippers. It got to the point where I was essentially writing my weekly sermons with just one person in mind. Rebekah Winchell." The pastor's leg was bouncing wildly. Obviously he was still bothered by the woman's effrontery.

"So she quit your church because she didn't like your sermons? Probably not the first time a minister lost one of his flock because of it."

Pastor Josh took in a deep breath. "There's more to it. Not many will forget the last time Rebekah Winchell set foot in Union Church. But even to this day I'm puzzled by the woman's extreme reaction to what I said."

"And that was?"

"I was at the front doors of the church following worship, greeting the parishioners as they left. When Rebekah approached next in line she began chastising me for once again getting it wrong. I felt it was imperative to take charge of the situation before I lost the respect of my entire congregation. So I gently laid my hand on her shoulder and quoted the disciple Luke. 'Whoever is not with me is against me, and whoever does not gather with me scatters.' She evidently took offense because her reaction was quite violent."

"Violent?" Homer's sensors went on alert. "In what way?"

"She pushed my hand away and in a rather sinister voice said, 'Don't touch me with your filthy hands.' And then she slapped me across the face." Pastor Josh shook his head as if still in disbelief.

Homer had to agree it was an unduly harsh reaction. "Then what?"

"She had some parting words of her own. 'And I will punish the world for their evil, and the wicked for their iniquity; and I will cause the arrogance of the proud to cease, and will lay low the haughtiness of the terrible.' Isaiah 13:11." He offered the Bible verse out of habit.

"Did you ever see her again?"

"After Pearl's funeral. She wouldn't come to the church, but she did hover in the background at the cemetery during the interment." The minister turned to ask, "Is Rebekah in any kind of trouble?"

"Not to my knowledge. I just like to gather information on anyone who might have contact with my ex-convicts. Do you think a relationship exists between Rebekah and Samuel or Timothy?"

Pastor Josh shrugged. "I can't be certain. I've never seen her out there, but I only make the trip once a week."

"Do you plan to continue those weekly visits?"

"Absolutely. Timothy needs me now more than ever."

"I believe you're right about that. If you see anything out of the ordinary, get in touch with me immediately. Even more important than keeping your eyes open? Don't turn your back on Samuel."

The minister became sallow at the inference to the elder Rawlins boy's capacity to bring harm.

After dropping Pastor Josh, Homer decided to stop home for lunch on his way back to the office. When he walked into the kitchen Benjamin and Sara were squabbling over plates of macaroni and cheese.

"What's going on here?" he asked in his commanding voice.

"Nothing," the youngsters said in mumbled unison.

"That's what I thought." Homer began shuffling through the stack of mail and asked, "Where's your grandmother?"

"Out in the garden," Benjamin answered.

Homer walked from the kitchen to the back porch and saw Frannie resting in one of the two Adirondack chairs facing the western hills where sometimes they enjoyed a cocktail at sunset. He sauntered over but his wife hadn't heard him. When he sat down in the companion chair he reached across to take her hand.

Frannie pitched forward and brought her other hand to her chest. "Oh. You startled me, Homer."

"I can see that. I didn't mean to wake you."

"I wasn't asleep," she said, sinking back into the chair.

"I know. But you *were* someplace else."

He watched a tear trace the curve of Frannie's silky cheek. Homer loved that face, even as the years laid claim to it. He would do everything within his power to protect this woman with whom he'd made a life. But he'd learned long ago how powerless he was to completely erase her sorrows and regrets. He reached over to caress away the dampness and that was when he saw the cause of his wife's tears. The handwriting was unmistakable. Another missive from Sophia lay slightly crumpled in her lap.

"May I read it?" His voice was gentle.

With a quivering hand she surrendered the paper life-line from her daughter.

"Will you send the money?" Homer asked after reading Sophia's appeal.

"We agreed not to enable her." She used both hands to comb back her thick hair in a gesture of frustration. "But tell me, how can I allow my own child to live this way?"

"She has a choice," he reminded her kindly.

"Does she? Has she ever truly had a choice?" Frannie snatched the letter back. "Let's face it. It's not Sophia's fault she's troubled. And you and I both know who's to blame."

# RUSSELL

"WHERE THE NOVELIST FEARLESSLY PLUNGES INTO THE WATER OF SELF-EXPOSURE, THE JOURNALIST STANDS TREMBLING ON THE SHORE IN HIS BEACH ROBE. THE JOURNALIST CONFINES HIMSELF TO THE CLEAN, GENTLEMANLY WORK OF EXPOSING THE GRIEVES AND SHAMES OF OTHERS."

JANET MALCOLM

Russell Paine had returned from Camp Davis with plenty to cogitate over. Even though he'd set a deadline for tomorrow morning, he decided to put the article about the protestors on the back burner for now. One of the many advantages to being editor and chief of *The Murphy Post*.

"I'll just run the paper a day late," he'd proclaimed aloud as he prepared his crisps and peanut butter sandwich, a guilty pleasure exposing his more humble East London beginnings. "Nothing like a little trailer park cuisine."

He filled a chilled mug from a bottle of oatmeal stout which he took along with his sandwich into the den and flipped open his laptop.

"Let's see now." Russell was poking around in his favorite search engine as he munched. "What can you tell me about Lucinda Cooper? Ah. She's one of the trustees for Camp Davis. That must explain why she has a home out there."

He jotted a note to himself to check on whether the camp was open year-round and if there were any full-time caretakers. Could Lucinda Cooper have been there all along, right under his nose? What a find! He turned his attention back to the computer screen.

"It says here Ms. Cooper is a talented medium who shares her spiritual knowledge and insights with members and visitors." He continued to read aloud, "One man who came to the camp with the intention of making peace with his long dead mother claimed a visit to the healing rock with Lucinda to be a most spiritually uplifting experience. Blimey. I'll have to check this out myself. I've always wanted to ask Uncle Albert where he hid his gold."

He snickered then leaned back in the soft leather desk chair and sipped his stout while letting his mind develop the character. Then he opened a Word document and began typing at lightning speed. He worked non-stop until it was necessary to turn on the lights and then he continued on through the night. This was just the break he was looking for. He'd hit a block in the book he'd been writing, but now it had been dynamited away because of one Rebekah Winchell, and he would be ever so grateful to her when he accepted the *Edgar Award* for best mystery novel. He closed his eyes and got lost in the never achieved but long sought after dream of writing *the* great novel. While hovering in a state somewhere between fantasy and forty winks, the chair tipped back precariously and brought him back to the real world.

"That reminds me," he said after saving and closing the document. He revisited the search engine and after nearly an hour, removed his glasses and wiped them with the scrunched up napkin he'd used earlier before refocusing on the monitor.

*Brown bread? No way. Can't possibly be dead.* Russell was clearly perplexed. He took his plate and mug to the kitchen and rinsed them off as he considered what he'd just read. He popped the top off a second oatmeal stout and leaned against the kitchen counter, deliberating whether it was too late to make the call.

"Aw, shove it," he said after taking a long gulp of ale. He

reached for the phone and punched in the familiar numbers. "B.W.? It's Russell. Sorry to call so late. - - - That's what I thought." He laughed.

"So how's life? - - - Really? You must be knackered out, then. - - - Hey, I need your help. It's payback time, mate. Got a pencil? I need everything you can get me on a Lucinda Cooper and a Rebekah Winchell." Russell laughed again. "Yeah, yeah. Just a couple of birds I've been hangin' out with. - - - Oh, God, I'd forgotten all about that. - - - Yeah. And there's one more person, a family actually. The last name is Rawlins."

Russell then proceeded to give the pertinent details he'd already gathered and instructions on what information to look for specifically.

"You've got a good nose. Let it be your lead. Follow any threads that look interesting. - - - What's it for? That depends on what you're able to deliver. It could end up being big. Really big. Think Truman Capote and *In Cold Blood.* Seriously, now. Can you manage? - - - Great! - - -When do I need this? Yesterday, mate, yesterday."

*I will be rich. I will be famous again.* He licked his lips in anticipation of all that would be his. But for now, he must successfully lure his prey. But which one first?

# CORDELIA

"THOSE WHO PAY ATTENTION WILL NOT DIE,
WHILE THE CARELESS ARE AS GOOD AS DEAD ALREADY."

BUDDHA

"Can I hold her?" The calmer gentler Rebekah reached for the still sniffling Gabriella. Peeved with me for abruptly interrupting her play time, my daughter went readily into the arms of the other woman, giggling happily as her tiny toes were tickled. It was amazing how quickly children developed a sense of self-importance and how easily they learned to dole out punishment for slights committed against them.

"You're very good with her, you know?"

"Am I?" Rebekah smiled with pleasure as she focused her attention on Gabriella. Then suddenly she seemed to remember she was in the presence of a sinner and cast a wary look in my direction. "I left the paint cans in the truck. You might want to get started."

And thus, the sinner was dismissed.

"Sure, I'll go change right now." I ran upstairs to find a secure hiding place for the letters. When I came back down I slapped my leg and said, "Let's go Handsome."

But the dog wouldn't budge. Ever the faithful guardian, he remained fixed to a spot where he could keep a watchful eye on his precious ward.

I concluded my labors for the day as the sun began to slip behind the barn. I lingered in the shower, the hot water feeling good against the hard-worked muscles that would surely tighten up by tomorrow morning.

"I've already fed the baby," Rebekah informed me as I entered the kitchen.

"How was her appetite?" I leaned down to kiss Gabriella who was intently piecing together a puzzle.

"Fair, I'd say. Although she ate nothing green." She scraped vegetable peels into the compost pail. "You can set the table."

I took from the cupboard the monogrammed plates and shuddered as an odd feeling crept over me. But before I could pinpoint the cause Rebekah said, "Bowls tonight. I made potato soup."

"Perfect. It's gotten a bit chilly." I pulled the belt of my sweater tighter. "How long have you lived here?"

"I was born here."

"In this house?"

At first, Rebekah was confused by the question. "What? This house? No. No. Not here."

"I assumed you were born here in Maine. I was just curious how long you owned this farm."

"Long enough to call it home." Rebekah answered abruptly. She opened the heavy oven door to check on the bread and a tempting aroma escaped.

"You bake delicious bread. I'd love to have your recipe."

"Nothin' in writing. My Aunt Lucinda taught me when I was probably no more than eight. I had to stand on a stool to watch her. Those hands could make magic out of any dough. I always thought she should have opened a bakery instead of…" Rebekah stopped short.

I pretended not to notice and suggested, "Maybe I could watch you make it next time."

"We'll see."

Further attempts at dinner to draw my taciturn hostess into conversation about her past proved futile. Rebekah had almost let something slip, leaving me only to speculate, but it wasn't enough.

"Let me clear the dishes and wash up," I offered. "I know someone who might want a playmate."

"All-righty." Rebekah pushed her chair back and carried Gabriella closer to the wood stove. "It's nice and warm over here. Shall we make something with the clay?"

"These are lovely dishes. My mother had a similar pattern."

"That was my own mother's set," Rebekah said absently as she created a creature with the Play-Doh.

"Was your Aunt Lucinda your mother's sister or your father's?"

"Daddy's." The voice was childlike and for an instant I thought Gabriella had spoken the word. But it had been Rebekah, and having let the modeling clay drop to the floor she began twirling her fingers through her long silver-striped locks and stared vacantly upward. Then she said it again, ever so softly. "Daddy."

Whatever spell Rebekah had been under, it was broken by my next question. "So where is your Aunt Lucinda now? Does she live nearby?"

Rebekah snapped to attention and brusquely announced, "I think it's time for this little girl to go to bed." And she promptly whisked up Gabriella and walked toward the stairs.

"I'll be up as soon as I take Handsome out," I called after her then clipped on the leash before he had a chance to race up the steps. "Oh, no you don't. You've got some business to take care of first."

The dog let out a resigned whimper and pranced toward the door. He quickly took care of his needs and ran back inside. I set him free and barely saw his tail as he rounded the stairway landing. I finished the kitchen clean-up before quietly creeping up the stairs where I peeked into the guest room from the hallway.

"And do you remember who built the ark?" Rebekah asked in playful voice.

"Nooo." My daughter was sitting in Rebekah's lap.

"That's right. Noah."

"And how many of each animal came with him?" Gabriella responded with the correct two fingers. My daughter was a quick study, even though I wasn't thrilled with the subject matter.

But I felt a shiver race up my spine when Rebekah hugged Gabriella close to her chest and said, "That's right my little gem."

I stayed up late into the night poring over the letters I'd taken from the storage pantry. But I couldn't figure out who this Betsy Cooper was. A friend? Another relative? Most were addressed to 'Daughter of mine' and signed 'Yours in God's love, Mother' and the writer was urging Betsy to repent for her sins and turn her life over to the Lord.

There were also several letters written by Lucinda, who I gathered was one in the same as Rebekah's aunt since it wasn't a common name. Lucinda had told Betsy, "I am trying to make contact with the child. Never lose faith in the Spirit. The child cannot be lost to you as long as the spirit is alive. Death is truly the birth of the spirit."

As I reread those last words of Lucinda's message to Betsy Cooper, I began to tremble.

*Death is truly the birth of the spirit?*

# REBEKAH

"AND THE PRAYER OF FAITH SHALL SAVE THE SICK."

JAMES 5:15

"What's wrong?" Rebekah burst into the guest bedroom without bothering to knock.

"She has a fever." The child was lying on the bed wailing in distress as her mother searched furiously through the backpack.

"You sure about that?"

"If you don't believe me, feel her forehead." Cord was unable to hide her exasperation.

Rebekah drew nearer to the screaming child and indeed could feel the intense heat before her hand even reached the hot, clammy skin.

"There, there," she said, trying to offer comfort, but the little one would have nothing to do with her. In fact, she would only let Handsome come near her and he was displaying his concern by alternately licking her face and fretfully circling the little ball of fire.

"God damn it!" Cord yelled. "I can't believe I left the first aid kit in the car."

Rebekah recoiled from the sacrilege, but then felt a touch to her arm and she turned to look at the anxious young woman.

"I'm so sorry." Cord did not remove her hand. "I didn't mean to offend you. I'm just worried about Gabriella."

Rebekah dipped her head slightly to indicate the apology was accepted.

"Do you have any *Tyleno*l?"

"Tylenol?"

"For the fever."

"No." Rebekah had no need of medications. Not since the terrible headaches went away.

"Advil? Anything?"

"I don't have any pills." She shook her head then sank to her knees and began to pray. "Dear Lord, we beg of you to do as your disciples proclaimed. 'And he laid his hands on every one of them and healed them.' Lord, have mercy on this innocent and heal her diseased body."

She reached out and placed her hand on the scorching hot skin but the sobbing child pushed it away.

Cord left the room and returned within a minute holding a damp washcloth wrapped around ice cubes. She gently applied the coolness.

"Here baby. Let mama help you." The crying had subsided, but the child was still moaning in her suffering.

Rebekah was overwhelmed by a sense of helplessness, an old haunting feeling that she wished would go away. She closed her eyes and resumed her spiritual entreaty. It was the only thing she knew to do in a crisis.

"Rebekah?" Cord kneeled down beside her and quietly interrupted the silent litany. "Please listen to me. One of us has to go to town. My baby needs medicine."

She was preoccupied with her prayers and hadn't even realized Cord left the room again until she heard footsteps running up the stairs.

"Rebekah, where are your truck keys?"

"The hook. They must be on the hook," she finally answered but never opened her eyes.

"They aren't there. I've looked in the truck, the kitchen, the living room. Could they be in your pocket? Did you leave them in your bedroom?"

But she couldn't remember what she'd done with those keys. She couldn't think. She had to pray. Prayer was the answer. God would intervene.

"Rebekah, help me. Please." Cord's plea was becoming desperate.

"Dear Lord, take away these demands on me." She unclasped her hands and brought them to her head. "I can't cope. I can't cope."

"Yes you can. I can help you."

*Had she spoken those words out loud*, Rebekah wondered.

After a moment of stillness, Cord asked, "Would you do it for your little gem?"

Rebekah's eyes flashed. "What. Did. You. Say?"

"Would you do it for your little gem?" Cord repeated softly.

The movement of her arm was involuntary. She hadn't been conscious of her action until she felt the sting of her palm against the young woman's cheek. Immediately she brought the offending hand to her mouth, as if it were words and not physical violence she'd hoped to take back. She now saw the reflection of a different kind of fear contort the young woman's face.

# CORDELIA

"BEWARE OF THE ANGER OF THE MOUTH. MASTER YOUR WORDS."

BUDDHA

"I HOPE THAT WASN'T A BAD move," I said to Handsome as we bookended Gabriella on the bed, not so close as to make her more uncomfortable with our own body heat. The fever hadn't broken and without a thermometer there was no way to know how high the temperature had soared. But cool cloths were effective in sedating the hysterics for the time being.

"But I had no choice." I continued my one-sided conversation. "I needed her to wake from that...that fugue. I had to take the risk." But Rebekah's violent reaction had enhanced my intrigue over just who the child in that picture frame could be. *My little gem.*

I gingerly touched my smarting cheek. Could it possibly be the child Lucinda spoke about in her letter to Betsy Cooper? If so, then how is Rebekah involved?

*The letters.* This would probably be my only opportunity to replace them. I lifted the mattress to remove the packet then bent over my baby and caressed the warm, damp tresses that had curled from the sweat of fever.

"Would you like some juice, sweetie?"

My little girl nodded, which I took as a hopeful sign.

"Okay. Mama will be right back."

Finally one bit of good luck on this awful day: the storeroom door had been left unlocked again. I retrieved the manila envelope to replace the letters I'd taken the day before. But then I couldn't help myself and grabbed another handful. The craving to learn more about this Betsy Cooper person had become insatiable.

In the kitchen, I poured some juice and water into a sippy cup and took down a plate for a slab of bread cut from the leftover loaf. I thoughtfully considered the monogrammed C on the dishes. *Cooper?*

# RUSSELL

"JOURNALISTS ARE LIKE DOGS, WHENEVER ANYTHING MOVES THEY BEGIN TO BARK."

ARTHUR SCHOPENHAUER

"WELL, WHAT DO YA' KNOW," Russell murmured as he arrived at the offices of *The Murphy Post*, which happened to be located to one side of *The Apothecary*. "Our paths are crossing quite a lot these days, Ms Winchell."

Rebekah was scurrying from the pharmacy just as Russell was pulling his Aston Martin into the Reserved for Editor parking space. Not that parking was an issue in Murphy, but he appreciated the sense of importance attached to having his own space. The Town Council deliberated for months to approve the sign and might never have done had Russell not put on the pressure with his editorials. Hail the power of the pen!

The woman was in such a hurry she paid no mind to a slip of paper that fell from the bag she was clutching as she hoisted herself up into the truck. But fortunately, the Pagan Fox had been on the alert and was able to surreptitiously retrieve the receipt before it blew into the drain grate. His brow furrowed as he reviewed what Rebekah had purchased. To cast a better light on this puzzle, Russell ambled into the pharmacy to nose around a bit.

"Isn't it a great morning my fair Maid Marian?" He said to the pharmacy assistant slash check-out clerk slash wife to Pharmacist Wyatt Kilcane.

"That it is Mr. Payne. Here's your *Times*." The attractive woman with the comely shape and pert little nose tapped a pile of newspapers on the counter top.

"Aha. So it is. And since there's another copy right beneath mine, I gather our fine officer of the law has not yet been in to collect his own paper this morning."

Marian looked at the clock and said, "That is unusual. Sheriff Pruitt always stops in within minutes of the paper drop."

Russell threw down a five dollar bill and said, "Since I have some business to discuss with him, why don't I just deliver this to the good sheriff of Nottingham."

"And who do you fashion yourself to be in this little charade? Robin Hood?"

"M'lady doubts me?"

Marian giggled.

"What? Do I amuse you?"

"It's the accent. It tickles me."

"I'll tickle you all right," he said in a randy voice.

"Mr. Payne, need I remind you, my husband stands but a few feet away?"

"That's right, Russell. You better watch out lest someone tampers with your next prescription." Wyatt looked up from his task of precision pill counting, his usually pleasing face distorted by an evil grin.

"What a great headline that would make. Druggist hangs for newsman's death!" Russell returned the grin.

"But who would write it?" Wyatt raised one eyebrow to take on an even more menacing expression.

"Ahem. Yes, I see your point, chap. However, might I argue that this is not the first time you've made such an egregious threat against my life? And yet here I stand before you, healthy as an ox."

"It's also not the first time you've flirted with my wife."

"But who could resist?" Russell winked at Marian and the three of them laughed at the little scene they'd just played out. "Honestly, morning stops at *The Apothecary* are the highlight of my days. Sense of humor DNA seems to have been bred out of the *Main-ahs'* genetic pool. At least those who live in Murphy."

"Ah, they're not so bad," Marian said. "You just have to figure out what they consider to be funny."

"Pssshh. Even if you did figure it out, there wouldn't be enough to fill one of Wyatt's pill bottles."

"You've hung around here a long time. It must suit you." Wyatt observed.

"Are you kidding? I adore it here."

"I detect a hint of sarcasm."

"A hint, you say? Oh, by the way, as I was pulling in I happened to see Ms. Winchell rushing from the store and this slipped from her bag or pocket or something." Russell produced the receipt. "I was afraid it might have some credit card information so I thought I should bring it in to you."

"You can toss it. She paid with cash."

Russell made a pretense of starting to tear up the receipt but stopped to take a curious peek. "Children's Tylenol? Children's Cold and Flu medicine? I say, does Ms. Winchell have a family?"

"Not that I know of," Marian said.

"I thought it was a bit strange myself," Wyatt agreed. "But I didn't see any reason to question her. They're all over-the-counter products."

"Of course, then it must not be anything serious." Russell planted the seed of doubt.

"Although." Marian pursed her lips. "She did seem a bit flustered, didn't she honey?"

"That's because she didn't know which product to purchase."

"Planning ahead for visitors or something?" Russell asked

offhand as he feigned fascination with a story on the front page of *The Times*.

"No. She was definitely buying to treat someone."

"Hmm? Why do you say?"

"Because she asked me to recommend the best product for a child with a fever."

The phone rang at precisely the perfect moment as far as Russell was concerned. He had learned all he was going to from the amiable Kilcanes and he didn't want to draw further attention to his interest in Rebekah Winchell. He pondered over the connection between her visit to the pharmacy and her appearance at the Spiritualist Camp yesterday. But before he got bogged down in the mystery of Ms. Winchell, he needed to see Homer about a revelation he'd unearthed.

# HOMER

"CIRCUMSTANTIAL EVIDENCE IS A VERY TRICKY THING. IT MAY SEEM TO POINT VERY STRAIGHT TO ONE THING, BUT IF YOU SHIFT YOUR POINT OF VIEW A LITTLE, YOU MAY FIND IT POINTING IN AN EQUALLY UNCOMPROMISING MANNER TO SOMETHING ENTIRELY DIFFERENT."

SHERLOCK HOLMES IN ***THE BOSCOMBE VALLEY MYSTERY***

"IS THE DINER CLOSED?" OLIVIA asked, unable to hide her surprise by Homer's early arrival to the office.

"I've got some phone calls to make. Got any coffee?" The sheriff settled himself behind the massive desk and began to sort through paperwork.

"I'll brew a pot." His assistant busied herself at the kitchenette.

"Strong please."

"You got it." Olivia finished her task and was leaning against the door frame. "So how'd it go yesterday over at the Rawlins' place?"

"We should never underestimate the corruptness of that man's soul. I guarantee you, Samuel Rawlins will be back in prison. Let's just hope it happens before someone gets badly hurt."

"Or worse."

"Or worse." Homer was of the same mind. Since yesterday he'd been shadowed by a thick haze of dread that indeed it might come to such a tragic end. "When you've worked in the system for as long as I have, it's not hard to get a sense of someone's capacity for violence simply by observing them unguarded for one minute. And Samuel Rawlins? He's the nastiest."

Olivia swallowed hard. "Murphy's a nice little town. How did we end up with such a horrible being living in our midst?"

"Sadly, Liv, monsters lurk where you'd least expect them. That's what makes them especially dangerous."

The phone rang and his assistant looked relieved to have a diversion from the unpleasant topic of Samuel Rawlins.

"Boss? It's a Mr. Quinten. From the FBI?"

Homer nodded. He'd been expecting the call. "Put him through."

When the call was disconnected, Homer closed his eyes and tilted his chair back, causing the worn leather to creak. He cogitated over the conversation until the wafting aroma of coffee broke his train of thought. When he opened his eyes, Olivia's pleasing face was staring back at him across the desk and a steaming cup of Joe was set before him.

"So?" she asked.

"So what?" He took a swig of the hot pick-me-up.

"Don't you think you should let me in on what's going on in that brilliant mind of yours?"

"You first."

"What do you mean?"

"You were going to do some digging around about Rebekah Winchell. Turn up anything of interest?"

"Is that why the FBI called?"

"You do the talking and I'll ask the questions."

"Such a charmer. I can see why Frannie fell for you."

Homer raised his eyebrows and made a circling motion with his hand indicating he wanted her to carry on.

"First, let me say for the record, I don't understand why you're paying so much attention to Ms. Winchell. She's never brought a bit of trouble to this town, she pays her taxes on time and she keeps to herself."

"Duly noted." Deputy Bishop was an excellent assistant, efficient in her duties, and Homer would have been lost without her. But she could be a soft touch. "I hope your tenderhearted nature never interferes with uncovering the truth."

Olivia pulled a face. "I've worked for you for over ten years now."

"Twelve, actually."

"My how time flies," she said in a sulky tone. "Haven't I always been fair-minded in my work?"

Homer nodded his assent.

"Okay then."

"Did you ever stop to think that I might in fact be looking out for Rebekah?"

"How's that?"

"Russell's been showing more than a passing interest in her and I don't like it. But since he's sniffing around there might be something to it and wouldn't you agree it would be better for the woman if we discovered what it was before he does?"

"Look who's being all compassionate now." Olivia crossed her arms and leaned back in the chair. "I'm sure our steel trap of a town clerk won't give Russell access to anything she isn't required to by law. And she would never let it slip that I've been gathering information."

"Agreed. Did you learn anything else?"

She looked down at her notes. "The deed to the farm isn't in Rebekah's name. Lucinda Cooper holds the title."

"The Camp Davis Lucinda Cooper?"

"None other."

"Curiouser and curiouser," Homer mused.

"There's more of a connection there, but first I've got to tell you what happened yesterday with my mother. She's positive Rebekah isn't who she's saying she is."

"Your mother? And how would she know about all this?" He didn't hide his displeasure.

"Have I ever told tales out of school?" Olivia bristled.

"No, but there's a first time for everything."

"Either you trust me or you don't, and if you don't you can find yourself a new assistant deputy. I'll call Mr. Payne right now and make sure there's an ad in the classifieds tomorrow."

Homer couldn't suppress a grin. He liked feistiness in a woman, but couldn't guess whether the flush flaming Olivia's face was from annoyance or the denial of an attraction he sensed. There was no denying he enjoyed the admiration of this younger woman with whom he spent more time than his wife, but it also wasn't prudent to encourage it. He'd learned to tread carefully in the comfortable familiarity which had developed over time.

"Don't go getting your panties all in a bunch. I trust you."

She replied with a dubious look.

"Completely." He held up his hands in surrender. "My most humble apologies. Now can we get back to the discussion at hand?"

Fortunately, the pouting session was short-lived.

"How *my mother* became involved is because my car's still at Fred Taylor's shop. You don't even want to know." She rolled her eyes. "Anyhow, I needed a lift home yesterday and as we drove through town we passed Rebekah in front of Jake's loading paint cans into the back of her truck. And Mom said, 'I went to college with that woman.' At first I wasn't certain who she meant because there were other people milling about. But then I saw she was pointing directly at Ms. Winchell."

"Where did your mom go to college?" Homer interrupted.

"In Lewiston."

"She went to Bates, too?"

"Double legacy. Only she graduated." Olivia had dropped out in her sophomore year to pursue coursework elsewhere in criminal justice before landing in Murphy when she answered the ad for Assistant Deputy. When her parents retired from teaching professions in Massachusetts, they followed their only child to the state of Maine.

"I thought it would be a good opportunity to do some poking so I suggested we stop and say hello. But my mother couldn't remember her name and thought it would be embarrassing to put her old classmate on the spot."

"So you let her off the hook and told her the name."

"Yep, but she insisted Rebekah Winchell wasn't right."

"She could have taken her husband's name if she married."

"True, but it was the first name my mom couldn't get past. She was certain it was not Rebekah because that was her roommate's name and there were no other girls in her dorm named Rebekah. By the time she dropped me at my place Mom had recalled the woman's first name."

"Which is?"

"Elizabeth."

Homer sighed. "People change over time. How likely is it any of us would recognize someone we hadn't seen for over thirty years in a quick drive by?"

"That's what I told her. But she's positive that our Rebekah and her Elizabeth are one in the same."

"My bet is it's a simple case of mistaken identity."

"Or twins separated at birth." Olivia grinned mischievously.

"Now *that* sounds like a story for Russell."

"My mom has the tenacity of a pit bull. As we speak, she's rummaging through boxes of college memorabilia that have been mildewing in the attic. She'll continue to search until she finds evidence proving she's right. There will be no giving up until this mystery is solved to her satisfaction."

"Maybe I should hire her."

"You couldn't handle the both of us."

"I have no doubt." Homer took a swallow of coffee. "You mentioned another connection with Lucinda Cooper?"

"My friend Emerson…"

"When are you going to give up and admit you two are more than just friends?"

Olivia leaned her crossed arms onto the desk and gave him a look that read: *I am so bored with those inferences.*

Emerson Collins was the youngest son of a wealthy family down in Portland who Olivia met at Bates. Emerson had followed her to Murphy and everyone assumed a romantic link. But Olivia refused to discuss the matter, never confirming nor denying the rumors.

"So how's that job search of his going?" Homer teased, for Emerson was a bit of a slacker.

"If he didn't have that damn trust fund." The whole idea was repellant to her. "He has no incentive to work. However, what Emerson lacks in ambition he makes up for with his passions."

"So what's his cause du jour?"

"Well, what I started to tell you is that he was part of that animal rights protest going on out to Camp Davis."

"Animal rights? I thought it was a group of fundamentalists who were protesting."

"There were two groups out there. *The New Christian Soldiers* is the organization objecting to the Spiritualists' practices of healing through mediumship. But *PETA* was also there because of a rumor about animal sacrifices taking place during some of the ceremonies."

Homer winced. "Do they?"

"Who knows? That's one wacky group of people. Anyhow, Emerson told me Rebekah was out there yesterday."

"Is she a member of *PETA* or this church group that was

protesting?" In Homer's mind, as strange as the woman might be she didn't fit the animal activist profile. However, from what Pastor Josh had shared she apparently had narrowly interpreted religious beliefs.

"I'm inclined to think she's not associated with either."

"So what was she doing out at the camp?"

"Emerson didn't know, but she wasn't there for the protests. According to Em she drove through the camp gates like a bat out of hell and stayed for a couple hours."

"Maybe she was paying a visit to her benefactor?" Homer scratched his chin.

"Don't know. But I plan to do a little more digging on that today."

"Good job."

"And one more thing. Guess who else was out at Camp yesterday?"

"The Amazing Kreskin?"

"You're not too far off. Russell Payne."

Homer frowned.

"He might have been working on an article for the paper."

"You're probably right," he said, hoping Russell hadn't been there when Rebekah made her appearance.

"I've lived up to my part of the bargain. Now it's your turn. Spill."

"There's not much to tell." He sipped his coffee to hide a smile, watching over the top of the mug as Olivia seethed at the injustice.

"Don't mess with me, Homer," she challenged through clenched teeth.

"Okay. Okay." He chuckled, setting the mug down on the desk. "But bear in mind, this is just a notion on very shaky footing. In fact, it might not even have legs."

"I get it. We're talking conjecture, a hypothesis." Olivia was growing impatient.

"As I mentioned, there were three stories on the news tape that could create a reaction like the one I observed from our Ms. Winchell."

"Yes. The Camp Davis thing and Samuel Rawlins are the two that come to my mind. Have you ruled those out?"

"Not yet. Especially now that your man Emerson has added this significant tidbit about her showing up out at the camp."

"Look, I've watched that tape twice now. And to my mind there's not another story that could be linked to Rebekah, unless perchance you think she's the arsonist behind the fire down in Kittery." She paused and looked askance at Homer. "Is that what you were discussing with Mr. Quinten?"

"Checking facts, seeing if they had any leads. Basically, I was looking for a reason to rule it out."

"And was the FBI able to give you that? Can you cross it off the list?"

"Not yet. But what I did learn ..."

Homer didn't have a chance to finish what he was about to share with his assistant deputy because Russell Payne burst through the door.

"Good morning faithful civil servants. Sheriff Pruitt, I've brought your *New York Times.* And greetings to the particularly fetching Miss Livvy." Russell bowed dramatically.

Olivia blushed from the pleasure of the compliment. "Good morning, Russell. Care for a cuppa?"

"No thank you, luv, but I would appreciate a private word with the good sheriff here. I've a little nugget of information he might find particularly useful." He gave an exaggerated wink.

"In that case, I've got some research to complete." She raised her eyebrows at Homer and closed the office door.

"So, what exactly is this little nugget?"

"Did I say nugget? I meant to say a real gem." Russell settled himself into the chair across from Homer. "It has come to my attention that Murphy's most notorious criminal, one Samuel Rawlins, has an even darker past than you might imagine."

"I have a fairly fertile imagination, especially when it comes to our Mr. Rawlins. Though I'm game to hear what you've uncovered about the creep."

"Well, there's so much I hardly know where to start."

"You can begin by telling me what you expect in return." Homer finished off his now tepid coffee with one gulp.

"Why Sheriff, you insult me," Russell huffed.

"No games, Rusty. Ever since you arrived in Murphy you've been coming to the table for scraps."

"But haven't I scratched your back as well?"

"I'll admit our arrangement has been one of a symbiotic nature. So I repeat, what do you need from me?"

"At present, I have no need for your assistance. Let's just say I'm *paying it forward*."

Homer mulled over the offer, tapping his fingers on the desk top. "Okay, so what have you got on Samuel Rawlins?"

"You're only half correct, Guv. It's Samuel, all right, but his proper surname is not *Rawlins*. And he was just a young chap when he hopped aboard the train of immorality. That one's got a rather long history of loathsome transgressions. And by the by, have you never wondered what happened to his papa?"

# RUSSELL

"EVERY JOURNALIST OWES TRIBUTE TO THE EVIL ONE."

JEAN DE LA FONTAINE, 17TH CENTURY FRENCH POET

RUSSELL WAS WHISTLING A CHEERFUL tune when he left the Sheriff's office, confident he'd planted the seed for an expanded investigation. He suspected Homer had a strong desire to get the monkey off his back, and Samuel Rawlins was a particularly repugnant little chimpanzee at that. He saw it as his duty as a citizen of Murphy to do what he could to help local law enforcement promptly escort that pimple on society back to his cozy little eight by ten cell.

All the better for Russell if Homer was to pick up the ball and run with it. He delighted in knowing someone else would be doing the grunt work for him. It was a talent he'd honed early on in his career; figuring ways to get others to carry the burden. But he didn't imagine Homer would see it that way. No, the sheriff would be grateful for the assistance he'd provided and in exchange would permit unrestricted access to the information he'd need for his book.

Russell could see no flaw in this reasoning, but on the slim chance Homer became stingy, he'd keep veiled the juicy details he learned about Lucinda Cooper and Rebekah Winchell. A perfect bargaining tool to his way of thinking, for surely the information he possessed about the two women would be more valuable to the sheriff than what he would eventually turn over in kind about Samuel Rawlins.

He imagined himself visiting the evil one in a dungeon of an interview cell; seducing him into believing he was a friend and supplying him with permitted tokens from the outside world. After all, Samuel had already proven himself to be easily corruptible. If he could kill his own father over a bottle of whiskey, just think what kind of information a few cartons of cigarettes would buy.

Russell was playing out the scene in his head as he ambled slowly toward his office, wearing a self-satisfied smirk. It would be easy to convince the little monster that his was a story of legendary proportions. There might even be a movie deal down the road and Samuel could have a say in who would take the leading role. When he had his quarry drooling at such prospects, it would be the perfect time to lay the trap. Samuel would need to turn to someone with experience and connections to document the account and get it published. But being a man with no means, the only possession of value was the story itself. When the vision of fame was all but certain to fade away, Russell would offer the deal: he would accumulate all the research, write the book, and adapt it for the movie, the whole job in exchange for the rights to the story.

Russell's head was so high in the clouds he hadn't even noticed Francesca Pruitt exiting the pharmacy until he had literally bumped into her.

The sheriff's wife let out small cry of alarm as she dropped her bag of purchases. "My goodness, you gave me a start, Russell."

"I say, I did more than startle you. I nearly knocked you flat on your arse."

Francesca's hands were trembling as she tried to collect the items.

"Allow me," he said, taking the bag from her grasp and

replacing the items that had fallen to the ground, noticing they were the very same products Rebekah Winchell had purchased earlier.

"I hardly recognized you without your two little accessories," he said playfully, handing over the bag. "Sara and Benjamin?"

"Oh, yes. They're home with a sitter. I'm afraid they've both come down with a virus going around." She looked everywhere but directly at him as she spoke.

Russell tut-tutted and wished the children well. "You and Homer should be commended. It's a selfless deed taking on the responsibility of raising your grandchildren."

"We're happy to do it. Really, we are," she said as she hunted in her purse and retrieved her car keys.

"So tell me, what is *So-phi-a* up to these days?"

Francesca's head snapped up and her eyes narrowed as they found his. Her expression answered so many questions. She cleared her throat and out of habit pushed her hair behind her ear. "We don't hear much from the children's mother."

"That's a pity." He thought it odd she referred to Sophia not as her daughter but as the mother of her grandchildren.

"Is it?" she asked in a whispered tone.

"I was thinking of the children."

"As was I." A curtain of sorrow had lowered over Francesca's face and marred her lovely features. She looked down at the shopping bag and was prompted to bid adieu. "I really must be going."

"My best to the little kiddles." Russell dipped his head and blatantly stared as Francesca walked off, admiring her luscious curves. When she drove away he reminded himself he had a newspaper to get out and proceeded to his office. He was whistling again as he bound up the stairs. Was there anything more thrilling than knowing the private, intimate details of other people's lives? Especially when they have no idea you know? Well, he could think of one thing better.

Yes indeed, Francesca Pruitt was sexy, beautiful and forbidden. A mighty scrumptious canary for a rather ravenous cat.

# REBEKAH

"THERE SHALL NOT BE FOUND AMONG YOU ANYONE WHO BURNS HIS SON OR DAUGHTER AS AN OFFERING,
ANYONE WHO PRACTICES DIVINATION, A SOOTHSAYER OR AN AUGUR,
OR A SORCERER, OR A CHARMER, OR A MEDIUM ,
OR A WIZARD OR A NECROMANCER. FOR WHOEVER DOES THESE THINGS IS AN ABOMINATION OF THE LORD."

DEUTERONOMY 18:12

When Rebekah walked into the farmhouse from feeding the animals she found Cord taking the scissors to the listless child's head.

"What on earth are you doing?" she exclaimed.

"She's miserable," Cord gave as the only explanation for shearing Gabriella's head.

"But why?"

"The medicines you bought yesterday aren't working. We have to get her to a doctor. Today. She needs antibiotics." Cord was speaking with calm authority. "You said there could be people searching for us. But they will be looking for a little girl, right?"

Rebekah nodded, recalling how she'd embellished the story of a door-to-door search in order to manipulate. The tactic had worked to her advantage two days before, but now it appeared to be backfiring.

Cord finished the haircut and removed the towel to reveal an outfit of t-shirt and OshKosh overalls. Then she took some

Vaseline and styled the child's hair to stand up like a crew cut. "There. What do you think?"

Rebekah had to admit, the transformation might fool anyone who didn't know the little girl, but she was also overcome by sadness.

"It's the best I can do."

"But how will you disguise yourself? They'll ask for some type of identification."

"I'm not going to take her." The young woman came to her and said directly. "You are. You're known in this town."

"No. No. That won't do." She didn't recognize her own voice, pitched as it was with fright. "I can't do it. I can't."

"Yes, Rebekah, you can. I've seen how attached you've become to Gabriella in this short time. You couldn't live with yourself if anything happened to her."

"People will ask questions." She began to pace.

"And you'll have answers. It will be easy to explain. I'll help you."

Rebekah was feeling caged in. She closed her eyes and began reciting The Lord's Prayer. She felt Cord take her hand and heard the young woman's voice in unity with her own. After they spoke the Amen she opened her eyes to look upon the beseeching expression of a desperate mother. It was a familiar reflection, mirroring her own personal anguish and fear many years earlier.

"You must do this, if not for us then because it's an act of Christian charity."

Rebekah inhaled deeply then puffed out a resigned breath. "What will I say?"

"It's best to keep the story as near to the truth as possible. Do you have any relatives that you could say are visiting?"

Rebekah could only think of Aunt Lucinda, a mention that would be unwise. Then she remembered a cousin she'd once been close with but hadn't seen for many years.

"My cousin Ruth. Last I heard she moved to Vermont with her husband and children."

"All right. Your cousin Ruth has taken ill and you've been asked to look after her grandson while her daughter takes her to a specialist in Boston. Is that something you could repeat if asked?"

Rebekah hesitated before responding. "Yes. My cousin Ruth has cancer. Her daughter took her to Boston to see a specialist. They left her little boy with me to look after for a while."

"Perfect. And what shall we call our little boy?" Cord kissed Gabriella's forehead.

"Jacob." In the Bible, Rebekah's favorite son was Jacob. She began to massage her temples to push back a nagging memory threatening to surface.

"So you simply tell the doctor that *Jacob* came down with a fever which hasn't responded to *Tylenol* and you felt a doctor should take a look at him. If they ask his age, he's two and a half. If they ask for insurance information, say you'll pay with cash. Same with the pharmacy if the doctor writes a prescription, which I'm sure he will." Cord handed her a considerable amount of money.

Rebekah pocketed the bills and reached for the little body which had become dead weight. "Let's go, honey."

Cord picked up the backpack designed to carry her child and said, "Since I left the car seat in my car, we need to rig up something that will be safe to transport her."

On the way to town, Rebekah considered the transformation of her lodger from hazy daydreamer to composed and responsible parent, tenderly ministering to her daughter. The little girl's illness had apparently snapped the young woman awake to reality. The previous night, Cord had maintained a cautious reserve, neither of them acknowledging the mention of Gemma.

Of course, now she was doubtful she'd heard correctly. How could this stranger possibly know?

Rebekah rehearsed the story Cord invented but did not relish committing a gross disregard of the commandments. Maybe she should end this torment right now by going to the sheriff and telling him the truth. But they'd take the girl away, and she couldn't bear the thought of losing her.

The waiting room was vacant for which Rebekah whispered a prayer of thanks. A pleasant middle aged woman wearing nurses' scrubs slid opened a glass window and asked if she had an appointment.

"No. This is an emergency. I'm babysitting for my cousin's grandson and he's taken ill with a fever."

"What's your name?"

"Winchell. Rebekah Winchell. My address is number 11 Route 79. No phone."

The woman peered at her intently over half glasses. "And the baby's name?"

"Jacob."

"Last name?"

Rebekah's throat went dry. They hadn't discussed a last name. But she did not want the nurse to become suspicious so she blurted out the first thought that came to mind. "Cooper."

Dr. Metcalf had seen them immediately and after a quick examination confirmed there was a virus going around and the little tyke's symptoms were in line with what he'd been seeing. He wrote out a prescription and advised her to bring Jacob back in if the fever didn't break within 48 hours. The doctor also made some other suggestions which he wrote down on a blank prescription form. Nobody questioned her when she paid cash for the visit at the reception desk, but by now the waiting room was overflowing with mothers and children.

She ducked her head and made for a quick exit when the

nurse called out across the room. “Ms. Winchell? You forgot Jacob’s prescription.”

Rebekah had not been pleased to have attention drawn to her at the doctor’s office and she wasn’t relishing a long wait in the pharmacy under the watchful eyes of town folk, especially with a toddler in her arms. But she was in luck because there were no customers waiting and the pharmacist took care of her right away.

“I guess the Tylenol didn’t work for” - he looked again at the form - “little Jacob.”

She looked up into the kind face of the man who had helped her yesterday. “Fraid not.”

“What a cute little guy,” the woman who took her money yesterday had come from behind the check-out counter and playfully grabbed the little feet. “What are you doing with Dora the Explorer on your shoes? I’ll bet these once belonged to your big sister, huh?” The woman smiled at Rebekah and then added, “I remember what that’s like. I was always getting the cast-offs of one of my older brothers or cousins.”

“Times are tough,” she agreed but was grateful not to have to converse further as the bottle of liquid medication was passed down from the pharmacist. “What do I owe?”

“Do you have an insurance card?”

“I’ll just pay cash and take the receipt. His mother can sort out the details when she comes back for him. I’m just babysitting for a spell.”

“Lucky you,” the woman enthused. “Such a beautiful child.”

Rebekah secured the little one into the makeshift car seat and opened the bottle to dispense the first dose. “Here you go.”

But Gabriella was not cooperating and began crying. “Mama. My mama.”

Feeling the judging eyes of town folk upon her, she hopped

into the front seat and put the car in gear. She'd stop outside of town and try to persuade the child to take the medication.

"Settle down, honey. I'm taking you to Mama now." But the howling persisted to the point where Rebekah thought she'd start screaming herself.

"What to do? What to do?" She was tapping the steering wheel. When she arrived at the crossroads, it was as if she had no power of her own to guide the wheel and instead of turning off toward her property she stayed straight. "Dear Lord, please forgive me."

When she drove through the gates there were no groups assembled, however there were plenty of people strolling the camp grounds. She glanced at the dashboard clock which told her services had probably finished and her best chances of finding Lucinda would be at the cottage. As she rounded the bend of the dusty drive and approached the stone building, the piercing shrieks brought her aunt running from within.

She averted her eyes from Lucinda's questioning gaze and lifted the toddler from the truck cabin, making shushing sounds.

"Rebekah, what have you done?" her aunt's tone blended concern with accusation.

She handed the child over and said, "Auntie, you must help me. Let us take our baby to the healing stone."

Lucinda's soothing tone had calmed the little girl enough to be persuaded to take the medicine. She then drank a cup of milk and fell into a deep sleep. The two women remained speechless on the walk through the woods until arriving at the substantial slab of granite upon which the slumbering child was laid. As her aunt began the rituals of communing with the spirit world, Rebekah slowly surrendered to the healing words and those old familiar chants.

When they returned to the cottage, Lucinda made sandwiches

and the two ate quietly as the child continued to sleep. Her aunt still possessed an ethereal aura, although she had aged considerably over the years.

"Shall I do a reading? It might be helpful." Lucinda did not wait for an answer. She removed the plates and returned with her Tarot cards.

Rebekah knew she should resist, but instead concentrated on the cards being laid on the table before her by frail but still graceful hands.

"You must be shrewd around this woman," Lucinda cautioned, tapping the middle card.

"But *The Fool* means innocence," Rebekah objected.

"So you still study the cards?" Her aunt nodded solemnly.

"No!" Her reply was harsh. She was ashamed to admit having held on to the cards given to her so long ago, when she had foolishly veered from the path of righteousness. Although she had on rare occasions taken them out for a quick look, she had just as quickly shoved them back into the drawer. She added more gently, "Not for years and years."

Lucinda studied the cards. "Pay heed to *The Fool's* perspective. It's reversed and she is headed for a downfall. *The Hermit* is positioned prominently with *The Tower* and *The Moon*. You mustn't let her take you down with her my dear one."

Rebekah had been soothed by the experience and felt she knew what had to be done. But on the drive home, cracks began to materialize in her veneer of serenity, which completely dissolved by the time she arrived at her sanctuary.

"What have I done?" She was swept away by guilt and confusion. "If you are a forgiving God, I beg you to absolve me of my great sins. I witness to you that I have partnered with demons but I vow never to have fellowship with the devil again." She broke down and sobbed, covering her face in shame. When she absently leaned forward she wasn't even conscious of sounding the Silverado's horn.

# CORDELIA

"DO NOT LIVE IN THE WORLD, IN DISTRACTION AND FALSE DREAMS."

BUDDHA

HANDSOME HAD CLIMBED ATOP THE back of a wing chair to watch as Rebekah drove away with Gabriella. He let out a woeful whine as he pressed his nose against the front window.

"You're already on Rebekah's bad side. She won't be happy to see your tell-tale smudges on the window." I sidled up beside the pooch, scratching behind his ears, trying to tamp down my own misgivings.

So many questions were swirling in my head. What if Rebekah gets pulled over and arrested for not having a legal child safety seat? What if the doctor does a thorough examination and discovers Gabriella's true sex? What if it's determined my baby has a serious disease and is rushed to a hospital? Why was it taking so long to get the car repaired? How had Rebekah explained the out of state license plates?

"Come on boy, we need a distraction." With the round trip to town plus stops at the doctor and the pharmacy, I calculated there to be more than enough time to hike to the clearing and back. Besides, there was no way for Rebekah to reach me without a phone so I saw no point in being cooped up in the house with my tormenting thoughts.

As I walked toward the path, Handsome let out a yelp. I turned and saw a car arriving at a distance so I scooped him up and darted into the barn. My heart was racing as I peered through a crack between the wall boards. From this vantage I couldn't see the vehicle but seconds after the thump of the car door the driver came into view. The visitor was a stocky, middle aged man, dressed in khakis and a polo shirt. He walked casually to the door and when there was no answer he thankfully left without a glance in the direction of my hiding place.

"That was close," I said to Handsome, adrenaline propelling me up the hill at such speed that I needed a good stretch to work out a pain in my side when I reached the top. I slowly edged toward the clearing to survey the downward slope and was surprised by the shallowness of the river.

Handsome came up beside me and nudged my hand. "Well, what do you think buddy? Could we cross over if we need to?"

Voices boomed from the other side. I lowered myself behind a mountain laurel bush when two men charged out of the run down cabin. Though I couldn't make out the words, there was brutality in the tone. As the quarreling intensified I revised the query. "Should we even consider crossing it?"

When we returned to the farm, there was no truck nor were there any signs indicating Rebekah may have returned and then left again. I considered resuming the painting project but felt too restless with worry. To distract myself further, I retrieved the letters from beneath the guest room mattress. I'd been finding it a challenge to navigate the blurry details of a mystery unfolding within the missives. As I shuffled through the bundle, a newsprint article slipped loose. I searched for a date or the name of the newspaper, but the article had been clipped from somewhere in the middle of the page. "Tragedy Claims Life of Local Minister" read the heading.

> The reverend Matthew Wayne Cooper, much admired pastor of the First Baptist Church, was

> pronounced dead upon arrival at St. Barnabus Hospital last night just before midnight. Volunteer firefighters were called to the scene at 10:15 PM after a 911 report of flames appearing from the second story window of the church rectory by a neighbor who'd been out walking his dog. In a statement, Chief of Police Thomas Williams said the initial coroner's report suggests Rev. Cooper died of a gunshot wound to the chest before the fire was started. At present he cannot confirm any suspects but reported that no staff or family members were present at the time of the tragedy. Anyone with information or who might have seen any suspicious activity is urged to come forward and contact the police immediately. Rev. Cooper is survived by his wife, Estelle, a daughter, Elizabeth, and a sister, Lucinda.

I could at least eliminate one of my earlier hypotheses. Rebekah could not be related to this Betsy Cooper person through marriage because there was no brother listed in the article. However, both Rebekah and Betsy Cooper had an Aunt Lucinda so I had to presume they were cousins. And yet, there was no other sibling listed for Reverend Cooper. My eyes were bleary when I finished reading the second pile of letters, but I was no closer to figuring out the relationship between the two women.

I rubbed my neck and looked at the clock. "Where on earth could they be?"

I returned the letters to the envelope in the storage room and then opened the box with the photographs to take a closer look at the images. Tucked to the side at the bottom was a leather bound book I must have overlooked before. It was a journal; a journal that just might hold the answer to the Betsy Cooper mystery. I stowed the diary in my hiding place under the mattress then returned to the family room and sat down cross-legged in the middle of the floor and began to draw in deep breaths the way my foster father, Chung Wu, had taught me so long ago.

"Jing-jing-jing-jing-jing-jing-jing-jing," I repeated the mantra quietly. Jing was the Chinese word for calm. I was out of practice but had a great need to take myself away from terrifying thoughts of all that might have gone wrong today.

The unrelenting blare of a car horn coupled with Handsome's furious barking abruptly interrupted the deep meditative state I'd achieved. I sprinted out the door and pulled Gabriella from the back of the truck.

"Baby, baby, baby. Mama missed you so much." I held my daughter close. She was still warm to the touch and began to cry. "Hush now, sweetheart. You're safe with me now."

I rushed to revive Rebekah from her collapsed position, which wasn't easy considering the whimpering child in my arms and an overly eager pooch circling my feet.

"I have sinned." Rebekah covered her face and sobbed. "Behold, the whirlwinds of the Lord goeth forth with fury. It shall fall with pain upon the head of the wicked."

"I'm sure you've done nothing that can't be forgiven." Wasn't the Christian God a forgiving being?

Rebekah wiped her tears with her shirt sleeve and said in a childlike voice, "That's exactly what Auntie always says. But I should never have tried to cross over. Daddy warned me: 'God is a righteous judge, a God who expresses his wrath every day.' I just can't figure out who to believe anymore."

"You've been gone so long. I'll bet you haven't eaten since breakfast." I helped Rebekah from the truck, thinking her confused state might be caused by a dip in blood sugar.

"Baby needs her medicine." Rebekah reached back in the cab for the pharmacy bag.

"Let's get you both inside. I'll fix you some supper and a nice hot cup of tea."

Once inside, I put the kettle on before reading the dosing directions of the antibiotics. "Has she had the first dose yet?"

Rebekah was lost somewhere in her mind. I had to gently shake the woman to bring her back and asked again about the medication.

"Yes, she took it for Auntie."

*Auntie?*

"What did the doctor say?" I asked, coaxing Gabriella to swallow the medicine.

"A virus is going around. The office was full of people." Rebekah's voice was mechanical.

"So you had a long wait to see the doctor?"

"No. We got right in and out."

"Really? But you've been gone for hours."

"Have I?" This ever more bizarre persona wore a mask of bewilderment.

I quickly slapped together a sandwich and poured a cup of tea, hoping some nourishment would reawaken the crotchety old Rebekah.

"Are you hungry baby?" I turned my attention back to Gabriella. "How about a PBJ?"

"She had some crackers."

"Where?"

Rebekah didn't answer and pushed the sandwich aside. But she did appear more relaxed when she finished drinking her tea. "I'm going to the weaving room for a bit."

Gabriella ate a few bites of her sandwich and then fell promptly to sleep. I nestled her into the bed and Handsome snuggled in beside her, finally content now that his charge had been safely returned to him.

Later, when I took the dog out for his evening business, light was still shining from beneath the weaving room door. I collected the medication to take upstairs and took a closer look at the prescription form, finally noticing the last name Rebekah had chosen for an alias. Jacob Cooper. One more connection to Betsy Cooper heightened my misgivings about this extended stay in Murphy, Maine.

# RAMON

"MEN'S VOWS ARE WOMEN'S TRAITORS."

WILLIAM SHAKESPEARE, ***CYMBELINE***

"IT TOOK YOU LONG ENOUGH to answer," Ramon shouted into the phone to be heard above the airport din. "You have to talk louder."

He flashed a quick grin. "And here I thought I was your top priority."

"So have you heard from her? - - - Nothing at all? - - - What new development?" Ramon listened for a moment then kicked at the floor. "Damn. That is definitely not the best news you could have given me. - - - Yes, it is delayed and no estimates for when it might take off. - - - More like Typhoon Cordelia. - - - I'll call you before I board, but if you hear anything, anything at all, call me. - - - You as well. Adios."

Ramon disconnected the call and raked his hands through his hair. Normally, he wouldn't mind being stranded on a foreign continent. He'd look upon it as an adventure of sorts. Maybe use the time for uninterrupted work. But today he felt completely powerless, and sick with worry.

*Where the hell are you, Cord?*

He slumped onto the only remaining chair in the corner of the Delta Sky Club and looked out upon the gloom of tropical storm force winds holding him hostage. He couldn't help but be reminded of similar circumstances years before when he'd been stranded in D.C. by another ill-timed storm.

Leaning elbows onto thighs, Ramon clasped his hands together and sucked in a deep breath. He'd certainly slammed the door on possibility back then. If he had the opportunity for a do-over would he make the same choice to reconnect with Cord? And what about her perspective of that long ago weekend when the innocence of their friendship had been transformed forever?

He rubbed the woeful lines creasing his forehead. He must not allow himself to be pulled under by the strong currents of regret. All energy must be positively directed toward forming a plan. When the plane landed at JFK he would hit the ground at full speed.

# HOMER

"IT IS ALWAYS AWKWARD DOING BUSINESS WITH AN ALIAS."

SHERLOCK HOLMES IN *THE ADVENTURE OF THE BLUE CARBUNCLE*

"I'M ON MY WAY OUT to the Winchell farm," Homer reported in to Olivia. "I want to see what she can tell me about the Rawlins boys and how well she knew Pearl. See if I can shed a little more light on what Mr. Payne had to share."

"Do you think it's true?" she asked.

"I haven't checked it out yet, not even sure if I can get access to the information. I'm afraid we've arrived at an unfortunate juncture in our culture where the press has more power than the law. But my gut is telling me the whole sordid tale Russell unearthed is factual."

"Speaking of unearthing buried secrets, I have something interesting..."

"You're breaking up." Homer had entered no man's land.

He thought again about the horrific details Russell had shared about Samuel Rawlins. But he suspected the Pagan Fox was holding something back. Either a bargaining chip for something yet to come or the reporter wanted a head start on some new information. He turned down a winding dirt lane that passed for Rebekah's driveway. As he rounded the last curve, the house came into view, as did someone with short blonde hair darting into the barn. His detective antenna was on alert, but the wisest tactic was to let the person believe they hadn't been seen.

Homer sauntered up to the porch and knocked on the door even though the truck was nowhere in sight. He was tempted to pretend to go looking for Rebekah in the barn, but trusting his instincts he got back into the cruiser and left. When satisfied he'd driven out of sight, he parked and backtracked on foot, creeping along trees to keep his body camouflaged. After waiting several minutes, his patience was rewarded when the petite figure cautiously emerged, a small dog following close behind. From the shape and posture he determined the subject to be a young female. The girl gazed intently down the drive for a few seconds then quickly vanished behind the barn.

He didn't know what to make of this unexpected development. At the moment he had bigger fish to fry, but he'd be back again. Unannounced.

"Don't make this a habit," Homer grumbled at Russell, who was sitting at the diner counter. When he stopped at *The Apothecary* Marian told him his paper had already been picked up.

"My apologies for presuming to do a chap a favor," Russell said as he handed over the morning *Times*. "I did stop by your official digs first, and when I didn't find you there I assumed you'd be in your usual spot."

Homer ignored the subtle jab and settled into his corner booth, sending the message he was in no mood to play.

Apparently Russell didn't take the hint and called out across the diner. "I believe you'll find the puzzle on page 11 of section B today, Guv."

This provoked a mixed reaction from the other patrons. Those who considered Russell a slimy character or had at one time been maligned in the *Murphy Post* rolled their eyes disdainfully. But others found his insults to be entertaining and were amused by the comment.

As owner of the establishment, Becky had to give the appearance of remaining neutral, but while filling Homer's cup he muttered under his breath, "One day he will cross the wrong fellah in he-ah and I promise to wait at least five minutes before I call the law."

"And if I'm sitting here when it happens? I'll just keep my head buried in the paper until you give the signal," Homer said with a wink.

The bell above the door jingled and Homer looked up to see Frannie and the kids walking toward the booth. Another set of eyes were covertly watching over his laptop but she whisked the children straight past Russell without acknowledging his presence.

"Mornin' Ms. Pruitt." Becky raised the coffee pot and asked, "Can I get you a cup?"

"No thank you, Becky. I must get these two home and back into bed. I just wanted to give Homer an update."

"Have they come down with the nasty flu bug goin' round?"

"Unfortunately, yes. So we won't tarry."

When Becky sashayed over to fill another customer's cup, Frannie gave Homer a quick rundown of what the doctor had said. Before she turned to leave she added, "You will never guess who was there."

"Okay, then tell me."

"Rebekah Winchell. And she had a little boy with her."

Homer glanced in the direction of the counter where Russell was absorbed in his typing. Following his gaze, Frannie easily interpreted the signal to change subjects. More than anyone, she knew her husband's country bumpkin routine was a ruse and one that had always worked to his advantage. She momentarily lost herself to contemplating the heights her husband's career might have reached had it not been for one serious misstep. And to be fair, it wasn't his blunder. Had he not volunteered for overtime that long ago night, they would never have heard of Murphy, Maine.

"Hey kids, let's get you two out to the car." Homer gently took his wife's arm but whispered sharply into her ear, "Frannie."

He knew she was unaware of how uncomfortably long she'd escaped within. Before he was able to get his wife's attention, Russell looked up from his laptop and peered at them knowingly.

Homer escorted Frannie to the car, questioning her about Rebekah and the little boy. When he waved her off, instead of returning to his crossword puzzle and coffee, he continued in the direction of his office. Something about the reclusive woman had always gnawed at him, but she had kept her nose clean for all these twenty years. In spite of that, his detective's nose was picking up on a peculiar scent blowing around the Winchell farm. All those visits to town recently, her distressful reaction to the news report earlier in the week and showing up at Dr. Metcalf's office with a small boy. Not to mention the unidentified young woman he'd spied hiding in the barn this morning. There was no question he'd be making a return visit to Ms. Winchell and whoever else might be living out there.

When he walked into the Sheriff's office, Olivia was waiting for him.

"Remember how I told you my mother would not give up until she solved the mystery of Rebekah Winchell to her satisfaction? And by satisfaction I mean until she could prove she was right."

Homer nodded.

"Look at this." Olivia handed him a student directory from Bates University, 1970. "Can you pick out Rebekah on this page?"

"Well, well, well. What do ya' know? So Rebekah Winchell is

an assumed name. Okay. You know the drill. Get me everything you can on one Elizabeth Cooper."

"Already working on it, boss."

"If I wasn't married and you didn't have Emerson…" Before he could finish, a ticket book whacked him squarely on the head.

# RUSSELL

"WE JOURNALISTS DON'T HAVE TO STEP ON ROACHES. ALL WE HAVE TO DO IS TURN ON THE KITCHEN LIGHT AND WATCH THE CRITTERS SCURRY."

P.J. O"ROURKE

RUSSELL WAS UNSETTLED BY FRANCESCA'S glacial stare. He didn't know how long she'd already been glaring at him when he looked up from typing his article. It was as if she hadn't actually been looking at him but into the depths of him, which felt oddly intrusive and yet intimate. He couldn't help staring back, not only because she was exotically beautiful, but also because she fascinated him. Francesca had become his most challenging case study and one that bordered on obsession. Her coupling with such an average-Joe sheriff had been particularly baffling. And it annoyed him to no end that Homer chose to call his wife by the incongruously frumpy shortened nickname. *Frannie* just didn't suit her.

As Russell chipped away at the mountainous obstacles to the truth - or rather, he should give some credit to his investigator buddy B.W. - an intriguing story was on the verge. However, the intangible thread needed to tie the fragmented facts together remained beyond his reach. But he was getting closer. Until then, the already unearthed secrets of Francesca's life would be guarded with the greatest care.

What was even more interesting to Russell at the moment was what Francesca had said to Homer. He couldn't be positive, but he thought he heard her mention Rebekah Winchell. It wouldn't take long for tongues to be set a wagging. With Murphy being such a small community, it wasn't out of the ordinary for folks to feel a sense of entitlement about everybody else's business. It was one of the perks of being a small town journalist. He closed his laptop and gathered his notes, shoving both into his messenger bag and sauntered across the street toward his office. But first he took a detour into *The Apothecary*.

He slowly walked the aisles gathering miscellaneous items, eavesdropping on his neighbors, hoping someone would reward him with a morsel of information. He wasn't there but five minutes and BINGO!

"Hello, Mrs. Kepler. Are you feeling any better today?" Marian asked as she tallied up the octogenarian's purchases.

"I was, but since I was in Dr. Metcalf's office with all those flu germs flying around like bats at midnight I'll probably be next."

"Why don't you buy a bottle of this hand sanitizer? It's on sale today."

"Well, if you think it will help." Ida Kepler leaned in conspiratorially, though she was hard of hearing and still spoke loud enough for everyone in the store to hear. "Guess who was at the doctor's this morning?"

"From what I hear? Nearly everyone."

"It was that Winchell woman. Hardly ever see her in town, but I did recognize her. Anyhow, she had the cutest little girl with her."

"Not to contradict you, Mrs. Kepler, but it was a little boy."

"Are you certain?" The woman's brow wrinkled in doubt.

"The child's name is Jacob. She brought him in here to pick up some medication. I think he's got the bug, too."

Wyatt walked up with a package. "You forgot this Ms. Kepler."

"You're an angel. I would have had to drive all the way back for this." Again the woman whispered loudly. "Marian tells me that was a little boy with Rebekah Winchell."

"That's right," the pharmacist answered.

"Goodness. I guess my eyes aren't what they used to be."

"They're all so cute at that age, sometimes it's hard to tell," Marian patted the old woman's hand.

Russell and his half-filled basket of unneeded toiletries were next in line. "So the mystery continues."

"Mystery?" asked Marian.

"You know, yesterday? Ms. Winchell? The receipt for children's products?"

"Mystery solved." Marian began scanning the items. "She's babysitting while the little boy's mother is out of town. Unfortunately, he came down with the flu."

"A relative?" he asked as he opened his wallet and handed over two twenties.

"Could be. Not the same last name though."

Russell was itching to inquire about the child's name, but he didn't want to risk crossing the line between innocently curious neighbor and nosy reporter digging for dirt. He'd figure another way to get Marian to spill. But now wasn't the time, especially with a line of customers eager to make their purchases.

# REBEKAH

"WHOEVER CAN BE TRUSTED WITH VERY LITTLE CAN ALSO BE TRUSTED WITH MUCH,
AND WHOEVER IS DISHONEST WITH VERY LITTLE WILL ALSO BE DISHONEST WITH MUCH."

LUKE 16:10

THE HOUSE WAS COMPLETELY DARK when Rebekah walked out of the weaving room. She looked at the clock with amazement, having been absorbed with her project for hours. Still, she had more she wanted to accomplish and went to the store room in search of a special yarn.

She checked the knob as was her habit before inserting the key, but the handle turned and the door opened easily. Had she forgotten to lock the door? She kept the lone key on a chain around her neck at all times. There was no other possibility.

Rebekah clucked aloud, "You aah becoming careless."

To find the perfect skein of wool she pulled out several boxes, exposing the space under the empty shelves where a photograph caught her eye. She picked it up to inspect more closely, the image provoking such an upsetting memory it became a struggle for her to maintain equilibrium.

"Gemma," she gasped, grabbing hold of the shelves to stop the spinning, and thus pulling a section crashing down upon herself.

Cord appeared with the dog at her heals and began to clear away the debris.

"Rebekah! Are you okay?"

She was anything but okay. Seeing the long ago snapped photo of Gemma was the catalyst to release a maelstrom of memories.

"Why Daddy, why?" she sobbed.

"Let me help you up." The younger woman reached out her hand.

But Rebekah remained fixed to the floor, rocking her body and clutching the photo to her heart. She couldn't be certain how much time had passed when the sound of the front door closing brought her out of the stupor. Most everything in the pantry had been picked up and resettled on the shelves. Her knee was bleeding, probably having been scraped by the metal unit when it fell. She hoisted herself up and spied something in the corner behind the door; an item Cord must have missed as she was picking up the mess. She leaned down to collect the child's little red ball. *But how did it get in here?*

She placed the crumpled photo of Gemma on the table and began smoothing it out with her hands before tucking it into her Bible. She was much calmer by the time she heard footsteps on the porch.

"I fed the animals," Cord informed her as she washed her hands.

"That was kind of you. A righteous man cares for the needs of his animals. Proverbs 12:10," Rebekah recited the quote in a quiet voice.

"I was glad to do it. Besides, you've been good to us. Do unto others, right?"

As the young woman set about to make breakfast Rebekah asked, "Last night the store room was unlocked. Would you know anything about that?"

There was an ever so slight hesitation in Cord's movements before she answered, "Actually, I didn't know you kept it locked."

"So you've been in there?"

Cord turned and looked at her directly and said, "No. Never."

# CORDELIA

"HOW LONG THE NIGHT TO THE WATCHMAN, HOW LONG THE ROAD TO THE WEARY TRAVELER,
HOW LONG THE WANDERING OF MANY LIVES
TO THE FOOL WHO MISSES THE WAY."

BUDDHA

I'D BEEN HOVERING AT THE threshold of piecing together the connection between Rebekah and Betsy Cooper when the commotion of storage shelves tipping over interrupted my reading. There'd been a letter tucked inside the back cover of the diary addressed to the Kentucky District Attorney from a Dr. Ryan and typed on letterhead from Arbor House – A Private Psychiatric Treatment Facility for the Criminally Insane in Louisville. It was a letter of recommendation to the State Department of Corrections.

> "After six years of a court ordered psychiatric treatment program, I consider Elizabeth Cooper to be rehabilitated. There has been no evidence of dissociative fugue in the past five years nor any lingering signs of psychosis or delusions. The patient has demonstrated an ability to take ownership for her actions and to separate her acts from those of others. She now understands the timing and circumstances surrounding the deaths of her father and daughter and she has

come to terms with the more recent passing of her mother. I present copies of my professional notes for review by the state. In my qualified opinion, Elizabeth Cooper is no longer a threat to herself or society. My recommendation is for Ms. Cooper to be released from her state mandated treatment program."

This Dr. Ryan, presumably the psychiatrist assigned to the case, figured prominently in Betsy Cooper's writings.

September 17th ~ Dr. Ryan told me if I want to get better so I can go home then I have to find the truth. But home to what? Where? There is no place for me. He said by writing down what I remember we can uncover what really happened and that I don't have to share what I write with anyone else unless I want to. I'll bet someone will come snooping into my room at night and read this while I'm drugged with sleeping pills. Well, if they do - and I mean you nurse Mildred Ross - it will be on their conscience not mine. Who cares anyhow? Besides, this is a waste of time since I already know the truth. I am a great sinner and now I'm being punished. Daddy's death is my fault. Whether or not my finger touched the flame that burned his soul, it was my bidding. I hated him so much after he made me give up my little girl. I lay in bed night after night, praying to a God that had betrayed me to strike my father dead. And for once in my whole life God did what I asked. And I was glad for it. An eye for an eye.

September 18th ~ I read to Dr. Ryan what I wrote last night. Why not? His spies would get to it anyway. He asked me why I consider myself a great sinner. Getting pregnant out of wedlock is a sin and my part in Daddy's death is the biggest sin, but he already knows about those. I didn't want to talk about my partnering with the devil. According to Daddy all the things I did with Aunt Lucinda were abominations. So I didn't answer. Then Dr. Ryan asked me to focus on my maternal obligations. I imagine he thinks I should never have let them take my daughter away in the first place. He's right because then none of this would have happened. But I was weak. Daddy terrified me with his fit of rage and Mummy totally took his side. I had nobody to turn to after they sent Lucinda away.

September 25th ~ A letter came today from Aunt Lucinda. She said not to despair. My little girl lives on. I wonder if she's seen her. I will write and ask her to please tell her I'm sorry for everything and that I never meant to let her go.

September 26th ~ Dr. Ryan asked to read Aunt Lucinda's letter. I could tell by the way he closed his eyes and rubbed the bridge of his nose that I shouldn't have let him. He asked if I remembered about when they took my baby away. I've told him so many times and I don't understand why he keeps asking me these questions over and over again.

Why did they take her away? Because Daddy said she was a product of sin and Mummy told the people I was unfit to care for a baby. But that's not true. I loved my little girl. Only those two times did I lose track of her. But I was tired and confused. If only I had gotten some sleep.

Where did they take her? To a foster home.

Did you ever see her again? Yes. Aunt Lucinda took me for visits at the park.

When was the last time you saw her? Her third birthday. She was crying because they took away the present I brought for her. They told me I had to leave. That I was upsetting her. Liars!

Where is she now? Gone. Gone. Gone. I never meant for it to happen. Mommy's so very sorry, Gemma.

What at first seemed a preposterous notion that Rebekah Winchell and Betsy Cooper were the same person now had adequate evidence to legitimize the alarming theory. Rebekah had selected Cooper for a last name for Gabriella's prescription and there was the *C* monogram on the china to consider. Not to mention this shared Aunt Lucinda without a reasonable explanation. And why else would she be in possession of the letters and diary? If the theory proved valid, Rebekah had served time in a facility for the criminally insane. But for what? Murdering her father? According to the newspaper article, Reverend Cooper had been shot to death and the author of the journal claimed responsibility for his death. But even more a concern, what happened to Gemma? In his letter, Dr. Ryan had indicated his patient had taken ownership of her actions and understood the circumstances of her daughter's death. Could Rebekah have done the unimaginable because of some psychotic episode?

I was overcome with sick dread. I'd taken refuge with - *and worse* - exposed my daughter to a very sick woman, one possibly capable of murder. Or murders. Now my fear was that I'd been witnessing the reemergence of the psychoses Dr. Ryan had referred to in his report. Ever since Gabriella became sick, Rebekah had grown increasingly anxious and agitated. And last night she'd appeared completely unhinged, mumbling about her Daddy and Auntie and talking about sinning and crossing over. But even more disturbing, how many times had she called Gabriella *her little gem*?

My little Gem. Gemma. Gone. Gone. Gone.

But where and how?

Rebekah mustn't guess I've learned her secret.

I clasped my hands together to ease the trembling. I had to keep it together until my baby got well and I figured a way out this nightmare.

# HOMER

"IT IS OF THE HIGHEST IMPORTANCE IN THE ART OF DETECTION TO BE ABLE TO RECOGNIZE, OUT OF A NUMBER OF FACTS, WHICH ARE INCIDENTAL AND WHICH ARE VITAL."

SHERLOCK HOLMES IN *THE ADVENTURE OF THE REIGATE SQUIRE*

HOMER MADE THE LONG DRIVE out to the Winchell farm for the second day in a row and was relieved when the truck came into view as he rounded the last curve of the dirt road. He wouldn't have called even if the woman did have a phone, always preferring the element of surprise. If only what he was investigating was a little less ambiguous, aside from the fact Rebekah Winchell was not who she portrayed herself to be.

He heard foot shuffling before the door cracked warily open.

"Good morning, Ms. Winchell." He offered his friendliest smile.

"Mornin'." Rebekah twisted her long graying mane into a knot. Homer thought about Olivia's description of the woman as old. Aside from the worry-wrinkled forehead, the rest of her face was free of age lines. It was the silver streaked hair that belied her true age.

"How've you been?"

"No complaints." She scratched her chin and said, "What brings the sheriff all the way out to these parts?"

"I was on my way to Camp Davis."

Rebekah's head jerked at the mention of the Camp.

"I'm doing a favor for a colleague down in Washington. He's

looking for someone and there's reason to believe the person might have headed up north. It's doubtful anything will come of it, but with all the out-of-towners visiting the Camp this weekend I thought it was worth a try. Anyhow, since I was passing by your place, I figured I might as well stop here."

Homer handed over a copy of the bulletin that had come across his desk earlier in the week. He'd needed a ruse for visiting and the *Amber Alert* flyer was the best he could come up with on short notice. "Have you seen anybody resembling this little girl and her mother?"

Rebekah stalled a moment, making a show of looking for her glasses. "Ah, here they are. Let me take a look."

She became absorbed in her study of the photo, seeming to forget Homer was standing there. He cleared his throat, rousing her from her spell.

"Haven't seen them," she snapped and handed the paper back.

He waved it away. "You keep it. I've got more in the car. It was a long shot, but thanks for indulging me."

A child's cry could be heard from somewhere within the house and Homer aimed a questioning look at Rebekah.

"Well, I must go tend to my little grand-nephew." The woman took hold of the door knob as if to close it, but as he made no move to leave his place inside the threshold, she sighed with resignation. "I'll just go see after him."

Moments later Rebekah returned holding the still fussing toddler in her arms.

"What's his name?" Homer asked, softly taking hold of the little boy's shoe to get his attention. The child turned to look but then quickly buried his head back into Rebekah's shoulder.

"Jacob. He's not feeling so good today."

"Maybe he has the flu that's going around?"

"I wouldn't know about that." Rebekah smoothed back the child's damp hair. "It's probably nothing."

"My grandchildren are both down with it." He reached over and felt the child's forehead. "He's feverish. You should take him in to see Doc Metcalf."

Rebekah tensed like a hunted animal sensing a trap.

Homer pretended indifference and changed the subject. "By the way, Pastor Josh mentioned you used to be friends with Pearl Rawlins?"

"Did he, now?" Her look soured. "Pearl and I were cordial."

"You know her son was released from prison?"

"I'd heard," she said as if she'd just swallowed something distasteful.

"Is there anything you might be able to tell me about Samuel?"

"Like what?"

"For starters, where the Rawlins' came from?"

"I think it was Minnesota. No wait." She closed her eyes a second. "It was Wisconsin. I remember 'cause we had a discussion once about which cheese was better, Wisconsin or Vermont made."

"Did she ever talk about her husband? Were they divorced or was she a widow?"

"I'm not a busybody, Sheriff." A flush came to her face. "I never asked anything of a personal nature and she seldom offered."

"What about her sons?"

"She didn't have to say anything for me to know she had trouble on her hands with the both of them. Samuel's as loathsome a creature there ever was. Can't imagine why he's been let go."

"I'm not pleased about it either," he agreed. "Did he ever threaten or harm Pearl?"

"Sent her to an early grave is all."

"You think he killed her?" In light of what Russell had shared this wouldn't come as a shock.

"One way or t'other. A heart can only heal so many times."

"And Timothy?"

"He's a strange one. Can't tell you much more than that."

"We're keeping close tabs on Samuel, but to be safe you best lock your doors at night and let me know if there's any trouble at all." Homer turned to go but before stepping off the porch asked, "You sure you don't want to see about putting in a phone out here, Ms. Winchell? I could have the phone company come right out."

Rebekah waved the idea away as she would a pesky mosquito. "I've managed out here for twenty years, haven't I?"

"I guess you have." He gave her a respectful bow of the head.

She shifted the child to her other arm so Jacob was facing him again. He waved but the little boy quickly twisted away.

"You'll let me know if anything comes to mind about Samuel Rawlins?" he called out over his shoulder.

Rebekah nodded and abruptly closed the door.

Homer pulled the same maneuver as the day before and trekked back to watch the farmhouse from the bordering trees. This time his wait was fruitless, so he ambled back to the car, mulling over what to do next as he headed back to town.

"Yes indeed, something stinks at the Winchell farm," he murmured aloud, certain Rebekah was withholding something about Pearl Rawlins. And a nagging at his brain told him something didn't fit with the story she was spinning about the little boy. Of course, she wasn't aware he had the advantage of knowing another person was staying out there, even though he hadn't a clue how the young woman fit into the picture. But for now it served him well for Rebekah to relax in the comfortable assumption she'd pulled the wool over his eyes. It wouldn't do to scare her off before he had all his ducks in a row.

# CORDELIA

"CAN YOU HIDE FROM YOUR OWN MISCHIEF?
NOT IN THE SKY, NOT IN THE MIDST OF THE OCEAN, NOR DEEP IN THE MOUNTAINS, NOWHERE."

BUDDHA

"WHAT DID THE SHERIFF WANT?" I asked, freeing Gabriella from Rebekah's tight grasp. Handsome was running in circles, delighted to be free from his confinement in the upstairs closet.

"How did you know who it was?" Rebekah narrowed her eyes in mistrust as she tucked a folded slip of paper into her sweater pocket.

"I peeked through the bathroom sheers and saw the markings on the vehicle."

Rebekah continued to stare mutely.

I was disconcerted but managed a calmly concerned tone. "I hope nothing's wrong."

"Wrong?" She frowned. "Nothin's wrong. He's just asking around about the Rawlins boys. You remember my telling you about the property across the river? Well, the older brother's been paroled."

"Yes, I remember. But you never told me what he did." I filled a sippy-cup with juice and sat down at the table with Gabriella. "Drink up honey."

"Assault and attempted rape. Disfigured the girl pretty bad."

"How?"

"Deep scar on her face. He was going for her throat but she fought against him too hard."

"That's appalling." I felt sick to my stomach, and with good reason.

"He's an appalling man. The girl's lucky to be alive. Just a young thing, too."

"How could someone who committed such a vicious crime be released from prison?"

"I can't figure it out." Rebekah shook her head. "But we'll start locking the door at night."

"Didn't you mention a minister stops by their house now and then?" I asked casually.

"Every Monday morning, just like clockwork. Ten on the dot. Somebody has to make sure Timothy gets fed."

"That's an awfully nice gesture."

"Do you know what I think would be a nice gesture? Getting my house painted. I'll look after her." Rebekah reached for Gabriella again. "Maybe you can get the porch finished today."

"Sure." I hadn't had the nerve to ask again about my car, but as I saw it, there was nothing to lose now. "You were going to check on the part for the Corolla. Did it come in yet?"

I was desperate to hear an affirmative answer, but it was not forthcoming.

"Luck is not with you on that car," Rebekah said as she bounced my daughter on her knee.

"How's that?"

"The shop's closed until further notice. Both Fred Taylor and his son Willy have come down with the flu."

As I climbed the stairs to change into painting clothes, I pulled from my pocket the newspaper scrap ripped from the back of an article I'd discovered while snooping in Rebekah's files. It was an ad with a number for a local taxi company. The delusional writings of my captor were enough of an incentive to flee this loony farm and the arrival of the police was the jolt I needed to hasten the plan I'd been formulating.

Monday would be the day. Gabriella should be well enough to travel by then.

# REBEKAH

"AND THEY BLESSED REBEKAH AND SAID TO HER, "OUR SISTER, MAY YOU INCREASE TO THOUSANDS UPON THOUSANDS; MAY YOUR OFFSPRING POSSESS THE GATES OF THEIR ENEMIES."

GENESIS 22:60

"Let's get you in the tub." Rebekah peeled away the toddler's clothing, damp from fever. An old song came to mind and she hummed the calming tune as she bathed the listless child.

"From your head to your toes, goodness knows, you're so precious to me." She sang the words while dressing the child in pajamas. Then she toted the sleepy little girl down to the weaving room and tucked her onto the settee.

"Well, I might as well do a little more work on your blanket," she cradled the child's soft head in her hand before leaning in to kiss the top of the newly shorn locks. "You be still."

She turned her attention to the weaving and contemplated what to do about Cord's lies. She had to have been snooping around in the storeroom. How else to explain the loose photo? She checked the boxes containing her personal concerns and nothing looked amiss. Still, she couldn't take any chances. Perhaps it was time to destroy those private matters. She'd tried before, but just couldn't bring herself to do it. Auntie had offered to burn them once. Maybe that was what she should do.

As Rebekah wove the colorful threads, her mind set adrift on a sea of long ago memories. She didn't know how much time had passed when her little girl began to fuss.

"Hush now, Gemma, Mommy will be right there." She knotted the yarn and turned to tend to the baby, but was aghast to find someone lifting the child from the settee. "Put her down!"

The frightened young woman clutched Gemma even tighter.

"Rebekah. It's me. Cord."

Then that mangy little dog dashed frantically into the room and reminded her who the woman was.

"Sorry. It must have been all the talk this morning about Samuel Rawlins. Has me jittery." Rebekah explained away the odd behavior.

"I didn't mean to startle you." Cord rocked the child in her arms.

"I got lost in my weaving." Rebekah rubbed her face. "Happens sometimes."

"Sure. I understand." Cord said in a placating voice. "By the way, I finished painting the porch."

"That was quick. Let me repay your hard work by fixing you a proper meal." She herded them all from her work space. "Why don't you get washed up? And I'll go see about supper."

Rebekah continued to brood over what happened in the weaving room. And she didn't like the way Cord had looked at her, or rather hadn't looked at her, all through dinner. If only she could recall more clearly what had been said, but the dull beginning of a headache was hindering her concentration.

"I'll do the dishes," Cord offered.

"Well, then, why don't I take this one up to bed? Looks like her appetite is returning." She hefted Gabriella from her makeshift highchair. "What a good girl for eating all your carrots."

"She doesn't feel as warm, either. The medication seems to be working."

"Praise God."

Rebekah sat with the child in the rocking chair and began flipping pages of a large illustrated Bible. "What story should we read tonight?"

Her heart filled with joy when her little gem pointed to the picture of a beautiful woman standing by a well, holding a pitcher of water for a shepherd.

"You want to hear the story of Rebekah?"

The little girl placed her tiny hand on Rebekah's chest. "Becca?"

"That's right. This Rebekah" - she pointed to the picture – "was giving water to a man named Isaac who she later married. After many, many years she finally found out she was going to have a baby."

"Baby," Gabriella repeated.

"She praised God for her good fortune because Rebekah didn't have just one baby. She had two." Rebekah raised two fingers. "Twin sons named Esau and Jacob, who was her favorite."

She continued to rock quietly for several moments before resuming the story, her voice faint yet anxious. "But something had gone terribly wrong. The doctor told her the babies had stopped breathing, even though she'd carried them for months and months. I never even got to hold them. I didn't do anything to make them stop breathing. Truly I didn't. You've got to believe me. It wasn't my fault."

As Rebekah brushed away tears, from the doorway came a shadow of motion. She twisted around to see that woman again, lurking nervously, a troubled look on her face.

*Dear Lord, what have I said?*

# CORDELIA

"AN IDEA THAT IS DEVELOPED AND PUT INTO ACTION IS MORE IMPORTANT THAN AN IDEA THAT EXISTS ONLY AS AN IDEA."

BUDDHA

I'D LEAVE TONIGHT IF THERE was a way. Stealing away with the truck was my first thought, but the key wasn't in its usual place on the hook by the door nor had it been left in the ignition. The thought of Rebekah guarding it made me even more uneasy. I had to hope the woman wouldn't break before Monday morning. I couldn't chance showing up at the Rawlins' house before then. I was relying on the security offered by the presence of the minister.

Gabriella's fever finally broke and she slept peacefully. Whereas I was so unnerved by Rebekah's bizarre behavior I couldn't possibly allow myself to succumb to sleep. To occupy my mind I had two choices, the Bible or Betsy Cooper's journal, so I selected the more compelling of the two. A love interest had entered the picture. Betsy's mother had introduced her to a man named Ted Walsh, the single son of an evangelical minister. It had been Mrs. Cooper's plan for him to offer influence over Betsy's spiritual redemption, but Ted apparently had other intentions of a romantic nature.

I know it's shallow to say this, but Ted's a handsome and attentive man and his grandmother's diamond ring has the most delicate antique setting. Still we haven't known each other very long so I must consult with Dr. Ryan and write to Aunt Lucinda. But it's Mummy's blessing that's most important. She promised to give it prayerful consideration, but I can tell she's more worried about the salvation of my soul for what I did to Daddy.

There were no journal entries for several weeks. The next time Betsy wrote it was about her mother's sudden death.

I can't believe Mummy's gone. Now I'm all alone, except for Lucinda, who's obviously unable to be here right now. But Auntie did write to me, warning me not to rush into marriage. She said I'm still too fragile, but she doesn't understand how lonely it is here. No friends except for Ted, only nurses and Dr. Ryan. Mummy's dying words were, "Tell Betsy I forgive her. Please God, someone must watch over her." I think it was her way of giving her blessing for the marriage. Ted will be the one to watch over me now.

A section had been ripped from the diary and the next written account of Betsy's life started nearly two years later, leaving me only to speculate what those missing pages may have revealed. Presumably the state of Kentucky had agreed with Dr. Ryan's recommendation and released Betsy from treatment to marry Ted Walsh. But when the journaling picked up again, she was back under Dr. Ryan's care after her brief union had come to an unfortunate end.

Ted brought nothing but misery to my life. He was an agent of the devil and that's why he's dead now. It was God's will and that which we cannot question. Ted only married me for my inheritance, an inheritance I hadn't even known about. He admitted it the day the twins died, after blaming me for their deaths. I should have listened to Aunt Lucinda's warning, but I was weak. And in that weakness I tried to put a stop to my agony once and for all. But I failed miserably, and now my wrists bear the scars of shame, a forever reminder of my great sin.

But I have a guardian angel and his name is Dr. Ryan and he's helping me to focus on the positive and look to the future. He calls me "The Heiress" which is ironic seeing as I grew up in such a stark household from Daddy's stern vow of poverty. Now I'm well-off by comparison. Mummy always talked of her family working the mines of Kentucky, but never had she mentioned they actually owned the mining companies.

But material wealth cannot help me. It cannot take away my grief. It cannot cure me. I'd give it all away to have my babies back. I wonder if Gemma is watching over her little brothers now. I sometimes imagine my three little ones holding tight to one another as they float on angel clouds. If only I could be with them. But I must wait for the hand of God to take me, no matter how difficult or long the wait might be.

I must be patient as I wait for Auntie to be free again, to bring me back home. Back to Maine.

"Mama." Gabriella was awake and reaching out to me.

I put aside the book and when I turned to cuddle was comforted by the feel of soft, cool skin.

"Play time," Gabriella squealed and Handsome hopped up on the bed.

"Shhh."

My child held her finger to her lips, mirroring my shushing gesture.

It was early so I decided a hike might be the best way to entertain my daughter and avoid waking Rebekah. I dressed quickly and situated Gabriella into the backpack carrier. I snatched a juice box and an apple from the kitchen, careful to close the door quietly as we set off. The sun's rays were barely stretching to the horizon, casting only just enough light to make out the path. I would climb to the clearing for another look and to run through the plan in my head once more.

As I trekked up the hill my thoughts were centered on Rebekah. Irrational as it was, I felt a twinge of pity. I was no less fearful of what she might do, but was there any wonder the woman was unraveling? She'd lost three children, been accused of killing her father and had spent nearly a decade in a psychiatric institution. Not to mention that opportunist Ted Walsh preying upon her when she was most fragile.

All the same, the journal bears the one-sided ramblings of a psychopath. Details surrounding the deaths of her father and children were too ambiguous to dismiss Rebekah's involvement. *Bearing the scars of shame.* She was always nervously pulling at the cuffs of the long sleeved shirts worn even on the warmest days. Were those self-inflicted wounds a result of a crushing guilt from the heinous crimes she committed? I shivered involuntarily.

Gabriella began to sing the *Itsy Bitsy Spider* while Handsome scampered off the path to chase a squirrel, his tail wagging with excitement. To have the innocence of a child or the oblivion a dog possessed would most certainly be blissful.

The sun was peaking above the hills when we reached the clearing. I settled Gabriella on the ground near the edge and offered the juice box, which was greedily sucked down. Then I began to slice the apple with my Swiss Army knife, sharing bits with Handsome. I stared down at the ramshackle house, those telephone wires our only lifelines at the moment.

Timing was crucial. It was imperative we make it down to the house at precisely ten o'clock tomorrow morning. If Samuel Rawlins was as dangerous as Rebekah promised, our arrival must coincide with the minister's to ensure a safe rescue.

I scanned the hillside and determined the best path down to the narrowest and most shallow part of the river for crossing. I would take the bare minimum and leave the rest behind. Except for our identification documents and my cell phone, there was nothing irreplaceable.

"What do you think? Can we do it, boy?" I scratched the dog's ears and he moaned with pleasure.

Now that the route and timing had been plotted, only one sticky issue remained. I needed to be convincing in my strategy to get Rebekah out of the house early enough for us to make our escape. My stomach soured at the thought of all that could go wrong. Handsome nuzzled my arm as if sensing my fear.

"One more day to get through, buddy. Just one more day."

# RUSSELL

"THE JOURNALISTS HAVE CONSTRUCTED FOR THEMSELVES A LITTLE WOODEN CHAPEL, WHICH THEY ALSO CALL THE TEMPLE OF FAME, IN WHICH THEY PUT UP AND TAKE DOWN PORTRAITS ALL DAY LONG AND MAKE SUCH A HAMMERING YOU CAN'T HEAR YOURSELF SPEAK."

GEORGE LICHTENBERG

"That's brilliant, BW, absolutely brilliant." Russell had just taken a call from his ace investigator. "What am I going to do with it? I'm going to win a fucking *Pullitzer* that's what I'm going to do."

"Let me just get my pad and pencil. I want to make sure to get all this down correctly." He walked briskly with his cordless phone from the outside porch to his study. "No, don't send anything over the wires. Overnight it, but keep a copy in your safe just in case. I'm not the hugest fan of your United States Postal Service. Okay, I'm ready now. Kentucky, you say? How'd she get there? Uh huh. Uh huh. No. What kind of hospital? - - - No kidding? - - - Uh huh. Blimey! I could kiss you."

"You've certainly made my day, ole' boy." Russell reached into his desk, pulled out a cigar and bit off the tip.

"Now on that other matter. The Pruitts?" He lit the cigar, leaned back in the chair and kicked his legs up onto the desk. "No, this one's strictly personal. So, what've you got?

He listened for a few moments, puffing contentedly. "Send that along, too. We're getting close, but I still need more. What else have you got going that's more important than me?"

Russell didn't have an exclusive with BW, but he paid him well and expected his full attention.

"Are you serious? I haven't heard that name in ages. I didn't know you were still connected. What's he doing these days?" Russell tapped an ash off the end of the cigar. "So he's a proper journalist now? He always was a bit too squeaky clean for the likes of us."

"Okay, then. Get back with me as soon as you have more. It's important. Ta-ta."

Russell stubbed out the half burned cigar and considered the wealth of information BW had provided. He pondered for a moment over the findings about Homer and Francesca. Then he marched to the kitchen wearing a most satisfied grin and pulled a bottle of Dom Perignon from the refrigerator. It had been a Christmas gift from the editor of *Short List* magazine, the British equivalent of *GQ* or *Esquire*, where he wrote satirical essays under his nom du plume, *The Pagan Fox*.

"I can't think of a better time." He popped the cork and poured himself a flute of the bubbly. "Or a better reason."

# HOMER

"IT'S ONE OF THOSE INSTANCES WHERE THE REASONED CAN PRODUCE AN EFFECT WHICH SEEMS REMARKABLE TO HIS NEIGHBOR BECAUSE THE LATTER HAS MISSED THE ONE LITTLE POINT WHICH IS THE BASIS OF THE DEDUCTION."

SHERLOCK HOLMES IN ***THE CROOKED MAN***

"DO YOU HAVE ANY IDEA what time it is?" Frannie leaned against the kitchen jamb, arms folded and eyes only partially open against the glare of the overhead light.

"Three-thirty?" Homer pushed back from his puzzle and massaged his own tired eyes.

"Close enough." She shuffled to the refrigerator, took out a carton of milk and filled two glasses. "Maybe this will help."

They touched their glasses together after Frannie seated herself next to him in the nook.

"So what is it?" she asked.

"Hmm?"

"The case you're working on."

"No case." He drummed his fingers on the side of the glass. "Just something bugging me."

"Would you like a sounding board?"

Homer placed his hand on top of his wife's. "You're sleepy. Go back to bed."

"I'm up now, so you might as well take advantage."

"I'd rather take advantage of you back in bed." He suggestively caressed her arm.

"You'll be no good to me until you get it off your chest."

"Ouch."

"No ouch. I can just tell you're distracted." She rotated her glass on the tabletop.

"How's that?"

"When was the last time I caught you up in the middle of the night working puzzles? If you can't remember, it's because we were in New York and you were working a homicide case."

Homer took a large gulp of milk.

"The greatest criminal mind in the city and the department ruined it." Frannie had never assuaged her resentment even though two decades had passed.

"Water under the bridge, babe. Water under the bridge."

"Do you miss it?"

God he missed it. He missed it so much his teeth ached. But it wouldn't be good for his marriage to admit it.

"Nah. Let's face facts. Had I stayed I'd probably be dead by now. The stress was killing me. And believe me when I say, there's no place like Maine to even out the blood pressure. I love it here."

Frannie narrowed her eyes skeptically, but let it go. Maybe because intuitively she understood it was a risky subject to pursue.

"And Murphy really is a great town to raise Benjamin and Sara," he added.

"It wasn't exactly the best place for their mother." A sad frown distorted her beauty.

"It wouldn't have mattered where we lived. Sophia was destined to follow fools."

For several minutes neither spoke.

"What are you thinking about?" Frannie interrupted the quiet interlude.

"Genetics." Homer said, which he immediately wished he could retract when a shadow of despair darkened his wife's eyes.

"You had a choice."

"And never a regret." He gently squeezed her hand; a subtle apology.

"So?" she asked.

"What?"

"Are you going to tell me what's at the root of your insomnia?"

He was trapped by guilt now. "I hesitate to bore you because it's just a gut feeling."

"Your gut feelings usually lead to important discoveries."

"All right. It has to do with Rebekah Winchell, but I can't pinpoint exactly what's bothering me."

"I wondered why all the questions. Does it have anything to do with the little boy she brought to Dr. Metcalf's office?"

"Possibly. But there's more to it. I took a ride out there today and something's not right. She's acting odd."

"She's an odd woman."

"Yes, but in her oddity she always maintained a certain routine. Something has happened in the past couple of weeks to shake her out of that comfortable cocoon."

"What did she tell you about the little boy?"

"That he's her grand-nephew."

"Nothing more?"

"She omitted the detail about her visit to the doctor. That's about it." Homer refrained from mentioning the young woman he'd spied sneaking into the barn. "I didn't want to appear overly curious. Better to..."

"...let her think you have no interest." Frannie finished the sentence. "Then she's more likely to slip up and reveal a clue."

Homer smiled. "You know me well."

She nodded. "Why did you go out there anyway?"

He shrugged. "I wanted to do a little probing about Samuel

Rawlins. According to Pastor Josh, Rebekah was friendly with his mother. I thought I might learn something useful."

She cocked her head to the side. "Do you think she's somehow involved with those two boys?"

"No, but I think she's holding on to some confidences about their mother's past. Russell paid me a visit the other day. He was able to uncover some information about Samuel that had been sealed by the courts and supposedly destroyed." Homer made air quotation marks. "You know how that can go."

"Do you trust anything that man has to say?" Frannie spit out the words.

He ignored the venomous attitude but didn't expect his next words to flame the fire. "I was telling Olivia it's become a sad world now that journalists have better access to information than law enforcement officials."

"I hope your detective nose has exposed Little Liv's true intentions."

"And that would be?" His eyebrows arched.

"Your little assistant's aspirations go beyond the *professional.* She has her sights set on being more than just your deputy."

"Olivia?" he scoffed. "About that, you're wrong. She's head over heels for Emerson."

"That's not the scuttlebutt around town."

Homer didn't put much stock in the comment because his wife wasn't in any local social loops. She was a loner with no close friends in town. Having moved to the quiet outer sticks from culturally vibrant New York City, she didn't connect easily with the folks of Murphy. Initially her primary focus had been Sophia and her issues. And now, although involved with Benjamin and Sara's school activities, the other mothers were much younger and again there was little commonality.

"You'd best be careful with that little flirt," Frannie warned.

"There's no need. I've only had eyes for one woman my

entire life," he said, trying to coax her out of her sullenness. "I think that's all I need to say…Francesca."

Her head jolted, a blend of anger and surprise twisting her features. He had broken the longstanding rule by using her given name.

"Okay?" He lifted her fingers to his lips and looked searchingly into his wife's eyes. Through three decades of marriage she had remained an enigma. Her capricious nature and fiery temperament left him in a perpetual pre-emptive state.

He held her gaze and after a time her expression softened.

"Okay." Frannie leaned in and brushed her lips against his, but in doing so knocked over her half filled glass of milk.

They laughed as they grabbed for napkins to mop up the mess before it reached Homer's paperwork.

"What's this?" The *Amber Alert* bulletin had caught her eye.

"Child abduction out of the Washington area" As he looked at the flier his wife was holding, a flash of something familiar came to him, but her next comment swept it from his mind.

"Cute little girl. She looks like somebody." She shook her head and handed it back. "Maybe Sara at that age?"

"Little bit." He shoved the flier into his briefcase as Frannie stood and walked toward the archway.

There was a nagging at the periphery of his subconscious mind, but it wouldn't surface.

"You coming?" she asked, casting a provocative glance over her shoulder.

Whatever it was, it would have to wait.

# PART FOUR

## TRAPPED IN THE BELLY OF THE WHALE

# CORDELIA

"FEW CROSS OVER THE RIVER. MOST ARE STRANDED ON THIS SIDE. ON THE RIVERBANK THEY RUN UP AND DOWN. BUT THE WISE MAN, FOLLOWING THE WAY, CROSSES OVER, BEYOND THE REACH OF DEATH."

BUDDHA

"I HATE TO IMPOSE ON YOU again. Why don't I drive in this time?" I was certain the suggestion would be denied, but hoped the mere act of offering would allay any suspicions.

Rebekah frowned and her hand went automatically to her pocket, creating a jingling sound. Ah. The truck keys.

"You might be identified."

"I can wear a ball cap and sunglasses."

Rebekah clicked her tongue at my proposal. "Even if you weren't recognized, they might not give you the medicine. At least they know me at the pharmacy and believe the story I told them."

"Can you imagine? The entire bottle of antibiotics poured down the toilet." I shook my head. "But Gabriella could get worse if she doesn't finish the whole prescription."

"No. We can't have that." She scowled. "I'll go."

"If you think it best." My plan to get Rebekah out of the house also had to buy a large window of time. "Um, could you pick up a few other items while you're there?"

Rebekah took the proffered list and exclaimed, "More disposable diapers? Lord she goes through those things fast."

"She hasn't been easy to potty train. That's how the medicine ended up flushed down the drain. I turned my back for one second, and down it went."

"Quite a few things on the list. It might take a while."

"Here's some money." I handed over a sum much larger than she'd need. "Maybe the repair shop's open again and you can check on when the car will be fixed. Hopefully soon you can return to your peaceful existence."

"I'm not complaining." Rebekah began bouncing Gabriella on her knee. "I love having sweet little girls staying with me. Are you a sweet little girl?"

"She threw out the medicine before I could give her the dose this morning. I'd hate for her to go too long without it." I didn't want to appear pushy, but I needed to get Rebekah on her way so we could make it to the Rawlins house at the same time the minister arrived. *Just like clockwork. Ten on the dot.* The words echoed in my head. "Are there any chores I can do while you're in town?"

"There's the painting." Finally, the woman surrendered Gabriella with a kiss atop her head. "Bye-bye, sweetie-pie. You be my best girl."

The backpack had barely a hair of room to spare, but at the last minute I ran upstairs for Betsy Cooper's diary. I wasn't sure why, but I felt more secure taking it with me.

"Damn." As I retrieved the journal from its hiding place beneath the mattress I managed to cut my finger on the sharp edge of the bed frame. Handsome sounded a warning bark so I had no time to bother with a Band-aid.

As I reached the porch I heard the remote toot of a car horn. It was an odd sound and I felt a flutter of reassurance it wasn't Rebekah's truck.

"Let's go." I slapped my thigh and Handsome followed as I jogged to the path behind the barn, never looking back.

Besides Gabriella's essentials, I'd packed a change of clothing, all our documents, the cash, some snacks and water. The added weight was making the trek much more taxing than usual and I was winded when we reached the top of the hill. I needed a moment's rest before climbing down to the stream. As I released myself from the carrier-backpack and eased it to the ground, I noticed Gabriella was holding a balled up piece of paper.

"What did you get into?" I untwisted it to make sure it wasn't something important. My stomach flipped over when I saw my own face looking back from a recent photo, with the words *Wanted by the FBI* printed beneath.

"Where did you get this, honey?"

"Becca's pocket." She'd been sitting in the chair where Rebekah had draped her sweater, the one in which she'd stuffed a folded piece of paper after the sheriff left yesterday. That must have been the real reason for his visit. But why would Rebekah lie about it? She'd already seen the alerts.

My resolve was even stronger. I had to get us out of here. I felt in my own pocket for the bit of paper with the number of the taxi company. Our ticket to freedom.

"You ready, boy?" Handsome's wagging tail and wiggling body was answer enough.

It was not an easy descent and I was forced to crawl down backwards at times because of some unstable boulders. Making it especially difficult was the top heavy load I was carrying. Except for nearly slipping once on algae covered rocks, crossing the stream was easier than I'd anticipated. When I approached the house there was no sign of a car, so I ducked into the bordering woods and checked my watch. Ten o'clock. We had made it.

Twenty minutes later there was still no sign of the minister and I was only narrowly winning my battle with panic. If forced to abandon the plan now, I'd never make it back to the farm before Rebekah. Who knew what such an act of betrayal might do to her? Certainly, we'd never be given another opportunity for escape, and worse, what if she snapped? The woman was already unstable. No, returning to Rebekah's was not an option, for so many reasons.

What was it Ramon had said to me on the phone the day I fled from my life with Aiden?

"You must follow the law of Cortez," he had counseled.

"The law of what?" I'd asked.

"Not what. Who? Did they not teach you anything in that fancy prep school you attended? Hernando Cortez was the Spanish explorer who conquered the Aztecs. When he reached Mexico he had his men burn their ships to prevent any thought of retreat or abandonment of their cause."

"So you're saying I need to burn all bridges back to my old life."

"Once you make this decision, you have to see it through. Are you prepared to do that?"

I had been prepared, or at least that's what I believed when the choice was made. It had been so much easier when I knew Ramon was going to be on the other side. Today I was venturing into dangerous and unknown territories alone. If only there was some way of reaching Ramon. A moment to speak with him would renew my spirits. I closed my eyes and made myself hear the soothing tones of his voice. Then I tried to clear my head with some meditation exercises. Finally, I said a prayer to my parents' Christian God. Today I would seek help from all channels.

Another fifteen minutes passed and still nobody had shown at the Rawlins' property.

*Okay, then. It's time to burn the ships.* I stood and hitched the backpack onto my shoulders, careful not to wake my peacefully slumbering daughter.

I swallowed back the taste of bile when my tentative knock was answered by the personification of evil. The young hoodlum's lip curled in a nasty smirk as he picked at one of the multiple piercings. The body mutilation continued with sinister images tattooed on the exposed parts of his arms and chest. But most alarming was the combat knife jammed into the waist of his jeans.

"You lost little girl?" His wicked laugh turned into a smoker's violent coughing fit.

I looked beyond the man into the house and saw a wall phone beyond the living room at the entrance to the kitchen. I judged my lifeline to be within twelve feet.

"I'm not lost. I know where I am and who you are," I said with all the bravado I could muster.

"You do now?" he sneered.

"Yes, Mr. Rawlins. I'd like to ask a favor, please."

"*Mister* Rawlins? That's a new one. I don't trust strangers much. So, why don't you tell me your name?" He brazenly touched my cheek with his forefinger. "Then we won't be strangers."

It took the utmost control not to recoil. "Cordelia."

"Well, you are the first Cor-deel-ya I ever met." The coughing resumed. "What do you want Cor-deel-ya?"

"I would like to use your phone."

The man continued to study me in a way that made me extremely uncomfortable before he finally became aware of Gabriella who was awaking from her nap but still groggy enough to remain quiet.

"Who's this?" He reached toward her but Handsome's deep growl stopped him. He scowled at the dog. "Watch yerself, mongrel."

"The dog can stay out here." Relief nearly overcame me when I heard the crunching sound of automobile tires on gravel. Finally, the minister had arrived.

"Go ahead." Samuel reluctantly agreed, thumbing over his shoulders in the direction of the kitchen. "But no funny business."

I now felt safe enough to enter the grimy rooms which reeked of tobacco. I was confident the plan was going to work. The minister could drive us out to the main road where we'd wait until the taxi arrived.

The screen snapped shut behind me and the awful young man stepped briskly across the rickety porch. I glanced back and spied Handsome's faithful head outside the door.

"Good boy," I called out as I leaned the backpack holding Gabriella gently against the wall by my feet and fished the paper with the number from my pocket. I lifted the outmoded handset from its cradle, the dial tone a sweet sound and the tonic I needed.

"Thank you," I whispered when I heard the ringing. One step closer. "Hello. I'd like to order a cab…"

From nowhere a force thrust me into the wall. And then I was gone.

# RUSSELL

"BAD MANNERS MAKE THE JOURNALIST."

OSCAR WILDE

TWICE RUSSELL MISSED THE TURNOFF because there was no signage, but finally he spied the dirt road that would take him to the Winchell farm.

"Move you little rodent," Russell yelled out the window. But the rabbit wouldn't budge from the center of the lane. He hit the horn and the bunny scampered off into the brush. *So much for the element of surprise.*

Russell was making an unannounced visit. He wasn't certain Rebekah would even know who he was, which didn't matter a weasel's whisker to him. He just wanted to catch the woman with her guard down when he dropped the bombshell.

He was ready with an explanation for stopping. He'd tell the old hermit he was helping with a genealogy project for a friend back in jolly old England. Said friend had found a connection between an ancestor who'd come to Maine in the late 1800's and the founding of Camp Davis. She'd been hoping to attend the annual Spiritualist gathering at the Camp to conduct her research, but alas, illness kept her on the other side of the pond.

He rehearsed what he planned to say one last time. "While studying the file my friend sent me, I stumbled upon the oddest coincidence. The first spiritualist leader at Camp Davis was a man by the name of Thomas Winchell and his last known descendent was a Rebekah Winchell. Only *that* Rebekah Winchell died over 40 years ago and is buried up at Camp Davis in a secluded family plot. Of course, you probably already know all that since you're a Winchell and it's a rather unusual name. In fact, you're the only other Winchell I could find still living in these parts. So I was hoping you might be able to help me close some gaps in your family history."

He envisioned several possible scenarios to follow. Rebekah may well be rendered speechless or all twitchy with nerves. She could slam the door in his face or order him off her property. The woman might even grab her shotgun and shoot him on the spot. He was rather hoping for one of the former possibilities for obvious reasons. Any would adequately corroborate the fact that Rebekah Winchell ain't Rebekah Winchell after all.

Yes indeed, he had unearthed a genuine diamond this time.

"Bloody hell!" he swore when he arrived to see the truck was gone.

"Double bloody hell! I don't need this agro," he shouted when there was no answer to his knock on the door. His carefully laid out plans were now going to have to be delayed.

"Maybe I'll just wait her out." Russell walked around the property, stirring up the chickens and goats by dragging a stick against the fence posts like a petulant little boy. He opened the barn door for a quick look but nothing caught his eye. When he came upon two bowls at the side of the house with water and kibble he thought it odd. There was no flea-bitten farm dog anywhere around and he'd never seen Rebekah toting around a canine companion in her truck. He walked back up onto the porch and peered into the windows before trying the door knob. Of course, it was unlocked. After all, this was Hicksville, USA. He debated for all of three seconds before slipping into the house.

# REBEKAH

"EVEN MY BOSOM FRIEND IN WHOM I TRUSTED, WHO ATE OF MY BREAD, HAS LIFTED HIS HEEL AGAINST ME."

PSALM 41

REBEKAH WAS STRUGGLING WITH THE burden of her deception. The kindly pharmacist and his wife had easily accepted her lies, but afterward she lacked the spirit to face anyone else in town. She reasoned it was more important to return quickly with the medicine than to waste time picking up the other items. Cord could surely wait one more day. When she steered the truck onto the long dirt road that would lead her home she down shifted to a slower speed and surveyed her property. It was a lot of acreage to oversee and she would someday have to consider what to do with all this land.

A terrible ache came to her heart at the thought of what might have been. Hers had been a lonely life and she could no longer deny the comfort she'd found in her recent companionship. Not that she completely trusted Cord. The woman had lied to her on several occasions. But was that any worse than the lies she herself had been telling lately? When she collapsed the other night, Cord had taken good care of her, without judging. And she was a hard worker who never complained about the chores she was asked to do, including painting the house which was no easy task. And Lord, how she was falling in love with that sweet little girl.

Nonetheless, Lucinda's stern warning against getting

attached continued to echo in her head. "I guarantee there will be nothing but regret to come of this. Encourage them to move on, my child. You must protect your heart."

But could she trust her aunt any better than the stranger who had wandered into her life? She felt certain the arrival of the woman and child, even the strange little dog, had been part of God's plan for her. She parked the truck and reached for her small companion Bible to search for a verse.

> *For I know the plans I have for you, says the Lord, plans for welfare and not for evil, to give you a future and a hope.*

Rebekah contemplated the words and realized how much she wanted a hopeful future with Cord and the baby. And yet, Lucinda had been her protector, coming to the rescue so many times. It was Lucinda who figured a way to bring her home to Maine so she wouldn't have to go through that ugly trial. She looked again to her Bible. It opened easily to a passage she had consulted countless times.

> *Do not turn to mediums or seek out spiritualists: you will be defiled by them. I am the Lord your God. If a person turns to mediums, I will set my face against that person and will cut him off from among his people.*

How could she rely on the counseling of a woman with whom God would forbid her to consort? She bowed her head and prayed fervently for guidance. When she opened her eyes moments later she felt certain the answer had come to her.

Rebekah clucked in annoyance as she rounded the curve and saw the front door was wide open. Then she remembered Cord still had the trim to paint and assumed she left it open to dry. But that assumption was soon nullified as she stepped onto the porch and took in the old chipping paint around the door.

"I've brought the medicine," she called out. Then she yelled from the bottom of the stairs, "You up there?"

She walked back out to the porch and glanced about the farm yard before checking to see if Cord had collected the eggs from the chicken coop, a duty she had taken over every morning since she arrived. The eggs had not been touched. She grabbed a basket and set about the task while considering where the woman could have gone. Surely she wouldn't have risked a hike with a sick child.

Rebekah returned to the house and put the basket down on the kitchen counter before slowly climbing the stairs to the second floor. She was surprised to find the bed still unmade since her guest had always been exceptionally tidy, but was relieved to see neatly folded items of clothing still in the bureau drawers. She sat on the foot of the bed and took an inventory of what was missing. The backpack was gone and so were Cord's red jacket and the baby's blanket. What about the leather pouch where she hid her money? Not that she needed to hide it. Money was something for which Rebekah had little use. She kneeled down beside the bed and nervously pulled out the suitcase and checked the outer zipped compartment which is where she found it when she first searched the room. But the pouch was no longer there.

Rebekah rested on her heels and noticed the first drop of blood just inches from her foot. She gingerly touched the small wet splotch then stood and studied the area until she spied another out in the hallway. The trail led down the stairs and to the porch, but no further traces of blood could be seen once she got to the dirt driveway. However there were some footprints too large to be Cord's or her own and when she squatted down to inspect more closely she also made out some fresh tire marks not matching the treads of her truck.

When she stood she could see there were two separate sets of footprints, one aimed at the house but another pointed in the direction of the animal pen. She followed the tracks and as they veered toward the barn door her heart began to race. She cautiously opened the door, and even though she couldn't detect any footsteps on the barn floor, she marched quickly to the back where the hay bales were stacked. Nothing had been disturbed. Crossing one worry off the list she returned to the house.

She began to pace as she mumbled to herself.

"The sheriff might have come back. He could have arrested her." She suddenly felt chilled and pulled her sweater from the back of a kitchen chair.

"Nah. The sheriff wouldn't have taken the dog along," she argued against the first possibility as she pulled on the sweater and plunged her hand in the pocket for another look at the flyer he'd left. It was missing.

"Cord must have discovered the bulletin." That would have been enough to scare her into finding another hiding place. Yet it didn't explain the footprints or the other vehicle that had been here. Or the blood.

Rebekah closed her eyes to think. *Who could have been here?*

"Oh my God," she gasped as the horrible truth came to her. Without hesitation she snatched up the truck keys and rushed from the house.

# HOMER

"IT IS A CAPITAL MISTAKE TO THEORIZE BEFORE YOU HAVE ALL THE EVIDENCE. IT BIASES THE JUDGMENT."

SHERLOCK HOLMES IN ***A STUDY IN SCARLET***

HOMER DECIDED TO RETURN A third day to the Winchell Farm. He hoped the thread of a frustratingly elusive clue would be drawn to mind if he looked again with eyes more acutely focused. Again he arrived to find the truck gone, but this time he tried the door.

"Hello? Anybody here?" he called out as he entered the still house. Not surprising, there were toys scattered about the family room and *Yo-Baby* yogurts in the refrigerator. A door leading from the kitchen to what he presumed to be a closet was locked. With just cause Judge Bennett would issue a search warrant, but so far he had nothing to go on. Another door off the living room opened to a space crowded with looms and weaving supplies, but nothing suspicious was found there.

He climbed the creaky stairs and turned to the left into a stark, nearly sterile bedroom with but one picture of Jesus hanging on the wall and a well used Bible on the side table. The bed linens were so tightly tucked it would have brought tears of pride to any army sergeant. The closet was lean of belongings and the only item of a personal natured was an antique music box atop the lone chest of drawers.

Homer walked to the other end of the hall to a second bedroom. In the bureau he found a pair of khaki trousers, a polo shirt and a t-shirt he presumed belonged to the woman he caught sneaking into the barn the other day. He lifted the pillow and found a pair of pink pajamas sized for a toddler. He sat heavily on the bed, staring at the Dora the Explorer image.

"How could I have missed this?" The fact that had escaped his detection was now as clear as spring water. He shook his head in disgust.

He'd seen the Dora logo on the child's shoes yesterday but hadn't made the connection. Not even last night when Frannie pointed out the similarity between Sara and the photo of the child in the FBI alert. Sara had worn nothing but Dora the Explorer attire for nearly two years, but a little boy would never be dressed in Dora togs.

He replaced the pajamas and covered them with the pillow and thoroughly searched the remaining drawers and closet. Under the bed he found a suitcase but nothing within provided anything helpful. Then in the corner he spied a scrap of paper. He pulled the bed from against the wall and reached down to collect what turned out to be a newspaper clipping. He skimmed it quickly before tucking it into his wallet for safe keeping. He'd get Olivia working on it as soon as he reached an area with cellular service.

Before he turned toward the stairs he noticed a small, dark red speck on the floor.

"It's blood, all right," he said upon examining it more closely. He retrieved a tissue and gently blotted at the sticky smudge, trying to estimate its stage of coagulation. Then he traced the tiny red patches until they ended near the front stoop.

He looked sharply at the out buildings, wondering if the person leaving the trail of blood might have sought sanctuary when they heard or saw his car. Striding swiftly across the farm yard, he decided to check the barn first. When he opened the door, the dust motes were glimmering in the bright rays of sunlight shining through cracks between the wall boards. When his eyes adjusted he followed a beam of light to some exposed specks on the floor, but they were dry to the touch. He took out his small magnifier and examined the markings more closely. The stains were black, probably motor oil, with striations through the droplets giving the impression of having been swept over by broom bristles before they'd dried.

Homer followed the marks to the back of the barn where they ended at a deep stack of hay bales. He climbed the ladder to the loft, but there was no evidence anyone had been hiding out. After searching the chicken coop and an old shed, a nudging brought him back to the mountain of hay in the barn and he began pulling down the bales. His intuition and labors were rewarded and after he'd examined his discovery, he replaced the bales and swept up the loose pieces of straw, leaving the barn as he'd found it.

He returned to his vehicle and jotted some notes on the back of the FBI flyer. He flipped it over for another look. Indeed the little girl in the photo was wearing the very same Dora shoes. He examined the child's face. The hair was obviously different now, blonde and cut like a little boy's. Anyone would have been fooled by the attempt to disguise, even if they had seen the flyer. But now he had little doubt the child Rebekah was looking after was the missing Gabriella Martelli. And no doubt the woman he'd glimpsed hiding in the barn was Delia Carlyle. But how on earth did they end up here?

Olivia was going to have a very busy day.

# RAMON

"LOVE GOES BY HAPS; SOME CUPID KILLS WITH ARROWS, SOME WITH TRAPS."

WILLIAM SHAKESPEARE, ***MUCH ADO ABOUT NOTHING***

"I'VE JUST LANDED AT JFK," Ramon spoke into his cell phone. "I still have to clear customs, but should be back at my place within an hour or so. Can you meet me there? - - - Great. You can update me then. I've got two more calls to make. - - - Okay. Adios."

As the line inched forward Ramon punched in another number. "Mama? I am home. - - - Of course, you were the first person I called. - - - Not tonight. All I really want to do is fall into my bed and sleep for a week. - - - Yes, I took those herbal supplements for the jet lag. - - - No, Mama. I am just tired and this is going to be a busy week. Why don't I come over this weekend? You can finally teach me to make empanadas. - - - Maybe. But it might be just me. We will see how it goes. Love you, too."

Ramon knew his mother was desperate for him to marry again. And she was especially eager to see him back with Gina. But that would change if ever she learned the true reason for the divorce. The generally accepted presumption by family and friends was that the blame fell heavily on his shoulders because of his demanding work schedule and extensive travel. He'd taken the high road and allowed the misconception to stand.

Gina had recently begun stopping by the loft on various

pretenses. To ask him to photograph some of her work for a promo piece of an upcoming exhibit. To bring her agent by to see the paintings she'd left. Just to pop in with takeout from their favorite Caribbean restaurant because she was in the neighborhood. It had been gradual, but his ex-wife had cleverly insinuated herself back into his life and they'd fallen into a comfortable companionable association.

One day Mama had shown up while Gina was visiting.

"I stopped at the panaderia, the one nearby that you like so much?" His mother had bustled in with a basket bursting with all his favorite Spanish baked goods. She set the basket on the kitchen island and began to display all her purchases "Pan rustico, pan de leche, chocolate conchas and your favorite. Polvorones!"

"Thank you, Mama." Ramon had folded her into a hug.

"Mi'jo guapo." She reached up and gently pinched his cheek then looked beyond into the heart of the loft and saw Gina. Ever since, Mama had been not so subtly hinting about a possible reconciliation. But Gina would need more than an alliance with Mama to raze the mountain of doubt she'd created with her betrayal. And her quest would be more challenging now that Cord was back. Well, not exactly back, but she had returned to his thoughts and to his heart. He was beginning to believe the old adage about never getting over a first love.

But what had happened to Cord? No doubt she'd veered from the plan. Any number of unforeseen obstacles might have forced her to improvise a new strategy. He could only hope she hadn't stumbled into danger. Ramon pushed from his mind the possibility it was her intention from the beginning to vanish without telling him, or worse, that he'd never see her again.

# HOMER

"WHAT ONE MAN CAN INVENT ANOTHER CAN DISCOVER."

SHERLOCK HOLMES IN *THE ADVENTURE OF THE DANCING MEN*

When Homer entered a cell service area he called the office to hand down Olivia's assignments.

"Where've you been?" she asked before he managed hello.

"The Winchell farm. Why, what's up?"

"Where are you now?"

"I just turned onto Route 79."

"You might as well pull a u-turn now and take the River Road bridge over to Route 22. That will take you to…"

"I know where that will take me," Homer said, mastering a two-point turn. "But why am I needed out at the Rawlins' place?"

"Jimmy Kramer called for backup. He's called several times to set up Samuel's weekly parole meeting and there's been no answer. So he drove out there today and found no sign of him. Plus, the brother is acting strange. That is, stranger than usual."

"I'm on my way."

"Hey, Sheriff." Jimmy got out of his Jeep Cherokee as the sheriff's cruiser parked beside it.

Homer nodded. "So what's going on?"

"Something stinks, but I'm not sure what. I thought it'd

be smart to have the local law present if my nose is telling the truth."

"Background?" he asked as they walked toward the house.

"Samuel hasn't been answering the phone so I drove out to see why. There's no sign of him and the brother's more nervous than usual. Keeps looking off to the woods," Jimmy pointed to where Samuel sped out on his bike the other day. "And they have a dog."

Homer shrugged dismissively. "Strays frequently hang out at old farm houses."

"This one has a collar. At any rate, I'm more concerned about what my parolee has cooking out in those woods."

Homer rapped his knuckles against the screen door bringing both Timothy and the scrappy little dog to life.

"So where'd this little guy come from?" Homer raised his voice to be heard over the yapping.

"He was locked in the closet," Timothy said as if it was a perfectly reasonable response.

Jimmy and Homer exchanged a look. Samuel may have been born fully evil but Timothy had entered this world only half baked.

"How'd he get in the closet?" asked Homer.

Timothy raised his shoulders. "I suppose Samuel put him there."

Jimmy asked, "And just where is your brother?"

"He likes to hike in the woods." The words were spoken in monotone, as if he'd been programmed to repeat them.

"Maybe we'll just have a look around." Jimmy walked in the direction of the barn.

Timothy nervously rubbed his meaty hands together and craned his thick neck to watch where the parole officer was headed. The younger brother was tall and burly whereas Samuel was shorter with a wiry build. Their physiques may have differed considerably, however nearly identical faces would preclude any doubt they were siblings.

"Everything okay out here, Timothy?" Homer asked.

The young man swallowed hard, tears forming in his eyes.

"Maybe that man should stay away from there." Timothy opened the door to see better and the dog darted to freedom. "Oh, no! Come back little guy."

"Could be he's looking for greener pastures," suggested Homer, thinking the dog was smart to want to flee the likes of Samuel Rawlins.

The dog dodged Jimmy and scampered into the surrounding woods.

"But his owner might come looking for him." Timothy was becoming even more agitated. "There'll be a signal."

Before the last comment registered, Samuel emerged from the side of the barn holding the mutt by the scruff of his neck. "Lookin' for this mangy critter?"

Timothy lumbered to the dog's rescue and cradled him like a baby.

"We got business?" Samuel's lip curled as he spoke.

"I've been trying to reach you. We need a face to face every week," Jimmy reminded him.

"Don't this count?" Samuel spit out a wad of tobacco. "I'm seein' your ugly face now."

Homer placed a calming hand on Jimmy's stiffened shoulder. "Why don't we all go inside?"

With a haughty swagger Samuel entered the house and flopped down on the grimy sofa while Timothy took the dog into the kitchen for some water.

"Do we have to remind you of the consequences of a parole violation?" Homer asked.

"How've I VI-O-LATED my parole?" He inspected his dirty fingernails.

Jimmy swore under his breath, "You vi-o-late the earth."

"Say what?"

The parole officer composed himself. "You haven't been here."

"I's under the impression I been released from prison."

"On the condition you report in to me every week."

"I've been out communing with nature." Samuel's chortling set off a coughing spasm.

"You'd be doing yourself a great service by being a little more cooperative and a lot less confrontational," Homer suggested, casually walking to the kitchen archway where something caught his attention.

He stooped to pick up a pink rosebud appliqué and placed it in his shirt pocket. While keeping his eyes trained on Timothy he said, "Let me ask you Samuel, in your *communing*, have you by chance come across a young woman and her child?"

Timothy's head jerked, eyes darting quickly from Homer to Samuel and then to the ground as he nervously petted the dog.

"What's she look like?" Samuel grabbed a pack of Marlboroughs and tapped one free.

"Cut the games." Homer commanded. "You know very well what she looks like."

"A'right." Samuel struck a match and lit his cigarette, inhaling deeply. "Short, blonde hair. Cute, but not my type."

Jimmy hadn't a clue where Homer was headed with this new direction of questioning, but it didn't stop him from lobbing a sarcastic barb. "Too old for you?"

"That's right. I do like 'em young." A nasty grin distorted Samuel's face into an even uglier caricature of himself. "Don't you have a sweet little teenage daughter, Jimmy?"

Homer noticed the bulging neck veins and clenched fists. If Jimmy snapped, there'd be no preventing him from strangling the contemptuous creature.

"I'm asking the questions here." Homer stepped between the two men. "Where was this woman?"

Samuel picked a bit of loose tobacco from his tongue. "She came to the door. Asked to use the phone."

"And?"

"She made a call. Then she left."

"When was this?"

"Couple hours ago."

"Who did she call?"

"Dunno."

"Did she have the child with her?"

Samuel nodded then took another puff.

"Has anyone used this phone since?"

"Not me. Any of yer girlfriends call you today?" Samuel called out to his brother.

Timothy blushed crimson provoking a twinge of pity from Homer.

"Did you see the woman come to the house?" he asked the younger brother.

"No."

Homer raised a brow, not certain he believed the answer. "Have you made any calls today?"

Timothy shook his head.

"Nobody touch this phone," instructed Homer, then to Jimmy, "Drive down to the intersection of routes 79 and 22. Call Olivia. Tell her I need a crime scene unit out here on the double."

The parole officer sent him a questioning look.

"I'll explain later."

When Jimmy left, Homer turned his burning gaze on Samuel. "Let me be clear. If any harm has come to that woman and child, you can kiss your ass goodbye."

"What the fuck? I dinn't do nothin." Samuel stood and flung

over a coffee table tattooed with cigarette burns, scattering an ashtray overflowing with stubbed out butts.

Homer reached into his hip holster, firmly gripped the Beretta and said in a deadly calm voice, "You're getting on my nerves."

# CORDELIA

"FRESH MILK TAKES TIME TO SOUR. SO A FOOL'S MISCHIEF TAKES TIME TO CATCH UP WITH HIM. LIKE THE EMBERS OF A FIRE IT SMOLDERS WITHIN HIM."

BUDDHA

I COULDN'T SEE. I STRUGGLED TO open my eyes, felt as if I was blinking, but there was only blackness. Had I been blinded? By what? I tried to sit up, but the pain was so intense I couldn't keep myself upright.

"Master your senses. What you taste and smell, what you see and hear, in all things be a master." I whispered these words repeatedly until I felt less nauseous. I couldn't guess how much time passed before I tried again. At last I managed to pull myself up into a sitting position, but had to rest before gingerly sliding my legs over the side of whatever I was lying on.

"Aaahhhgg!" My bare feet were slapped awake by a floor so cold I nearly wept. The shock caused my legs to kick up involuntarily, toppling me over again. *What happened to my shoes and sox? And where was I, in a freezer?*

It took a while to recover for another attempt at standing. Able to bear the cold enough to edge my way around the small space, I could feel no corners, and worse no openings, no door or windows. I was trapped who knew where. And I was alone. I slid down onto the cold surface, holding my aching head, finally coherent enough to understand my grim reality.

*Where's Gabriella? Who has my baby?* A memory surfaced. I

was crossing the river to...*Oh, please no. Why hadn't I heeded Rebekah's warning? Oh, Buddha, I've played the fool.*

I rubbed my face to drive away the image of that vile creature's face, the menacing knife he carried. Then I remembered the crime he'd committed and could no longer contain the sobs.

"Please don't harm my baby. I beg you, please don't hurt her." My wails echoed off the dungeon walls. But could anyone else hear my plea?

# RUSSELL

"THE PRESS IS LIKE THE AIR, A CHARTERED LIBERTINE."

WILLIAM PITT

"CRIKEY! A VIRTUAL GOLD MINE," Russell marveled as he sorted through the documents and photographs he'd pinched from Rebekah Winchell's store room. He'd figure a way to sneak it all back once copies were made, and hopefully before the woman noticed anything amiss.

He was pleased to come across articles confirming his earlier research. But the letters. Oh, the letters were a magnificent find. The gods were looking upon him favorably. Unearthing the remarkable story of Samuel Rawlins would have made him happy enough. But now he was over the moon with the discovery of the completely barmy Rebekah Winchell a.k.a. Betsy Cooper, and practically in his own backyard.

"You are a clever and resourceful man," he congratulated himself as he cataloged his materials, reflecting at the same time on the future. The name Russell Payne may very well be added to the list of highly acclaimed true crime writers. It was thrilling to think he could one day be compared to the likes of Truman Capote, Norman Mailer, Ann Rule and Vincent Bugliosi.

Yes, his prospects were looking very bright indeed.

# HOMER

"THE DEVIL'S AGENTS MAY BE OF FLESH AND BLOOD, MAY THEY NOT?"

SHERLOCK HOLMES IN *THE HOUNDS OF THE BASKERVILLES*

"I WANT EVERY DETAIL." HOMER HAD moved Samuel into the kitchen with Timothy while the crime scene unit did their work. "What was the woman wearing?"

Samuel had become a bit more cooperative with a Beretta aimed in the direction of his manhood. "Jeans. T-shirt."

"Color?"

"Blue, I think. Red jacket tied round her waist."

"And the child?"

"I couldn't see. She was in one of those kid carrying backpacks."

Homer's eyes narrowed. "Why did you say *she*?"

"What?"

"You inferred the child was a girl. Why? "

A momentary flicker of panic crossed Samuel's face. "A guess. It's not like I was paying close attention or nuthin."

Homer segued to another question. "What kind of car was it you *think* she left in?"

"I don't *think* she left in it. I *know* so." Samuel was becoming agitated.

"And how's that?"

"When she came in to use the phone, I went out on the

porch because I heard a car drive up. I dinn't recognize it so I went to the barn to check on somethin'."

"Why didn't you wait to see who it was?"

"Cuz I wasn't feelin' sociable."

"Then what?"

"When I came back out there were tail lights rounding the curve. I never saw her again after that."

Homer wasn't buying the story and he also felt certain Samuel was hiding something out in that barn. He'd find out soon enough what, though his stomach turned at one of the possibilities.

"The child was gone, too?" he asked.

Samuel scoffed. "Why would she leave the kid?"

"Why would she leave the dog?" Homer countered.

"Beats me. But ev-i-dent-ly she dinn't want to take him along because we found him in that there closet." He pointed to a tiny coat closet near the door.

"Jimmy," Homer called out. "Have the guys get prints off the closet door and then check the inside for any evidence."

He turned back to Samuel. "A description of the vehicle she left in?"

"Dinn't get a close look, but I knew it weren't My Man Josh's car 'cause his is white and this one was dark. 'Sides, he drives a compact."

"Was it an SUV?"

"Could be."

"So what were you checking on in the barn?"

Samuel took a drag off his cigarette which gave rise to a coughing fit. A stall tactic.

Homer prodded for an answer. "These detectives are moving on to the barn. Is there anything you'd like to share with me before they go?"

"You got any girly magazines hidden out there Timmy boy?"

In a charade of good natured fun, he punched his brother in the arm, but the gesture was rebuffed.

Homer turned his attention to Timothy. "Where were you when this all happened?"

"Out walking."

"Where?"

Timothy contemplated Samuel who was sending him a fiercely threatening look.

"In the woods."

"Can you take me there?"

"You know the drill. Hands behind your back." Jimmy was grinning as he placed the handcuffs on Samuel Rawlins' wrists. He was read his Miranda rights and tucked into the back of the patrol car.

To Homer's surprise and great relief, the crime scene unit turned up no bodies in their survey of the Rawlins property. However, Timothy guided them to a sizable field of marijuana plants.

"Who's been tending your little agricultural project while you've been in the big house?" The plants were too mature to have been propagated within the past week since his release.

"Maybe you should ask the good reverend?" Samuel smirked.

Homer would do just that, but in the mean time, everyone would rest easier with Samuel Rawlins back behind bars.

# CORDELIA

"A WISE MAN, RECOGNIZING THAT THE WORLD IS BUT AN ILLUSION, DOES NOT ACT AS IF IT IS REAL, SO HE ESCAPES THE SUFFERING."

BUDDHA

"JING–JING–JING–JING–JING." I DRAGGED MYSELF BACK onto the platform where I'd been lying when I regained consciousness. I was trying to calm my fears and clear my head through meditation. But the throbbing pain was making it impossible. I needed to think, to come up with a plan. The screaming hadn't summoned anyone nor had it helped my headache.

I yawned and caught myself drifting off. *I mustn't fall asleep.*

I forced myself to stand and move. With great effort I started to walk along the perimeter of my small space, holding onto the wall for balance as I was still unable to see. Then to try and gauge the size of my prison cell, I let go and tentatively crossed the width, but stumbled over a lump and fell to the ground. It took me a moment to reorient and crawl back to the object that had tripped me up.

*My backpack!* I'd packed water and snacks. I wouldn't perish. There'd be Advil. I unzipped it and rifled through the contents, searching for the pain pills, finding a water bottle and a bag of trail mix. My thirst was fierce and I was already suffering the dizzying affects of dehydration, but I only allowed myself a few sips. Then I counted out ten pieces of nuts and dried fruit and chewed each one deliberately. As I continued to feel for the pain medication, my hand came upon a small bottle. I shook it. Liquid. I could feel a taped-on label.

*Oh, no.* Gabriella's antibiotics. She could relapse without finishing out the prescription. How would Samuel Rawlins know to care for her if she gets sick again? My mind was wandering dangerously close to the awful man's motivations for taking my daughter. To protect myself from such terrorizing thoughts, I took myself back to the very beginning of this whole mess. Why hadn't I stayed and faced the consequences? I might have found a really good attorney with the ability to persuade a sympathetic judge of my innocence. Even if Gabriella had been taken away, at least I'd know she was safe. That was more than I was assured of in my current desperate mess.

A subliminal whisper of my mother's wise words helped redirect such destructive thoughts: *You can't go back. No sense wasting time worrying over how things might be different. Use your energy to fix the problem.*

I needed to form a strategy, but first I had to do get rid of this headache so I could focus. Finally, the bottle of Advil. I swallowed three capsules with another gulp of water. Still plenty left. I allowed one more sip before another desperate thought came to mind.

*What if I run out of air?*

"Jing–jing–jing–jing–jing."

# RAMON

"THERE'S BEGGARY IN LOVE THAT CAN BE RECKONED."

WILLIAM SHAKESPEARE, ***ANTONY & CLEOPATRA***

RAMON KNEW BEFORE HE OPENED the door he'd find Gina inside. Her perfume was heady and unmistakable.

"Welcome home weary traveler." She was sitting on one of the pleasingly worn leather sofas with Ting purring contentedly in her lap.

"Weary is exactly the right word." He chucked his suitcase just inside the door and reached for the stack of mail on the console table. "I see our little friend came out of hiding."

Gina lifted the cat off her lap. "Ting was easy, but I do miss my little Guapo."

Ramon watched admiringly as his beautiful ex-wife swept across the loft in a saunter that perfectly melded grace and sensuality.

"But not nearly as much as I missed you." Gina put her arms around his waist and raised her face to his.

He could not deny an attraction to this woman. But desire alone couldn't carry a relationship, especially when one had betrayed the other's trust. He'd given Gina a decade of his life and wasn't convinced she was worthy of another significant chunk. He softly brushed his lips against hers and followed with a brotherly hug.

"Is it always going to be this way?" she pouted, releasing him from the embrace.

"Like what?"

"Me coming to you . You pulling away."

Ramon ran fingers through his thick, wavy hair. "Look, I am exhausted. I need a long, hot shower and about 48 hours of sleep. I do not think this is the best time for a relationship talk."

"You're right. You hop in the shower and I'll go get us something to eat." She picked up her purse as if it was settled. "How does *Giuseppe's* sound? A nice bottle of Chianti?"

"Not today."

She took in a deep breath, as was her habit when trying to calm a surging anger.

"I have a business associate stopping by. There is much more to do on this project. And as good as linguine with clam sauce sounds, I do not think my stomach is up for a big meal."

"Maybe later in the week?" Gina reached up and caressed his cheek.

"I will call. And by the way, thanks for coming to Ting's rescue."

"As I said before, *Ting* was easy." She left floating between them the implication that he was not.

Ramon checked the clock. There was time for a quick shower, which he needed for more reasons than the obvious. When he emerged from the bathroom wearing just a towel, his guest had already arrived and was sitting in a bar stool at the kitchen island, a frosty cold mug of beer in hand.

"Why don't you make yourself at home, Badger?"

"One step ahead of you," the scruffily bearded man raised the mug in a toast.

"You always are. Give me a minute." Ramon quickly donned a pair of chinos and a polo shirt and slid his feet into some Docksiders.

"We're going for the preppy look today?" Badger teased.

"You're not the only chameleon around town." Ramon opened the refrigerator, empty but for liquid consumables.

"Join me in a brewski?"

"I'd like to stay awake for at least the next ten minutes." He grabbed a can of Pepsi and popped the tab. "Okay, so what have you got?"

"Nothing beyond what I've already told you."

"Do they suspect her?"

"Duh." Badger spread out all the newspaper clippings and e-mail documents on the island.

After perusing the highlights Ramon smacked his hand on the polished concrete. "I do not understand why she is not answering her cell. How could she just vanish?"

"Are you sure it wasn't her intention all along? To slip away under the radar forever?"

"I have considered the possibility." Ramon thought hard for a moment. "But we have a history and my instincts tell me she is in trouble."

"What's this?" Badger made a face when Ting hopped up on the other barstool. "And what happened to that great dog you had?"

Ramon snapped his fingers and pointed to the cat. "Cord would never leave her cat behind. You should have seen how distraught she was when she could not coax it down from the duct work."

"Maybe she was distraught because she knew she was never again going to see him, her, whatever. You've got to face facts. She might have done it."

"Do not piss on my parade, Badge."

"You've got the hots for this woman."

"She is a very old friend. As I said, we have a history."

Badger rolled his eyes. "The hots."

Ramon tried the number again. "Straight to voicemail."

"What kind of phone did you get her?"

"The one you recommended. Basic flip phone. No data, no frills."

"Do you remember which model? Do you still have the box or instructions, anything that came with the phone?"

"Only if nobody thought to throw out my trash." Ramon turned to the receptacle and opened it, happy for once about his cleaning lady's neglectful ways. He sorted through until he uncovered the box and brushed off a few dried coffee grounds before handing it across to his friend.

While Badger skimmed over the phone instructions Ramon took a closer look at the articles lying before him. *What had Cord been thinking?*

"This is prime."

"What?"

"The phone your friend is toting around has the *Guardian Angel* feature."

"Is that supposed to mean something to me?"

"It's tracking software. We might be able to locate your little girlfriend. That is, if it was activated."

# HOMER

"WHEN YOU FOLLOW TWO DISPARATE CHAINS OF THOUGHT,
YOU WILL FIND SOME POINT OF INTERSECTION WHICH SHOULD APPROXIMATE THE TRUTH."

SHERLOCK HOLMES IN *THE DISAPPEARANCE OF LADY FRANCES CARFAX*

"YOU'RE MAKING A BIG MISTAKE," Samuel Rawlins yelled from the locked chamber. Except for the occasional drunk driver or disorderly, the two holding cells usually sat unoccupied. But they were designed to securely detain the most egregious offenders.

"Can you handle him?" Homer asked Olivia when they were out of ear shot.

"I know how to use this." She patted her revolver. "If that's what you're asking."

"It's not, but good to know you passed that part of the training," he said dryly. "His PD will be here in an hour. She's not to be allowed in the cell."

"Maureen Cuthbert?"

Homer nodded. "They can talk through the bars. I want no opportunity for escape."

"I doubt she'd ever want to get into a cell with that creep. Why would they assign a woman?"

"Strategy. If a sexual offender has to appear before a jury it's more favorable if there's a female defending him."

"But this is an unrelated charge. Won't the judge simply rule it a parole violation and order him back to jail? Unless..." she left the thought unspoken.

"As much as I'd like to make sure the degenerate never again leaves the confines of a prison, I hope it's not for those reasons."

"So you think he's done something to that woman and her baby?"

Homer chewed the inside of his cheek, bothered by his inability to answer Olivia's question definitively. Samuel Rawlins was indeed capable of the vilest crimes, but they needed evidence, or in the best case scenario to find the missing woman and child unharmed.

"So far the bloodhounds have led us down the road to nowhere."

"Speaking of hounds, what are you going to do with your new best friend?" She pointed to the corner where the dog he'd taken from Timothy Rawlins pranced anxiously.

"I have plans for him. What've you got for me on Betsy Cooper?"

Olivia handed him a file. "Fascinating reading material."

Homer flipped it open and skimmed over some of the information, his forehead creased with worry wrinkles. "What have we got on our hands, Liv?"

"When it pours the river runs wild. Oh, and the license plate you asked me to trace? The car belongs to a Ramon Alvarez."

"The city?" Homer asked, remembering a car with New York plates passing through town last week. The memory hadn't occurred to him when he'd uncovered the car beneath the piles of hay.

"Greenwich Village. A free-lance photographer. No criminal record and I haven't found a connection to Betsy Cooper or the missing woman. Maybe the car was stolen."

"Certainly a possibility. Have you contacted the family?"

"I have a call in to her parents." Olivia glanced down at

her notes. "The Carlyles. Arlington, Virginia. They've gone underground since their daughter took flight. An attorney's handling the media and running interference with law enforcement. A brief statement was issued and apparently Delia Carlyle had been estranged from her parents for years. I'll continue to pursue it."

"Good. Listen, I've got some people to see. Could you call Frannie and update her? Tell her Samuel's locked up." He grabbed the handle of the dog's leash and whistled. "Let's go, Bugs."

Olivia scowled. "Your wife is not exactly my number one fan."

"Give it time. You'll grow on her." He winked then ducked out the door before his assistant could launch the nearest hard object.

Homer's first stop was at Fred Taylor's auto repair shop.

"How do, Sheriff. Am I in trouble or does the cruiser need a tune-up?" Fred offered a toothy grin as he wiped his hands on an oil cloth.

"Neither today. But could you take a look at this receipt?" He handed over the slip he'd removed from the car hidden in Rebekah's barn. "You did the work?"

The mechanic pulled a pair of smudged cheaters from his shirt pocket and studied the paper. "Yep. Why you askin'?"

"I'm hoping to track down the owner of the car."

"Ms. Winchell said it belonged to her niece." He returned the receipt.

"She mention a name?"

Fred's lower lip protruded as he considered the question. "Not that I can recall."

"What happened to the car?"

"Remember that thick fog rolled in here last week? Seems

her niece was driving on Old County Road of all places. You know, out by Ms. Winchell's place?"

Homer nodded.

"Anyhow, she hit a deer. Banged up the front fender pretty good. But she didn't want no body work done. I told her to have her niece get it fixed soon as she got home, othern'wise it'll rust out."

"How long did you have the car?"

"Oh, it were an easy job. Had it ready the next day. She picked it up real early 'cause her niece needed to get on the road. No skin off my nose cuz I'm always here at the crack of dawn." He wiped his brow with the oil cloth. "Is Ms. Winchell's niece in some kinda' trouble?"

"I'm not sure, Fred. But I'd appreciate if you kept this conversation between us."

"Sure thing, Sheriff."

Homer drove in the direction of Rebekah's farm, on the lookout for Old County Road which he thought had been closed years ago due to an unstable bridge. He pulled onto the road, barely noticing the stacked cement blocks on either side because of overgrown bushes and vines. Lying a few feet to the side was a corroding metal sign.

"You're a slippery little devil." The dog tried to worm his way free when the car door opened. "Now stay."

He turned the sign over - *Road Closed* - then propped it up against the blocks and discovered the remains of the wooden rails rotted and splintered into pieces on the ground. He'd notify Public Works to get out here and replace the barricade.

The road was heavily rutted which forced him to drive slowly. When he came upon some deep tire treads running off to the side, he stopped and hooked the leash. The dog began circling the area, sniffing and whimpering.

"Hold on there." He grasped the leash firmly, not wanting to lose his important piece of evidence. Although the dog represented a puzzling aspect of the case since the FBI flyer reported the woman and child to be traveling with a Bengal cat.

He inspected the tread marks and determined the car had ended up lodged in the ditch. There was a second set of larger treads, almost certainly the towing vehicle, and he would lay high odds they matched the tires of a certain Silverado.

"Come on, Bugs." He lifted the dog into the cruiser and continued down the potholed road until he came upon a farm. Viewing it from a different perspective, at first he didn't realize it was the Winchell property. The road ended, but tire tracks had left an imprint in the field so he followed them to the rear of the barn.

"This must have been how she got the car into the barn," Homer was thinking aloud. "But why go to the trouble of hiding it under stacks of hay?" None of the possible scenarios coming to mind fit with what he already knew.

The dog was becoming frantic as they neared the house.

"I don't think they're here anymore, buddy." He reached over and gave the dog a pat.

A chat with Rebekah had been next on his list. How convenient to have happened upon a short cut. He needed to pry from the woman everything she knew about this Delia Carlyle-Martelli person, including how she ended up in the middle of nowhere. There must be some type of personal connection with Rebekah, or with Betsy Cooper. Whatever it was, he aimed to expose the link that tied these two women together.

He was experiencing the exhilaration that always accompanied an investigation. He just hoped he would unravel this mystery before anything happened to the missing woman and her child. If he wasn't already too late.

As he drove around to the front of the house he felt deflated by the absence of Rebekah's truck.

"For a hermit, she sure doesn't stay home much," he said to the dog who was panting eagerly to be released. "Okay. Let's check it out."

Homer was tugged up the porch steps and when the door swung open he let go the leash and the dog darted frenetically from room to room in search of his people.

He noticed at once the previously locked door off the kitchen had been left ajar. The storage room shelves were filled with canning jars, spools of yarn and several boxes. He lifted the lids and quickly shuffled through the personal paraphernalia. Since Olivia had arranged for the issuance of a search warrant he decided to remove them now.

After loading the cartons into the back of the cruiser he returned to find the dog nosing around the weaving room. There was a small chest next to one of the looms and in one of the drawers he found a photo of a little girl and a letter, the subject of which was a person named Gemma. The words made little sense to Homer but he pocketed both. Before leaving he checked the barn one more time to ensure everything was as he left it earlier.

"Let's go, Bugs." He slapped his leg and the dog came running. "One more stop, boy."

# REBEKAH

"THOU ART MY HIDING PLACE; THOU SHALT PRESERVE ME FROM TROUBLE; THOU SHALT COMPASS ME ABOUT WITH SONGS OF DELIVERANCE."

PSALM 32:7

WHEN LUCINDA OPENED THE DOOR of the old stone cottage, Rebekah glanced suspiciously over her aunt's shoulder into the room beyond.

"Are you alone?" she whispered.

"Yes, of course."

Lucinda took in the disheveled appearance of her niece. Rebekah's long hair was uncombed, her clothing wrinkled and mismatched. She looked as if she hadn't slept and her eyes had a disconcerting wildness to them.

"Rebekah what's happened?"

"Oh, Auntie, I'm so confused." Rebekah covered her face and began to weep.

"Come here my darling girl." Lucinda gently pulled her into an embrace and began slowly swaying from side to side, humming an old familiar tune that had always had a calming effect when Rebekah became distraught.

It seemed to work because before long, Rebekah's crying ceased. She released herself, but still held on to Lucinda's hands as she spoke her peace.

"I can't help but fear for your soul because your ways are sinful in the eyes of the Lord."

"Shush about that. I thought we agreed I'd worry about my own soul."

"Still, it's not fair of me to judge you and then ask for your help. But that's what I've come to do."

"I'd give my life to help you." Lucinda brought Rebekah's hands to her cracked, aged lips. She turned the wrists upward and kissed the scars and said as if she herself had inflicted the wounds. "Forgive me. You have always been my very own."

Rebekah stared, bewildered.

"It's no longer enough simply knowing you are near. Promise me we will never again be estranged because of our beliefs."

"I promise, Auntie." Rebekah broke down again and for a short while completely forgot the reason she'd come.

"I'm filled with joy now that you've come back to me." Lucinda wiped away the last of the tears and said, "Come, sit with me and tell me how I can help. Is it about the little girl? Has she become sick again?"

Rebekah squeezed her eyes closed and shook her head. "It's much worse than that."

# RUSSELL

"YOU CANNOT HOPE TO BRIBE OR TWIST THE BRITISH JOURNALIST.
BUT SEEING WHAT THE MAN WILL DO UNBRIBED, THERE'S NO OCCASION TO."

HUMBERT WOLF

Homer Pruitt was standing at Russell's front door holding a small mutt under one arm and a bottle of Glenfiddich.

"Well, well, now. Have Dorothy and Toto landed in Oz?" Russell asked.

"I thought you might get lonely out here so I brought you a companion." Homer set the pooch down as he walked through the threshold and immediately the dog lifted his leg on a leather armchair in Russell's family room.

"Bugger off you little twit." Russell made as if to kick the creature. "Not to look a gift horse in the mouth, but I daresay Guv, you'll be taking that one back where it came from."

"Give him a chance. It's a sign of acceptance. He did the same thing at the office." Homer handed over the bottle and made for the kitchen and a roll of paper towels. "Maybe you'll appreciate this more?"

"Acceptance, my eye." Russell peered at the label. Homer must want something. "Fifteen year old scotch whiskey. Old Solera Reserve at that. Lovely. Not too early for a wee dram?"

"Not to my mind." Homer blotted up the dribble and washed his hands.

Russell opened the bottle at a rustic sideboard that served as a bar and poured an inch of whiskey into two rocks glasses. He handed one to Homer and said, "To your health."

Homer took a sip then admired the remaining amber fluid in his glass. "Mighty good scotch."

"Have a seat." Russell rested his form on the couch and the dog jumped up beside him, wriggling his body affectionately.

"See he likes you."

Russell preferred cats. He identified with their sly natures. But he couldn't deny this odd little mutt had an appealing charm. "What's his name?"

"I've been calling him Bugs."

"It fits. He is a buggy-eyed little creature, isn't he?" Russell scratched the dog's head and was rewarded with a whine of pleasure.

"To what do I owe the pleasure of your visit, Sheriff? Besides the oh so generous gift of this canine companion."

"I have a story for you."

Russell leaned forward. "I'm all ears."

Homer raised his hand in a halting gesture. "I'm offering the story as a trade. In exchange I need you to dig up some information for me."

Just as he'd suspected. Now they were getting to the motive behind the scotch whiskey. "What kind of information?"

"It involves someone in town."

"And who might that be?"

"You'll agree to keep it completely confidential?"

"I'm not agreeing to anything until I know the scoop is worthy."

Homer took another sip.

They had arrived at an impasse.

But evidently the sheriff was more desperate for help than

Russell was for a story. And thus, he began to share the particulars of what had transpired out at the Rawlins place.

"So that's where this little guy came from." Russell had been scratching the back of the dog's neck and felt a small pellet just under the skin. Bugs had been micro-chipped. He decided to keep the discovery to himself. "Frankly, I'm going to need more than a simple marijuana bust."

"Nothing's simple as it concerns Samuel Rawlins. People around here were awfully upset about his early release. They'll be pleased to know he's going back where he belongs."

"But the whole bit about a woman and her child appearing out of the blue and then locking the dog in the closet before disappearing? Complete rubbish. What can I make of that?"

"There's more to the story."

"And that would be?"

"I can't reveal anything further until I've confirmed the facts. But when I do you can rest assured it will be a worthy story; farther reaching, beyond our quaint little burg."

"When can I print it?"

"Probably next week, but I've got loose ends to tie up first. Then I'll give you the rest of the details."

"So what are you expecting in return? That is, if I do accept."

"It's delicate. Can you promise complete discretion?"

"What do you say here in the states? Scout's honor?" Russell touched three fingers to his head in a proper salute.

"Rebekah Winchell is an assumed name."

Russell covered the gasp that escaped by pretending to cough. "What makes you think so?"

"She was recently identified as Elizabeth Cooper by someone who went to college with her. Liv and I have done a little research but we've hit some roadblocks."

Russell was wondering just how much the sheriff already

knew and how far he was willing to go. "Surely you could call in the real sleuths at the FBI to gather this information."

"I want to avoid drawing unnecessary attention until I know what I'm dealing with. It might be harmless, and if that's the case, I'd like to see it swept under the rug. The woman's done no harm that I know of."

*That you know of, right.* Russell was thinking how fortuitous it was to have such a considerable head start into the subject of Rebekah Winchell aka Betsy Cooper. As for the matter being swept under the rug, well now, that was highly unlikely.

"What are you looking for?" he asked.

"The type of information someone would have buried deeply. If it even exists."

*Oh, it exists.* But Russell had no intention of letting Homer Pruitt throw a spanner in the works. Still he hoped to tease a bit more out of the good sheriff. "I don't think you've dangled a big enough carrot with the Samuel Rawlins slash marijuana slash mystery woman and child business. You've got to cough up a bit more collateral if I'm going to drop everything for some investigative work."

Homer downed the rest of the scotch. "Mind if I have another?"

"Go ahead. Hell, I might as well get pissed, too."

After the drinks were poured and the two men touched glasses again, Homer pulled some papers from his pocket and began to unfold them.

"As I told you, Samuel said he'd never seen the woman before she showed up asking to use the phone. But he did give a description to a sketch artist with the crime scene unit." Homer placed the drawing on the coffee table.

Russell picked it up to scrutinize closely but didn't recognize the pretty face looking back at him. "And Samuel claims he never actually saw the woman leave, right? She and the child simply left with an unidentified person driving an unidentified car after locking this little guy in the closet and all the while he was in the barn presumably hiding evidence of his marijuana empire."

"That's what he said. Except for the last part."

"And you believe him?"

"I believe the woman and the child were in the Rawlins' home."

"Why?"

"I found a small piece of evidence. And then there's this." Homer placed another sheet of paper on the coffee table aside the sketch artist's rendering. It was an FBI *Amber Alert* flyer.

"Bloody hell," Russell whispered. "Not likely a coincidence, is it?"

"I don't believe in coincidences; especially not one so weighty as this."

"What about the brother? Did he see anything?"

"He claims he was out walking at the time. Even so, I'm not sure Timothy would be a very reliable witness."

Russell stared at the photo and the drawing for several minutes. "Let me ask you this, Sheriff. Do you think there are bodies to be found somewhere on the Rawlins farm?"

Homer finished his scotch. "So far, the search dogs haven't turned anything up."

"That doesn't answer my question."

# HOMER

"THE PRESS, WATSON, IS A MOST VALUABLE INSTITUTION, IF YOU ONLY KNOW HOW TO USE IT."

SHERLOCK HOLMES IN ***THE ADVENTURE OF THE SIX NAPOLEANS***

HOMER WORE A SATISFIED SMILE as he drove away from Russell Payne's lair. He was confident the microchip had been detected, which was exactly what he'd intended, though he had Timothy Rawlins to thank.

"There will be a signal." Timothy's words hadn't registered right away. But with the help of the Internet he was able to detect the presence of a chip. Now the newsman's nose would track the dog's original owner, which would surely produce an important cluc about the presumed victim of Samuel Rawlins. He would just have to be clever enough to get Russell to hand over his findings.

He had some juicy morsels of his own to barter with if it came to that, having withheld several crucial pieces of information including the fact he'd already been in contact with the FBI. He also hadn't revealed the missing woman and her child had been Rebekah's house guests, nor had he mentioned the boxes he'd confiscated from her storage closet. He had however detected a subtle shift in Russell's demeanor at the mention of Rebekah's name and suspected the journalist was holding onto a secreted bit of information. But Homer wasn't worried. It would eventually come out.

Another aspect he failed to share with Russell was Samuel's

insistence on taking a lie detector test. He hoped to convince the PD to postpone the test for as long as possible. Homer would prefer to get a confession out of the little creep; or at least force him into tripping up on his account of what happened. The longer he sweated it out in a cell the better the chances of breaking him.

He was careful to exclude details concerning Pastor Josh's alleged involvement, which would indeed be a scandalous story to report. Instead he intended to extend the benefit of the doubt, thinking it possible the minister had been used as a pawn in Samuel Rawlins' evil little game. Still, he would be questioning the pastor.

Homer checked the clock. The day was getting away from him and there was still much to do. He hadn't counted on two straight double scotches and would need to clear his head before checking in with the search team for an update. However, if the news was bad he'd be glad for the dulling powers of the liquor.

# CORDELIA

"IN THE SKY, THERE IS NO DISTINCTION OF EAST AND WEST;
PEOPLE CREATE DISTINCTIONS OUT OF THEIR OWN MINDS
AND THEN BELIEVE THEM TO BE TRUE."

BUDDHA

I AWOKE FROM A NIGHTMARE ONLY to remember I was stuck in one of my own making. As I reached into the backpack for more Advil my fingers brushed against something cool, metallic. *My cell phone.* I grasped the device, nearly weeping from relief when it lit up. My sight had not been lost from the impact of whatever knocked me unconscious. I opened it to get a better look at the cold chamber in which I'd been imprisoned, but it was only marginally helpful. I could only confirm the depressing absence of doors and windows. I checked for service bars. Exactly none. What was I expecting in this tightly sealed cavity?

I felt a vibration, a pounding from above.

"HELP! HELP! I'm in here!" I pounded my fists against cold, stone-like walls. "Please help me!"

I stopped screaming only when I felt the pelting of something pebble-like showering down upon me. When the brief downpour stopped I brushed the muck from my face and head, spitting out dirt. It took a moment for my eyes to adjust, but when I looked upward there was a shaving of light shining in.

"Dé!" A Chinese expression for misfortune slipped out. *I've been buried underground.*

I was hit with another cascade of sandy gravel and fell to the ground, using my arms for a shield. When I was able to look up again, someone was peering at me from the opening above. Even at a distance I could make out the face and it was not one I was pleased to see.

Samuel Rawlins had returned for me. To what? Finish me off? But I would not cower in fear.

"You listen to me," I growled deeply. "I want you to get me out of here this instant and I want my little girl back."

"She's gone." The sound echoed off the walls.

"What do you mean she's gone? What have you done to my baby?" I screamed.

"Nothing. I didn't do nothing to her. But I did lose your dog."

"GET…ME…OUT…OF…HERE."

"Can you reach my walking stick?" The voice had changed, perhaps distorted by the echoes of the cavern-like pit, but the disdainful tones had softened.

I hesitated, considering it might be a trick.

"You've gotta try." The voice above pleaded.

I managed to pull myself atop the platform I'd been lying on, but it wasn't high enough. Then I tried the backpack as a boost, and that still fell short.

I slowly stepped back down, firmly pressing my body against the wall and closing my eyes to calm the wooziness. My head was throbbing again.

"Is there a rope down there?"

I took two deep breaths and reached for my cell phone to better light the area.

"There's nothing down here." And then it dawned on me. "Shouldn't you know that since you put me here in the first place?"

"No ma'am, I did not."

I studied the face as well as I could from this distance and concluded the man looking down at me was not the degenerate who had thumped me on the head and dropped me down a hole in the ground to die.

"You're Timothy?" I barely got the question out before a wave of vertigo sent me spinning.

"Yes, ma'am and I promise to get you out of there. I'm going to find a rope but I'll be back. Here's a candy bar in case you get hungry."

Something dropped at my feet.

"Hello? Did you hear me?"

But there was no response.

# HOMER

"LIFE IS INFINITELY STRANGER THAN ANYTHING WHICH THE MIND OF MAN COULD INVENT."

SHERLOCK HOLMES IN ***A CASE OF IDENTITY***

"Pops is home," Homer could hear little Sara's squeal of excitement before he even opened the kitchen door.

"That's right. Pops is home." Sara took a running leap into his arms and he bear hugged her until she begged to be released.

"Hey, Pops." Benjamin was sitting at the table, grinning, but not willing to leave his chocolate sundae for a hug from his grandfather.

"You two must be feeling much better. At least you're well enough to be eating ice cream again." He walked over and stole a bite from his granddaughter's bowl.

"I don't think you should be sharing food with these two germ factories." Frannie was drying the last of the supper dishes.

"I come from hardy stock." Homer leaned in for a kiss. It was tepid at best.

"Well, that's a good thing, because Pops *isn't home* for long." Frannie folded her arms and leaned against the kitchen counter.

He raised his eyebrows in question.

"I just had a call from Pastor Josh."

"Interesting." Homer was assuming the minister had heard about Samuel's insinuation and was calling to either exonerate himself or to confess.

"He's out at the Rawlins' place."

"Did Olivia…?"

"Yes. She called." Frannie clapped her hands together, slowly and deliberately. "Job well done. Congratulations on earning *everyone's* undying gratitude for arresting Samuel so quickly."

He perceived more than a suggestion of sarcasm laced into her words of praise.

"Thank you?"

"Anyhow, you'd better call Pastor Josh right away. He stopped out to check on Timothy and found him in an extremely agitated state. He wasn't making sense."

"And that's unusual?"

"He claims to have found a woman in the ground."

It was dusk when Homer pulled up to the Rawlins house for the second time that day. He'd put more miles on his cruiser in the past week than in the last three months. He parked beside a white Prius and took in several deep breaths to steel his nerves for the details he was about to learn.

"Pastor Josh." Homer acknowledged the minister then turned his attention to Timothy. "Do you mind if I sit down here with you?"

"What did you do with the dog?" Evidently he'd not been forgiven for confiscating the young man's new best friend.

"He's being taken good care of by a friend of mine." Homer pulled out a chair from the rusting chrome table and sat across from Timothy. "I understand you have something to tell me?"

"I found the woman you were looking for this morning." Timothy was finger doodling on the table, avoiding eye contact.

"But I thought you hadn't seen her." Homer bent his head down in an effort to get the young man to look up.

"I hadn't seen her *here*. That's what you asked."

Technically, that was the question he had posed. "So you saw her somewhere else?"

Timothy nodded as he continued to outline the tabletop pattern, but was not forthcoming with any specifics.

Homer was coming to realize he was going to have to work for every morsel of information. "Where did you see her?"

"She was crossing the Argyle River and then I saw her go into the woods."

"Where were you when you saw this?"

"I already told you. I was walking." Timothy was growing impatient.

"That's right. You'll have to forgive an old guy like me for not remembering everything."

For the first time a smile brightened the young man's face. "I'll try."

"Did she have her little girl with her when she crossed the river?"

Timothy bobbed his head.

"But not when you found her tonight?"

He shook his head.

Pastor Josh apparently sensed Homer's weariness of the point by point probing. "Why don't you tell the sheriff everything that happened just as if you were telling a story? Start from when he left earlier today and take us through what happened up until right now."

Timothy closed his eyes and sucked in a deep breath and began to narrate the events of his day. "After they took Samuel and the dog away I didn't have anything much to do, so I waded across and climbed to the top of the hill where I'd seen her once before. I found a path and figured that must have been where she came from. I hiked down a ways until I came to a fork and wasn't certain which one to take until I saw a few broken vines of toxicodendron radicans."

"Toxic what?"

"Poison ivy. There were tons of both the trailing vine and

shrub varieties, but it was the torn vines that made me think that was the way to go even though the path wasn't well cleared. I followed the trail but when it ended I got lost. That's how I ended up pushing through to a clearing. There were some bales of hay, stacked apple baskets, a couple of buckets, that kind of junk." Timothy took a swallow of water and said no more.

Homer misunderstood the pause. "And that's where you found the bo…found the woman?"

Another bob of the head.

"Do you think you could take us back there?" Pastor Josh asked.

"I tried to go back with the rope, but I got lost."

Homer frowned. "Why were you taking a rope?"

"To get her out of there."

He still wasn't following. "How would a rope help? Wouldn't a shovel have been more useful?"

Now Timothy stared at him as if *he* was the one who wasn't quite right.

Homer rubbed his forehead and tried again. "Exactly how were you going to use the rope?"

"I was going to throw it down to her and pull her up."

"Where is she? In a well?" His tone sarcastic.

"Yes. She's in a well." Timothy was nodding his head, clearly excited now. "But it's no longer working. I mean there's no water in it. I think the spring dried up. Anyhow there was a thick plank covering it, to keep people from accidently falling in I s'pose. But somebody shoveled dirt and stones on top of it. I never would have thought to look if the woman hadn't screamed."

Timothy took another swallow of water while the sheriff and the pastor sat in stunned silence.

"Are you saying," Homer cleared his throat, "the woman is still alive?"

"Yes. Why wouldn't she be?"

*Because when you hear a woman has been found in the ground you don't automatically assume she's alive.* "And you had a conversation with her?"

"Mostly she yelled at me. Until she figured out I wasn't Samuel. But she might be hurt. She didn't sound so good when I left. That's why I called Pastor Josh. I've got to get that rope to her. I promised."

"Okay, then. Let's go find her."

The three men tried to retrace Timothy's route using high intensity searchlights Homer kept in his cruiser, but they failed to locate the well.

The young man was on the verge of tears. "But I promised her I'd come back with the rope."

"And you will," Pastor Josh assured him. "There will be a better chance of locating her in the daylight and we will get her out with this very rope."

"We aren't giving up." Homer grasped Timothy's shoulder. "Now here's the plan. You are going to get some rest because you'll need your energy tomorrow. I'm going to arrange for those tracking dogs to come back first thing in the morning. I'll see you right here at seven o'clock. Is that a fair deal?"

Timothy held out his hand. "Shake on it?"

"Sure thing. Now get to bed."

Homer and Pastor Josh watched Timothy slowly trudge off and then the sheriff said, "I think after we solve this piece of the puzzle you and I need to have a little talk."

"About Timothy?"

"No, I think Timothy's going to be okay once his brother's back in State, which shouldn't be too long. Things are bad enough for him and if the woman doesn't make it through the night, it goes without saying, he's a goner."

"Samuel's diseased soul may be a lost cause. But I will pray for the young woman. And her missing child."

"We'll take all the help we can get." Homer decided to cast out a little bait. "Makes the marijuana find seem trivial."

If it hadn't been the inky dark of midnight, he probably could have watched the color drain from Pastor Josh's face.

"What marijuana?" A wretched croak of a voice posed the question.

"There's a small greenhouse hidden beyond the barn with about two dozen mature plants. But more concerning are the two large fields of seedlings we happened upon about a half mile away. Probably a couple acres in total. Except Samuel swears the plants aren't his."

"Who else could they belong to?"

"Don't know. We'll have to see how Samuel's polygraph goes."

"Polygraph?"

"Yep. If you think of anything that might shed some light on our little discovery, let me know."

Homer wasn't laying odds on what the minister would do. At the moment he was just too damn tired to care.

# RUSSELL

"WHERE ELSE IN SOCIETY DO YOU HAVE THE LICENSE TO EAVESDROP ON SO MANY DIFFERENT CONVERSATIONS AS YOU HAVE IN JOURNALISM?"

BILL MOYERS

"CAN YOU SEE ME BW?" Russell was speaking with his ace investigator, his face right up to the camera.

"Back up a little bit. All I can see is your right nostril, and trust me, it's not your best feature."

"Sorry, mate. Is this better?" He moved his chair back a foot or so.

"Cool, man. I can't believe you finally hooked up the webcam. What's it been, like six months now?"

"I'm a bit slow at these high tech gizmos. But I wanted to try it out with you first."

"Well, it's working. I can see your ugly mug."

"Speaking of ugly, what's with the scruffy beard? You look like a blooming hobo."

"Good, that's the look I'm going for. So was the information I sent useful?"

"Quite. Now I have another task for you. I've come into possession of a little pooch. A stray I thought, until I spotted his micro chip. Anyhow, I took him to a local veterinary clinic and they had a device to read the chip and determined the original owner lives in New York City of all places."

"Crazy, man. How'd he end up in Maine?"

"That's the mystery. Anyhow, I've been unable to track down these people. Of course, if they've moved and haven't registered the new address, there's practically no way of locating them through this system. Can you see what you can do?"

"Sure. What have you got?"

"Thomas Smith. I know." Russell's voice dripped incredulity at the ridiculously common name. "There must be ten thousand Thomas Smiths in the city that doesn't sleep."

"Or more. Middle initial?"

"Nope."

"Of course not."

"The phone number is now someone else's listing, but here it is." Russell read off the number and the last known address provided by the microchip registration. Then he held the dog in view of the webcam. "BW, may I present the newest member of the Payne household?"

"Again, all I can see is his nose. Move back a little."

"Like this? Isn't he a funny looking little bugger?"

"Hey man. That dog looks familiar."

"Really? Well, he is from your neck of the woods."

"This is way out there man, but does he by chance have a wide black stripe at the base of his tail?"

Russell aimed the dog's derrière directly at the camera. "Indeed he does."

"Way too close, man." Then BW called into the microphone, "Hey, Guapo!"

The dog responded by twisting around and whipping his tail briskly against Russell's face.

"Crikey! You already know this Tom Smith fellow? Now that is a bit fluky, isn't it?"

"To be honest, I don't think I know any dudes by that name."

"How's that?" Russell wasn't following.

"Sometimes this kind of shit is just too bizarre for me." Badger White shook his head in total disbelief.

# CORDELIA

"YOU ARE FAR FROM THE END OF YOUR JOURNEY. THE WAY IS NOT THE SKY. THE WAY IS IN THE HEART. SEE HOW YOU LOVE."

BUDDHA

I OPENED MY EYES TO TOTAL blackness and it took a moment to gather my wits and call to mind where I was. I lifted my hands to touch the wall and then it all came back. I'd somehow been dropped to the bottom of an underground vault; unless of course, Timothy Rawlins showing up last night had been a hallucination.

What had he said about Gabriella? Only that *he* hadn't brought harm to her. But there was no mention of whether or not my little girl was safe; and nothing about his brother. My whole body began to tremble at the prospect of my baby in the arms of that sinister man.

*Do not imagine the worst.* I forced aside those thoughts to keep from going mad. What day was it? It had been Monday morning when I left Rebekah's. But how long had I been unconscious? And when did Ramon say he was returning to the states? Was it Tuesday? Oh heck, what difference did it make? He was a resourceful man, no question, but how could I bring myself to hope he could track me down? Why would he even try? By now he must realize I'd forsaken the plan he so carefully laid out for me. How could I blame him for losing faith in me? But hadn't I forgiven him a far more wounding betrayal?

My brooding propelled me back ten years to that disheartening weekend in Washington. I'd not yet met Aiden and hadn't had any serious relationships to speak of; rare for someone in her mid-twenties. I was beginning to agree with my mother that I was emotionally unavailable. When the phone rang I'd been in a sulk and let the call go to the answering machine. But when I heard the soft, familiar voice of my childhood friend I leaped for the receiver.

"I'm here! I just walked in the door."

"You were out in this weather?"

Busted. But how had Ramon know about the blizzard? I guessed it was big news everywhere when the nation's capitol was snowed under.

"Hey, when there's a storm, you must be prepared. And by prepared I mean a two week's supply of bread and milk."

He laughed. "Are you mocking my mama?"

"Never! So, what's the momentous occasion?" Never before had the two friends telephoned at any other time during the year besides New Year's Day.

"Guess where I am."

"Tahiti?"

"Not so exotic as that."

"Good, because I'd be jealous. Russia?"

"Nope. But the weather is similar right now."

"It's a big world. You've got to give me a hint."

"I will do better. I am at Dulles and stranded for at least the next twenty-four hours."

I chattered on idly for several minutes trying to summon the courage to invite him to my place.

"I rely on public transportation to get around or I'd offer to come get you."

"No worries. There are a few cabs running." And so it was settled.

I scurried around to make the apartment look presentable before checking the fridge to see what I might whip up to impress for surely he'd be hungry. And I was right, he was ravenous, but not for food. This unforeseen development in our relationship had been both terrifying and thrilling. In my mind our coupling went beyond impassioned, pent up sexual attraction, and I was basking in the delusion that Ramon shared that view. However, on the last day of his visit I was rudely slapped back to reality.

"Cord, I need to tell you something."

We'd been snuggled together in front of the fireplace. "You sound serious."

"It is serious. Did you expect this" -he pointed to himself and then to me- "that anything would happen between us?"

"No." I wanted to admit that it was something I used to hope for, but I'd been shy about sharing the truth. "Did you?"

He shook his head.

"I'm glad it did though. Aren't you?"

"Of course, mi querida. I can promise you I will never forget this time together." He brought my hand to his lips for a kiss then folded it firmly against his chest. "I have always had this special compartment in my heart reserved for you. But it was protected."

"What do you mean by protected?"

"I am not sure how to explain it. When we were younger, after you left? Well, I'd fantasize that we would someday meet again and be together."

"Like now?" I nestled in more closely, bursting with such happiness that Ramon had shared my same desires.

He sighed deeply. "Yes, like now."

"I wish I'd known."

"It would not have changed anything. The two of us? Together? It was never meant to be. You moved on. I remained."

I did not like where I sensed the conversation was headed. "Only because of circumstances not of our choosing."

"That is true about most of life. However, we inhabit two vastly different worlds."

"But what counts is we come from the same place. You and I…"

"It cannot be."

"I don't agree." I turned to look at him more directly, but he averted his gaze.

"Cord." He held up his free hand to stop me from saying anything further. "I am engaged to be married."

I'd been stunned by the declaration. A sense of boundless loss and betrayal rendered me unable to articulate my distress. The cliché about timing being everything certainly held true on that day when the phone interrupted the excruciating long moments of silence that followed Ramon's wounding confession.

"That was Continental. My flight leaves in two hours."

I'd remained a dead weight on the sofa while Ramon called a taxi then showered. Thirty minutes later he was gone and I hadn't seen him again until last week.

The fissure in my heart had only partially healed as the years passed, leaving a scar that would not let me forget the deep and tender connection we'd briefly shared. A connection I'd never felt with anyone else, not even the man I married.

Being with Ramon again had resurrected a suppressed longing, but the two of us seemed destined to forever travel divergent paths. I was filled with deep regret that my love for him would remain eternally unrequited. I wiped at the tears that were dampening my cheeks.

*Why am I even thinking about this?* Time to concentrate on my present quandary, which was far more distressing than a lost love.

A beam of sunlight began to illuminate the dungeon from

above. Timothy must have left the covering off. I sat up quickly but the pain in my head forced me back down.

I was going to have to take this slowly. At least the dizziness had passed. Little by little, I propped myself up on my elbows and reached for the backpack. I popped three Advils with a few sips of water. The light filtering in from above reflected on a silver object on the ground. A Three Musketeers Bar. *At least now I know for sure Timothy was here last night.*

He'd tossed something down to me before leaving to retrieve a rope to pull me free from this underground prison. Wouldn't it be ironic if the brother who according to Rebekah 'wasn't right in the head' turned out to be my liberator?

But what was taking him so long to return? My worst fear for Timothy was that Samuel had harmed him. My worst fear for myself was that Samuel would be coming back for me. I could wait no longer. I had to figure my own way out.

I tore open the candy bar and ate it hastily then finished the last sips from the water bottle before trying to stand. I took in my cave-like surroundings. The platform I'd been lying on turned out to be a stack of pallets. I couldn't fathom their purpose but was struck with an idea of how to use them. First I dug down deep into my pack and removed a pair of Tevas I was now glad for shoving in at the last minute.

Normally it would have been an easy task, but my movements were lethargic as I maneuvered the pallets upright into a makeshift ladder. I struggled to pull on my backpack and cautiously climbed upward, slipping once and nearly toppling the precarious structure.

I was crying when I finally saw blue sky, from a combination of pain and the unexpected joy of hearing birds chirping in the trees. With my last remaining will I managed to pull my body out from the dank prison cell. I laid there for several moments, breathing hard while taking in my surroundings. That's when I realized the awful truth. Samuel Rawlins had thrown me down an old abandoned well and left me there to die.

*But where exactly was this well?* I pushed through brush until I came to an old stone wall which I followed at a snail's pace as it wound through the woods. Eventually I arrived at another small clearing. It felt familiar. I pushed the heels of my palms into my eyes trying to grasp the elusive memory of when I might have passed by this place. Nothing came to me. I continued to plod along until I reached a stream that branched off from the river. Something didn't seem right though. I looked to the sky to check the sun's position, but that confused me even more. Probably dehydration was hindering my ability to focus. And if I was going to find Gabriella, I needed to focus. I dropped down and drank thirstily, dipping my head under the cold water to rinse away the dirt caked onto my face and hair. It was a much needed jolt to awaken my senses.

I could think of only two options, the first being to plead for Rebekah's forgiveness and help. The second was to return to the Rawlins' place and demand to know where my daughter was. Neither choice was particularly appealing given that I was practically as frightened of Rebekah as I was of Samuel Rawlins.

Before I could make up my mind I heard a distant howling. I remembered Rebekah telling me about a hiker who'd recently been attacked by coyotes. I changed course and began moving in the opposite direction. However, aside from my inability to move quickly, I was also even more disoriented. Instead of moving toward the river I had arrived at the boarder of a large meadow. The animals were fast approaching from the woods, only now I felt certain the sound was not a pack of coyotes but baying bloodhounds following a scent. *Mine?*

If I crossed the meadow I'd be easily spotted. I faltered a second, unsure which way to flee. The decision was taken out of my hands when an ATV thundered toward me and skidded to a stop.

The driver flashed a badge and commanded, “Get in now.”

I was too exhausted and frightened to do anything but obey.

# HOMER

"THERE IS NOTHING MORE STIMULATING THAN A CASE WHERE EVERYTHING GOES AGAINST YOU."

SHERLOCK HOLMES IN ***THE HOUNDS OF THE BASKERVILLES***

A WHOLE TEAM FOLLOWED THE BLOODHOUNDS and their handlers, some on foot and others on ATV's. Homer and Timothy kept up a good pace behind the tracking dogs.

"Is any of this starting to look familiar?" Homer asked.

The young man nodded then began to point excitedly. "There's the fork. Right up there."

"Well, let's see how good these hounds are." And sure enough they dragged the group through the brush and poison ivy until they reached the clearing Timothy had described earlier.

"The hatch is moved." Timothy lumbered to the well, nearly tripping over the dogs and peered down into the dark hole. "I don't think she's down there anymore."

Homer aimed his flashlight into the now vacant cavity. "Looks like your girlfriend's pretty clever." *Or she had help.*

Timothy blushed crimson. "She's not my girlfriend."

He ruffled the young man's hair. "Just a figure of speech."

The rest of the crew arrived and Homer began to issue orders.

"Miller, you go down and collect what's down in the well." As the man anchored a rope ladder and descended Homer shined the light on a water bottle. "Bag that bottle while you're at it. Might as well offer the dogs a fresh scent to follow."

"Where's Boatman?"

The forensic tech had just pulled up with Pastor Josh. "Over here."

"Miller's down the hole. Collect what you can around the scene. Check the baskets, buckets, everything. I'll take Feller with me in case we come across any other evidence. When you're done, go back to the Rawlins' place and wait there."

Jimmy Kramer had volunteered to come along. "How the hell did he know about this abandoned well?"

"Good question." Homer called out to Timothy who was listening intently to something Pastor Josh was saying. If he could be a gnat buzzing about over there he'd probably be hearing something about a little lady named Mary Jane.

"Yes sir?"

"Does Samuel ever go hiking in these parts?"

He frowned. "My brother spends most of the time sitting on the couch smoking cigarettes and drinking Budweiser."

"I'm just trying to figure out how Samuel may have known about this place." Homer had forgotten he needed to be more direct in his questioning of the young man. "Any ideas?"

Timothy blinked several times as he mulled the question, probably fearful of saying something that might keep his brother out of jail. Who could blame him?

"How about when he was younger? Do you think he might have come here with friends to hang out?"

"He used to hunt and do some trapping. Maybe that's how he knew about it."

"And looky what's right over there." Jimmy Kramer was smiling triumphantly as he pointed to some rusted out traps at the edge of the clearing. "It's not looking too good for our Sammy boy now is it?"

*It also wasn't looking so good for little Gabriella Martelli.*

Homer shouted to the crew. "Okay, where's that bottle? Let's move!"

Boatman handed him the bag and he in turn gave it to the dog handlers. Seconds later they were off again. The hounds reacted fiercely when they reached a stream and forged on through the woods until they arrived at a field. And there the dogs stopped, sniffing in circles, nosing at their handler for more scent clues.

"Let's fan out and see what we can uncover." Homer issued the order when he caught up.

Feller came across some tracks. "Looks like an ATV wheel."

"Can you tell if it matches ours?"

The tech was able to confirm they were not a match to the crime scene team vehicles.

"How fresh are they?"

"That's going to be hard to tell. It's lucky we even saw them."

"Can you get an imprint?"

"That I can do," Feller said and began to take out the materials he would need to cast a tire print.

Homer walked over to where Timothy was kneeling.

"You okay, son?"

"I think that VTA was here today."

"You mean ATV?"

"That's what I said." Timothy's defensive response gave Homer pause. Could this boy's problems be as simple as a learning disability like dyslexia?

"Anyhow, look at this branch. It's broken which is very rare for the hamamelis virginiana."

"Virginia who?"

"Hamamelis virginiana," Timothy repeated slowly. "The common witch hazel plant. See how flexible the branches are?" Timothy demonstrated by bending several branches. "Archers used to make their bows from these trees. But this one snapped off."

"So it would have taken some force to break it. Like a vehicle of some type."

"Yes. And here you can see the white sap. This branch was broken very recently." He inhaled the scent of the plant. "Witch hazel."

"How did you know that?"

Timothy shrugged modestly. "I read a lot."

"Good job."

"This will help you find the woman?" Timothy looked up, squinting from the sun's glare.

"We'll see."

"What about the little girl?"

"One missing person at a time, Timothy. Once we can talk with the mother she might tell us something that will help us track down her daughter."

An hour later the crime scene team compared notes back at the Rawlins' house. The bloodhounds hadn't picked up another scent direction and the vehicle tracks disappeared at the paved road.

"Feller I want you to rush that imprint and start checking the makes and models to match the tire and start narrowing down owners by searching purchases of the vehicle in this general region. I need that information straight away."

As the crew began to scatter, Pastor Josh approached.

"Is there anything I can do? I feel so helpless. I keep thinking about the little girl…"

Homer rubbed his chin as he considered the wisdom of what he was about to ask.

"There's no way Samuel would have been considered for early parole without an advocate, right?"

"Yes, that's true." There was wariness in his tone.

"It might be quicker for you to check out if he was counseled by someone who might have been sympathetic enough to offer a recommendation. I'd really like to get my hands on the file. Can you do that for me?'

"But those documentations are confidential." The minister had taken out his handkerchief and began blotting at his perspiring forehead.

"You're right. I'll just have Olivia get a court order."

"No." Pastor Josh cleared his throat. "What I mean is, maybe I can circumvent the red tape."

"That's what I was hoping."

"Great," Homer mumbled to himself when he closed the door on his cruiser. Now he had another bone to chew during his drive back to the office. Could Pastor Josh be hiding more than his involvement in the marijuana operation? He picked up his cell phone and punched in Olivia's number.

"I need you to get Judge Bennett to sign a warrant for the release of Samuel Rawlins' files from Warren. Pronto."

It was imperative to get hold of those documents before anything happened to them. Like being conveniently misplaced or vanishing altogether.

# RUSSELL

"I HATE JOURNALISTS. THERE IS NOTHING IN THEM BUT TITTERING JEERING EMPTINESS. THEY HAVE ALL MADE WHAT DANTE CALLS THE GREAT REFUSAL. THE SHALLOWEST PEOPLE ON THE RIDGE OF THE EARTH."

WILLIAM BUTLER YEATS

RUSSELL COULDN'T BELIEVE HOW IMPECCABLE his timing had been of late. He'd been out for a bit of a joy ride when he spied a person limping through the woods. As he closed in, his trained eye identified her from the FBI flyer shown to him by Homer yesterday. She wasn't in great shape, which would work to his advantage and make for an easier interrogation.

He pulled the ATV into the large detached garage, turned off the engine and gave his captive an appraising look.

"Let's get you inside and clean up that gash on your head." Russell guided the young woman into his cabin and set about gathering antiseptic cream and bandages.

"Who are you?" She dropped her backpack by the sofa table and began rubbing her arms. "What do you want with me?"

"It's my job to ask the questions. How did you end up wandering the woods? You were on private property. My property as it stands." He was lying. His cabin was several miles from where he found her. In reality, he'd been the one trespassing when he'd happened upon the woman.

"You're English." She winced as he dabbed at the wound.

"Clever girl. Now answer my question."

"Somebody hit me over the head, shoved me into an old deserted well and kidnapped my little girl."

Russell's eyes popped wide. You can't even make up stories like that. "You expect me to believe such rubbish? First, prove to me you have a child."

The woman reached into her backpack and pulled out a bottle of antibiotics.

"A little girl, you say? This prescription was written for someone named Jacob."

The woman closed her eyes and sucked in her bottom lip. "Look, it's complicated. The person who took my baby took all her stuff, too."

"And left you with only a bottle of medication?" He perused the label again, frowning as he took note of the last name of Cooper. Puzzle pieces were clicking into place in his mind.

"You don't understand."

"What I understand is you are in big trouble."

"Why am I in trouble? The man who kidnapped my little girl and then threw me down a well to die is the person you should be after. You should be helping me."

"Save your breath." He escorted her across the living room where he opened double doors to another room and motioned for her to go in.

In seconds, the little pooch practically flew up into the woman's arms and began licking her face with enthusiasm.

"Oh, Handsome." She hugged the dog and scratched his ears.

*Handsome?* Russell thought not.

"If you're okay, then maybe..." She began to cry. But a moment later a horrified expression distorted the pretty features. "How did you...? You're not really the police, are you?"

"No, I'm not. But I do know all about you. Delia Carlyle."

It seemed hardly possible, but the woman's complexion became even more pallid.

Of course, he was bluffing. He knew her name and other odd bits and pieces, but it would be enough to coerce some information out of the woman. "And I can help you. But first, you're going to help me."

"Why did you call me by that name?" Her eyes narrowed but her voice was thick.

He walked to his desk and produced the flyer Homer had left with him. "Your hair is a different color and you've cut it short, but there's no doubt."

She looked at but didn't touch the paper. "So why the games? You know who I am, that I have a child, why not just turn me in to the real authorities?"

"Let's just say I have a soft spot in my heart for runaways; especially those who are useful. And as I said, you scratch my back and I'll..."

"You'll do what? Let me go?"

"I'll help you find your daughter."

"How?"

"First things first." Russell took her by the elbow and guided her to his assembled display of storyboards set up on easels throughout the large space. This was how he worked. Right now he was choosing his next project out of several possibilities so there was a lot to take in. He pushed her toward the first display and scrutinized her reaction.

She took in the collage of older and more recent snapshots then directed a fiercely distrustful look his way. "Why do you have all these photographs?"

"I've taken a personal interest in Ms. Winchell. Actually, I find her to be a fascinating subject. Don't you?"

"How would I know?"

"Come now, you recognized her. How did you come to know her?"

"I don't really *know* her."

"Is that so? Funny. I paid a visit to her just yesterday. Popped over to ask a few questions."

"About what?"

"Well, you see, I'm writing a book." He waved his hand as if to shoo away a thought. "Doesn't really matter because she wasn't home. I daresay that was convenient for me though. I was able to collect a great deal more information with her gone. Don't you agree?" He pointed in the direction of his next display, the subject of which was Camp Davis with a time line of sorts representing the various spiritual leaders. Beside this easel was a stack of materials he'd snatched from Rebekah's storage room.

She bent down to sort through the pile. "You stole this."

"Hmm. Makes me think you've been doing a little poking about yourself."

The woman glared defiantly but didn't deny the accusation.

"I'm merely borrowing the materials. I'll happily return them when I'm finished. So now that we're both on the same page, so to speak, why don't you tell me exactly what your connection is to the woman."

"I don't have a connection," she continued to insist.

"I think you're lying. Do you want to know why?"

"Not particularly."

"No? Well, I do think you'll be interested in what I happened to come across while I was visiting the Winchell farmhouse."

The Englishman opened a drawer in his massive desk and plucked out a tiny pink polka-dotted t-shirt.

# CORDELIA

"A DOG IS NOT CONSIDERED A GOOD DOG BECAUSE HE IS A GOOD BARKER. A MAN IS NOT CONSIDERED A GOOD MAN BECAUSE HE IS A GOOD TALKER."

BUDDHA

"WHERE IS SHE?" I LUNGED.

"Cor blimey! You're a feisty bird, aren't you?" The man was taller and easily dodged the attack.

But Handsome began to circle, barking wildly until he managed to latch onto a pant leg.

"Belt up, you little bugger." The man was unsuccessfully trying to shake the dog loose. "Haven't I been taking good care of you?"

While the dog's antics were causing a distraction, I grabbed hold of the man's shirt and shouted, "Tell me where my daughter is."

The Brit managed to pull free and dragged the wriggling pooch out of the room, closing the door to keep him at bay. He brushed with annoyance at his now disheveled clothing.

"No need to get your knickers in a twist. On my honor, I did not kidnap your child. But if you calm down and promise to be good, I might be the one to help you find her. I am closely associated with the local law enforcement and I will call in the troops and get them cracking on the case."

"I already know who has her."

"How can you? A moment ago you thought I took her."

I looked past the man and took note of a familiar looking woman in one of the photos on the Camp Davis storyboard. I stepped closer to read the name. Lucinda Cooper. Pressure began to build at my temples. What did this man know and what did he think I knew?

"You said you were writing a book. What's your name?" I continued to scrutinize the Camp Davis collage of photos and documents.

"Russell Payne. I'm a virtual unknown on this side of the pond. But not for long." He shook his finger. "You'll hear my name again one of these days."

I circled the room, closely studying each of the boards. When I reached the last easel I was overcome by terror.

# RAMON

"LOVERS EVER RUN BEFORE THE CLOCK."

WILLIAM SHAKESPEARE, ***THE MERCHANT OF VENICE***

"I'M LOOKING FOR THE SHERIFF." Ramon offered a most engaging smile.

"He's working a case right now but maybe I can be of help. I'm his assistant, Deputy Bishop." The woman's diminutive frame and amiable demeanor didn't fit with her title, but the pistol in the holster belt confirmed her position of authority.

"Do you have any idea when he'll be back?"

"Sorry, I don't."

"I could go meet him where he is." Ramon suggested hopefully.

"I'm afraid you're going to have to tell me the reason you need to see him and let me make the judgment as to how the two of you can arrange a meet up."

"It's a delicate and confidential matter."

She gave him a look that said *I've heard it before.*

"Also quite urgent."

"I'm sure it is."

The phone rang.

"I shouldn't be long. Have a seat."

Ramon didn't like being at the mercy of somebody else's command. Not when he intuitively knew Cord was in trouble. He picked up a magazine, flipped the pages and then put it back down and began to pace the waiting area. He stopped cold when he saw the *Amber Alert* posted on the bulletin board. Maybe this had been a mistake. Having no idea what type of predicament Cord had landed herself in, he'd hoped to ferret out some general Intel from the local police.

He edged closer to the office door which had been left ajar so he could hear the officer's phone conversation. She was discussing a warrant for documents from the state prison. He felt relieved it had nothing to do with Cord.

Then he took a seat in the corner and waited. Just as the deputy ended her phone call, a tall and stunning middle aged woman entered the building and walked purposefully to the office.

"Have you heard from Homer about the abducted woman?" Her manner was brusque and her voice frosty.

He strained to hear but couldn't make out what the deputy was saying because the other woman's body was blocking the sound.

"That couldn't have made his day."

More inaudible chatter.

"Where are they looking?"

The deputy must have walked closer to the door because he heard her say, "Along the Argyle. They'll find her eventually."

"Hopefully before it's too late. What about the little girl?"

"No sign of her."

They had to be discussing Cord and Gabriella. Ramon stood and the two women turned to look at him, one just remembering he was there and the other noticing him for the first time. He felt his face grow warm under their scrutiny.

"I'll just come back later to see the sheriff." He turned toward the door but it was flung open before he reached the handle and in walked a man whose average stature belied his commanding presence.

Nobody spoke as the man, presumably the Sheriff, sized up the situation. First he glanced at the two markedly different women. The tall, sophisticated brunette shot him a fierce look while the petite blonde smiled awkwardly.

"Ladies," he said before turning his attention on Ramon. "You here to see me?"

Ramon quickly contemplated his options and decided his best course of action would be an honest and direct approach. Besides, on first pass this imposing man of the law gave the impression he could smell a scam for miles. He'd take his chances Sheriff Pruitt would appreciate forthrightness.

"It's about the *Amber Alert.* I have a way to locate Cordelia Carlyle."

# RUSSELL

"BAD MANNERS MAKE THE JOURNALIST."

OSCAR WILDE

"We're buggered now. The coppers have arrived." Russell couldn't guess what brought Homer back so soon, but the sight of the cruiser coming down the lane made his stomach turn.

"Where can I hide?" the woman asked, looking about the room desperately.

"From this sheriff? Nowhere. He'll sense something's amiss the minute he crosses that threshold. I'm sorry, but the jig is up."

"If you don't save me then I can't help you." It was a threat. A damn good threat.

They'd barely scratched the surface of what this fugitive could share about Rebekah Winchell. When she'd seen the photos of Samuel Rawlins they'd struck a deal. She'd tell him all she knew if he'd help her find her little girl and get them safely out of the country. Not to mention the diary she claimed to possess and was holding as collateral. If Homer arrested her Russell could surely kiss that little goldmine goodbye.

"Time to duck and dive." He pointed to a back door and tossed her the ATV keys. Then he picked up the pooch and went to greet his visitor. "I'll stall him best I can."

"Back for some more Glenfiddich?" he called out from the porch and walked down the steps to hinder ingress.

Homer was sporting what Americans so aptly describe as a shit-eating-grin.

"I'm on the wagon today, Rusty."

"Francesca must prefer her men completely sober." He couldn't resist an opportunity for a dig about Homer's wife.

"If that's what you want to think."

Uh oh. The sheriff wasn't playing today.

"So what brings you back out to my humble digs?'

"Oh, I think you know exactly why I'm here."

"Actually, I don't have a clue," he admitted truthfully. "So perhaps you could be so good as to enlighten me?"

"I've come for Delia Carlyle."

"Who?" *How on earth could Homer have figured out she was here?*

"Don't play games with me. The woman in the FBI flyer I showed you yesterday."

"Oh, yes, of course." Now he'd have to apply his finely honed acting skills. "But I'm still unclear about…you think she's here?"

"Let's go inside."

Russell walked slowly toward the door and took his time entering in front of the sheriff. Bugs or Handsome, or whatever the heck his name, was squirming to be set free. But he held tight for fear the dog's sniffing nose might alert the sheriff to the escape route. Thankfully the woman was not in sight, though he felt a surge of alarm when he saw her backpack lying on the floor. He subtly nudged it under a chair when Homer stepped out of the room.

"I hope you're happy," his tone indignant, after the sheriff had searched everywhere save the den which was where he was headed next, much to Russell's dismay. He didn't wish to explain all the storyboards about Rebekah Winchell and Camp Davis.

"I'll be happy when..." Homer's hand was on the doorknob when the sound of an engine to the side of the house interrupted him. "What the...?

The sheriff barreled through the door and Russell reluctantly followed, his mind churning up a plausible explanation. However, by the time he walked onto the porch, Homer was already charging for the cruiser.

"If it turns out you are any way involved with this, I'll see to it you serve time."

Russell responded with the best guise of innocence he could muster.

"And you can forget our deal."

"That's okay," he said as the sheriff peeled down the lane. "I've struck a much better deal with our little run-away."

Then he remembered the backpack and dashed inside to claim his prize.

# CORDELIA

"FOR A WHILE THE FOOL'S MISCHIEF TASTES SWEET, SWEET AS HONEY. BUT IN THE END IT TURNS BITTER. AND HOW BITTERLY HE SUFFERS!"

BUDDHA

HOW ON EARTH DO YOU *operate this thing?* Alarm was setting in. I searched for the ignition and tried to figure out the gears. After finally managing to start the engine I awkwardly steered the vehicle behind the garage and hit the accelerator until I was hidden by the woods.

*Crap.* In my hasty departure I'd forgotten the backpack which held all the documents needed to get through Customs and into Canada.

When I'd made it deeper into the forest I brought the vehicle to a stop and idled for a few moments to think through my dilemma. I couldn't chance returning for fear the sheriff would still be there, or worse, that he'd found the backpack and had confiscated the papers. I felt inside my jacket to ensure the sacred prize was still secure.

Russell had left me alone only for a moment to retrieve some antiseptic and bandages at which point my first impulse had been to remove Rebekah's diary from the backpack and tuck it into an inside pocket. Why I had chosen it over my identification papers I couldn't say, but there was a silver lining. Now Mr. Payne had a substantial motivation to find me before the sheriff did.

He'd practically salivated when I'd told him of its existence.

But I hadn't shown it to him, only dropping hints about what Rebekah had revealed in her journal.

"You mean Betsy Cooper," he said to remind me he'd already learned quite a bit about the reclusive woman.

But I knew the entire absurd tale wouldn't be discovered in the boxes Mr. Payne had purloined from Rebekah's storage room. It was the diary that held all the elements needed to fulfill the man's ambitions for the sensational story. For now though, it would be to my advantage to secure the journal in a place where it would never be discovered. I had the perfect location in mind, but the risks in getting it there were high.

I hesitated only another brief moment before shifting into gear and continuing on. From Russell I'd learned I was back on the east side of the river, implausible as that was, and that his property was south of the Winchell farm. When I arrived at the meadow where I'd first come across the strange Rebekah, I parked the vehicle behind a copse of trees and set off on foot. It would take much longer to walk, especially in my condition, but I didn't want the sound of the engine to alert Rebekah.

I approached cautiously. The truck wasn't there but the front door of the house had been left wide open. Inside, nothing had changed since I left Monday morning. Even the breakfast dishes were as they'd been left, unwashed in the sink. The only items missing were the boxes from the storage room. I stepped into the spinning room where the blanket Rebekah had been weaving was folded neatly on a chair. I brought the feathery soft spun coverlet to my cheek and took it with me as I walked back outside. The goats and llamas huddled together near the gate of their pen.

"Are you hungry?" I called out softly.

I filled buckets with feed and watched as the animals jockeyed for position to gobble it up. Then I checked the hen house where there was a surplus of uncollected eggs. Before I could begin to consider what had happened to Rebekah I heard the distant sound of a car and ran for the trees behind the house. I wasn't willing to wait and see who the driver might be, especially since the sheriff would have had adequate time to complete his search of Russell's cabin and this might be his next stop.

I was done in when my escape vehicle came into view. On the arduous return trek a plan had formed. I'd return to Russell's cabin and force his hand. If he wanted the diary bad enough, and I was positive he did, then he'd have to make good on his promise. Only when he succeeded in delivering Gabriella would I comply with my end of the bargain. As for getting out of the country, all I'd ask for would be the return of my documents and his car. Then I'd tell him where he could locate the precious chronicle of Betsy Cooper's tragic life.

When I arrived at the ATV, I hopped on to rest a moment before reaching to turn the ignition.

*Please, no.*

The key was gone.

# REBEKAH

"...AND YE SHALL BE TORMENTED WITH FIRE AND BRIMSTONE IN THE PRESENCE OF THE HOLY ANGELS AND IN THE PRESENCE OF THE LAMB. AND THE SMOKE OF THEIR TORMENT GOES UP FOREVER AND EVER..."

REVELATIONS 14:10-11

"I MUST RETURN TO THE HEALING rock," Lucinda said. "Take this time to think about your options."

Rebekah's pleas to join her aunt had gone unheeded and she about went mad waiting in the cottage while her aunt communicated with the spirits for guidance. She tried prayer to calm her frayed nerves, but so great was her fear of God's wrath, she couldn't concentrate.

Her aunt returned looking old and weary. "I should never have given in to your need to hold on to the past. It was a mistake."

Rebekah started to protest, but Lucinda cut her off with a firm decree.

"Go home and remove all the letters, the photos, everything from your past. Bring it all back here so we can destroy it." She handed over the keys to her old Buick. "Take my car. We don't want anyone recognizing your truck.

*Why couldn't Lucinda do this?* Rebekah was fretting over her mission to collect all the memories she could never bring herself to cast away. As she neared the house, the sight of all the animals corralled in the farm yard reminded her she'd neglected her stock.

She walked briskly to the pen and was surprised to see the goats, the llamas and the hog already gathered around their buckets.

"Cord must have come back," she whispered before rushing inside. Everything was completely still with no sign the woman had been there.

"But how could she have?" Rebekah chewed on the notion as she fished the chain with the storage room key from around her neck. But again she found the door open and her distress was compounded by what she discovered.

"Please God, no," she moaned. The boxes she'd been sent to retrieve were gone. What would Aunt Lucinda say if she returned without them? Sinking to the floor, she curled up into a fetal position, not even hearing the door creak open.

# RAMON

"SPEAK LOW IF YOU SPEAK OF LOVE."

WILLIAM SHAKESPEARE, ***MUCH ADO ABOUT NOTHING***

RAMON HAD ANTICIPATED A NUMBER of different reactions when he revealed the location pinpointed by the tracking program on Cord's phone. The one it provoked was unmitigated wrath.

"Damn that lying sack, son-of-a-bitch," Homer Pruitt shouted, slamming his fist down on the desk. Then he'd turned a hard gaze on Ramon. "Do I have to put you in a holding cell or will you play nice and wait here until I bring her back?"

"I've nowhere to go." Ramon offered an exaggerated shrug of the shoulders. "I'm the one who came to you, remember?"

He figured if he didn't argue it would be all the easier to slip away. For five agonizing minutes after the sheriff left to pursue the lead, Ramon waited under the watchful four eyes of Frannie and Olivia before making his break.

"Is there someplace in town where I can get a decent cup of coffee?" he asked, casually stretching his back.

"Becky's Diner," the tall, cool Frannie answered.

"I can brew a pot here," Olivia offered simultaneously.

"It was a long drive and I could use some fresh air. I'll just walk over to the diner." Ramon looked up and down the street from the front window. "Where'd you say it was?"

He watched in the window's reflection as the two women

exchanged looks. It was Frannie who gave the green light. Evidently in the little burg of Murphy, Maine the sheriff's wife trumped the assistant deputy.

"Walk to the corner and go right. One block to Main Street and you'll see it just a bit down to your left."

"How do you ladies take your coffee?" he asked, jotting down the orders as if he meant to return. By the time they realized he was gone, he'd be far enough on his way.

Fortunately, he'd already programmed his phone GPS to track the signal from Cord's cell phone. However, he kept losing the signal and after repeatedly retracing a circuitous route he was beginning to lose heart.

"Where in God's name is this place?"

A moment later Ramon saw an SUV turn out onto the main road about a half mile ahead. He could see the official insignia and the strobe lights atop the cruiser. Luck was with him as the vehicle turned in the opposite direction. But the signal was getting stronger so he tried the unmarked lane where the cruiser had emerged. He drove through a heavily treed area before arriving at a clearing where a rustic cabin set on a small lake came into view. Having no idea what he would be walking into, he reversed his rental car so it would be camouflaged by the woods and made his way to the cabin cautiously on foot.

The first porch step groaned, alerting a canine resident within. Ramon braced himself for a barrage of barks and growls as the sound of clicking claws drew nearer. But when he saw the wiry little dog he could hardly believe it was his own Guapo. *One step closer to finding Cord.*

He opened the screen door and the pooch sprang up into his arms, lathering him with a loving tongue.

"How's my boy?" he whispered, offering pets and soft

soothing words to calm the overly excited dog. "Shhh. Quiet now."

Not having a clue what to expect next, he clutched the dog tightly in his arms and crept through the cabin, hoping the aged pine planks wouldn't announce his presence. Rustling noises drew him to a doorway on the far end of the living room where he watched as a man rummaged through a backpack, pulling out its contents in a haphazard fashion. Ramon sensed a familiarity in the man's silhouette.

"Bloody hell!" The man heaved the bag across the room and only then became alert to the fact he wasn't alone.

The two men stared in complete astonishment.

"Russell?"

"Bloody hell!"

"So you said."

"Rammie Alvarez? Is it really you, or have I gone barmy?"

Ramon smiled and freed the squirming pooch. "It's me, in the flesh."

The two men sized each other up for a moment before Russell strode across the room and picked up Ramon in a painful man hug. "What's it been ole man? Seven years? Eight?"

"Pretty close." Ramon was thankful to be released from the uncomfortable embrace. "The Fergie Affair?"

"Quite right. After that you left me for greener pastures."

"My conscience was starting to get the best of me. I had to start sleeping at night."

"Never mind all that. Must be sleeping now. You look great, mate."

Ramon couldn't shake the ludicrousness of crossing paths with his old boss. But how on earth did Russell get involved with Cord? His bewilderment must have shown, but was being misinterpreted.

"What? I look that bad?" Russell feigned annoyance.

"You look the same, but what are you doing out here in the boondocks of Maine? And how the hell did you come to have my dog?"

"Yours?" Russell scratched his head. "BW didn't mention..."

"You have been in touch with Badger? That son of a gun."

"Maybe a drink will help us sort this all out." Russell grabbed a bottle of scotch and poured two fingers.

"No time. We can unravel all the twists of fate later. What I really need is for you to tell me where Cord is."

"So she's Cord now?"

"Short for Cordelia, but let's not beat around the bush. She was traveling with my dog and since you have Guapo she must be here, too."

"She was." He took a gulp of the scotch.

"Did the sheriff take her? Because I told him to look for her here."

"How's that?" Russell looked perplexed.

"I tracked her cell phone to this location."

"Aha." Russell downed the liquor and pointed over his shoulder. "It's in her bag. And the sheriff did not apprehend your little felon. She fled the scene so to speak."

Ramon took three quick strides to collect the backpack that had been flung against the wall and began rifling through it for clues, visibly troubled when he came up with nothing that might help him locate Cord.

"It's all there, mate. Everything except the one thing I was looking for anyway," he muttered under his breath. "So tell me, what's this woman to you?"

Ramon ducked the impossible question that had been haunting him his entire life.

# HOMER

"AND YET THE MOTIVES OF WOMEN ARE SO INSCRUTABLE."

SHERLOCK HOLMES IN ***THE ADVENTURE OF THE SECOND STAIN***

"THE PAGAN FOX STRIKES AGAIN." Homer grumbled as he drove down the lane. "What I'd like to do to that slime-ball."

He'd pretended not to notice when Russell kicked the backpack under a chair, thinking it best to leave the bait in its trap. He was hedging his bets Delia Carlyle had left it unintentionally in her hasty escape and undoubtedly would be returning for her belongings. But where would she hide until she felt it safe to return? He absently tapped the steering wheel before turning onto Route 79 toward the Winchell farm.

He decided on a last minute detour, turning sharply down the unofficially closed Old County Road. The decision paid off when the lowering sun's rays glanced off an object concealed in a thicket near the edge of a fallow field. He was doubly pleased when he uncovered an abandoned ATV. Homer wouldn't require a forensics report to learn Russell Payne's name was on the list of matches for the tire print taken from the scene earlier.

"I wonder what brought her back here," he mused sarcastically. He proceeded cautiously to the farm house and parked out of sight behind the barn. After sneaking in for a quick check behind the hay stacks – it was still there – he walked around to the front of the house where an unfamiliar car was parked.

"Hello," he called in through the screen door. "Anybody home?"

When there was no answer, he unsnapped his holster and with one hand on the Berretta entered the house. He heard a muffled sound coming from the storage room and crept in that direction while keeping a watchful eye to his surroundings. He pushed at the slightly opened door and found Rebekah Winchell in a sobbing heap on the floor.

"Ms. Winchell?" He kept his voice gentle so as not to startle her.

The woman didn't respond so he left her for a moment to secure the perimeter. When he felt assured there was nobody else in the house, he snapped the holster closed and went to the kitchen faucet for a glass of water. The untidy state of the house was not lost on him.

He knelt down on the floor facing the crumpled form and offered the glass. "Sit up and drink this Rebekah."

When she remained unresponsive he tried another tactic to awaken her from the trance. "Betsy?"

She turned her head sharply and whispered, "It's all gone. Everything is gone. Everyone is gone. It's over. Don't you see?"

"What's gone? What's over?" Homer pried. "Where's your little nephew, Jacob?"

"Jacob is gone. Both the twins." She shook her head then looked at him with wide, red rimmed eyes. "But I couldn't help that. And Gemma, too. She never stopped crying. But then she came back. Auntie said she had. I was a good mommy. But Daddy didn't understand."

Her jumbled thoughts were teeming with resentment. But the anger quickly seeped from her voice and was replaced with a sorrowful sigh. She pulled herself into a sitting position with her back against the wall, hugging her bent legs close to her chest.

She laid her forehead in defeat against the tops of her knees and said, "I didn't mean to hurt Daddy. I truly didn't."

Homer reached over and touched the woman's arm. "I'm sure you didn't."

"Yeah?"

"Everything will be okay, Betsy."

She turned her head slightly and looked intently at Homer. "I know you?"

"Yes."

When recognition registered she rolled her head away and pleaded, "Leave me. Please, leave me."

He went in search of a phone but then remembered there was none. Now he was in a fix. No cell service and he couldn't leave Rebekah alone in such a state. He walked out onto the porch to consider his options and was shocked to see his wife's RAV pulling up to the house.

"Frannie, what's going on?" he asked when she met him half way.

"I'm afraid our Mr. Alvarez flew the coop." She held up her hand as he started to fume. "I take full responsibility. Olivia hadn't wanted to trust him, but I overruled her."

"How did you know to come here?"

Frannie rolled her eyes. "Part of Olivia's plan. She thought it likely he'd follow you to Russell's so she went in that direction and sent me here in case this would be your next stop."

Homer was thinking, but didn't dare say, how impressed he was with his deputy's thought process.

"Who's minding Mr. Rawlins?" he asked.

"Jimmy Kramer stopped by with a report for you and was only too happy to be of service. Oh, and by the way, Olivia asked me to pass on a message. Apparently Wonder Woman has arranged to have Samuel's file delivered by the end of the day."

"I'd say Olivia's more like an older version of Nancy Drew."

Homer took his wife's hands. "But you? Well, you're Emma Peel through and through. Tough, smart, sexy. My fantasy woman as a young boy."

Her sidelong glance held equal measures of pleasure and skepticism.

"But today you're an angel of mercy." He pulled her toward the house. "I need a big favor."

Frannie had been wonderful with Rebekah. She'd convinced the distraught woman to move to the kitchen table for a cup of tea and some toast. She promised to stay until Homer returned, even though he couldn't be certain when that would be. As he was leaving, Olivia's cruiser came into sight and he motioned for her to stop at a distance from the house. No need to give either woman inside any more reason for suspicion.

"Frannie told me about your quick thinking. Good work."

Liv pulled a face. "Don't be too quick with the praise. Nobody was at Russell's by the time I arrived."

"Did you go inside?"

"The cabin was locked, and without a warrant..." she let the thought drift."

Homer rubbed his chin. "Why don't you head back to town and make sure that file arrives?"

"What are you going to do?"

"Not sure yet, but I'm hoping an idea will come to me soon." He winked at his assistant and rapped the fender of her car as a signal for her to take off.

That idea came sooner than Homer could have hoped. As he rounded the barn to return to the cruiser, he spied a flash of red darting into the woods at the far edge of the hay field. He hopped into the SUV and drove across the field, turning the car onto a deserted trail and driving as far as he could until the vegetation became too thick for the vehicle. He'd have to continue the pursuit on foot, but it didn't take long before he caught another glimpse of the limping form weaving through fallen trees and brush. The woman had to be in pretty bad shape after being tossed down a well. He was within ten yards when she sensed his advancing presence and looked over her shoulder. She tried to speed her pace but in doing so her feet became tangled in a root and down she went.

Homer pulled out his badge and reached down to give the woman a hand up. "I'm Sheriff Pruitt. And you, I presume, are Delia Carlyle."

# CORDELIA

"IF THE TRAVELER CANNOT FIND MASTER OR FRIEND TO GO WITH HIM, LET HIM TRAVEL ALONE RATHER THAN WITH A FOOL FOR COMPANY."

BUDDHA

THIS TIME THERE WAS NO question the man helping me to my feet was holding an authentic law enforcement ID. I recognized him from the quick glimpse out the window when he stopped at Rebekah's a few days earlier.

"Yes, I'm Cordelia Carlyle." I brushed myself off, feeling a deep sense of defeat.

"I'm sure I don't have to tell you how much trouble you're in."

"Do what you want with me, but my little girl has been taken and..."

"First, you've got some explaining to do, sister." He took a firm grip of my arm and escorted me back down the overgrown path. This man meant business.

"Please listen to me. A man name Samuel Rawlins has kidnapped my daughter."

"Mr. Rawlins has been arrested."

I nearly stumbled at this encouraging news but the sheriff was quick to keep me upright.

"Have you found Gabriella?" *Please, please, please say yes.*

"Not yet. We were lucky to find you before..." The thought

hung suspended. "Anyhow, it's *Timothy* Rawlins you can thank for saving your life."

"Yes, if Timothy hadn't opened up that well." I didn't want to think about how my life would have ended. "But what about my daughter? Is anyone looking for her?"

"I'm the one asking the questions here. The more you cooperate, the sooner we can narrow our search."

So they *were* looking for her.

The sheriff secured me into the passenger seat of the cruiser and then reversed out of the woods and drove across the field toward Rebekah's barn. I couldn't begin to guess why and wasn't prepared to face the woman after deceiving her.

"What make and model car do you drive, Ms. Carlyle?" he asked.

"A Honda CRV," I answered absently. I was so thirsty. "Can I have a drink of water?"

"In there." He pointed toward a compartment in the passenger door. "You were driving a CRV when you had your accident last week?"

This Sheriff Pruitt knew a lot about me. Perhaps Rebekah had finally blown the whistle. "Oh, no. That was a Toyota Corolla."

"Beige? Registered in the name of Ramon Alvarez?"

I nodded.

He got out of the car and came round to open the door. "I need you to look at something."

He pulled open the barn door and led me to the back where the hay was stored and began removing bales from the stack, perspiring from the effort. Before long he had exposed the front fender of the car that was supposed to be at the mechanic's shop awaiting a part.

"Is this it?" he asked, wiping his brow.

"It is. But I don't understand."

"Well, that makes two of us."

I looked at him and then back at the car, completely baffled. *How did it get back here? Why was it hidden? And why had Rebekah lied about the part.*

"How did you come to be in possession of the car?" He led me back to the police car.

"It's mine. I mean I paid for it. It was only registered in Ramon's name. He's a friend."

"How did you end up here?"

"I was driving to Canada and became lost when a fog rolled in. After I hit a deer with my car I came across Rebekah and she towed it to town to have it repaired. She pretty much insisted we stay with her while we waited." It was an extremely edited down version. "She said a part had to be specially ordered and then the repair was delayed further because the owner of the shop became ill. I can't imagine how it ended up back in her barn."

The sheriff's incredulous expression was proof enough he wasn't buying my story.

"Why would she lie to you?" he asked.

"I don't know. Rebekah was a very strange woman. At first, she was quite aggravated to have to deal with us. I was under the impression she wanted us on our way quickly. But then..." *How could I explain the change that came over her?* And why bother? If he wasn't accepting what I was telling him about the car, he'd never believe all the rest, especially about Rebekah's alter ego, Betsy Cooper. I'd only be making it worse if it seemed I was fabricating a tall tale.

"Was Ms. Winchell holding you against your will?" The sheriff started the car and drove back across the field, circumventing Rebekah's house.

"Evidently. She hid the car didn't she?"

The sheriff dropped that line of questioning. "How do you know Russell Payne?"

"The British guy? I don't know him. I just wandered into his path. I'd never seen the man before today."

"It was his ATV you were driving?"

"Yes. But I don't see how any of these questions will help Gabriella."

"All right. When and where did you last see your daughter?"

"Monday morning at the Rawlins' house." How I wished I could turn back time.

"How did you get there?"

"On foot. I crossed the river."

The sheriff sent me another skeptical look. "What were you doing there?"

"Using the telephone."

"Why?"

"Because I needed to make a call and Rebekah doesn't have a phone and there's no cell service out here."

"Who were you calling?"

"A taxi company."

"Why?"

"I needed to get away from here. I didn't trust Rebekah. She'd been acting odd."

"In what way?"

The questioning was becoming tedious and my head was aching again. "Can we please get back to my daughter?"

"We will. But I'd like to know how you could think someone as dangerous as Samuel Rawlins would be more trustworthy than old Ms. Winchell?"

He was misunderstanding. I took in a deep breath and tried to focus on selecting the right words to explain.

"I couldn't imagine I'd be coming face to face with the devil, but when Samuel opened the door to his house?" I shook my head to dislodge the image. "I just know he's responsible for taking my baby."

"He's a pretty nasty character," the sheriff agreed. "Why didn't you run?"

"I heard the pastor's car pull up the driveway. I felt safe then."

They had reached the main road, but the sheriff put the car in park and turned to address his next question directly. "You're saying you saw Pastor Josh there?"

"I didn't actually *see* him. But Rebekah told me he arrived every Monday morning to deliver food. That's why I planned to show up at that time."

He nodded for me to continue.

"So I put Gabriella down just for a second while I was using the phone. And that's the last time I saw her." I could no longer hold back the tears. "It was a mistake. I admit it, but you've got to help me."

"You don't remember how you came to be in the bottom of a well?" We were driving again.

"I remember nothing after dialing the phone." I wiped my wet face with the cuffs of my jacket. "What has Samuel said? Surely you've questioned him."

"He denies having anything to do with kidnapping your child. He says that whoever drove up the driveway took you and your daughter."

"The minister?"

"Pastor Josh wasn't there Monday morning. He had a meeting and couldn't deliver the meals until later in the day."

I was becoming nauseous. "Who was it then?"

"Samuel said he didn't recognize the car and didn't wait around to see who it was."

I held my head in my hands. "How could you believe an animal like Samuel Rawlins?"

"I'm reserving judgment until after his polygraph test. And let me remind you of your own status. You're a fugitive who kidnapped your child and were about to flee the country. For all I know you could have staged this."

I gasped. "And then I had the person knock me out and throw me down a hole in the ground? What a great plan."

"It could have backfired."

"Look. I had no phone, no computer, no way of communicating with anyone. How could I arrange anything?"

"You appear to be fairly resourceful. By the way, why did you disguise your child to look like a boy, Ms. Carlyle?"

"Rebekah told me about the missing persons alerts and flyers in town. We didn't want anyone to recognize her."

"You must have done something pretty bad to let a total stranger take over the health and well being of your child. Especially someone you claim to have distrusted."

Was he purposely twisting my words or was this what my predicament looked like to an objective observer?

"Rebekah was very caring toward my daughter. I didn't become wary of her until I learned some information about her past. That's when I knew we had to escape. And I didn't do anything bad. Yes, I admit I was running away from something. Someone. But it was to protect myself and my daughter."

"I guess that didn't work out so well for you, did it?" the sheriff scoffed.

"I don't mean to be disrespectful, but how is this line of questioning at all constructive?"

"I'm still trying to eliminate you as a suspect in the disappearance and possible harming of your daughter."

For a second I thought my heart would burst from my ribcage. I laid my hand against my chest to calm the tremors within.

"I – would – never harm my daughter." I turned to face my captor. "What can I do to convince you?"

"You can start telling me the truth."

"I *am* telling you the truth." It was looking as if my only chance to save myself was to reveal everything. "Let me explain why I ran away. Then maybe you'll understand I could never hurt Gabriella. My husband was not a nice man and not only was he trying to take my baby but he was also plotting to do away with me."

"He was going to kill you?" he asked in a patronizing tone.

"Not by his own hand. Look, I have proof in the trunk of the Corolla. If you turn around and go back, I can show you."

"That won't be necessary. Your husband is not a factor."

I was frustrated by the sheriff's dismissive attitude. "How can you say that?"

"I can say it, Ms. Carlyle, because he's dead."

# RUSSELL

"ABSOLUTE TRUTH IS A VERY RARE AND DANGEROUS COMMODITY IN THE CONTEXT OF PROFESSIONAL JOURNALISM."

HUNTER THOMPSON

"LOOK, MATE, I'M AN OPEN book," Russell said before knocking back another glass of Dutch courage. "You need only ask."

"Where is she?" Ramon asked.

"I was afraid that would be your question, as it's the one I cannot answer. I honestly don't know. I can only offer you proof that she was here." He indicated the backpack.

"How did she end up at your place?"

"I was out blowing off steam on my Suzuki Quad when I happened upon her in the woods. She was not in the best of shape I might add."

Russell didn't miss the tensing of Ramon's jaw at this news. "Again, I must ask, why are you pursuing this woman?"

"She's an old friend."

"I see. Then you are probably aware that your *old friend* is in a bit of a jam."

"Yes, I know. What did you talk about? Did she share anything with you?"

Russell gave Ramon a brief synopsis of what he'd pieced together from his conversations with Homer yesterday and with Ms. Carlyle just a short while ago. But he didn't mention anything about the symbiotic arrangement he'd struck with the woman. After all, a man's got to eat. And he still wasn't clear on his old colleague's role in this unfolding drama.

"How did she leave?" Ramon asked.

"When the sheriff arrived she ran out the back door and stole my all terrain vehicle." He'd already decided he'd deny any accusations to the contrary. It would be his word against hers.

"Do you have any idea where she might have gone?"

Russell mulled the question for a moment. "I can think of two possibilities."

"Well, what are you waiting for?" Ramon was already walking towards the door. "Let's go."

# REBEKAH

"BEHOLD, CHILDREN ARE A HERITAGE FROM THE LORD, THE FRUIT OF THE WOMB IS A REWARD."

PSALMS 127:3

"WHAT DID YOU SAY YOUR name was again?" Rebekah squinted at the unfamiliar woman who was sitting across from her at the old claw-footed oak table she'd inherited with the house.

"Frannie, or just Fran. How about you? What would you like me to call you?"

*Now there's a question.* She dunked her tea bag in the hot steaming mug as she contemplated her answer.

"Maybe you could call me Betsy."

"Is that your given name?"

She nodded. "Elizabeth Cooper. Betsy for short. " She hadn't said the name or even thought it for so many years. *Betsy Cooper.*

"I'm pleased to meet you, Betsy."

The two women sat in silence for a few moments. But it wasn't uncomfortable. It was nice. Companionable but not threatening. Maybe it was the pill Fran had given her. She'd promised it would make her feel better. And she did.

"Do you have any children, Fran?"

"I have a daughter. Sophia."

"Where is she?"

"I don't know." The woman closed her eyes before saying, "She's lost to me."

Betsy could see a reflection of her own pain etched in the woman's features.

"I'm sorry."

Fran opened her eyes and replied with a small sad smile.

"I know what it's like to lose a child." She knew what it was like to lose everyone.

"Would you like to talk about it?"

Betsy stared at her image in the cup of hot liquid, deciding there was little harm in telling. "All my babies died. First Gemma, then my twin boys. The boys were only infants. But Gemma? She was my special girl."

"I'm sure she was." Fran hesitated a moment before asking, "How did she die?"

"It shouldn't have happened. If Daddy hadn't taken Gemma away and given her to another family she wouldn't have gotten sick. He said I was a bad mother, but it's not true. I only made one mistake."

She brushed away a lone tear and Fran reached across the table. "Is it too painful?"

"I had a breakdown. It took me a long time to get better, but I did. And then I came back here and did the Lord's work. And he rewarded me for my goodness and brought her back to me." She took a large gulp of tea and smiled beatifically.

"I'm not sure I understand what you mean."

"I have a picture of her. Do you want to see it?" She reached into her pocket and withdrew a piece of paper. She unfolded it on the table and caressed it lovingly. A peculiar giggle slipped off her lips. "Her name isn't really Amber."

Fran stared first at the photograph and then at her. Betsy didn't like the look in the woman's eyes. Maybe it had been a mistake to tell her about Gemma.

# REBEKAH

"HE GIVES THE BARREN WOMAN A HOME, MAKING HER THE JOYOUS MOTHER OF CHILDREN. PRAISE THE LORD!"

PSALM 113: 9

"YOU CAN'T IMAGINE HOW MUCH I appreciate this, Fran." She hadn't even had to ask. The nice woman who made her tea had offered to take her to see Gemma.

"I understand how hard it is to be separated from a child. I'd want to be with my daughter if I could. You'll have to direct me, though, because I've never been out to Camp Davis."

"It's very peaceful. You'll like it." She pointed. "Turn here and drive to the end of the road."

"It's a lovely property. How long has your aunt lived out here?"

"Ever since I can remember." Except for those years when they both were sent away. But she didn't see the point in going into all that with a stranger.

"I'd think it would get lonely."

"Aunt Lucinda is never truly alone. She's a medium." This admission came out a guilty whisper.

"A medium?" Fran's forehead crinkled.

"She communicates with those who have passed over to the other side."

"Like conducting séances?"

"Sometimes. I used to study with her until Daddy put a stop to it." They'd arrived at the cottage. "Just park here."

When they entered the house there was a note left on the kitchen table from Aunt Lucinda which read: I took the child to the healing stone. Wait for me here.

She crumpled up the note and picked up a plate of cookies. "Snickerdoodle?"

"Maybe later." There was concern in Fran's voice when she asked, "Is something wrong with the...with Gemma?"

"Her fever's back and we can't get her to settle down. But the healing stone will calm her cries." She walked to the window and pushed the curtain aside. "Here they come now."

Aunt Lucinda hadn't been able to hide her surprise nor her displeasure to see a stranger sitting at her kitchen table.

"This nice lady is Fran. She drove me back here so I could see Gemma.

"Mama," the little girl shrieked.

"Let me take her." She reached for the wailing child. "What a fussy little girl you are."

Lucinda offered a curt hello then pulled Rebekah into the living room to ask in a whispered tone, "Where are the boxes?"

"I know how important it was to bring them to you, but I couldn't." She was trying to keep her voice down, but it was difficult with the baby fussing.

Lucinda pursed her lips and gazed contemplatively out the window. Then she walked back into the kitchen and said to the visitor, "I see that you drove my niece out here in my car. I have an errand to run. Can I give you a ride someplace? To your car maybe?"

Fran directed her gaze at the troubled woman who was trying desperately to quiet the screaming child. "Maybe I should stay here and help Betsy with Gemma until you get back."

"Betsy?" A strange look darkened Lucinda's features. She glanced at her niece and then studied Fran before sighing resignedly. "That would be very kind. Thank you."

"Where are you going?" Betsy followed her aunt outside, still holding the whimpering baby in her arms.

Lucinda caressed her face and said, "I have something to take care of. But it's nothing for you to worry over. Promise me you'll stay here until I get back?"

Her aunt's expression was achingly familiar. She'd seen it before. Long ago when she still used traps for hunting, she'd come across a rabbit that had just been ensnared. For months afterward she'd been haunted by the look of terror in the eyes of the poor captured creature. Right now she felt as if she was looking into those same frightened eyes.

"Auntie, tell me what's wrong?"

"You should take the little one inside. There's a chill in the air. And don't forget you have company. Why don't you offer your friend a cup of coffee?"

Her aunt hugged her quickly and left. But Betsy remained outside, watching until she could no longer see the taillights. She didn't know how long she stood there before Fran came to her side and guided her back into the kitchen.

"I don't know what's wrong with her." The child was becoming even more agitated.

"Maybe she's hungry," the woman suggested. "Where's her food?"

"Food? Oh! I think there's some yogurt. She likes yogurt."

"Why don't I take her for a moment while you fix her something to eat?" Gemma went readily into the stranger's arms but the crying didn't stop. "Hush now, honey pie."

While Betsy was slicing some bananas on top of the yogurt, Fran walked to the old fashioned rotary phone and lifted the receiver.

"I'm just going to call my husband and tell him I'll be late." The call was answered after one ring. "Is Homer there? Hello?" She started as she felt someone's breath on her neck.

Betsy held her finger on the disconnect button. "You mustn't tell the sheriff about Gemma."

# RAMON

"LOVE LOOKS NOT WITH THE EYES, BUT WITH THE MIND, AND THEREFORE IS WINGED CUPID PAINTED BLIND."

WILLIAM SHAKESPEARE, ***A MIDSUMMER NIGHT'S DREAM***

"IF ONLY I HAD AS much energy." Russell remarked with complete admiration as Guapo bounced from one side to the other in the back of the car, sticking his head out the windows as dogs are want to do.

"Where do I turn?" Ramon was driving the rental car because Russell, fond as he was becoming of the little dog, wouldn't let him near his Aston Martin.

"We'll cross the Argyle at River Road." Russell made a clucking sound. "Mainers are so obvious when naming their roads. It's about a mile up on the left."

"Unlike in England where every other lane has Ivy or Rose in its name?"

Russell responded with a pompous wobble of his head.

"So tell me about this guy Timothy," said Ramon.

"He's a little, how should I say, off? But fairly harmless."

"His brother is the bad seed?"

"Samuel Rawlins is the worst of the worst. And trust me, I know."

"Do you think he's capable of kidnapping a child?" Ramon asked.

"Capable? Without doubt. Besides which, your girlfriend is certain he took her and he's the sheriff's prime suspect."

"Prime? There are others?"

Russell frowned but didn't answer.

"Are you holding out on me?"

"Here's your turn."

Ramon steered the car over the rickety old bridge. "So tell me your theories?"

Russell tapped his steepled fingers together before he asked, "How well do you *really* know this bird?"

Ramon considered for a moment what he did know about Cord and her life and came up wanting. But his natural sense told him she was an authentically good person, and his instincts were usually pretty sharp. "I have known her since I was thirteen years old."

"That is a long time." Russell lifted his hands in a gesture of capitulation. "So, there you have it."

"She would not hurt her child," he insisted.

"Who are you trying to convince, mate?" Then Russell pointed to the left. "That's your road."

"You call this a road?" Ramon took in the squalor as he drove up to the house. "I cannot believe people actually live here."

"Welcome to the Appalachia of the North." Russell got out of the car while Ramon leashed the now frantic dog.

"Calm down, buddy."

They rounded the side of the house to find a large young man sitting on the porch swing, inspecting some creature captured in a Ball canning jar. He held it up to them and said, "The River Jewelwing. Odonata or more commonly, damselfly. See the white wing tips?"

"What does it mean?" Russell leaned in to inspect.

"It's a female. You can always spot the females in nature."

"So true, lad, so true."

"Hey boy!" Timothy finally spied Guapo and Ramon released the leash. The dog leaped up onto the young man's lap and began licking his face. "Are you the guy Sheriff Pruitt said was taking good care of him?"

Russell nodded. "But this is Ramon and he's the dog's rightful owner."

"No he's not." Timothy didn't look up from his attentions to the pet.

"Pardon?" Russell asked.

"He belongs to the blonde lady. She left him here but the sheriff took him away."

"That's right." Ramon sat gingerly on a loose porch step hoping to be casual and put the peculiar man at ease. "And she is the reason we are here. She is lost and we are trying to find her. Have you seen her?"

"Not since the well." Timothy refused to make eye contact and continued to administer pets to Guapo.

"The well?" Ramon asked, but the only response was a firm nod. "When was that?"

"Yesterday."

"Was she okay?"

"She was hurt. She couldn't stand very well but she spoke to me. It was dry though."

"What was dry?"

"The well." Timothy rolled his eyes scornfully.

"Crikey." Russell whistled. "Are you telling us she really was down in a well when you saw her?"

"Uh huh. She told me my brother put her there. But she got out before I could bring the rope. Someone else found her first."

"Some open book," Ramon mumbled as Russell's face turned a deep shade of red. Then he handed his card to Timothy and said, "If you see her again show her this. Or call me if you think of anything that might help us find her."

Timothy stared at the card. "She won't be coming back here,

Mr. Alvarez. She don't know Samuel's back in jail." Then his face brightened with the most pleasing smile.

"Well, that wasn't very enlightening," Russell was picking dog hair from his sharply creased trousers.

"No?" Ramon shot his passenger an accusing look. "I felt it was a rather revealing conversation."

"Now hold on," Russell managed an indignant tone. "You knew she'd been at my house. And I did not rescue her from some abandoned well. Like I told you, our paths fortuitously crossed in the woods."

Ramon's grip on the steering wheel tightened so that his knuckles turned white.

"Relax, mate. You'll have a coronary if you keep this us."

"You said there were two possibilities. Where do we go next?"

"Head back toward my place. The Winchell farm is a few miles beyond."

They drove in silence until Russell said, "There's something you're not telling me about this whole affair. I mean, I know it's crucial to rescue your friend and her little girl, but what else?"

Ramon looked out the rear and side view mirrors as if he was concerned about being followed. It was a hazard of his occupation, always on the alert for the competition. Being first on the scene usually equated with job security.

"I am surprised you do not already know. Are you not the *Pagan Fox*?"

"Look, I just learned about your little friend yesterday and I've been extremely busy on some other projects so I didn't take the time to do any research. However, that being said, I can Google her now." Russell pulled out his iPhone.

"Put it away." He felt as if he was betraying her, even though he knew full well that one touch of the Google screen would bring up the headline. "Cord's husband was murdered."

He could feel Russell's penetrating gaze.

"Dare I ask when this occurred?"

"Last week. The day she left him."

"That's not good."

"No, it is not good at all."

Russell turned in the car seat to face him. "So my friend, tell me, did she do the deed?"

Ramon was about to answer, but when they reached the other side of a hill they could see huge flames dancing above the tree line.

"Bloody hell!" Russell shouted. "That's the Winchell place."

# PART FIVE

## THE FOOL'S TRUTH

# HOMER

"ANY TRUTH IS BETTER THAN INDEFINITE DOUBT."

SHERLOCK HOLMES IN ***THE YELLOW FACE***

"No. No. You're wrong. Aiden can't be dead." The Carlyle woman's voice was deep and hollow, her head moving slowly from side to side. "It's not possible."

Homer was trying to judge the sincerity of the reaction, but with the winding roads it was a challenge to keep his eyes trained on his captive. "There's a copy of the death certificate on my desk. We'll be at the station soon enough and you can see for yourself."

The woman hugged her knees to her chest and leaned her head against the passenger window.

"When was the last time you saw your husband alive?"

"The day before I left." Her voice was quiet, vague, as if she was speaking to herself.

He barked his next question with the intent of reviving her. "Where was this, Ms. Carlyle?"

She sat up straight, but still spoke softly. "I'd just finished work and was walking to my car. I passed a little bistro on Wisconsin Avenue and there he was, sitting at a window table sipping martinis...with her. Aiden had told me he was leaving on a business trip early the next morning. I supposed he was having a send-off with his mistress. They both lifted their glasses to me and started laughing. Can you imagine?"

She rubbed her temples and laughed, but it was a vacant, humorless sound. Homer was about to ask another question but she continued her hazy narrative.

"My husband has a charismatic personality. But underneath the veneer of charm is a cruel and calculating man. He's the quintessential Venus fly-trap; superb in the art of seduction with a keen sense of targeting his victims. But once he possesses the unsuspecting prey, when they're comfortable and content? That's when he strikes without warning and destroys them to satisfy his own selfish means."

"I can see why you despised him." He'd hoped to inflame her vitriol; to provoke a rage that would lead to a confession. But the tactic had the opposite effect.

She responded meekly. "Aiden had the power and the will to hurt me. Fear, not hatred, was my motivation for leaving."

Homer sensed the woman's gaze and when he glanced over, he found himself looking into the eyes of a conquered soul.

"How? How did he die?"

"Ms. Carlyle." He paused for effect. "Your husband was murdered."

She stared down at her open palms, and in nearly a whisper, "When did this happen?"

"His body wasn't discovered for several days, but the coroner estimates the time of death to be early morning on the last day you were seen in the D.C. area. There's a video of you and your daughter leaving a First Bank branch in Richmond at 9:30 that morning carrying a rather large duffle bag."

He'd let her chew on those details for a while. He picked up his cell phone and checked for service then punched in speed dial for the office.

"I'm on my way in, Liv, and I'm not alone. - Yep. - Might as well get the Interview Room ready. And I need you to call the secretary over at Union Church. See if you can verify Pastor

Josh's meeting Monday morning. And that he attended the meeting. Thanks. Should be there shortly."

He'd made a mistake taking for granted Pastor Josh had been telling the truth about his alibi.

Homer glanced over at his passenger. Her presence in the car was merely physical. He could only guess where her mind had taken her, but he'd give the questioning a rest until she was settled in the interrogation room. He'd send Olivia in first with her soft glove style.

The phone was ringing when Homer escorted his prisoner into the station. Olivia came running from her office.

"Russell Payne's on line one. He's a bit frantic. Something about a fire."

"Then why not call the fire department," he grumbled. "Ms. Carlyle, this is Deputy Olivia Bishop. She's going to take care of you, get you some coffee, whatever you need."

The woman tilted her pathetic face and said, "I need you to find my baby. I'm begging you."

He took one look at his tender-hearted assistant and changed his mind. "Put her in Cell B."

"What?" Olivia was horrified. Homer had hired her because she was smart, efficient and believed in fair and quick justice. But he soon learned she was a compassionate soul and not quite as tough as she made herself out.

"You heard me," he said as he lifted the receiver. "Pruitt. What? Rusty, stop. Listen to me. You've got to turn around and get back to that farm *right now*. Frannie's in the house."

Homer slammed down the phone.

"Call the fire squad, Liv! Send them out to the Winchell farm." He issued the order and sprinted out the door.

# CORDELIA

"IT IS A MAN'S OWN MIND, NOT HIS ENEMY OR FOE, THAT LURES HIM TO EVIL WAYS."

BUDDHA

"WELL, LOOKY HERE. I GOT myself a new neighbor. And she's a purdy one, too."

I turned away in disgust as the prisoner in the cell across from where I was being led licked his lips in a vulgar manner.

"Leave her alone," the assistant deputy warned.

"Yes, ma'am." The man offered a ridiculous salute.

"Ignore him. I'll be back in a minute with some water and a snack."

"And an aspirin?"

"Sure thing." After Deputy Bishop closed and locked the outer door, my fellow inmate forced his face as far as it could go through the bars, which distorted his already sinister features.

"So we're getting special treatment?"

I turned my back to the man and closed my eyes, trying to clear the fog. Gabriella missing. Aiden murdered. And had she heard the sheriff correctly? A fire at Rebekah's farm? Maybe it was all a mistake.

"Hey, 'member me?"

"Please," I hissed. "I need to think."

"Think about what? Cor-deel-ya."

"How do you know my name?" I whipped around to face

my tormenter. He'd removed his face from the bars and finally I recognized the evil being who left me to die at the bottom of a well. I'd been so preoccupied with Aiden's death I'd forgotten Samuel had been arrested. "Samuel Rawlins."

"The one and only. At least you can hope." He let out a raucous whoop and then started hacking.

I grabbed the bars of my cell and pleaded desperately. "Where's Gabriella? What did you do with my little girl? Please tell me. Please."

"Please. Please." He repeated in a high-pitched, mocking tone.

"If you tell me where she is, I'll help you get out of here." It was a lie born of desperation.

This provoked another fit of riotous laughter. "What are you gonna do? Break us outta here with your super powers?"

"I can either lie or tell the truth when I'm on the witness stand at your trial."

"What trial?" The man was taking me seriously now. "There's no trial for a parole violation."

"But there will be for the abduction of my daughter. If anything happens to her it will be even worse. Solitary confinement for the rest of your days."

Samuel was enraged. "I'm tellin' you what I told everybody else. ***I dinn't take her***. My lie-detector test will prove it."

"You'd better check with your attorney. I'm an eye witness and when I tell the judge and jury what you did to me, nothing will save you."

"Bull shit," he spit out the words.

I shrugged as if I couldn't care less. "Karma."

"What?"

"You've never heard of Karma? What goes around comes around? But hey, since you're not telling the truth why should I?"

Samuel picked up a bowl from his dinner and slammed it against the wall. After a couple minutes of brooding he acquiesced.

"All right. I'll give you somethin'." He looked sideways down the hallway. "I told the sheriff I didn't know the make or model of the car that drove up on Monday. But I saw it. I saw it clear as I see you."

I waited him out.

"It was a truck. A green fuckin' Chevy truck."

I tried to absorb everything his words implied. "You're sure?"

"Fuck yeah. I'm sure."

"Olivia! Deputy Bishop!" I began banging on the bars.

# HOMER

"WHAT WAS THE FAIR LADY'S GAME? WHAT DID SHE REALLY WANT?"

SHERLOCK HOLMES IN ***THE RETURN OF SHERLOCK HOLMES***

HOMER WAS TEMPTED TO IGNORE the incoming call from Olivia but since he would soon be out of touch he picked up. "Yeah?"

"Thank God I reached you."

"I'm just about to round Linden's curve. Talk fast."

"Two things. First, Ms. Carlyle is practically hysterical. Evidently, Samuel told her he lied to you about what happened out there Monday and now she has this crazy idea in her head that Rebekah Winchell took her little girl. She keeps shouting 'Tell the sheriff it was a truck. A green Chevy'. Do you know what she's talking about?"

"Not a clue." Homer had already been out to Rebekah's and he knew it to be a false accusation. "Okay, what's the second thing?"

"A call just came in but there was a child screaming near the phone and I could barely hear what the woman was saying. She asked for you but then the call disconnected."

His first thought was that it might be Sophia calling from some shelter. His second thought, "The Martelli girl?"

"It was coming from..."

"You're breaking up. Liv? Damn it!"

# RAMON

"LOVE IS BEGUN BY TIME, AND QUALIFIES THE SPARK AND FIRE OF IT."

WILLIAM SHAKESPEARE, ***HAMLET***

When Russell mentioned something about the 'Winchell place' being the location of the fire, Ramon hadn't made the connection.

"Do you know them?"

"Know them? That's where your little jam tart's been hiding out," the Brit exclaimed.

"What?" He was stunned for a moment. "Is that where you were taking me? Where you think Cord might be now?"

"That's what I'm saying."

"God, no." He hit the gas pedal and the car lurched and nearly spun off the winding road causing Russell to bang his head and propelling Guapo from the back to the front of the car. "Sorry boy."

"Yes, of course, by all means worry about the dog." Russell was rubbing a bump that was forming on his forehead. "Let's get there in one piece, shall we? You won't be of much help if you mangle this piece of metal into a tree."

Then Ramon heard him mutter out the window, "You'll never convince me you're not shagging this bird."

He'd let it go. Right now he was desperate to make sure Cord was not in danger. When they neared the house he saw an old woman, wrapped in a full-length cape, standing beside the animal pen with her arms held upward and her eyes closed. Russell and Guapo were right behind him as he ran toward her.

"Is anyone in there?" Ramon shouted, startling the woman out of her meditative spell.

After a moment of confused hesitation she shook her head.

"Do what you can to stop this fire," Russell pointed to the house which had just begun to burn whereas the barn and some out buildings were already fully aflame. "I'm going to go get help."

Ramon pulled out his cell phone.

"No service," Russell yelled over his shoulder, sprinting to the car.

Ramon wasn't about to rely on the strange woman's assurances so he threw open the front door and ran inside, the dog close on his heels. The fire was confined to the kitchen, but it was quickly nearing the center staircase. He bound up the steps three at a time and thoroughly checked the rooms and closets. While in one of the bedrooms, Guapo started to whine.

"They're not here, buddy."

He scooped up the dog and returned to search the main floor as best he could with the smoke thickening. He exited the burning house coughing but feeling assured neither Cord or Gabriella had been left inside.

Once outside, the dog squirmed free of his grasp and scurried to the back of the house.

"Come Guapo," he called, but to no avail. Ramon jogged in pursuit and found the pooch sniffing around the stone foundation of a small shed-like structure that had not yet caught fire. "Now is no time to be running off."

But as he bent down to grab the dog's collar he noticed a string of blue yarn dangling between two large stones at the base of the building. When he pulled at the top stone it easily came free allowing him to quickly grab the folds of woven material.

"So that's why you were so upset. Is this your little friend's blanket? " He stuffed it into his jacket without further examination or even considering why it was there and raced back to the farmyard where the woman had resumed her stance of supplication, eyes closed and lips moving ever so subtly. He decided to search the barn, but when he grabbed the metal door handle a searing pain drove him back.

"Damn it!" Whether it was from the shock of the burn, anger or sheer frustration, he began to kick at the door. If Cord was in there, he had to at least try to get her out.

"CORD!" He was barely aware of Guapo's barking. Finally, he managed enough thrust to break the door free. But the energy produced by the escaping wall of heat was so forceful it knocked him to the ground. He shielded his face with his hands and tried to get up but stumbled. He felt his body being dragged backwards and when he was able to open his eyes it was to watch the roof of the barn collapse, causing the entire building to topple onto its side in the spot where he'd been lying just seconds before.

"You are one bloody idiot." Russell was panting from the exertion. "If you want to commit suicide go ahead, but you nearly got man's best friend killed in the process."

"Where is Guapo?" he asked before he saw the poor little dog licking determinedly at his paws. "Hey, come here buddy."

Ramon examined the dog. Some of his fur was singed and the pads of his paws were irritated, but otherwise he was unharmed.

"This might help." Russell brought a bucket of water filled from the pump and squatted down to inspect. "That hand needs some attention. You've got some burns on your face as well. Minor stuff. I don't think there will be scars to mar that pretty Puerto Rican mug of yours."

He took the proffered handkerchief and dipped it into the water and dabbed at Guapo's feet.

"Who do you think you are? The Human Torch?"

"There's more than one car here and nobody was in the house. " Ramon started coughing.

"So you tried to be a superhero?" Russell scoffed. "I thought you had better sense."

"What if they're in there?" He was trying to tamp down the panic that was rising.

Russell looked at the burning rubble and shook his head. Then he quickly paced over to the older woman and began to engage her in an intent discussion. A few moments later he was back. "That woman is Lucinda Cooper. She's the aunt of the woman who lived here and she admits to starting the fire."

"Incredible. But why?"

"Oh, it's safe to say she had her reasons. But she claims there were no people in any of these buildings before she started the fire."

"And you believe her?"

"Yes. Because she was looking for crucial evidence of a sensitive matter which she wanted to destroy. And hence" -Russell waved his arms- "this spectacular destruction. But her intent was never to harm anyone. She even freed all the animals and led them away first."

"What do you know? There are compassionate arsonists in this world after all."

"Sarcasm won't help us find your friend," Russell reprimanded.

"Why do I have the feeling you've learned more about what's behind this fire than you're sharing?"

"Probably because that would be a correct assumption. But more about that later. Right now I have some loose ends to tie up with *my new best friend* before the sheriff arrives."

"Anything to do with Cord and Gabriella?"

"Not sure yet." Russell hedged. "But it's best you aren't found loitering at the scene of the crime, so to speak. Go back to my cabin and take care of those burns and I'll be right behind you."

Ramon was not pleased to lose control of the search and none too eager to let Russell out of his sight, even if he was right.

"If I don't hear from you, I make a return visit to the sheriff and tell him all about *your new best friend*."

"Relax mate, I won't let you down. But seriously, get a move on. Those sirens aren't too far off."

"Either find Cord or come up with a damn good strategy to do so." He picked up Guapo and walked swiftly toward the car yelling over his shoulder, "You have one hour."

"The *Pagan Fox* always has a card up his sleeve."

Ramon just hoped that card wasn't the Joker.

# HOMER

"I HAVE A THEORY THAT THE INDIVIDUAL REPRESENTS IN HIS DEVELOPMENT THE WHOLE PROCESSION OF HIS ANCESTORS, AND THAT SUCH A SUDDEN TURN TO GOOD OR EVIL STANDS FOR SOME STRONG INFLUENCE WHICH CAME INTO THE LINE OF HIS PEDIGREE. THE PERSON BECOMES, AS IT WERE, THE EPITOME OF THE HISTORY OF HIS OWN FAMILY."

SHERLOCK HOLMES IN ***THE ADVENTURES OF THE EMPTY HOUSE***

As Homer drove up the twisty lane toward the cloud of smoke billowing high into the sky he passed a group of goats that had clustered along the stone wall. He became nauseous as he rounded the last curve and Frannie's car came into view, but that didn't prevent his detective eyes from automatically taking in the surroundings. In his rear view mirror he caught sight of the fire trucks' flashing red lights advancing from behind as two llamas and some chickens scampered across the lane in front of him. Russell was standing well away from the house with a woman by his side, but he knew in an instant it wasn't Frannie. He leaped from the car as he was shifting into park.

"Where is she?" He had to shout to be heard over the howling flames.

Russell rushed over, making a placating gesture with his hands. "It's all right, mate. Francesca's not here. She's safe."

It took several seconds for the truth to register. He pointed to the car, "But where is she?"

"It's a bit of a story, but rest assured, she's not here."

Homer glanced at the woman who was staring at the fire.

Her face was unreadable but there was a vague familiarity about her. Then he sent a questioning look in Russell's direction.

"Later, mate."

The fire fighters had arrived on the scene and were quickly unwinding the hoses but their attitudes made it quite clear they felt the effort would be futile. The captain of the crew, Mike Green, ran over to ask, "Everybody out?"

Russell answered. "Yes."

"How about the animals."

The woman finally spoke. "I set them all free."

Homer narrowed his eyes suspiciously and was about to ask her what role she played in this fire. But Russell laid a hand on his arm and pulled him away. "You should wait."

"Who is she?"

"Lucinda Cooper."

"Rebekah Winchell's aunt?"

"Right. Anyhow, you don't want to upset her."

"And why's that?"

"Because she alone knows where your wife is."

# RUSSELL

"EVERY JOURNALIST WHO IS NOT TOO STUPID OR TOO FULL OF HIMSELF TO NOTICE WHAT IS GOING ON KNOWS WHAT HE DOES IS MORALLY INDEFENSIBLE. HE'S A KIND OF CONFIDENCE MAN, PREYING ON PEOPLE'S VANITY, IGNORANCE OR LONELINESS, GATHERING THEIR TRUST AND BETRAYING THEM WITHOUT REMORSE."

JANET MALCOLM

All that remained of the old homestead where Betsy Cooper had veiled herself under the alias of Rebekah Winchell for twenty years was the blackened stone foundations of the house and the barn. The firefighters were able to contain the fire to the buildings and thereby prevented it from spreading to the surrounding woodland area.

"We were lucky there was no wind today," Captain Green said as the crew was packing up to leave. "I'll send you a copy of the report, Sheriff."

Lucinda Cooper had done nothing to cover her crime of arson. Only Russell understood that it was part of her plan. Fortunately, he had been the one to arrive for her admission of guilt before the good sheriff descended on the scene.

"So how are we going to play this?" Homer had waved the fire trucks off and was now ready to deal with Lucinda and the business of determining where his wife had gone.

Russell looked in the direction of where Lucinda was sitting on the side of the stone well and folded his arms. "Ya' see, here's the rub."

"Why am I already not liking this, Rusty?" Homer grumbled.

"Oh, actually, you're going to *hate it*. She'll turn herself in and you will have a confession by the end of the day. She'll also reveal where Francesca is."

"So far I'm happy."

"The thing is," Russell cocked his head. "I've got to be the one to take her."

He watched the sheriff's face grow a dangerous shade of crimson.

"She wants to spend a couple of hours with Rebekah, er Betsy, to explain what she did and to make some arrangements for her niece."

"I can manage that."

"Sure you can, but I've earned her trust by promising to help her." He lowered his voice. "Look, I was able to keep her from running away. Give me some credit here."

"If you think for one minute I'm going to let you swoop in to the rescue and bring my wife home."

"It's not like that, Homer." *God the man could be an infuriating Neanderthal.* Although if Russell was being honest, he couldn't deny the mini fantasy playing out in his head about how grateful Francesca would be to him. "I don't imagine your lady looks upon me as anything but the annoying newsman about town. The problem is, this Cooper woman doesn't trust anyone in law enforcement. She's holding on to the only power she has at the moment to get what she needs."

Russell was wagering on Homer's rational side to overrule his pride and it looked as if he was going to cash in the chips.

"All right. But I want a call from Frannie as soon as you get to her."

"My solemn vow." Russell made a gesture of crossing his heart.

"And I'd like a word with Ms. Cooper before I go."

Russell wasn't too keen about the potential of Homer throwing a wrench into his scheme.

"Go ahead, Guv, if you think it wise." Russell hoped his expression radiated unqualified skepticism. "If it was me? Well, I wouldn't want to take the chance of spooking the woman."

The sheriff was wavering, but finally he relented.

"Okay, but I'm warning you." Homer jabbed his finger hard into Russell's chest to emphasize his point. "No funny business."

"Duly warned." Russell rubbed at the area he was certain would be sporting a bruise by morning.

"By the way," Homer said as he walked to his car. "Guess who's locked up in Cell B down at the station."

"I couldn't say."

"Your little visitor. From earlier today?"

"So you found her?" At least he could produce that ace for Ramon.

"Found your Suzuki, too. You're cooked Russell. And how I deal with that will depend entirely on what transpires in the next couple of hours."

"I assure you, I will return Francesca to you unharmed and I will not to let Lucinda out of my sight."

"It's your neck if you don't."

If Homer had a clue as to the personal motivation Russell had to keep a tight leash on the Cooper woman, he wouldn't give a titchy bother about it.

# RAMON

"DOUBT THAT THE STARS ARE FIRE, DOUBT THAT THE SUN DOTH MOVE HIS AIDES, DOUBT TRUTH TO BE A LIAR, BUT NEVER DOUBT I LOVE."

WILLIAM SHAKESPEARE, ***HAMLET***

RAMON CHECKED HIS WATCH. HE'D become absorbed in reading Russell's manuscript draft and missed the deadline he'd set. The sun was lowering and he hadn't a clue where to start looking for Cord. He heard Guapo's soft yelp from the family room so he followed the sound to investigate.

Peering through the slats of the wooden blinds, he watched as one of the cars he'd seen out at the Winchell farm came into view. Russell got out of the passenger side, opened the rear car door and lifted a small child from the back seat. Guapo about went mad when he saw Gabriella and it was all Ramon could do to keep himself from running out the door. But since he was uncertain who was in the retreating vehicle, his better judgment triumphed.

Russell walked through the door sporting a huge self-satisfied grin.

"We've got ourselves a plan, Stan."

Gabriella had been sniffling when Russell brought her into the cabin, but she perked up as soon as she saw her best buddy.

"Hansome!" the little girl squealed with delight.

"If ever there was a mutual admiration society." Russell watched in awe the interactions of the canine-toddler duo.

"I have a feeling I am never getting my dog back," Ramon lamented.

While Gabriella munched on dried apple rings - the only suitable snack offering in Russell's rather bare cupboards - and tossed the ball for the never-tiring, ever-retrieving pup, Russell brought Ramon up to speed.

"Who was driving the car just now?" he asked.

"Francesca Pruitt, A.K.A. the sheriff's spousal unit."

"How did she get involved in this?"

"She was left to babysit Rebekah earlier in the day. Evidently the poor woman had a meltdown just as the sheriff stopped by for an unannounced visit. His wife came to the serendipitous rescue when she drove out to report that one Mr. Ramon Alvarez had slipped through the fingers of Murphy's finest."

"What can I say?" Ramon declared in an affected tone. "I am that good."

"Right you are. Anyhow, Rebekah's ramblings about a little girl put Francesca on alert. As she probed she was able to assemble bits and clues that led her to presume the child was the missing little girl."

"But how did she end up with her?"

"The whole story is beyond belief and much too convoluted to get into now. I'll tell you when I get back from town. I've got a prisoner to spring." Russell arched his eyebrows mischievously. "Your little squeeze is in the joint."

"Cord is in jail? Now? At the sheriff's office?"

"Yes to all three. Indeed she is. I told you I'd come through, ye of little faith."

"Thank God she is safe." He felt his throat constrict.

"Don't tell me infamous tough guy Rammie Alcatraz has a soft side?" Russell punched him playfully.

He smiled at the mention of his old nickname and was glad for the bit of humorous respite to camouflage his emotions. "Don't push it Payne in my Ass."

"That's the spirit."

"So tell me, how do you plan to get the sheriff to release a woman who is wanted on federal abduction charges and is the primary suspect in the murder of her husband? I can imagine you trying to sweet talk the beautiful wife, even the pert young deputy, but Sheriff Pruitt? No offense, but I don't think you two are in the same league."

Russell's grin became rather sinister. "No need to worry. I have in my possession some long buried and permanently expunged records" –he made air quotation marks – "that will surely make the sheriff, how shall I put it? Much more accommodating."

"Sounds like you've been keeping Badger busy these days."

"He is a most valuable asset. And I'm extremely confident the good sheriff will be more than willing to trade Ms. Carlyle for the would-be damaging information I possess. Of course, I'll be renouncing all of my power over Homer, which will make my life quite dull around here in the future."

Ramon picked up the rough manuscripts. "You'll be busy enough."

"You approve?" The typically overconfident former editor's eagerness for praise was incongruous.

"It is amazing. You have a winner here."

"Who'd have ever thought an idea for a book could so closely replicate an awful and long forgotten truth?"

"I'm not sure who said it, but true crimes are much more fascinating than those invented by fiction writers."

"I believe you are quoting yours truly." Russell bowed with faux humility.

"Such a modest guy." Ramon jabbed sarcastically but was content to see the re-emergence of his old friend's authentic persona. Russell Payne without an overinflated ego would be a travesty. "Should we not get moving?"

"Sorry my man. You will only confuse matters and I would prefer not to go to bat with a sticky wicket."

"But I need to be there in case…" He didn't finish the thought.

"In case what?" Russell asked but when he got no answer went on to say, "I see. You don't trust me. Is that it?"

"Truthfully?" His history with Russell had revealed the man's great ambition and an often ruthless means of achieving his goals. "I've been a bystander to your scruples."

"I guess you have me there. But let me size up the situation frankly. Homer's the type of man who doesn't take kindly to disrespect. It's quite possible he'd detain you merely to settle the score for your taking off against his directive. And if you are behind bars then how will you escort your young lady out of Dodge, as you Americans like to say."

Ramon couldn't argue with the logic, but his heart was rebelling wildly. He couldn't bear the thought of anything going wrong while he was stuck out in the wilds of Maine twiddling his thumbs waiting for a man with the conscience of a starving alligator to bring Cord to safety.

He at last held up his gauze-wrapped hands. "You win. I'll hold down the fort."

"That's a good chap. I'll call my land line when I'm on the way back here."

After Russell left, Ramon counted to one hundred before picking up Gabriella and grabbing his car keys.

# HOMER

"...IT IS STUPIDITY RATHER THAN COURAGE TO REFUSE TO RECOGNIZE DANGER WHEN IT IS CLOSE UPON YOU."

SHERLOCK HOLMES IN ***THE ADVENTURE OF THE FINAL PROBLEM***

When Homer watched Russell walk through the doors of the station carrying a large manila envelope, he smiled inwardly. He'd known all along Russell had something on him. And he'd also done some checking with his contact at the bureau who found a connection between the journalist and Ramon Alvarez. That Mr. Alvarez was also connected to Cordelia Carlyle was a gift that fell into his lap. This would all play out to perfection.

"Can we talk privately?" Russell tapped on the door jamb.

"Sure. Have a seat."

Russell closed the door. "I trust Francesca made it back safely with Lucinda Cooper."

"She did. You kept your part of the bargain."

"Do you have her formal confession to the crimes?"

"Yes. I think it's a fair assumption Ms. Cooper will likely spend the remainder of her days in prison somewhere. Arson alone has a maximum penalty of thirty years in Maine. Murder is twenty-five years to life with no possibility of parole. The only uncertainty is whether Kentucky will file an extradition order. She'd face the death penalty there." Homer would be turning the prisoner over to the District Attorney's office in the morning. Lucinda Cooper had admitted to killing Rev. Matthew

Cooper, her brother and Betsy Cooper's father. It had not been a premeditated act, rather one of passion. Lucinda was reluctant to expound on what inflamed the rage, but after she pulled the trigger it appears she regained her wits enough to set the parsonage on fire to destroy the evidence.

"Fascinating, isn't it? What did she say about the Ted Walsh murder?"

"Nice try." If he wanted to dig into the murder of Betsy Cooper's husband in Kentucky twenty years earlier he could do it on his own time. Lucinda confessed to that murder as well, which also involved arson, but she provided no supplementary details.

Russell's expression was feigned innocence. "I'm only curious about what might have provoked her to murder a second time. No worry. At least we can agree she was pretty handy with the matches. What do you think she was hoping to destroy out at the Winchell farm?"

Homer was thinking Russell already knew a lot more than he was pretending. "I guess we'll never know. So, where's Rebekah now?"

"She's being taken care of. It was a promise I made to Lucinda."

"In exchange for what exactly?"

"Why, Homer. You insult me."

"I just know you, Rusty." He looked pointedly at the file Russell was holding. "I take it you're here to see me about another matter."

"That's right." Russell leaned back in his chair and casually crossed his legs. "I want you to release the Carlyle woman."

This was unexpected. "Now why would I do that?"

"She's a young mother who's running scared. You're familiar with that scene."

Homer bristled. "Leave my daughter and my family out of this discussion."

"Okay, I'll try not to make this personal. But what would it hurt to let her leave the country with her little girl?"

"Might I point out the smallest problem with your request?"

Russell politely dipped his head in consent.

"The child still happens to be missing."

"Not a true statement. Little Gabriella is safe. I've seen her with my own eyes. You may call off your search."

Homer's insides were roiling with fury but he made every effort to remain calm. "Would you care to elaborate as to where she's been the past three days and more importantly, where is she now?"

"She's in good hands, but as you might imagine, the sad little thing is distraught over being separated from her mother. That's all I'm at liberty to share."

Homer narrowed his eyes, wary of the cavalier attitude. "You're violating Federal law. If you don't bring the child in you might be joining Lucinda Cooper in prison. Kidnapping is not taken lightly."

"I said only that I've seen her and she's safe. I have not kidnapped the Martelli girl. However..." The man suspended conversation to inspect his cuticles.

"However?" His patience was wearing.

"Oh right. Well the fact is somebody did kidnap her and it wasn't me nor was it our Mr. Rawlins."

Although Homer found Russell's swagger infuriating and he detested relinquishing control particularly on his own turf, he leaned back in his chair with a false air of nonchalance. "You're apparently running this show, so by all means, the floor is yours."

"Only since you insist." He cleared his throat dramatically. "So you see, Guv, it was Rebekah who showed up out at the Rawlins' house, knocked Cordelia out and left her in that well.

Long ago, she lost her own little girl, Gemma her name was, when she was about the same age as Gabriella. It was quite traumatic and she ended up in psychiatric care for many years."

"Gemma?" Homer remembered Rebekah mumbling the name in her mental collapse earlier in the day. Plus, wasn't that the name in the note he'd taken from her weaving table?

"Anyhow, she took the young mother and child under her wing when they ended up lost on her property. But according to Lucinda, in this disruption of a regimented and lengthy solitary existence, Rebekah's carefully fashioned façade started to break down. She began to experience delusions and was confusing her made-up self with her true identity, Betsy Cooper. She even hid Cordelia's car to prevent them from leaving because she was convinced the spirit of her long dead child had returned in Gabriella."

Homer hated to think Russell's account might be adding up. "In the barn?"

"In fact, yes. How'd you know?"

"I'm a detective. It's my business to know."

"Right. Anyhow, when Rebekah arrived home on Monday and found the house empty, her first thought was that Samuel Rawlins was somehow involved. She'd been preoccupied by his release from prison, so she drove over to the Rawlins' place with a rescue in mind. But Rebekah walked in while Cordelia was talking on the phone to a cab company and basically panicked. Ask Francesca. She'll verify the story."

He was even more displeased by this revelation. Why had Frannie kept this bit of information from him?

"Don't be too hard on her." Russell had read his expression well. "I lied to your wife. I told her you had already figured out who was behind the kidnapping and assault. But I suggested she might want to let you tell her yourself. I made you out to be quite the brilliant detective. You should be thanking me."

"I'll send you a sweet note." It wasn't worth mentioning he had in fact already uncovered a good part of the truth, and had Russell not intervened, he would have readily solved the mystery on his own.

"Don't be sore, Guv. As I see it, you're going to be quite busy with Lucinda Cooper's drama to sort out, the Samuel Rawlins score to settle and, oh yeah, that little marijuana bust to investigate. More than enough to occupy even the most ambitious forensic mind, wouldn't you say? One needs to keep those skills sharply honed." Russell rubbed his hands together briskly.

"I appreciate your looking out for my interests." He hoped the sarcasm hadn't bounced off Russell's inflated ego. "But let's not forget Rebekah Winchell or Betsy Cooper, as the case may be. We need to bring her in for questioning. You've just fingered her as a kidnapper and Frannie as a witness."

"Tsk. No can do. Betsy Cooper is untouchable."

"We'll see about that."

Russell bowed his head again, this time in a patronizing manner. "Back to my original plea for Ms. Carlyle. Why not let her go?"

Homer pounded his fist on the desk. "Because it's my job to ensure justice is done. She's a person of interest, essentially the prime suspect, in her husband's murder."

"Lots of murderers get away with the deed, don't they?" Russell stared hard as the question was left floating between the two men.

A nearly imperceptible nod from the sheriff prompted him to continue. "And most of them remain a danger to society. However, if this young woman is in fact guilty, which is doubtful, it would likely be a case of self-defense against an abusive spouse. From what I understand, there was proof her husband had some nefarious plans in store for her, but alas, said evidence was in the trunk of her car, which as we both know was blown to bits by the fire."

"Is that what her boyfriend told you?"

"Who?"

"Mr. Alvarez. He was here earlier today. I'm sure he's somehow involved in this mess and I want him back in for questioning, too. Have you by chance seen him?" He waited for Russell to squirm, but the bait was left dangling on the hook.

He merely sighed. "Again we digress. Cordelia Carlyle has only one aim, to leave this country and start a new life. You know what that's like, don't you? To get a clean slate? A new beginning?" He pulled a file from the envelope and set it on the desk.

Homer chuckled. "I've been waiting for this day ever since you arrived in Murphy."

"Have you really?"

"So you've dug up some dirt on me. What is it? The truth behind my sudden departure from the NYPD? I'm sure anyone with enough time on their hands could unearth those files. You really do need a hobby, Russ."

"Oh. I've got a hobby. But, you're right. The information regarding why you were asked to resign your shield to the NYPD's Commissioner was relatively easy to trace. I've known the particulars of your downfall from the toughest beat for quite some time now. But what hasn't been so easy to unearth is the solution to a mystery that has been secreted away in obscurity for nearly three decades."

Homer felt every hair on his body rise to attention. "You're talking in riddles."

"Now that is an ironic assertion, and coming from the king of the brainteaser himself." Russell drummed his fingers atop the file in an intimidating gesture.

"Can we get to the point?"

"Okay. I'll bottom line it for you. William Robbins."

Homer couldn't get his lungs to take in oxygen. It was as if all the air had been sucked from the room. Good God, what could Russell have uncovered about Bill?

"I can see why the name would have an untoward effect on you. After all, wasn't he *Francesca's* first husband? *Sophia's* real father? *Your best friend* at one time?"

He was floating in a vacuum, willing himself to be awakened from this horrible nightmare.

"But he was a man with secrets, wasn't he? Horrible, dirty little secrets, this Bill Robbins fellow had. Who could have blamed someone, *anyone*, for wanting him dead?"

"Stop it. Now." The low, painful moan of his voice was nearly unrecognizable.

"You ready to make the swap?" Russell inched the file closer. "Let the woman go and you can keep the file."

"This would ruin me."

"Damned if you do, but more damned if you don't. I do think you're overreacting though. Let me play devil's advocate."

"A good role for you."

"Don't be a flatterer." Russell made an affected gesture then leaned his arms onto the desk. "Look, who's going to know you even had the woman in custody? I'm guessing no official paperwork has been filed yet. As for Francesca and Miss Livvy? They'll never reveal anything. It's plain to see your little deputy has a hero worship thing going on with you, so she'll accept whatever you tell her. And your wife has as much at stake as you in returning this information to the vault. Even if she doesn't have the benefit of the entire truth."

Homer had underestimated his opponent. He felt certain there was no bluffing going on about the evidence contained in the file. His Achilles heel had been exposed and he doubted not at all Russell's capacity to reveal the secrets that could devastate his life, and particularly his marriage.

"What about your friend, Mr. Alvarez?"

"Ramon hasn't a clue about any of this. His sole objective is getting his friend to safety."

"That leaves only one more person." Homer stared intently, forcing himself not to blink.

"I know it's asking a lot, but you're going to have to trust me when I tell you I'm done. I've been gathering this history of yours for years now, holding onto it like an insurance policy and waiting to cash in when the right circumstances arrived. I knew there was something more. But this?" Russell tapped the file. "I never could have guessed."

"Why now? What's your connection with this woman?"

"It's not what you're thinking. I've only met the bird today. But I've known Ramon for years and if he vouches for her then his word is enough for me." Russell rubbed his face in his hands. "Believe it or not, I'm tired of the rubbish. I figure for once I might as well use the evidence I've collected to help someone instead of whipping up a scandal."

"But you'd have no qualms about using this against me." He reached for the file but stopped short of touching it.

"You're not a bad bloke, Homer. You've always played the game squarely and I have no desire to hurt you. I'm simply offering you a very powerful motive to comply with my appeal for the young woman's liberty."

"This is nothing short of blackmail, and you know it."

"Let's consider it more like" -Russell paused to compose his thought- "Karma."

"Karma?" Homer shook his head in disgust.

"Don't you see? We'd be burying *your* skeletons forever and at the same time giving someone else the same chance your family once had. It's all for the greater good."

Decades passed through Homer's mind during the moments the two men locked eyes. It was Russell who finally broke through the silence.

"I can't see that you have a choice, Guv."

# CORDELIA

"DO NOT DWELL IN THE PAST, DO NOT DREAM OF THE FUTURE, CONCENTRATE THE MIND ON THE PRESENT MOMENT."

BUDDHA

"WHAT JUST HAPPENED?" I ASKED my liberator.

"Don't look back. Just keep walking." Russell was propelling me down a side street.

Minutes ago Deputy Bishop had opened the door to my holding cell and escorted me to the waiting area where Russell Payne was waiting by the door and told me I was free to go.

"The sheriff didn't even question me," I whispered.

"We're just down this way. I'll explain everything in the car."

"Does this mean? Is she?" I couldn't bring myself to speak the unthinkable. *Had they stopped looking for Gabriella? Or worse, had her body been found?*

"Get in." Russell nearly shoved me into his car and rushed to the driver's side. Once the car was moving he said, "Your little girl is safe. I'm taking you to her now. She's with Ramon."

I couldn't suppress a loud sob. Then I grabbed Russell's arm, even though at this point he was trying to steer the car.

"She's really okay?"

"I promise. Your daughter is more than okay. She and that little rat of a dog, Handsome, or whatever you all call him, well the two of them are like a tiny yin and yang."

I had to smile at his choice of metaphors even though

the tears were flowing freely. My baby was safe. Nothing else mattered now. I silently said a particularly comforting Buddhist blessing. *By the power of every moment of your goodness, may your heart's wishes be soon fulfilled as completely shining as the bright full moon, as magically as by a wish-fulfilling gem.* Gem. My little gem.

When I'd quieted my tears and calmed my mind, I turned toward Russell. "Where did you say Gabriella was?"

"Back at my cabin."

I was afraid I'd misheard him earlier, and had to know for certain. "Did you say...?"

"Yes, she's with Ramon."

I rubbed the huge bump on the back of my head, suddenly terrified a concussion had thrust me into a sweet dream, one from which I'd be cruelly awakened. But Russell's lovely British tones were a reassuring interruption to my fears.

"Your Prince Valliant appeared at my door earlier today after escaping the watchful eye of the affable and kind-hearted Deputy Olivia."

So many questions were churning in my brain. Why had Ramon been at the jail to begin with and why had they been detaining him? How did he even find me? How had he and Gabriella ended up at Russell's? Why was I released without further questioning? And what had happened to Rebekah?

Russell correctly interpreted my introspective silence. "A lot has happened in a short time."

For the next thirty minutes I listened while this man I'd met only hours ago shared with me details of his long-standing relationship with Ramon and followed with an account of the events that had unfolded after I took off in the ATV.

"I'd become frightened of Rebekah, but never would I have dreamed she was capable of leaving me to die." I shivered. "I was certain it had been that horrible Samuel Rawlins. Surely he won't be set free again."

"Sheriff Pruitt has enough to send him back to prison. I doubt he'll pass the parole board quite so easily next time."

I was relieved for Timothy's sake. "And Rebekah?"

"She's become Betsy Cooper again. Right now she's on her way to Augusta where she'll be living in a private psychiatric treatment facility."

I shook my head. "It's a lot to process."

"And yet, the story doesn't end there."

The skies were dark, but the road Russell was turning onto was familiar. I could feel pressure building in my ears and was having trouble catching my breath.

"Why are you bringing me back here?"

"Closure, for lack of a better word. It's been a rough day all around. Ramon was even knocked flat on his arse trying to enter a burning barn to rescue you."

"The barn? I don't understand."

"You will in a minute." As the car rounded the final curve burning embers could still be seen glowing in the distance. "I thought you needed to see it."

Russell brought the car to a stop in front of the heap of charred wood and stone. *So I had heard the sheriff correctly.* It was hard to take in, even with the proof right in front of me.

"Nothing was salvaged?" I was disheartening to think everything I'd taken from Aiden's safe was gone, evidence of his scheme now just ash and soot.

"Only what I fortuitously removed yesterday."

"Does Rebekah's aunt know you have the boxes?"

"She does now. You see, we made a little pact. She's given me the rights to the story."

"Some story." I turned to look at Russell more closely. He

had a rather kind face. "I suppose that's your reward for rescuing a complete stranger."

"Are you going to go all Blanche DuBois on me?" He feigned a grimace.

"Not a bad correlation." I had been depending on the kindness of strangers since arriving in this tiny burg. I stared ahead at the rubble before us. "Rebekah may have been crazy, but she did take us into her home. Which as I see it now must have been very difficult for her."

"Probably her undoing," Russell mused, then quickly added, "Not that I'm blaming you. Your showing up just set off a maelstrom that sucked her under. She'd been a fugitive from herself for a long time."

"That's a great line."

"Isn't it? I was just trying it out on you. It's already down on paper."

"I wish I could do more than just say thank you for all you've done."

"I suppose it's a bit boorish to bring it up." Russell simultaneously raised his eyebrows and dipped his head. "But there was that, um, arrangement we had. About the diary? Unless, of course, the good sheriff confiscated it. And in that case I've already cashed in my last bargaining chip with him."

"The sheriff doesn't have it."

"Whew." He sank back into the leather seat. "That's a relief."

"But I'm afraid it's gone."

"Gone?" Russell's voice cracked like an adolescent boy. "As in, missing?"

I pointed to the remains of the burned out buildings before us. "Gone. As in, *up in smoke*."

"Bloody hell." Russell bemoaned in painful defeat.

# RAMON

"FOR WHERE THOU ART, THERE IS THE WORLD ITSELF,
AND WHERE THOU ART NOT, DESOLATION."

WILLIAM SHAKESPEARE, ***HENRY IV***

RAMON PARKED HIS RENTAL CAR in a space out of sight from the comings and goings of the sheriff's office. He had the Aston Martin in visual range, but it was dark and highly unlikely Russell would notice him. He felt certain his old friend was hiding something and he intended to determine exactly what that was. Plus, he was dubious Russell had the leverage he claimed to get Cord released. Now he was in a better position to intercede if necessary.

The wait was interminable, although a glance at the dashboard clock corrected the misimpression. He'd only been idling ten minutes. Fortunately, Gabriella had fallen asleep during the drive to town and Guapo had curled up beside her and was kicking his legs and whimpering the contented sighs of a dreaming dog. These little ones had been subjected to a fair amount of trauma in the past 24 hours and deserved some peace.

He spied Russell rounding the corner and instinctively slid further down in the driver's seat. But when Cord came into view under the street lamp he felt a contraction seize his chest.

"Gracias a dios." Ramon shifted into drive and the motion of the car alerted Guapo to hop up into the passenger side to oversee the navigation. "Perhaps I was wrong about my old amigo."

He allowed a lengthy gap between the vehicles, comfortable now that he was not being deceived, for they were heading in the direction of Russell's cabin. However, when he arrived there was no sign of the Aston Martin.

"Mierda," he hissed. "I knew it. But where did I lose him?"

He reversed the car and headed back to the main road. First he'd check the farm, but he'd be lucky to see the turn off in the pitch blackness of a starless night. After several passes he eventually was able to access the old dirt road.

"Okay. So you are back on my good side, Russell ole man." He coasted up behind where the Aston Martin's headlights were illuminating the remnants of the fire and parked a few yards back. He gently lifted the small, slumbering form from the back seat and carried her toward the lights. When he had traveled half the ground, the passenger door was thrust open as Cord leaped from the car and raced to meet him.

"Oh my baby. Baby, baby, baby."

Ramon watched in awe as the bodies of mother and child melded into one.

"Mama." Gabriella was groggy, but she understood she was home again. Home as defined by being in her mother's arms.

Ramon was there to hold on to them when Cord stumbled and nearly collapsed from the intermingling emotions of sweet relief at having her daughter back, sorrow about Rebekah's unfortunate life and worries for the future, all heightened by sheer exhaustion. He was uncertain how long they stood huddled together before Russell's voice interrupted their relatively brief interlude from the challenges they faced.

"Let's get them back to my place where they can have a proper rest."

"Tomato soup and saltines never tasted so good." Cord said between spoonfuls.

"A body cannot survive long on a mere handful of peanuts." Ramon smiled as he watched her slurp down the liquid nourishment.

"Don't forget the Three Musketeers Bar." Cord had shared with them only a few details of her drama, including the kindness of young Timothy Rawlins.

"I think the lad was rather sad he wasn't the one to rescue you." Russell remarked.

"Oh, but he did. He truly did come to my rescue." But Cord would elaborate no further.

Ramon held hope in his heart that one day she would feel safe in sharing the entire story of her ordeal. But he would never press her.

"Join me on the porch?" Russell twirled a couple of Cubana Torpados between his palms.

Ramon licked his lips. "I have not had one of those since..."

"We were celebrating..."

"Tony Blair!" They said in unison.

"So mate." Russell puffed animatedly as he lit the cigar. "Did she do it?"

"No."

"And you know this because?"

"I just do."

"Good enough for me. They're both asleep?" Russell asked.

"Out cold."

"Good. They'll need their rest. Tomorrow's a big day."

"At least it's not a far drive from here to Canada."

"God, these are fine smokes, aren't they?"

"The best." But Ramon was becoming somewhat lightheaded so he wasn't sure he heard correctly what Russell uttered next.

"What do you think about moving her to London?"

Actually, when it finally registered, he wasn't at all keen on the suggestion but he kept his thoughts to himself while his friend pontificated about the merits of the idea.

"I think Canada is just a smidgen too close for comfort. I mean, the US and Canada are kissing cousins, wouldn't you say? Especially as law enforcement goes. She's still being pursued here, but in the UK there would be the absolute assurance of anonymity."

"What if she wished to reconnect with her family? It would be easier for them to visit her in Canada. Besides, do you think it wise to isolate her on another continent and in a city as congested as London?"

"They do speak the same language." Russell stopped to relight his cigar. "I don't think you're giving Cord credit for being able to look after herself and little Gabriella. Hasn't she spent her entire adult life living near Washington, D.C.? She can handle London."

"But flats are impossibly expensive, if she can even find one."

The Brit blew out the match and flicked it into the ashtray. "She can have my flat. It's been vacant for a few years now. My sister's been looking after it and making sure it's kept up nice and tidy. I daresay it might be the perfect solution. I know people who could look out for her, help her land a job, that sort of thing."

Ramon was brooding. He could not deny it was an ideal opportunity for Cord. He just hated that she would be so far away.

Russell must have perceived the hovering cloud of discontent. "I might have some projects for a talented freelance photojournalist that would require frequent hops across the pond to keep the love lights burning."

"Do not read more into this. We are just friends."

Russell offered an *if you say so* shrug. "Well, in my opinion, friendship is the best foundation to build on."

"When was the last time *you* were involved in a serious relationship?"

"Valid point." He chewed the end of his cigar. "So what do you think?"

"The plan is a good one." He forced himself to say the words, trying to sound convincing. He had to put Cord's best interests before...before what? He didn't even know how she felt about him or a future together. After all, she'd abandoned their plan for Montreal without telling him. He hadn't had the courage to ask why and was left with plenty of possibilities to speculate over, none of them particularly reassuring.

"So it's settled?"

"Not my decision. But if Cord asks for my advice, I will support your proposal."

"She'll ask." Russell rose from the porch steps. "Come on, mate. We've got some work to do."

"*We*? Really?" Ramon smiled. "Or do you mean Badger?"

"Quite right. Want to talk with him while I've got him on the line?"

"Not tonight. I'm still pissed at him for not telling me about Guapo. But make sure he gets them first class tickets."

"Who's springing for this?" Russell asked, now leaning against the porch railing.

"Your idea. Your wallet. Besides, with two blockbuster books in the works I think you can afford it."

"Well, maybe only *one* best seller in my future. Remember how I was telling you about Betsy Cooper's diary?"

"Yes."

"Poof. Gone." Russell puffed out a chain of smoke rings for effect. "It had been stowed for safe keeping someplace on the Winchell farm. Need I say more?"

“That is a shame.” Ramon would show Cord what Guapo had helped him unearth from the foundation of the chicken coop and leave it to her to decide its fate.

# HOMER

"THE WORLD IS FULL OF OBVIOUS THINGS WHICH NOBODY BY ANY CHANCE EVER OBSERVES."

SHERLOCK HOLMES IN ***THE HOUNDS OF THE BASKERVILLES***

When Homer returned to his home late on that eternal day, he found Frannie sitting quietly in her favorite chair by the fireplace sipping red wine. It was May, but there was a chill in the night air and the warmth from the blaze was welcomed.

"Join me?" She lifted her glass.

"I could use something a little stronger tonight."

"You sit. I'll make it for you. What's your pleasure?"

He and his burdens crash landed into the worn, burgundy leather recliner.

"I think a Beefeater Gibson might be called for." Homer groaned with pleasure as warm palms and strong fingers kneaded his gnarled mass of neck muscles. He reached up for one of his wife's hands and brought it to his lips.

Frannie kissed the top of his head. "I'll get you that drink now."

He admired his wife's loveliness as she ministered to his drink at the small wet bar to the side of the hearth. She'd become even more beautiful with time and notwithstanding her tendency for aloofness, her features hadn't hardened as was often the case with those who isolate themselves. He'd observed this as an occupational hazard for women who partnered with men choosing law enforcement careers. Initial detachment began as a defense mechanism but often became a firmly ingrained trait.

For decades Homer had been plagued by doubt. When had Frannie begun to erect her walls of self-preservation? Was it before they were married? Had she decided never to completely trust another man after enduring an abusive relationship with Bill? He couldn't blame her for closing off her emotions, for not letting herself give in to the complete abandon of passion. Still, he had never been able to prevent his mind from wandering into the dangerous territory of questioning whether Frannie had responded to his marriage proposal like a cornered animal would search for the safest escape route. Would she have chosen him if circumstances had been different? If she hadn't needed him?

"Here you are." She handed him the drink.

Homer closed his eyes and savored the first taste. He heard the soft swoosh of air releasing from the plump cushions of Frannie's armchair. When he opened his eyes she was watching him inquiringly from her perch, long legs curled up beneath her body.

"Would you like to tell me what happened?"

Where to begin? He knew he couldn't tell his wife about Russell's success in blackmailing him. Or how close they came to having their long buried private affairs revealed. Sometimes he wondered if she had pushed the truth so far from her thoughts that she'd actually forgotten everything.

"Mother and daughter have been reunited."

"Where are they now?"

"I don't know."

"You don't know because? Is she already under FBI custody?"

He took a larger gulp. Dutch courage. Isn't that what Russell called it?

"I let her go."

"Why?" Frannie placed her hand at the base of her throat. A habit. She did this when she was taken aback.

"Russell came to plead her case and offered a very compelling argument in her defense."

"Russell? Really? Huh." She sat pensively for a moment. "I'm not certain if I'm more surprised by Russell taking up the cause of someone in a tight spot or that you would let him persuade you to go against your strict adherence to the code of law."

Had she always viewed his nature as so inflexible? He could think of numerous other occasions over the span of his career in which he had extended the grace of immunity. One very significant exception in particular was brought to mind nearly every day of his life.

"Rest assured, Russell had his own self-serving motives." He took another swallow of the gin. "Even so, my instincts were telling me there was more to her story. It was the right thing to do."

"Oh, Homer." Frannie leaned forward, lowering her hand from her throat to her heart. "I can't say why, but I'm glad."

He was surprised by her response. Instead of disappointment, Frannie had an almost triumphant reaction to his decision to turn a blind eye to Cordelia Carlyle's escape from justice.

"You agree it was the right decision?" he asked.

"Right? Wrong? I'm in no position to judge. It was certainly an unexpected choice."

There was an aspect of her attitude he couldn't quite read. It was almost as if his wife was feeling a sense of gratification to see another dimension of his personality exposed; one of vulnerability which he had skillfully kept hidden from her. Maybe they'd both been building defensive walls during the course of their marriage.

"I take that back," she said.

"You take what back?" He wasn't following his wife's train of thought.

"Let me rephrase that. I think you were faced with a hard choice and in light of my history, and the predicaments Sophia has gotten herself into over the years, I shouldn't be surprised you'd show compassion to someone in a similarly unfortunate circumstance."

It hadn't occurred to him that Frannie might have intuited Cordelia Carlyle's motives for protecting herself and her child by escaping an abusive situation. This new revelation put him in the unpleasant position of having to assess his integrity. When finally fueled with all the facts, would he have had the clarity of vision to empathize with the young woman? Or would he still have viewed her as a fugitive of justice through the cold eyes of a criminologist? He never thought the day would come when Russell Payne might be considered a finer human being than Homer Pruitt.

"Homer? What's wrong?" Frannie came and sat on the armrest of the recliner, wiping tears from his cheek.

"I'm just tired, baby. It's been a long day."

Tending to secrets was the hardest job in the world.

# PART SIX

## REVELATIONS

# CORDELIA

"HOLDING ON TO ANGER IS LIKE GRASPING A HOT COAL WITH THE INTENT OF THROWING IT AT SOMEONE ELSE; YOU ARE THE ONE GETTING BURNED."

BUDDHA

I'D BEEN LIVING IN RUSSELL'S London flat for six months when the liberating news arrived in the post. There was a newspaper clipping enclosed in the envelope. The headline was concise: *Powers Acquitted of Murder*! My heart quickened as I scanned the article.

> Aiden Martelli, celebrated D.C. attorney and son of Marco Martelli, the late illustrious lobbyist for the NRA, had represented the interests of the notorious Richard Powers. Mr. Martelli had reaped sizeable financial rewards from the association...

This I already knew. But according to the report, Aiden had become quite greedy, misappropriating funds from his client's accounts and severing the attorney-client relationship both permanently and tragically. I presumed Aiden possessed a far too intimate knowledge of his client's shady business dealings and killing him was the simplest means of silencing him. But then I read on to learn the defense strategy of Mr. Powers' mighty team of lawyers. They claimed Aiden's death had not been premeditated, but instead was an act of self-defense resulting from an altercation of passion. Mr. Powers had confronted Mr. Martelli after learning the attorney had been having an affair with, not Mr. Powers' wife but his mistress. Allegedly, their verbal quarrel escalated and became physical.

I skipped over the details of violence thinking how incongruously civilized the writer made it all sound through the simple insertion of the deferential title of *mister*. But I was hard hit by the validity of the article's ending sentence:

> Jealousy is often the catalyst that transforms a dangerous person's anger into homicidal vengeance.

My hands trembled as I folded the article and returned it to the envelope. Finally, my name had been cleared in connection with Aiden's death. My heart willed me to cartwheel across the back garden, but my conscience was doing battle with my joy. How sad for it to have been the family housekeeper who discovered Aiden's body several days after he'd been killed. And how could I celebrate the misdeeds of my daughter's dead father? He'd started out a good man, or at least that's what I was choosing to believe. I'd once been impressed by his passion for the law, and drawn in by his altruistic ambitions for the future. But sadly, when his father's health failed and Aiden was handed the legacy to the firm, he became swayed by power; a power which corrupted the moral code I felt certain existed at the beginning of our marriage. It would be the image of the younger Aiden I would cling to when someday Gabriella asked to know about the kind of man her father was.

I unfolded the note that had accompanied the article.

Maybe it is time? Ramon

This was the first I'd heard from him since he left a month ago after his only visit. He'd asked to come sooner, many times, but I had always put him off. My wounds were still raw from another obvious rejection. How else could I interpret his urging to change my escape destination to England?

I was trying hard to sweep away the remnants of my quashed dream of moving beyond friendship with Ramon, to be open to other possibilities. And I'd been successful in keeping him at bay until one day he simply showed up at the door unannounced.

"I was in the neighborhood, so I thought I would stop by." He'd been trying to come across casually witty, but there was an edge to his voice.

I couldn't have predicted my response to a surprise face to face encounter would be to break down and cry.

"Mi quierda," he had whispered in my hair as I leaned into him and sobbed desperately.

"Everything okay, deary?" The kindly but curious Mrs. Bannister called out from the flat next door. "Should I call a copper?"

I was fairly certain all Ramon did was turn his handsome face toward my neighbor and offer one of his charming smiles, because I heard Mrs. Bannister giggle before closing the door and then shout to Mr. Bannister who was hard of hearing, "Our little yank next door has a gentleman caller. Fine looking chap, this one."

At last I'd calmed down and had the presence to invite Ramon in from the hallway.

"How is Gabriella?" he asked as I made tea.

"I've enrolled her in nursery school. It was time." I tried unsuccessfully to stifle a hiccup. "I miss her terribly during the day."

"She will be home soon?"

"In about an hour. I walk to the school to pick her up." Trying to steady a shaky tray holding our tea cups, I guided him toward the terrace overlooking the expansive garden. "My favorite spot."

"I can see why." He followed my gaze to the hedge of bamboo.

"Beyond it is a small pond and a meditation garden established by one of my neighbors. He's a Buddhist monk."

"That is fitting."

I'd been studying with Chodak for months, but didn't want to talk about that aspect of my life with Ramon. It somehow felt too intimate. "How long are you staying?"

"I left the ticket open ended. I was not sure..." He shrugged uncomfortably. "As long as I am back for Mama's 70th birthday party a month from now."

"Are you here on an assignment?"

He reached across the table and gently squeezed my hand. "I am here for you, Cord."

I fought hard not to abandon my defensive walls and maneuvered the discussion to the safe topic of my new job. Russell had lined me up with an old chum who owned a small brasserie just down the street. I was the weekday lunch chef which fit nicely with Gabriella's school hours.

"You're lucky you caught me. I'd just gotten home when you showed up." I would later learn Ramon had already been apprised of my schedule from Russell's gang of mates who were keeping a close watch over *the young American and her little girlie.* Mainly we kept to ourselves and remained cautiously under the radar as I was still fearful of being recognized.

Ramon walked with me to the nursery school so he could present the gift of a stuffed dog he'd had made for her in Guapo's likeness. Because of the long quarantines required for dogs entering the UK, the poor child had been heartbroken to leave behind her very best friend. But she wrote to him care of the loft address where the pooch had finally arrived at a peaceful accord with Ting.

"Look who came all the way from America to see you." I reluctantly disengaged from my daughter's warm hug. At first Gabriella had hidden her face in my skirt, but when she saw the stuffed animal her squeals of joy brought a smile to all those passing by.

Ramon then escorted us back to the flat and wrote down the number where he was staying. I waited a week before making the call. Certain he would have given up and left by then, I was surprised to hear his voice on the other end of the line.

During the final weeks of his visit we spent a good deal of time together, whisking Gabriella off to enrichment pursuits at various famous locales around London, including the National Gallery and The Tate. We explored the exhibits at Wrest Park Gardens, visited Anne Boleyn's Hever Castle and what was to become Gabriella's favorite pastime, the Puppet Barge. For the first time since coming to England I'd felt safe.

Perhaps as if leading by example, he opened up to me about the professional life he usually kept closeted away. And the day before he left, at long last he divulged the whole story of his thorny on-again-off-again romance with his ex-wife.

"So she's still in your life?" I swallowed hard.

"When you reappeared, Gina was doing her best to make amends for her betrayal. I had never told anyone about the affair. My brothers, Mama, they all thought she felt abandoned because of my extensive traveling. And they were partly correct. Gina is a beautiful woman who enjoys attention. She was not used to being ignored and likely did feel neglected when I was away so often. An opportunity arose and she was easily seduced."

"You've forgiven her?"

He thought about it for a moment before answering. "I understand her."

I paused before asking the next question, uncertain how I'd

react to Ramon's response. "So, how would you describe the relationship now?"

"Not to sound trite, but we are friends."

"A broadly encompassing term." I hadn't disguised my skepticism.

"Okay. Let me put it this way, I have invoked the Law of Cortez." He winked at the reference he'd made when I decided to leave Aiden. "The ships have been burned. There is no way back to Gina. And it was liberating to light that match."

I accepted Ramon's promise he no longer had a desire to mend his broken marriage. However, when he departed I was still uncertain as to where the two of us stood. He hadn't professed his affections and he hadn't asked me about my own feelings. He had simply given me a letter to read, one he had written years ago, shortly after that imprudent fling in D.C.

"I may have lacked the courage to send this back then, but I have read and reread these words so many times I could recite them from memory. The point is, even though much time has passed, the message in this letter is still from my heart today." He set it on the table and said, "Whenever you are ready."

I had not yet opened the letter. Maybe it was time.

# HOMER

"THEY SAY THAT GENIUS IS AN INFINITE CAPACITY FOR TAKING PAINS. IT IS A VERY BAD DEFINITION, BUT IT DOES APPLY TO DETECTIVE WORK."

SHERLOCK HOLMES IN ***A STUDY IN SCARLET***

"A LETTER FOR YOU FROM," OLIVIA paused to read the return address. "Russell Payne? He couldn't be bothered to drop this off to you in person? Beware the deadly sin of slothfulness."

Homer was also curious about what Russell found necessary to send to him via the post office, but before he ripped open the envelope Pastor Josh popped his head into the office.

"Would you like an update on Timothy?" he asked.

"Shoot."

"Should a sheriff ever really say that?"

"You've got a point there, Josh." He was learning to appreciate the minister's ironically irreverent wit. "You were saying?"

"I've just met with his case worker and he's making great progress with the dyslexia. There are certain social skills thematic to autism that might have been corrected if they'd been addressed earlier, but his case is relatively mild. Still, she advises sessions with a counselor she's recommended in Augusta."

"Can you manage it?"

"It's only once a week. I'm more than happy to do what I can to help."

"Between you and Emerson, he can count himself a lucky

young man." Olivia's generous and goodhearted boyfriend, Emerson Collins, had taken Timothy on as a cause. Not only had he assumed the responsibility of legal guardianship, but Emerson also fixed up the apartment over his carriage house and offered it to the young man as a place to live. The farm had been sold and the proceeds had been established in a trust for Timothy's future.

"It's my penance, isn't it?" The minister's tone reaffirmed his humility.

"I think we both know you'd be looking out for Timothy regardless of the, um, other matter."

Pastor Josh had shown up at the sheriff's office just as Homer had been ready to close up shop the night he'd been coerced into setting Cordelia Carlyle free. He'd felt beaten down and had no inclination to hear the confession he'd been expecting. But the man of cloth had been so distraught he hadn't the heart to turn him away.

"You have to understand," he'd pleaded. "I truly believed what I was doing was completely legal."

"And what was that?" Homer asked, trying to speed the minister along.

"The marijuana was mine. At least the plants in the greenhouse were mine. I had absolutely no knowledge of the additional fields of plants you mentioned. That had to have been Samuel's doing."

As it turned out, Pastor Josh was the founder of an underground source for medical marijuana. Even though owning a small number of plants was legal in Maine for personal medical use, so many of the hospice patients to whom he tended spiritually were not up to growing and harvesting the plants. So with Timothy's knowledge of plants, he began to produce a small crop which he distributed to those who were suffering.

Homer had likened the minister's self flagellation to a child who had waited all day for his punishment only to learn the wait had been more severe than the punishment itself.

"Josh, I'm feeling generous today. I'm not going to arrest you. In fact, I'm not going to do anything at all about this. How could I penalize you for merely bending the law to help others?"

"There's no fine? No community service? No hair shirt to wear?" Pastor Josh was nearly giddy. An arrest would have damaged his reputation with his church and the community. And there was no question he'd have been dismissed from the prison chaplaincy program. Homer wouldn't have wanted to see that happen.

"You do realize you'll need to look into other options for supplying the medical marijuana?"

"Understood. I don't know how to thank you for sparing me from disgrace."

"I do. Why don't you see about arranging a healthier situation for Timothy? He deserves better than the life he has now."

And Pastor Josh had not disappointed. As Homer listened to the progress report, he was reminded that had Cordelia Carlyle not lost control of her car on Old County Road, Timothy might still be squirming under the thumb of his malicious brother. Perhaps he was being converted to the notion that things really do happen for a reason. Or what had Russell said? *Karma*?

After Pastor Josh left, Homer decided he needed a cup of Becky's coffee so he grabbed the *New York Times* and the letter from Russell and walked to the door.

"I'll be at the diner, Liv," he called over his shoulder.

"What did Russell want?"

He waved the unopened letter to indicate he'd not yet read it. "I'll let you know."

"Afternoon, Sheriff."

"Becky." Homer nodded and took his usual seat in the corner booth.

"Can I slice you a piece of apple pie to go with your coffee? Fresh out of the oven and still warm."

"I'm trying to cut back on the sweets." He patted his stomach. "Just the Joe, thanks."

"Let me know if you change your mind." Becky filled the mug with the thick aromatic black liquid Homer craved then returned to his debate with another customer about the new Red Sox manager.

He was eager to start the puzzle, but his curiosity about Russell's note won out. Inside the envelope there was an article from the Washington Post. "Well, I'll be damned."

He read the story of Aiden Martelli's murder which brought back sharply to mind Cordelia Carlyle's unwavering insistence she'd had nothing to do with her husband's death. He thought it strange to have reason to think of her twice in one day when for the past months all thoughts of the woman had been willfully forced from his mind. She was a humiliating reminder that he'd been tripped up by his past and held hostage by the incriminating secrets Russell had uncovered.

Homer removed the note scribbled in nearly legible handwriting.

> I guess it was a good choice after all. I'm in New York for a few weeks. The story was buried in the Times and I wasn't sure you'd see it. How about a drop of Glenfiddich when I get back? R.P.

He had missed the article, but he no longer combed the pages as he once did.

"Hey, Becky?" He called out.

"Yep." The diner's proprietor moseyed back over to the booth.

"I've changed my mind. I think I'll have a slice of that pie after all."

"Good news?" Becky nodded toward the note that had brought a smile to the sheriff's usually serious mug.

Homer laid his hand upon the envelope. "Let's just say it eases my mind about a decision I made a while back."

Becky nodded thoughtfully.

"Make it a large slice. Ala mode."

"Now Sheriff, that decision would surely ease any mind."

# RAMON

"LOVE SOUGHT IS GOOD, BUT GIVEN UNSOUGHT IS BETTER."

WILLIAM SHAKESPEARE, ***TWELFTH NIGHT***

"THE REVIEWS ARE IN AND we're going to a second printing! Not to mention, I just got the green light from my editor for book two." Russell burst into the loft past Ramon holding a prototype of the cover for his second book and a bottle of Dom Perignon. "Who wants some bubbly?"

Guapo greeted him wagging eagerly. "Hello there, Bugs."

Russell had become even more attached to Ramon's canine companion with his frequent stops in New York to meet with *his people* – agent, editor, publisher, publicist.

"I'll stick with a brew, thank you." Badger was sitting in a bar stool at Ramon's kitchen island with a half finished bottle of Stella Artois before him.

"You've already started celebrating?" Russell exclaimed.

"Badge is always celebrating something." Ramon took down from the cupboard some flutes and set them on the island.

"Don't damage too many brain cells," Russell waved a warning finger at his crack researcher. "I shall require your services again for my next project."

"And what will that be?" Ramon winced after taking a sip from his glass.

"I'm returning to the biz."

"You're not!" Badge was sitting at full attention now.

Russell's tabloid newspaper era had been especially lucrative for the young investigator.

"After a book tour I'll be returning to Fleet Street. Well. Not literally. I've got a new vision." He formed a box with his hands as a filmmaker might to view and center his scene. "No more gossip."

"Now that is a novel concept." Ramon opened the refrigerator and took out a bottle of beer for himself. "I am not the champagne type."

"Well, I am." Russell had already finished his flute and didn't hesitate before downing Ramon's cast off glass. He then delicately dabbed at the corners of his mouth.

"So what's this vision?" Badger asked.

"Actually, I've been offered an opportunity with the BBC, the focus on true crime investigation. I hope to put forward an aura of journalistic credibility and yet not overly sophisticated, if you get my drift." He gazed as if looking at himself in his future role. "Think Nancy Grace, only with British civility."

"A refined presence, but being a true East-Londoner, the common man will identify with you."

Russell made the universal sign of a gun with his hand and pretended to fire. "Right on target. Ramon, you'd make a fine PR man. Come with?"

"You'd best run that proposition past the common woman first." Cord had only caught the tail end of the conversation, having just come home from picking up Gabriella at school. Mother and daughter had returned to their natural hair color and length which suited them well.

"You get taller each time I see you." Russell squatted down to the child's eye level, competing with Guapo for her attention. "How old are you now, sweetie?"

The little sprout held up five fingers.

"Soon you'll be taller than Badger."

Gabriella swayed so she could have a peek at Badge who made a silly face, provoking a peal of giggles. Then she dropped Cord's hand and ran to Ramon. "Papa!"

He couldn't describe the emotion that swept over him every time he heard her tiny voice speak the word. The adoption had only recently been finalized but he and Gaby, his pet name for his new daughter, had readily formed a devoted alliance soon after returning from England.

"How was your first day of kindergarten?" he asked.

"Good."

"Were all the other children nice to you?" He'd become fiercely protective of her.

"Uh huh. Kimberly has a pet monkey."

"She does?" Ramon didn't miss Cord's furious head shaking. Saying no to this little girl was nearly impossible. However, Guapo and Ting were the only members of the animal kingdom he wished to welcome into the Alvarez family for the foreseeable future. He'd have no problem denying the impending request for an exotic pet.

When Cord returned to New York, it had taken some time to shake off the initial awkwardness. They were reestablishing their footing on a relationship path that had been littered with misunderstandings. Eventually, she began to discard the protective vestments she'd wrapped around her heart. Being back in the city she'd once loved was an advantage to Ramon's cause, as were the welcoming arms of his family. When she agreed to move from the tiny apartment around the corner and into the loft, he felt confident she had finally bundled up and set aside the bruised pride and hurtful memories. Years earlier, when on the cusp of becoming a man, he'd entertained fantasies of building a life with Cord. It was unfortunate he'd become sidetracked by Gina. And yet he was convinced their relationship would be all the stronger because it hadn't been an easy road back.

Weeks before the big move, they'd worked together in designing the perfect space in the loft for Gaby.

"She's going to be the luckiest kid in Manhattan." Cord admired the finished product.

"Luckiest kid. Luckiest guy." He embraced her from behind and rested his chin on her shoulder. "We really work, you know?"

"Yes, we've worked hard and she'd better appreciate it."

"That's not what I mean. We work as a couple. Beyond the romance, the lovemaking, which I might add is absolutely sensational."

"Well, you'd better say that." She turned around to face him without disengaging.

"And I mean it." He kissed her lightly on the lips. "But we also work as a family."

"I guess we do." She smiled then snuggled into his chest.

"I'm crazy about your kid."

"It's safe to say there's a mutual admiration thing going on there."

"Only when Guapo's not around."

"I hate to think of the day she starts school and has to leave him behind."

"Gaby comes from hardy stock. She'll handle it."

He sensed an immediate change in Cord's mood and wished he could backtrack the words.

She tilted sad eyes up at him and asked, "How will I tell Gabriella what happened to her father? I mean, she knows that he died, but someday she's going to want to know the whole story. I can't just blurt out *your father was one of the bad guys and got killed because of it.*"

"I trust you will know what to say when the time comes. Or you can let her read about him."

"Read about him?" She pulled away.

"I am supposed to prepare you. Russell wants to write a bio piece on Aiden. But not without your permission."

Her eyes darkened. "I'm not sure it's a good idea."

"Just give it some thought before you decide. In the mean time, I have a proposition."

"Okay. Tell me about this proposition." Thankfully the shadow had passed.

He'd been waiting for the right moment and hoped it was now. He kissed her on the forehead and pulled her in tight. "Why don't I adopt Gaby and become her new daddy?"

The delay in Cord's response filled him with anxiety. Maybe it was too soon.

She kept her face buried in his chest when she finally spoke. "But we're not married."

"That is true. A major obstacle, is it not?" He was being facetious. But when Cord finally looked up, her eyes brimming, he quickly put on his serious face. "Mi querida. It goes without saying, I would love to marry you. Will you have me?"

"I'll think about it." She was trying to punish him by lobbing a chilly retort back into his court, but she was too emotional to see it through. "Yes, of course, I'll marry you."

"Then you have made me happier than I have been since the day I first met you on Parsons Street."

A few months later Cord and Ramon, along with their best girl of honor and their canine ring bearer, hosted an intimate celebration of the beginning of their new life together. It was the first time since their teen years that both families had come together. Cord had reconnected with Ronald and Lorraine, and although the relationship was still fairly tenuous, they were proving to rival Ramon's mama in the department of grandparental devotion. To their credit, her parents surrendered to her wish to be called by her given name. She'd said it was liberating to permanently discard the ill-fitting Delia Carlyle and slip comfortably into who she was always meant to be. Cord Alvarez.

On the morning of their nuptials Ramon presented his new wife with the diamond pendant stolen the day she crash landed back into his life.

"Your mother need never know," he said as she removed the bow.

When she opened the velvet box she stared in disbelief. He imagined she was thinking back to the same day.

"I can't believe you found this." She blinked and looked again. "How?"

"Good Karma." He smiled as he gazed at their reflection in the mirror, clasping the necklace from behind then kissing her shoulder. "To fate and my good fortune."

"It makes my heart sick to think our paths might never have crossed again."

"Would this not be the perfect time for you to quote Buddha?" he teased.

However it was the wisdom of Lao Tzu, another great philosopher and the father of Taoism, Cord chose to recite in her vows.

"*Being deeply loved by someone gives you strength, while loving someone deeply gives you courage. Be content with what you have; rejoice in the way things are. When you realize there is nothing lacking, the whole world belongs to you.*"

And Ramon quoted, rather appropriately, from Shakespeare's *The Tempest.*

"*Hear my soul speak. Of the very instant I saw you, did my heart fly at your service. I would not wish any companion in the world but you.*"

# CORDELIA

"THOUSANDS OF CANDLES CAN BE LIT FROM A SINGLE CANDLE,
AND THE LIFE OF THE CANDLE WILL NOT BE SHORTENED.
HAPPINESS NEVER DECREASES BY BEING SHARED."

BUDDHA

"No champagne for me." I placed my palm atop the flute.

"You'll not raise a glass to toast this?" Russell held for all to see the mock-up book cover for *A Stop in Summerland: The True Story of the Medium Murderess.*

"I'm thrilled for you, really I am. Don't take it personally." I glanced coyly at Ramon.

"What are you two hiding?" Badger's nose was never off the clock. "Come on. Out with it."

Ramon smiled and shrugged. "We might as well tell them."

"Gabriella?" I summoned our daughter from playtime with Guapo. "Do you want to share our exciting news with Uncles Russell and Badger?"

She skipped over and patted my tummy possessively, smiling shyly. Then she squealed happily, as five year olds will do, "We're having a baby!"

"That's brilliant. " Russell refilled his flute. "All the more reason to let the bubbly flow freely."

"Congratulations, man." Badger gave Ramon a buddy hug and leaned in tentatively to kiss me on the cheek.

"I won't break, Badger." I hugged him close. "Think you're up for the whole Godfather routine?"

Badger responded with a look of astonishment, probably because he was well aware of my stance on religion.

Mama would be expecting a baptism with all the accoutrements including sponsors to look after the child's spiritual upbringing. I felt uncomfortable with the whole exhibition, but was certain we'd reach a middle ground. And I did like the idea of close friends chosen specifically to act as guardians over my child's well being. Before my mother abandoned me, it had only been the two of us. I have no memory of a father, aunts, uncles, nobody. Perhaps that was why it became so important for my own children to be offered as much love and support as possible. I'd put my foot down against baptism and Godparent nonsense when Gabriella was born. It was one of the few issues I ever controlled during my marriage to Aiden. Perhaps now I would make amends to that decision. If the new baby could have an abundance of hens looking out for it, why shouldn't Gabriella?

"Think about it." I advised Badger.

"No, no, it's cool. Really cool." Then he thought about it a moment longer. "You're sure you want *me*?"

"Anyone able to figure out a way to find me in the wilds of Maine during my direst hour? Yes, I'm sure I want you looking after my kids."

Ramon had been listening. He tapped his beer to Badger's. "Will you do it?"

"Sure. I'm up for it. Thanks, man."

"Then it's settled." I turned to Gabriella and asked, "Shall we make some snacks?"

"Yum, Mama."

As my sweet little daughter climbed up on a stool at the island and chatted about her day, I assembled a tray of tapas while the guys talked about old times. Ramon had already told me about his former days as a paparazzo. It had been a grizzly life – his description. He was lucky to have caught the eye of an editor at *Our World Magazine* and offered an opportunity for a serious photojournalism gig. But his assignments had taken him into some incredibly dangerous locations. When we decided to become a family, Ramon resolved to explore new ventures closer to home and in calmer waters. He landed at a mid-size publishing house as their Art Director where he was also putting together a book of his own photography. Now he was preparing for his first exhibit at a small but prestigious Manhattan gallery. So far he seemed content, or maybe he was just too busy to think otherwise. Either way, I'd keep my sensors acutely tuned.

After single-handedly downing the bottle of champagne, Russell's celebratory musings blurred the lines of propriety.

"No wonder you've been looking so happy, mate. And here I chalked it up to the increased regularity of shagging."

"I believe it's time to cut him off." Badger cringed. He probably enjoyed Russell's randier side when they were working, but right now he was horrified by his friend's tasteless words in mixed company. Apparently, he was already taking seriously his responsibility as protector of our family.

I waved away the remark. "I'm used to his drunken ramblings. This won't be the first time he's crashed in our guest room."

"Shorry, shorry," Russell slurred. "Too many drinky-poos on an empty stomach and not enough sleep."

"Here, eat this." I handed him a plate of bruschetta, which he immediately devoured then burped loudly, provoking a peal of giggles from Gabriella.

"You should just toss him on Gaby's upper bunk bed. He's acting more like the five year old in the group," Badger called out as Russell stumbled, with Ramon's help, toward his home away from home while in New York.

"Am I persona-non-grata this morning?" Russell asked sheepishly as he picked up Guapo and took the barstool beside Gabriella, who was enjoying a plate of chocolate chip pancakes. "Maybe I should check into a hotel."

I considered him intently as I flipped another pancake on the griddle.

"Do you remember the day we met?"

"Quite an unforgettable meeting, wouldn't you say?" He nabbed a veggie sausage from Gabriella's plate and shared half with the dog. "I kidnapped you."

"True. Then you helped me escape. But I'd left behind my backpack with all my identification documents and I was thinking: Great. Now I'll be completely reliant on that slimy conniver."

"Ouch. You really know how to hurt a guy."

"Were you or were you not scheming to steal Betsy Cooper's diary from me?" I countered.

He busied himself stirring sugar into the coffee cup I'd just set before him.

"Russell?"

"Oh, all right. Guilty."

"Now let's turn it around." I lowered my voice. "Didn't you believe I'd abducted" – I nodded in Gabriella's direction – "after committing the most unthinkable crime?"

"Well, yes, but..."

I cut him off before he could start spinning. "I'm just saying we were both wrong. But what counts is you trusted your instincts and somehow persuaded that sheriff to set me free. You saved us."

"What about Bugs here?" He patted the dog's head.

"He's my hero, too." I thought of our inauspicious beginning and how wrong I'd been about the little guy. He'd been looking out for us from the start. "The point is you are *always* welcome here. Consider yourself part of our family."

I was about to ask if he would join Badger in being a guardian for our children, but his eyes were already moistening. I'd save it for a better time. But to lighten the emotional moment I added, "Warts and all."

"Sloppy drunk and hungover." He chuckled and snuck his hand across to Gabriella's plate again and I had to smile when this time she swatted his hand away.

"Don't they teach tots to share in kindergarten?" he feigned an indignant tone.

"Old school, Russell. These days they teach kids to stand up for themselves." Ramon came in and offered a good morning peck. His curls were still wet from the shower and I breathed in his fresh, masculine scent, thinking how unfortunate it was we had company.

"Crikey." Russell interrupted my thoughts. "What's this world coming to?"

After breakfast, we three adults took our coffees to the comfortable sitting area where we lounged companionably by the fireplace.

"So tell me about *Evil Blood,*" I said to Russell.

"That it's going to second printing? You know that already."

"What's happening with the movie rights?"

"Still negotiating with the bugger." Samuel Rawlins had given Russell the book rights to his criminal life story, but he'd shrewdly withheld an agreement for the screenplay.

"I am amazed you were able to get him to divulge so many details." Ramon shook his head in disbelieving admiration.

"Those two girls in Wisconsin." I closed my eyes, still disturbed by what had been uncovered.

"I must confess it was a tough project to write. At least

the truth offered some closure for the girls' families." Russell had wanted to start with the book about Betsy and Lucinda Cooper, but Samuel had put pressure on him to focus on his story. "Rawlins is no dummy. He used the offer to reveal where the girls' bodies had been hidden as leverage to get his book published quickly. Apparently he was looking for the benefits of celebrity status in prison."

"I think waiting to write *Medium Murderess* worked to your advantage." I'd just finished reading the galleys for Russell's newest manuscript.

"Why's that?"

"There's more depth to your writing in the second book."

"Perhaps the characters are a tad more sympathetic, as well?" Ramon suggested.

"Isn't that the truth?" Russell agreed. "And yet, we're still talking homicidal tendencies."

"I was aware of certain aspects of Betsy Cooper's life before she took on the alias of Rebekah Winchell because I had the advantage of reading her diary."

"For which I will always be eternally grateful." Russell bowed in my direction.

"If I hadn't believed you would serve her well I wouldn't have given it to you. But I was horrified when I read about the cruelty and abuse she withstood from her father."

"No wonder she'd become delusional."

"I liked your tie-in to the Old Testament story about Rebekah."

"The biblical connection? Appropriate considering she was such a religious fanatic."

The biblical Rebekah was a beautiful and strong willed woman who was unable to bear children, which was considered a sign she was not favored by God. Finally, after many years she gave birth to twins, Jacob and Esau, but her story didn't have a good ending either.

"Yes. But the whole twin coincidence was really weird, especially considering she named one of them Jacob." I shuddered remembering when we disguised Gaby as a little boy to go to the doctor and Rebekah had chosen the name Jacob. "I hadn't known the second twin was named Joshua. That's why your chapter on the Gibeonites was so powerful. I like how you used it to emphasize the human inclination to hide the truth for self preservation."

Russell had portrayed an excellent metaphor through another biblical story of Joshua and the Gibeonites, a race of people who craftily disguised themselves so that Joshua would not take them down in battle.

"The Gibeonites were victims of persecution, forced to conceal their identities in order to spare their lives." Russell was explaining to Ramon who hadn't yet read the manuscript. "In the end they were punished and sentenced to a lifetime of slavery."

"Good use of symbolism." Ramon was refilling cups from the carafe.

"But Russell skillfully turned the ancient story into a fable for modern times. Anyone who veils their true character, regardless of the motivation, will end up being a slave to the deceit."

"As was the case for Betsy Cooper; as is the case with many of us." Russell shot me a meaningful look. "It's the *fool's truth*."

I hadn't thought about it as I read the manuscript, but I'd also been very much like the Gibeonites, forced to flee in order to protect my daughter, assuming a false identity to evade capture and punishment.

Ramon must have sensed the mood was turning somberly self-reflective. "Every time Badger enters a pick-up bar he becomes a Gibeonite."

"Ha-Ha. Very funny." I tossed a pillow at my husband.

Russell sat thoughtfully for a moment then said, "I think it's fair to suggest Betsy Cooper had discovered a peaceful destination when she climbed into the persona of Rebekah Winchell."

"If I hadn't come along, she might still be living peacefully. That poor woman."

"If you will recall" -Ramon reminded me dramatically- "*that poor woman* knocked you on the head, threw you into a hole in the ground and left you for dead."

"That's right," Russell agreed. "And she might have harmed somebody else one day. It's good this particular Gibeonite was unveiled."

"What's most astonishing to me is Lucinda. How does a spiritual healer summon such ferocity to murder not once, but twice?"

"She was passionate in her protection of Betsy. Wouldn't you kill someone to protect little Gaby?" asked Russell.

I looked to the den where Gabriella and Guapo were curled up together on the sofa watching a DVD. "I would hope to never be in that position, but yes, I'd do anything to protect my child. There's a difference, though. Lucinda was Betsy's aunt. She didn't possess a maternal bond with Betsy, the innate connection and instincts that come with giving birth."

"Didn't she now?" Russell's eyebrows were dancing wickedly.

Ramon leaned forward. "I know that look. What are you implying?"

I had a queasy feeling all of a sudden.

Russell rubbed his chin and gazed at us thoughtfully. "I really shouldn't do this. But hey, whoever said I was one of the good guys."

"But you are one of the good guys." I smiled encouragingly as Ramon cracked, "Not me".

Russell mockingly looked daggers at Ramon before clapping

his hands decisively. "I'm only sharing this because I trust you. As you said this morning, we're family. Am I right?"

"Of course." Ramon and I responded as one.

"This violates a condition upon which Lucinda turned over rights to her story. That and fifty percent of the proceeds from the sale of the book must go to Betsy's trust. But I digress. So you must take this juicy tidbit to your graves."

"Which might actually happen before you get around to sharing this confidence," Ramon deadpanned.

"Always the wise guy." A humorous glint brightened Russell's eyes. "Okay. So, Lucinda became pregnant out of wedlock when she was a teenager and was secretly dashed off to one of those homes for unwed mothers. After giving birth the child was adopted and here's the kicker. The adoptive parents were Rev. Matthew Cooper - Lucinda's brother - and his wife. They named the little girl Elizabeth."

I sat stunned by the magnitude of the revelation, unable to speak. It was Ramon who verbally connected the dots. "So Rebekah, rather Betsy, was Lucinda's biological daughter."

Russell pointed at Ramon. "Spot on."

"Then she was motivated by a mother's true instincts." I finally found my tongue. "She killed her own brother to protect Betsy. And then she killed Betsy's husband to protect her again."

"What I'm not exactly clear on is why Betsy needed protecting." Ramon was perplexed. "More likely others needed protecting from her."

Russell looked at me as if asking permission. I saw no point in concealing the reason and nodded my consent.

"You're going to read it eventually, mate." Still Russell hesitated before explaining, gazing over at our precious child, probably gauging Ramon's reaction. "There were unanswered questions about how Betsy's children died. Lucinda's actions were meant to silence those who might possess evidence; her aim to thwart any potential prosecution."

"My God." Ramon was staggered by the implication. "I knew the woman was crazy, but..." He looked at me in disbelief. "I do not want to even think about what could have happened to Gaby."

"I know," I whispered and covered his trembling hands with my own. "Let's don't."

"By the way, the real Rebekah Winchell died some fifty years ago." Russell made a smooth segue. "If you ever venture back to Murphy, Maine, take a stroll through the Camp Davis cemetery. You'll find her grave marker in the Winchell plot. Voila! Lucinda's inspiration for the alias."

"Why did you leave that out of the book?" I found it surprising.

"Dunno." He shrugged. "Maybe I didn't want to see a pilgrimage to the dead woman's grave. She had nothing to do with all this mess. Let the real Rebekah Winchell lay in peace, God rest her soul and all that."

"Russell, I am thinking you have become a convert," Ramon declared.

"I'll be a bloody heathen till the day I die. I'm going to hell. No doubt about it."

"There is no hell." I smiled. "Only Karma. And yours is looking pretty good these days."

That night Ramon and I stood together outside Gabriella's room, watching her sleep peacefully, Guapo snuggled up in the curve of her arm.

"How are we going to raise our children?" I asked.

"We are never going to let them out of our sight." He was still spooked by what he'd learned today about Rebekah.

"Yes, we will watch over them closely. But I was talking about how we'll raise them spiritually. I know Mama wants..."

Ramon cut me off. "Let's leave my mama out of this. We will help our children to become good people and expose them to the teachings of all the great spiritual leaders. And then we will trust them to make their own decisions."

I was pleased to know we stood in unison. "So you'll handle your mother?"

"She'll be fine. As long as there are no mediums in the family." He squeezed my shoulder playfully.

"Shouldn't be a problem," I laughed. "By the way, how many kids do you want?"

"I'm good with another two, at least."

"That's a relief."

He leaned in so he could look into my eyes. "Why?"

"Because, " -I sighed happily- "we're having twins."

"When did you find out?"

"This morning." I pulled the ultra-sound picture from my pocket and handed it to him.

Ramon squinted, closely examining the image. "Boys?"

I snatched it back. "Too early to tell. Besides, I don't want to know."

"If they are boys, just promise me one thing?" he asked.

I'd come to better understand my husband's sense of humor and guessed where this was heading. "We will not be naming them Jacob and Joshua."

"You are getting quicker." Ramon grinned, then reached down and caressed my tummy. "I am thinking my Karma's in pretty good shape these days."

I smiled up at him. "Oh yeah."

# REBEKAH

"NOW THEREFORE YOU ARE CURSED, AND THERE SHALL NONE OF YOU BE FREED FROM BEING SLAVES..."

JOSHUA 9:23

September 27th

I want to go home. I miss the farm. I miss my goats and chickens and the llamas. But most of all I miss my little Gemma. A letter came from Aunt Lucinda today. She was sending a warning in our special code. She says I must never tell anyone what really happened. But I can't see what difference it makes. Nobody ever believes me anyhow. Just like in the old days with Dr. Ryan, I've tried telling Dr. Steiner that I killed Daddy. Ted, too. But everyone thinks I'm either confused or making it up. "Delusional," I heard the nurse say. So I'm giving up. I'll not try to convince them of the truth anymore. Besides, maybe if I tell them what they want to hear they'll let me go home. Then I can see my Gemma again.

Betsy Cooper set aside her new journal, the one given to her by the nice Englishman who sometimes visited. From the small desk in her room she took out Aunt Lucinda's Tarot deck. The first card she laid out was the Queen of Wands, who used fire for good or evil. No surprise there. It always turned up. But today, for the first time since Aunt Lucinda warned her about the strange young woman named Cord, she flipped over The Fool card. It was upright. A good perspective for The Fool.

"I'm pleased." Betsy nodded as she gathered the cards. "That means she's taking good care of Gemma."

# RUSSELL

"JOURNALISM WILL KILL YOU, BUT IT WILL KEEP YOU ALIVE WHILE YOU'RE AT IT."

HORACE GREELEY

RUSSELL SCRIBBLED A QUOTE FROM John Galsworthy's *The Forsythe Saga* onto the cover page of a copy of *Evil Blood.*

> "There are moments when Nature reveals the passion hidden beneath the careless calm of her ordinary moods—violent spring flashing white on almond-blossom through the purple clouds; a snowy, moonlit peak, with its single star, soaring up to the passionate blue; or against the flames of sunset, an old yew-tree standing dark guardian of some fiery secret."
>
> Your only chance of keeping her is to trust her. Tell Francesca the truth. R.P.

He addressed the package to the personal attention of Homer Pruitt at the sheriff's office in Murphy, Maine. Just before boarding he dropped the envelope into one of the Express Mail boxes at JFK.

"Welcome to British Airways, Mr. Payne. I'm Laura. Let me take your coat."

"Thank you, Laura." Russell relinquished his Burberry but held tight to his laptop. He had some work to do on the flight.

"Can I get you a drink before we take off?" Laura asked.

"That would be lovely. Glinfidditch? Neat."

He stretched out in his first class seat and sipped the scotch while admiring the young and shapely flight attendant. It was a nice view. And in less than six hours he'd be in London.

"I'm back. And it's all good." He raised his glass in salute.

Maybe he believed in Karma after all.

# HOMER

"...WHEN YOU HAVE ELIMINATED THE IMPOSSIBLE, WHATEVER REMAINS, ***HOWEVER IMPROBABLE***, MUST BE THE TRUTH."

SHERLOCK HOLMES IN ***THE SIGN OF FOUR***

HOMER OPENED THE PACKAGE WITH a great deal of curiosity. *Evil Blood*. Rusty's magnum opus. He'd already special ordered the book when he'd read the review in *The Times*. Not one to hold a grudge, he was glad to know Russell's toil and strife of the past couple of years had paid off. The article said there was another book in the works set at a Spiritualist camp in Maine. He didn't have to use up too many brain cells to predict what the next book was going to be about.

Homer flipped open the cover and smiled when he saw that Russell had signed his copy. He grabbed his cheaters to read the inscription. The smile quickly vanished and was replaced by a dark scowl. He turned the page and read the preface which began with another quote. This one from Gilbert Parker, a British politician and writer.

> "In all secrets there is a kind of guilt, however beautiful or joyful they may be, or for what good end they may be set to serve. Secrecy means evasion, and evasion means a problem to the moral mind." But Samuel Rawlins' secret was not joyful and its

> beauty was only in the perfection of the cocoon that had protected it for over a decade…"

Homer flipped to the last page of the book where Russell had again quoted this Gilbert Parker fellow.

> "There is no refuge from memory and remorse in this world. The spirits of our foolish deeds haunt us, with or without repentance."

"Exactly who were you writing this for, Rusty?" Homer closed the book with a soft thump and pushed it away as if it was contaminated. He drummed his fingers on the desk, glaring at the book as one might face down a great adversary. Then he removed the envelope from the trash can and wrapped it back around the book.

"Going to Becky's?" Olivia called out as he marched in the direction of the door.

"No. I think I'll take off early today. Can you hold down the fort?" He didn't turn to face his assistant because if he did, surely she would recognize his panic.

"Will do. Is everything okay boss?"

"Just a headache. See you in the morning."

Homer had a small window of opportunity to take the book home and destroy it. Frannie would be picking the kids up from school but it wasn't a long drive so he'd have to work fast.

He unlocked his home office door and carried the package to his desk. He sat down and pondered the best strategy. Should he burn the book or simply tear out the first page with Russell's damning inscription? He casually flipped open the music box he'd purchased for Frannie years ago after she'd told him about her lonely childhood. She'd climb to the attic and play the record over and over, letting her mind carry her away to a safe place.

She'd been married to his best friend, Bill Robbins, when he'd given her the present. Bill had always teased him about having a crush on his wife, but he'd thought it was lighthearted and all in fun. Never could he have imagined that the innocent attention he paid to Francesca out of friendship had fueled an irrational jealousy that led to her tortured existence.

That horrible day, how many years ago was it now? Thirty-one? Thirty-two? The music box had been playing when he arrived, Francesca singing along with the tinkling notes.

"Sweet dreams till sunbeams find you, sweet dreams that leave all worries behind you. But in your dreams whatever they be, *dream a little dream of me*."

He'd never known if the music box had been the instigating source of the last brutal battle. Or maybe Bill had somehow learned about the arrangements Homer had made for Francesca and Sophia to go to a safe house. One morning after Bill had left for work, she had come to him for help. Her nose was broken and bloody and her dress had been torn. But evidently she'd taken plenty of that type of abuse before.

"It's not for me, Homer. It's Sophia." The toddler was screaming in her arms. "He touched her."

Homer had immediately understood what she meant, though it was unfathomable that his friend for life had molested a child. But there was no arguing with the red and swollen eyes that were pleading with him. Surely she hadn't punched herself in the face and broken her own nose.

"Why haven't you reported this?" he'd asked.

"You know why. He's a New York state's attorney. Who would believe me?"

"There are women's shelters. Everything is confidential."

"With *police* protection. Come on Homer. Do you really believe we could hide in one of those?"

"You're right." He hadn't really known what to do, but he

knew he had to come up with a plan. "What time does Bill leave for work?"

"Eight o'clock usually. Why?"

"I'll take care of it. All you need to do is be home tomorrow morning at nine o'clock. Until then, go about your normal routine. Don't do anything that might arouse suspicion and don't pack anything. Just be there."

But when he'd shown up, Bill was dead and Francesca had escaped to a safe place in her mind, singing along with the music box. When she'd finally awakened from a traumatized state, she believed Homer had killed her husband. Why hadn't he told her the truth then? It was a question he'd faced countless times throughout his marriage. She'd looked so incredibly fragile, as if she might shatter if she knew her hand had committed the deed. Or had he wanted her to envision him as her liberator from the hell of an abusive life? The truth had been deeply buried for so long. How could he possibly explain to her now why he allowed her to continue living a lie?

It had been his partner on the force who Homer had turned to for help. Fortunately, it hadn't taken much to convince Kevin McCarthy because Bill had once dated his sister and he'd been a witness to a foreshadowing of a violent and misogynistic pattern.

Kevin had taken one look at Francesca and said, "What do you need me to do?"

They had arranged the scene to look as if an intruder had killed Bill and they made the murder weapon disappear. Homer had never asked how Kevin disposed of the hand gun, but he knew it would never be found.

Because the crime involved one of their own, the NYPD expedited the arrest of a local group of repeat offenders and luckily a neighborhood store owner identified one as a shoplifter who had stolen a carton of cigarettes the same day of the murder. Prosecutors were able to convince a jury to send the perpetrator to prison for life. Homer and Kevin had no qualms about saddling the guilt to a thug who'd previously been convicted of assault with attempt to kill, armed robbery and attempted rape. In their minds he was the quintessential recidivist who would have ended up in the same place sooner or later. In fact, they might have saved someone's life by allowing this to go down.

When Kevin died after a brief battle with cancer ten years ago, Homer took on solitary ownership of the burden. He was the only living person who knew what had really happened to Bill Robbins. Or so he thought. He opened the safe and retrieved the file Russell had given him.

He might as well destroy this, too.

Apparently Kevin had harbored some misgivings about wrongfully sending a man to prison because he'd sought absolution from his confessor and priest before he died. And Russell had hired a very clever investigator who somehow tracked down the old priest and managed to coax another deathbed confession. Now the priest was dead and so was the secret. It was all there in the file.

Homer closed the music box as it wound down and gazed at the framed photograph taken on their wedding day. He'd always been in love with her, but a guy never admits to loving his best friend's wife, not even to himself. It's just not how men work. But a few months after Bill's death he'd been able to come to terms with his denial. He had to admit he'd been somewhat amazed when she accepted his proposal without hesitation. However, she had made one heartbreaking request. "I don't want to be Francesca anymore. I'd prefer if you called me Frannie from now on."

He opened the book and read Russell's inscription again: Your only chance of keeping her is to trust her. Tell *Francesca* the truth Homer.

He shook his head. "How long had he known?"

"How long had who known what?"

His wife was leaning against the door jamb, arms folded over her chest. He hadn't even been startled by her appearance. There was no denying how much he loved the woman standing before him. Maybe it was finally time to put to rest his terror of discovering she'd never loved him back. That she'd only viewed their union as one of convenience and security.

"Homer? What's wrong?" She inched closer. "Tell me you're okay."

There were tears streaming down Francesca's lovely face. Yes, she had always remained Francesca in his heart. Frannie was only a mirror image, Francesca's shadow. He'd done that to her. It was time to make amends.

"I have something to tell you."

"CAN A HUSBAND EVER CARRY ABOUT A SECRET ALL HIS LIFE AND A
WOMAN WHO LOVES HIM HAVE NO SUSPICION OF IT?
I KNEW IT BY HIS REFUSAL TO TALK ABOUT SOME EPISODES IN HIS AMERICAN LIFE.
I KNEW IT BY CERTAIN PRECAUTIONS HE TOOK. I KNEW IT BY CERTAIN WORDS HE LET FALL.
I KNEW IT BY THE WAY HE LOOKED AT UNEXPECTED STRANGERS."

SHERLOCK HOLMES IN ***THE VALLEY OF FEAR***

THE END.

ACKNOWLEDGMENTS

I am deeply indebted to my early readers, whose insight and keen eyes helped transform a work-in-progress into a layered novel. On this fun but at times thorny journey, Rosie Genova has been a most generous critique partner and friend. Thank you also to Sarah Pinneo for being an excellent resource in helping to navigate the challenging technical aspects of publishing.

I am privileged to have amazing friends ~ some who are as close as sisters, having shared our worlds since childhood ~ others I'm fortunate to have met along my meandering adult path. I can't thank you enough for your endless encouragement through this prolonged undertaking.

Certainly the person most affected by this trek toward publication would be my husband. You've kept me grounded through your uniquely humorous perspective about life. And I have benefited greatly from your especially keen editorial skills and for being my sounding board. Special thanks from *Lady Laptop* for indulging this passion and for so patiently allowing me to leave stacks of books, files and research scattered around the house and for not rolling your eyes as I toted my laptop along on every vacation and road trip.

My mother was a significant influence in my life and her recent death left a great void. But her nurturing essence endures, through quiet whispers not to give up, a gentle hand guiding me forward. I wish she had lived to hold this book in her hands. She would have been so proud.

There have been so many times I've thought to quit,

questioned why I was pursuing such a difficult course. Thank goodness the belief by others in my abilities as a writer has always overpowered my self-doubt. With love, I thank you all.

CPSIA information can be obtained
at www.ICGtesting.com
Printed in the USA
LVHW092302150219
607775LV00001B/7/P